D

dragonwitch

TALES OF GOLDSTONE WOOD

Heartless

Veiled Rose

Moonblood

Starflower

Dragonwitch

dragonwitch

TALES OF GOLDSTONE WOOD

†   †

ANNE ELISABETH STENGL

BETHANY HOUSE PUBLISHERS
a division of Baker Publishing Group
Minneapolis, Minnesota

© 2013 by Anne Elisabeth Stengl

Published by Bethany House Publishers
11400 Hampshire Avenue South
Bloomington, Minnesota 55438
www.bethanyhouse.com

Bethany House Publishers is a division of
Baker Publishing Group, Grand Rapids, Michigan

Printed in the United States of America

Library of Congress Cataloging-in-Publication Data
Stengl, Anne Elisabeth.
    Dragonwitch / Anne Elisabeth Stengl.
        pages cm.—(Tales of Goldstone Wood)
    ISBN 978-0-7642-1027-3 (pbk.)
    I. Title.
PS3619.T47647675D73 2013
813'.6--dc23   2013007324

Book design by Paul Higdon
Cover illustration by William Graf

Author is represented by Books & Such Literary Agency

13 14 15 16 17 18 19   7 6 5 4 3 2 1

To Manda,
for all those long walks,
daydreams,
and endless stories.

LEGEND OF TWO BROTHERS

LET ME TELL YOU A STORY.

In the days when the Near World was new and mortal men were young and frightened, Death-in-Life crept among the shadows and whispered darkness into their fears. So they hid themselves in caves and never dared to look above to the lights shining in the vaults of the sky; they could not hear the Songs of the Spheres.

The Lumil Eliasul, Giver of Songs, took pity on their helpless state. He sent his knights, the Brothers Ashiun. No one recalls their names before the Lumil Eliasul called them into his service. The elder he called *Akilun*, which is Wisdom; the younger, *Etanun*, which is Strength.

With these names, each brother was given a great gift. Into Akilun's hand, the Lumil Eliasul placed Asha, a lantern filled with the light of Hymlumé, the lady moon.

"Take this lantern, and with it disperse the shadows so that my children may see the Greater Lights. And when they see, they will hear the Songs I have sung for them and which the sun and the moon sing still. Thus they will have hope of life beyond the dust of mortality."

So spoke the Giver of Songs. Then he turned to Etanun, and into his fist he pressed the hilt of Halisa, a sword forged in the fires of Lumé, the lordly sun.

"With this sword," said the Lumil Eliasul, "cut down the monsters that plague their fears. Drive out the fires of Death-in-Life and his brood with a fire more pure, more dreadful, more sure. Thus my children will know the truth of the life to which they have been called, and they will sing with Lumé and Hymlumé."

At the behest of their Master, the Brothers Ashiun carried their gifts across the Final Water into the Near World. Etanun drove out the Faerie beasts that crawled along the mortal ground, devouring as they went, and even Death-in-Life drew back into his own dark kingdom, fearing the fire of Halisa. Akilun shone his lantern into the darkest reaches of the mortal realm, and people far and wide gathered to its light, marveling at the things they saw and heard of that they had never before dreamed. Together, the two brothers built the Houses of old, great halls with doors on either end that opened to the east and west. Akilun filled these Houses with the light of Asha so that even when the brothers passed on to distant realms, the mortals of every nation could still hear the Songs of the sun and the moon.

So Etanun and Akilun journeyed throughout the Near World, bringing truth and hope to the farthest countries, even to the distant isles across the wild sea. But Death-in-Life looked upon their work and gnashed his teeth. He hated the Songs of the Spheres almost as much as he hated their creator. When he had first seen the pitiable state of the mortals, he had thought to take them, to create a people after his own design who would serve and worship only him. But now, as the Houses stood tall and the mortals gathered to hear the Songs, Death-in-Life saw his nightmarish dreams begin to fade.

So he turned to another, an immortal queen of the Faerie folk, and he spoke his lies to her. Brokenhearted and filled with jealous anger, she heeded his words. And so he created his firstborn.

Hri Sora. The Flame at Night.

She set upon the Great Houses and burned them, scattering the poor mortals back into darkness. Heroes of old rose up to face this dragon, but none could match her flame. One by one, kings, queens, and chieftains of the Near World watched their holy places burn, sacrifices offered by Hri Sora to her Dark Father.

But Akilun and Etanun were not through with their work. Akilun shone Asha lantern, and mortals flocked to its light. And Etanun set out to slay Hri Sora. Armed with Halisa, he plunged into the darkest regions of the Near World. He found her at last on a cold mountain, and there he fought her. The fire of their battle melted the snow on the mountaintop, which ran like rivers down into the valleys below. Yet Hri Sora could not match the might of Halisa as wielded by the knight, and she fell beneath his blade.

But alas, Death-in-Life's firstborn could not be so easily destroyed.

Akilun the Elder, bearing his lantern, found his brother exhausted upon the barren slopes of the mountain. Etanun was near death, but under Akilun's gentle hand, he gradually stepped from the shadow back into the living world.

"I have killed her!" said Etanun then.

Akilun shook his head. "It is not so, brother. Hri Sora will return, I fear. You have only destroyed the first of her lives."

Etanun refused to hear his brother's words. His heart burned with a fire of his own, the fire of vengeance unsatisfied. "Halisa cannot be cheated out of such a victory!" he declared. Akilun could only wait in silence for Etanun to know the truth.

In time, the Great Houses were rebuilt. Kingdoms were established. Nations rose and fell and warred and made peace. But those mortals who heard and paid heed to the Sphere Songs prospered and gave thanks to the Song Giver. A hundred years spun across the face of the mortal realm.

And Hri Sora returned, even as Akilun had known she would.

In a rage of fire more terrible than before, she flamed into the Near World. All the rebuilt Great Houses she tore to pieces and then set upon those she had not touched during her first life. One by one she destroyed them, and though Etanun, incensed, pursued her with all the passion of his soul, he could not overtake her trail of fire.

At last there was but one House remaining in all the Near World. The people of that land knew of the destruction wrought by Hri Sora. Desperate, they did what no man had dared do in all the generations since the coming of the Brothers Ashiun. They shut the doors of the House, hiding the glow of Asha, damping the Songs of the Spheres. And their world plummeted into darkness.

Although Hri Sora searched far and wide, she could not discover the final House of Lights.

Thus thwarted in her goal, she flew to the wide green plain of Corrilond and set fire to its lushness, turning all from green to desert in moments. There at last Etanun found her, and there he fought her a second time. The fury of their battle was beyond all telling, and mortals fled from that land, not to return for generations. Once more Hri Sora's flame could not withstand the fire of Halisa. Etanun plunged the blade into the depths of the furnace within her breast.

For the second time, Hri Sora died and vanished from the Near World in a hurricane of ash.

Again Akilun sought out his brother, only to find him on the brink of death. Again Akilun nursed him back to life. But Hri Sora's claws had scored Etanun's body with deep wounds filled with dragon poison. Though Akilun ministered to his brother with great skill, when at last Etanun opened his eyes, they shimmered with the heat of remnant venom.

"I have killed her!" Etanun declared. "I have had my vengeance!"

But Akilun responded with great sorrow. "She will return more powerful than before."

Etanun surged to his feet then, ready to kill in his anger. "Where is your lantern?" he cried. "Where is the hope you spread to mortals? Will you profane it with this dooming prophecy? Or is it that you cannot bear the glory of my might, the gift our Lord bestowed upon me, as compared to your own paltry glimmerings?"

Akilun could not reason with his brother. They parted ways, Etanun declaring that he could no longer have dealings with Akilun, prophet of doom, who disgraced the light he bore. Etanun sheathed his sword, hiding its brilliance, and refused to fight as he once had. The bitterness of dragon poison filled his body; he lowered his gaze from the Spheres Above, and he stopped up his ears to the Songs in which he had once gloried.

It was then that he began to hear the voice of Death-in-Life for himself.

"You want power?" said that dreadful Father of dragons. "You want fire that cannot be quenched? Come to me. Receive my kiss."

Etanun plunged into the Netherworld, pursuing that voice and that false promise. "My Lord has betrayed me," he said to himself as he went.

"His gift, Halisa, has proven worthless. I will seek my own way now." With these black thoughts, he progressed down and down, driven by poison as he pursued the Dark Water.

But Akilun followed him.

The elder brother, Asha in his hand, stepped into Death's realm and chased Etanun down the long, dark Path. He caught him at last and pleaded with him to go no farther. "Turn your face away from this dire purpose!" he cried. "Turn back to the truth you know and humble yourself before your Lord."

"I will not be humiliated before all the worlds again!" Etanun cried, and he spat in Akilun's face, declaring that he would meet Death and take his kiss without fear.

So Akilun put his arms around his brother, clutching him fast. "I will not let you go another step."

Etanun struggled; Akilun held true. Etanun's strength was double that of his older brother, but Akilun's love was greater still. They wrestled in the darkness of Death's realm, Etanun resisting, Akilun restraining. All the light of Asha shone in Etanun's eyes, brighter and brighter, chasing away the phantoms of the Netherworld and their grim whispers. "Look at it!" Akilun cried, forcing his brother to face that shining purity. "Look at it and see the truth you once knew!"

Etanun fought but the light filled him even so. The brightness and beauty of it washed Hri Sora's poison from his veins, leaving him weak, trembling, but in the end . . . whole.

His muscles relaxed. Breathing with difficulty, he collapsed. Akilun let go his hold and fell beside him.

Generations had passed in the mortal world above as the brothers battled and then lay still. At last Etanun roused himself and turned to Akilun. "Brother, I have sinned," he began, but the words vanished from his lips.

Akilun was dead.

His strength broken from his great struggle for his brother's life, his spirit had flown across the Final Water to the Farthest Shore, where Hymlumé and Lumé sing before the throne of the Song Giver. But while his spirit flew free, his body lay in ruin beside Etanun.

Etanun wept. He wept at his folly, at the conceit that had led him and Akilun to this place. Even as he wept, the light of Asha rested upon him.

He dug a grave for Akilun on the Path to the Dark Water. He set a monument there, a stone carved with this legend:

> *Beyond the Final Water falling,*
> *The Songs of Spheres recalling.*
> *Though you walk the Path to Death's own throne,*
> *You will walk with me.*

He set Asha atop the stone and left it there, saying, "May you be a guiding light, a hope to those who find themselves drawn by Death-in-Life's foul work."

Then he turned and marched into the deep places of the Netherworld, and fiends and phantoms fled at his footsteps. He found a place where the Final Waters flowed, spreading from the realms beyond into the Near World and into the Far. In that place he built a chamber. Above the flowing water, he set an uncut stone.

"There rest, Halisa," he said, placing his sword atop that stone. "May you sleep a hundred years and more until Hri Sora returns to work her evil fire. Wake only when I or my heir comes at last to claim you."

So Etanun left Halisa waiting in darkness. He himself journeyed from the Netherworld into the realms above, passing out of all legends and tales and histories. Until the time of Hri Sora's return.

Until the time of her final death.

Part One

Chronicler

1

HAVE YOU EVER WATCHED AN IMMORTAL DIE?
You who have slain countless fey folk, tell me if you dare: Did you ever stand by and watch an immortal death? Did you see the blush of life fade to gray, the light of the spirit slowly wane? You have taken life, but have you seen it stolen from before your eyes?

I have.

Dawn in the North Country was beautiful, if chilly that spring, filled with birdsong and dew-shimmering flowers on the banks of River Hanna. The rising sun stretched out its rays to crown the high keep of Castle Gaheris. Tenant farmers, their tools over their bowed shoulders as they made their way to the fields, straightened momentarily, lifting their gazes to the sight. Their hearts swelled to see those austere stones glowing with morning glory, as though the sun itself bestowed a golden promise upon all who lived there.

The castle was home to Earl Ferox, who some said should be king.

The farmers smiled at this, their weathered faces cracking against the dawn chill, their breath wisping before their mouths. Honor though it was to be tenants of the most powerful earl in the North Country, how much greater would the honor be should they become tenants of the king himself?

So the sun rose and the farmers trudged on to their fields, and the servants inside Gaheris stoked fires in cold hearths and prepared for an important day, the day the envoy from Aiven should arrive. A day some might even call fateful.

And Alistair sat upright in his bed, screaming.

He realized what he was doing quickly enough, stuffed his fleece into his mouth, and bit down hard. He knew the servants had heard him, though. He could hear them in the chamber beyond . . . or rather couldn't hear them, for they had frozen in place, afraid to move. He heard instead their silence.

He coughed out the fleece and, though his heart trembled and his limbs shook, forced himself to utter a great, noisy yawn. It would fool no one. But the servants took it as a signal, and he heard them resume their tasks, setting his fire and filling his basin with fresh well water.

They knew better than to enter his private bedroom. He bolted it against them in any case.

Alistair waited until he heard them leave. Only then did he slip out of bed, wrapping the fleece around his shoulders as he made his way to the window. He looked out upon his uncle's lands: the fields, the hamlets, the groves, all of which he would inherit one day.

But he couldn't see them, nor the growing sunlight that bathed them.

He saw only a pale silver glow shining upon a child's face.

"Dragons blast it!" Alistair cursed and shook his head.

No more than an hour later, Alistair stumbled into Gaheris's library, startling the castle chronicler, who was at his desk, copying out some ledger or history. The Chronicler looked up in some surprise at the young man's entrance.

"You are early, my lord."

Alistair shrugged. The library boasted only three windows, mere slits in the stone, all west and south facing and admitting none of the morning light. Thus the room was full of candles sitting in wooden, wax-filled bowls. Their glow cast Alistair's face into ghoulish shadows, emphasizing the dark circles beneath his eyes.

The Chronicler frowned with measured concern as Alistair took a seat at the long table in the center of the room. "Another restless night?"

Alistair buried his face in his hands. Then he rubbed at the skin under his eyes, stretching his face into unnatural shapes, and ended by pulling at the roots of his hair. "You're an intelligent, learned man, are you not, Chronicler?"

"So some would say," the Chronicler acceded.

"Have you," Alistair continued, still pulling at his hair and studying the grain of the wooden table before him with unprecedented concentration, "in all your readings, picked up a word or two concerning dreams?"

The Chronicler set aside his quill and pumice stone, then folded his arms as he turned on his stool to more fully look upon the young lord. "What manner of dreams?"

"Recurring," said Alistair darkly. He stared at the table as though he should like to burn it with his gaze. The candlelight shone into the depths of his eyes, turning the pale blue irises to orange.

The Chronicler tipped his head to one side. "Are we speaking of a dream you have experienced, Lord Alistair?"

Alistair nodded.

"In this dream, did you see an ax, a sword, or any form of iron weaponry suspended above your head?"

"No."

"Did you see the face of one long dead calling out to you from behind a shadowy veil?"

"No."

"Did your last-night's supper confront you in an antagonistic manner?"

"What?" Alistair looked up.

"Did it?"

"Why would I dream something like that?"

The Chronicler leaned back on his stool, reaching to a near bookshelf from which he selected a volume. The vellum pages were neatly copied in a flowing, if shaky script, and all was beautifully bound up in red-stained leather. The Chronicler flipped to a certain page illuminated with images more fantastic than accurate. He read:

"Ande it dide com aboot that Sir Balsius, moste Noble Earle of Gaheris, saw withyn the Eiye of hyse Mynde a sertayn Mutton upon which he hade Et the night prevyus. And thyse Mutton did taxe Hym moste cruelly for having Gnawed upone its Joints. And it spake unto Hym thus, sayinge: 'And surely You, most jowl-som Lorde, will die upon the Morrow, and the Wolfs will Gnaw upon Thyy Joints.' So it dide Transpyre that Sir Balsius betook Hymselfe to the Hunt, and—"

"Wait, wait!" said young Alistair, his brow puckering. "You're telling me that this Earl Balsius—"

"Your great-great-grandfather, if I recall the chronology correctly," said the Chronicler.

"—dreamt about an antagonistic mutton and died the next day?"

"According to my predecessor, yes." The Chronicler shut the book and smiled a grim, mirthless sort of smile at the young lord. "But I give little credence to these so-called histories. Dreams are merely dreams, and stories are merely stories. They are subjects of curious interest but nothing upon which to base your life."

He shoved the volume back into its place with perhaps a little more vehemence than was called for. Alistair, however, did not notice. He was trying to recall what he'd eaten the night before.

"What about," he said, embarrassed but eager to know, "what about a pale-faced child?"

"Come again?" said the Chronicler.

"A pale-faced child. Paler than any child I ever saw. Like a ghost or a phantom. Running along the edge of a bottomless chasm, and . . ." Alistair stopped, his mouth suddenly dry, and stared into the flickering candle flame, unable to continue.

"Is this your recurring dream, my lord?"

"Perhaps. Some of it."

"Well, no doubt about it, then," said the Chronicler. "You're going to die."

"What?" Alistair nearly knocked the candle over as he spun to face the Chronicler. "Do you mean it?"

"You saw the pale-faced child beside the bottomless chasm?" The Chronicler selected another volume, slid down from his stool, and approached Alistair at the table. "Then there can be no doubt about it. You're going to die. A slow, lingering death brought on by study and academic application." He plunked the book down in front of Alistair. "As long as you're here, you might as well start reading. Open to the tenth page, please."

Scowling, Alistair watched the Chronicler climb back onto his stool, wishing he were clever enough this early in the morning to think of something nasty to say. But too many sleepless nights in a row, waking at dawn to frozen feet and nose, had sapped him of any cleverness with which he'd been born.

He should have known better than to confide in the Chronicler.

He opened the volume to the required page and stared at the words scribbled there. He pulled the candle closer, then reached for another. The added light did nothing to help.

"I can't read this," he said.

"Yes, you can," said the Chronicler.

"I don't know this piece."

"You know all the letters, and you know the sounds they make." The Chronicler, bowed over his work, did not bother to look around. His quill scritched away at a flimsy parchment as he made a copy, using the pumice stone to hold the page in place rather than risk greasing the delicate fibers with his fingertips. "Sound it out."

Alistair's scowl deepened. He did not recognize the hand in which this unknown text had been written. Everything put down on paper within the walls of Gaheris was either in the Chronicler's hand or that of his predecessor. But this hand, this wavering, watery script in faded ink, was not one he had seen before.

"I have time," the Chronicler said. "I can wait all day if necessary."

Alistair swallowed, trying to wet his dry throat, then took a hesitant stab at the first word. "Ta-hee."

"What sound does a '*th*' make?"

Blood rushed to Alistair's cheeks, turning their chalky pallor bright and blotchy. "*The!*" he read, as though he could kill the word with a single stroke.

"Go on," said the Chronicler calmly.

Setting his shoulders and rolling his stiff neck, Alistair drew a deep breath. "*The kin-gee . . . No, king. The king will find his . . . his way to the—*"

He stopped suddenly. Within that short phrase he recognized what he was reading. His embarrassment tripled, and he clenched his fists, glaring round at the Chronicler again. "I'm not reading this," he said.

The Chronicler continued writing without a pause.

"This is a nursery rhyme," Alistair said. "I'm not a babe in my nurse-maid's arms!"

"Shall I bear word to your uncle that once again you have given up intellectual pursuits for a pack of sorry dogs and a still sorrier fox?"

"Intellectual pursuits? This?" Alistair threw up his hands, leaning back in his chair. "Anyway, Uncle Ferox doesn't read. Neither does any other earl in the North Country. That's why we keep men like you."

The Chronicler said nothing. But he said it with such finality that Alistair sighed, knowing he'd lost the fight, and turned back to the book. He might as well ram his head against a brick wall as challenge the Chronicler.

Between them remained the unspoken truth: Earls may not read, but earls were not kings.

Well, neither was Alistair, but this argument would gain him no ground. Not with an entire nation's expectations resting on his young shoulders. So he bent over the old book again and strained his eyes in the candlelight to make out the scribbling scrawl.

"*The king will find his way,*" he read slowly, like a blind man feeling out an unfamiliar path, "*to the sw—swar—sword?*"

"Yes," said the Chronicler.

"*The sword beneath the floor. The nig-hit. The night. The night will flame again.*"

"Good," said the Chronicler, though Alistair knew the effort hardly merited praise. Even the simplest words gave him difficulty. He'd started learning too late, he thought. It came easy for someone like the Chronicler, who'd been apprenticed to old Raguel from the time he could speak.

Alistair had always had more important matters to occupy his mind, and only the daft whim of his uncle could have driven him to letters so late in his education.

"Continue," the Chronicler said.

Alistair ground his teeth. Then he began:

> *"The night will flame again*
> *When the Smallman finds the door.*
> *The dark won't hide the Path*
> *When you near the House of—"*

"Do you really think I am so easily fooled?"

Alistair stopped. He did not raise his head, but his eyes flashed to the back of the Chronicler's head. "I'm reading the rhyme," he said.

"No," said the Chronicler, still without looking around. "You are *reciting* the rhyme. You know it by heart. You're not reading at all."

With a curse, Alistair slammed the book shut and stood, nearly knocking the nearest candle over into its pooling wax. "If I already know the dragon-eaten thing, I see no reason why I should read it."

"Neither do I," the Chronicler replied, "so long as you are determined to be less of a man than you could be." He shook his head and assumed a patronizing tone, one that Alistair knew all too well and hated for the familiarity. "Do you not realize, my lord, that you only limit yourself by this stubbornness? Can you understand the wealth of worlds and lives available to you through the written word, waiting to be discovered?"

"Unreal lives," Alistair said. "Unreal, untrue, unlived. I have no interest in holing myself away in dark rooms, poring over pages of these fool letters. I have a life of my own to live."

"Unless, of course, this pale-faced child of your dreams has its way," said the Chronicler.

Alistair's cheeks drained of color. He looked sickly in the candlelight. "Don't mock me, Chronicler. Remember your place."

But the Chronicler was one of those people unable to be intimidated by rank. He turned and fixed Alistair with a stare, and Alistair immediately wished he could take back his words.

"You mock yourself," said the Chronicler, "wasting your energies worrying about dreams when there is work to be done. Or do you think the kingship will land upon you without merit? You, Earl Ferox's illiterate nephew?"

Alistair wanted to rage. But rage didn't come naturally to his nature. Besides, he was terribly, terribly tired. So he wilted beneath the Chronicler's stare and managed only a muttered, "I don't see how reading and writing will make me a better king. Will it strengthen my ability to lead earls, bind alliances, or battle Corrilond?"

"The Kings of Corrilond read," said the Chronicler.

"Well, then I won't be a King of Corrilond, will I?"

The Chronicler's mouth opened, and Alistair braced himself as for the whip. The Chronicler may not have possessed anyone's idea of manly prowess, but he did possess a tongue quicker and sharper than any cat-o'-nine-tails and a wit to match. Some of the tongue-lashings Alistair had received during library altercations left scars, and he did not relish taking another.

He was spared by a knock at the door and the entrance of his mother's page. Alistair turned to the boy with relief. "What is it?"

"Her ladyship wishes to inform you of the arrival of the envoy from Aiven." The page bowed quickly, his eyes darting from Alistair's furious face to the Chronicler's and back again. "Your bride, my lord."

"Oh." The heat drained from Alistair's body, leaving him suddenly cold and a little clammy. "Of course. Thank you, and tell Mother that I will be down directly."

The page left and Alistair, without a word to the Chronicler, went to one of the south-facing library windows and looked out. He heard the thump of his teacher sliding off his high stool, but he did not turn around. His gaze swept across the courtyards of Gaheris and down the path leading up from River Hanna. He saw the flag of Aiven, white with the crest of a griffin in red, and the retinue, some on foot, some on horseback. In the midst was a horse-borne litter in which he was certain rode Lord Aiven's eldest daughter, Lady Leta.

The entourage entered the outer courtyard, and Alistair could see the curtains of the litter drawn back. The Chronicler climbed up on a low step beside him and also looked out the narrow window.

"Well," said Alistair as the girl emerged. "There she is. My bride." He frowned a little. "What do you think of her?"

The Chronicler's eyebrows lifted, and his voice was as dry as it had ever been when he replied, "She looks a proper milk-faced lass. Just what you'd expect in an earl's wife."

"I suppose you're right," said Alistair, and while he felt he should be angry with the Chronicler, he couldn't work up the strength for it.

"You'd better go down and meet her," the Chronicler said. "Your lesson this morning is through."

"Maybe one more verse?" It was only almost a joke.

"Face it like a man," the Chronicler said, and though they had just been at odds, he clapped the young lord on the back. "You can't escape her now she's here."

"No. I suppose not."

Lady Mintha, sister of Earl Ferox, wrapped her fur-edged robe tightly about herself as she waited to receive the Aiven envoy. The cold morning tipped her features a raw red but could do nothing to emphasize the chill in the gaze she turned upon her son.

"Alistair!" she cried, her smile freezing his blood as Alistair, still buckling his cloak, hastened to join her in the inner courtyard. "You've kept us waiting in the cold, my darling. I was beginning to think your uncle would be obliged to escort Lady Leta inside himself."

"Forgive me, Mother," Alistair said, dropping a kiss on his mother's cheek . . . or rather, on the air just above. He feared his lips might ice over if he actually touched her. Then he offered a hasty bow to his uncle.

Earl Ferox, though he had been a magnificent man in his prime, trembled like a gutted old tree, still standing but only just clinging to life. His eyes, once bright with warrior's fire, were filmed over with dullness. A few years younger than his sister, he was not an old man. But the wasting disease struck even the mightiest, and neither leech nor herbalist could prolong the span of his days.

He kept living, however. Long after many had thought he would succumb, he continued his labored existence, day after dogged day. He had not yet seen the earls of the North Country offer the crown to Gaheris. He could not die. Not yet.

He nodded to his nephew and bade him rise. "This is a great day for Gaheris," he said, his voice quavering but determined. "Long have I wished to see the Houses of Aiven and Gaheris united in purpose. Today marks the beginning!"

Even as he spoke, he stepped aside. The hunched mass of his body moved to reveal the form of the maiden standing beyond. And Alistair had his first up-close look at his future bride.

Light of Lumé, she was much younger than he'd thought!

Or perhaps, he decided on second glance, she was merely small for her age. And the way she stood, head bowed and eyes downcast, gave her the look of a young girl rather than the woman he had expected. She wore a white barbet and veil that covered all her hair, decorated by a simple gold thread.

And the eyes she raised to meet his, though gray, reminded him of a fawn's timid gaze. The poor girl was at least as unhappy about this arrangement as Alistair, which was some consolation at least. Alistair offered her what he hoped was a friendly smile.

"Welcome to Gaheris," he said.

She opened her mouth. For a moment she said nothing, and he could see by the look in her eyes that she was trying to think of something clever, something charming. He braced himself. In the end, however, she managed only a weak, "I . . . I'm pleased to make your acquaintance, Lord Alistair."

He felt his grin sliding away, so he stepped forward swiftly and offered his arm. "You must be cold," he said. "Allow me."

She slid her hand up onto his wrist and walked beside him, her head scarcely coming to his shoulder, and said not a word the rest of the day unless spoken to. There was no doubt in Alistair's mind.

He would never love Lady Leta of Aiven.

In the gloom of night, a shed door creaked.

By the light of the moon above, a wizened, dirty figure emerged, toting a broom, a mop, and a leaking bucket. He shut the door and latched it firmly, then turned with a sigh to survey the inner courtyard and what the moonlight might reveal. River muck tracked everywhere! And who to clean it up? Certainly not the great lords and their great guests.

This was the work of a scrubber.

So the scrubber swept and mopped and scraped mud and horse droppings from the stone. As he worked, he turned his eye up to the castle keep. He saw a light on in the library, of course. Lifting his gaze one story higher, he saw another flickering candle in a window. Lord Alistair's room, he knew, and the candle his one feeble defense against the terrors of the dark and his dreams.

The scrubber looked for a light in the guest quarters. But Lady Leta must have been sent to bed, obedient little creature that she was.

The scrubber scrubbed on. More muck would be driven into the crevices come morning, and he would be out here at this same chore yet again. But that did not mean a man shouldn't try. So on he worked at his lonely task.

But he wasn't alone. Oh no! He had the moon above and all the starry host watching him. One star in particular, bright blue and low to the horizon, winked with curious interest. The scrubber looked up at it and smiled.

"Starlight, star bright," he whispered.

Let us out!

Across the way stood a heavy door, the entrance to the Gaheris family crypt. As the scrubber drew near, driving mud before him, whispers reached out to him from beyond the door, whispers no one else heard, perhaps because, in reality, there was nothing to hear.

Let us out!

"Keep your helmets on," the scrubber said, his bare feet squelching in the mud trailing behind his mop. "It's not time yet."

2

*T*HE PARASITE LATCHED HOLD OF ETALPALLI, *and I, for the first time, saw death in the eyes of my father, my mother. Immortal, they had ruled the City of Wings since before Time dared visit our demesne. They had seen the rise of the red spires and guided the growth of green things. They ruled from Itonatiu and Omeztli Towers and were, in my eyes, like the sun and the moon themselves.*

But the day the Parasite came, my parents looked from their two high towers and saw, for the first time, their doom.

When Leta's father came to her earlier that spring and said, "You are going to marry the Earl of Gaheris's nephew," her first instinct was to rebel.

"I am a person!" she wanted to shout. "I have my own desires, my own passions! I'm not a tool for the manipulation of alliances!"

But as always, it was practical Leta who responded instead.

"Very well, Father. This will be a great thing for Aiven House, will it not?"

"A great thing indeed. The nephew may be King of the North Country one day."

So Leta nodded, folded her hands, and resigned herself to her fate. After all, as her mother often told her, marriage was the only means by which a maiden might gain power to change the course of history. A strong marriage could be the making of a woman, and even a bad marriage was preferable to no marriage at all.

"And Lord Alistair of Gaheris is the best match to be had among all the earldoms," Lady Aiven informed Leta later that same day. "He is young, well-formed, strong, and will inherit all his uncle's estates."

"Did Earl Ferox never marry and have children of his own?" Leta asked, curious, for she knew little about this family that would soon be hers.

"Oh yes," her mother replied. "Ferox did marry. Pero was her name, Lady Pero. A charming, delicate thing she was! She was due to have a child too, but she died on the birthing bed, and Ferox never remarried. Brokenhearted, so they say."

"What of the baby?" Leta asked.

"Dead too, of course." Lady Aiven shrugged, then gave her daughter a sharp glance. "Don't look so dispirited. It makes you more whey-faced than ever, and no man wants to marry that. Why should you care about the death of a woman and child you never met? These things happen. It is our woman's lot."

"Our woman's lot," Leta whispered to herself on this, her second morning in Gaheris. The night before had passed in a blur, and although she'd sat beside Lord Alistair for the whole of a sumptuous banquet, she could not recall two words spoken between them.

She'd spent half the night staring at the drawn curtains round her bed and reviewing the evening's events without satisfaction. Now she sat, hollow eyed, in the privacy of her chambers and waited for life to happen. But life seemed as disinclined to happen that morning as it ever had in Aiven. Her lady had informed her that she would be invited to dine privately with Lady Mintha later that day and, until then, she must amuse herself in her own chambers.

Like a prisoner.

So much for a grand adventure, rebellious Leta thought bitterly.

What did you expect? practical Leta responded with annoying calm. *Romance? Intrigue? Silly girl.*

A knock sounded lightly at the door. Leta hesitated, uncertain what to do. Her lady had stepped from the room. Dared she answer the door for herself? A second knock. She couldn't very well pretend not to be in, could she? Feeling a bit bold, Leta crossed the room and cracked open the door.

She found herself face-to-face with Lord Alistair.

"Oh!" This was as far as her vocabulary would take her on short notice.

"Good morrow, Lady Leta." Alistair offered a friendly grin as he bowed. He wasn't a handsome man, though he was, as her mother had told her, well-formed and strong. His face was pleasant enough beneath a shock of bright red hair. Perhaps not what a girl envisions as her future husband or even, for that matter, her future king. But then, Leta knew very well she was no man's dream come true herself. And she would marry Alistair a year from this very day. Best to put a brave face on it. So she tried a smile of her own in response.

"I wondered," said Alistair, encouraged by that smile, "if I could interest you in a tour of Gaheris? As you are new to my home, I should like to do what I can to make you comfortable."

Leta looked him swiftly up and down. He was dressed in riding gear and even held a riding crop in one hand.

He wasn't intending to seek you out this morning, her practical side said. *His mother caught him on his way to the stables and sent him up to court you.*

Her rebellious side responded, *So what? At least he's an opportunity to escape these cold rooms!*

Leta drew a breath, all too aware she'd let the silence linger too long. "Um. Let me fetch my cloak," she said.

Alistair waited patiently until she joined him in the passage. Perhaps he was a little disappointed. By agreeing to his proposal, she had certainly deprived him of his last hope for a morning ride. Disappointed or not, at least he was courteous about it, and that could go a long way toward making a marriage bearable, Leta told herself. After all, plenty of young men would have ignored her existence entirely, before and after marriage.

And really, who could blame them?

Alistair led her down the passage, explaining how her chambers were on the same side of the keep as the family rooms. "Since you're to be family soon enough," he said with another of his vague but friendly grins, "my uncle thought it best that you be settled with us."

Leta floundered for an interesting response. "I am comfortable," she managed. It sounded just as insipid as she'd feared.

Alistair took her through the whole of the keep, pointing out the great hall, the passage leading to the scullery and kitchens. "And the most prized possession of all within Gaheris," he said grandly, opening a certain door, "the castle well."

Leta tried to demonstrate interest as she looked into the small, damp chamber housing the castle water supply. Like Aiven's, it was located within the keep itself so that should siege come upon the castle, the defenders could retreat all the way to the keep and still have everything necessary for life and defense.

"It's the best water you'll find anywhere in the North Country," Alistair claimed proudly.

Leta nodded. Then she asked, "Has this castle suffered under many sieges?"

"More than you can count, though not since my uncle's mastery," Alistair replied and seemed pleased to be asked. "And never once has Gaheris fallen!"

Leta knew he expected some comment, but she could think of nothing, so she smiled again.

"Yes," said Alistair, turning away from her with something of a sigh. "Shall we continue?"

They emerged at last through a door into the inner courtyard. Alistair waved a hand to indicate the castle's guest wing, where, he informed her, the steward and other servants of high rank lived. "The castle chronicler has rooms there as well, but he rarely emerges from his library," Alistair said. "And beyond that wall"—he indicated the opposite side of the courtyard— "is a sheer drop down to the river below. Another of Gaheris's defenses."

"What is that?" Leta asked, pointing to something along that same wall. It was a small mausoleum in marble with a heavy wooden door, rather finely made, eye-catching amid the harsh and militaristic lines of Gaheris.

"The entrance to the family crypt," Alistair replied, leading her toward it. "Beyond the door, a stairway leads down to the vaults where my ancestors are laid. My father is there. What's left of him."

Leta shivered at this and drew her cloak more tightly about herself. She felt as though she looked upon her own final resting place. After all, she would marry into the House of Gaheris and someday be laid among the lords and ladies of the castle. "Our woman's lot," she whispered.

"What was that?" her betrothed asked.

But she merely shook her head. He beckoned her to follow him to the outer courtyard, which was a veritable market square open to the farmers who tilled the fields beyond Gaheris's walls. The housecarls' barracks lined the north wall, with the stables and smithy on the west. It was all much grander than Aiven, though Leta knew her father was considered the second most powerful earl in the North Country. No wonder all talk of possible kingship centered on Gaheris House and no other!

"Do you hunt?" Alistair asked as they neared the stables.

"I . . . I never have," she replied, ducking her head before she could see the disappointment on his face.

"Well, never mind," he said, his voice cheerful if a little forced. "My mother dislikes the hunt herself. She calls it a bloody ritual of—"

"My lord! My lord Alistair!"

A stableboy came running up to them, bowing and touching his forelock and hardly sparing a glance for Leta. "It's your red hunter, my lord! Master Nicon wishes you to come at once!"

"Ah, the same old trouble, eh?" Alistair said, his voice light but with a trace of concern behind the lightness. He turned to Leta. "I must see to this. The stables are no place for a lady. Shall I . . . shall I escort you back?"

He looked frustrated at the prospect despite that ever-determined smile. Leta hastily replied, "Oh no, I can find my way well enough. And if I miss a turn, surely someone will direct me."

Relieved, Alistair bowed over her hand and kissed it in a distracted manner. The next moment, he was hastening off behind the stableboy, and Leta watched his red head disappear into the gloom of the stables.

There was nothing for it. She must return to her rooms and the boredom of a day highlighted only by a prospective supper with her future mother-in-law. "Our woman's lot," she muttered again and retraced her steps through the gates. Determined to ignore the crypt with its fine marble, she turned her head away and saw, on the opposite side of the inner courtyard, a humble shed.

Even as she watched, a wizened little man emerged from it, a lowly scrubber carrying a mop over one shoulder. He saw her too and grinned and bowed. What an ugly creature he was, as old as age itself! She gave a cool nod and hastened on to the keep.

Oddly enough, as she passed through the doorway into the dim and drafty halls, Leta met no one. She continued to meet no one as she climbed the first set of stairs and paused at the top, trying to remember from which way she had come. The passages right and left looked exactly alike to her, so she took the right one and went up another winding stair, though she was certain by then she'd chosen incorrectly. Arriving at a long, well-furnished passage that seemed familiar, she hurried to its end and opened the final door, expecting to come upon her own rooms.

She stood at the threshold of the castle library.

Leta paused, her mouth open and her eyes wide. What a wondrous sight! Why had Alistair, amid all his boasting of wells and defenses, neglected to show her this room? It was dark and dusty, lighted only by a few candles, but she could smell the wealth of knowledge contained therein. Volume upon bound volume filled the various tables and shelves lining the walls, and a hundred or more scrolls! A long table littered in papers took up half the floor space on one side, and a desk covered with inkstands and parchment was drawn up to one of the windows.

You should shut the door, practical Leta advised. *Shut the door, own your mistake, and retrace your steps. Someone will have noticed you're missing by now.*

Yes, and what a stir that will be! rebellious Leta thought, amused. And she stepped into the library and closed the door.

A book lay open on the long table, a candle lighting its pages. Leta approached with all the reverence due holy things and leaned over to look upon the written pages. One page boasted a fine illumination of a house, she thought, though it was turned away from her. With tentative fingers she gently moved the book to a better viewing angle.

And there it was. The House of Lights. She would recognize it anywhere, the heart of all North Country history and legend. The House of Lights, built by Faerie hands and filled with the light of a magical lantern. The illuminator had depicted it as it once was, its doors flung open and light pouring out in sacred brilliance that was almost song. Beneath it all were written words. Leta put out a hand as though to catch them even as they danced across the page.

"I wouldn't touch that if I were you."

"I'm sorry!" The words fell from Leta's mouth, as much a reflex as her hastily removed hand. She whirled about, expecting to see some stern figure standing behind her. But there were only more shadows and more books. "I'm so sorry. I have never seen so many books in one place before." She spun slowly as she searched the library for some sign of the speaker. "How many are there? A hundred at least, I should imagine. Two hundred even! Aiven cannot boast half that. Indeed, I think my father possesses no more than twenty bound volumes, even were you to combine all his estates."

There was silence for a long moment. Then the same voice spoke. "Ferox boasts the greatest library in all the North Country, as befits the greatest earl."

Leta, turning to the voice once more, looked up and realized that there was more to this library than she had first seen. The ceiling opened above her into a loft, a whole second level to this marvelous chamber. She could see no light up there, and the speaker stood beyond her range of vision.

Somehow, unable to see to whom she spoke, Leta felt emboldened. "You seem to take much pride in Earl Ferox's possessions," she said, tilting her head.

"Naturally," the speaker above her replied. "I copied many of them myself. Though they belong to the earl, they are a piece of me, and I alone can read them."

"And who are you, please?" she asked, moving around the table and straining for a glimpse.

"I am the castle chronicler."

The voice was deep but also rather . . . dry, Leta decided. It was the voice of one who spent most of his time in shadows and dust. "Have you no name?" she asked. She heard his footsteps above and thought he moved to avoid her line of vision. He gave no answer, and after a few waiting moments, Leta no longer expected one. She turned back to the table and the book with the illumination. Candlelight caught the colorful ink and made it shine.

Once more she traced the letters written beneath. She spoke softly:

> *"The dark won't hide the Path*
> *When you near the House of Light . . ."*

More footsteps creaked above, and the dry voice spoke again, this time with surprise. "Lights Above! Don't tell me you can read."

Leta withdrew from the table and folded her arms beneath her long cloak. "No," she said quickly. "Not I." She felt as though the rest of her was folding up as well. Folding up into the tiny lump of insignificance she had always been.

The thought made her angry, and the anger pushed her to speak again. "I am right though, aren't I? This is about the House of Lights?"

"It is."

"A funny thing," Leta continued, looking at the page but keeping her hands to herself, "writing down nursery rhymes. Are there not more important things to which you might turn your hand?"

"Always," said the Chronicler. "But sometimes even a chronicler needs to indulge in the unessential."

Leta's gaze ran over the lines and marks that flickered along with the candlelight. She had never been permitted into Aiven's library unescorted, and the old chronicler who'd holed himself away in there chased women out as a terrier might chase rats. Leta could not recall the last time she had been so near a book.

"And these marks and scratches," she said, speaking softly, "come together to make what I said. To make the rhyme." She shook her head, smiling in wonder. "That is magic, you know. And you are a wizard!"

Silence above, then shifting feet.

"My father's chronicler could not do this work," she continued, looking from one page to the next to see the wealth of text held there. "Father says he can scarcely put three words to a page, but he's the only man I'd ever met until now who could read or write." She looked up into the shadows of the loft again. "Did you teach yourself?"

"No," said the Chronicler. "I was apprenticed when quite young to Raguel, the former chronicler. When he died, I took over."

"Do you have a special gift? A magic that enables you to learn?"

"Anyone can learn to read or write." The voice was drier than ever. "Few bother to try. At Earl Ferox's request, I am attempting to teach Lord Alistair. But he can't be bothered to apply himself."

Leta felt cold suddenly, colder even than when she had stood in the great outer courtyard. "You don't think much of my lord Alistair, then?"

Once more that wall of silence was her answer. She wondered if the Chronicler had not heard her soft voice and opened her mouth to repeat her question when she heard from above:

"He will make a fine Earl of Gaheris one day. He is just the man old Ferox would wish to inherit, and he will earn the respect of all the North Country."

Leta waited, but the Chronicler said no more. She stood shivering in the candle's glow, studying the illumination of the House of Lights and wondering if the Chronicler found her tiresome. Perhaps it was time to return to her rooms, to her lady's scolding, to supper with Lady Mintha and a groom who did not want her.

Instead, she said, "Could you teach me?"

"What?"

The answer came quick and sharp, and Leta almost lacked the courage to continue. "Could you teach me?" she said, forcing herself to speak. "To read?"

"You?"

In rushed Leta's practical side, raging vehemently. *Don't be a goose! You are a woman. Don't forget your place. You can't learn to read and write! You are intended to marry and bear children.*

Leta cringed and almost bowed out then and there.

But her rebellious side replied, *Pttttthp!* with such clear articulation that her practical side was shocked into silence.

"Why not?" she demanded, a little breathless, as though she'd just run a mile in the cold.

Another long silence. Then the Chronicler said, "I've never known a woman to read or write."

"Does that mean it can't be done?" Leta asked, half fearing his answer.

At first, nothing. Then the stamp of feet across the loft. Leta turned and realized that there was a narrow, spiral staircase in one corner leading down to the floor on which she stood. She saw a shadow moving and knew the Chronicler was descending. He stepped into the candlelight.

He was young. She noticed this with a start, for she had assumed from his voice that he was older than her father. But indeed, he was as young as Alistair, younger even.

He was also a dwarf.

Though his face and features were fine, his body was disproportionate, his arms and legs too short, his chest like a barrel. He looked up at her, his eyes pale and bright in the candlelight, and they glittered with an expression she could not quite read. As though he was always angry and barely suppressing that anger even now.

Leta realized she was staring. She blushed and looked away.

The Chronicler's voice was dry as stone. "I'm sorry, Lady Leta of Aiven," he said. "I didn't quite catch that last bit."

"I said," she replied and forced herself to meet his gaze, "does that mean it can't be done?"

The Chronicler studied her, his eyes shrewd and missing few details. She felt unprotected somehow and wanted to hide. Instead, she held herself straight and hoped her face betrayed none of her many fears.

"No," said the Chronicler at last. "No, I don't think it means that at all."

3

*S*OME CALL HIM THE CROOKED ONE; *others, simply the Mound. He appears without warning, without premonition, a cancerous growth latching hold of the land. He is black earth covered in dead branches that rise like antlers to claw the air. No one knows how he comes uninvited into the protected realms of Faerie lords and ladies. When he appears, there can be no hope.*

I was scarcely more than a fledgling then, new on my wings, bright and full of the life I believed was to come. I had never heard of the Parasite, never heard the cursed breath of his name. But my mother whispered it even then.

"Cren Cru! Cren Cru has come among us!"

Standing with her on the rooftop of the Moon Tower, I looked out to the mound that had taken root in the center of Etalpalli. I thought it a strange, ugly lump, like a boil amid the green of our beautiful demesne. But I did not fear it then. I did not know. I was too young.

But I quickly learned.

The old scrubber was not permitted in the family wing of Gaheris Castle, but none was awake in the dead of night to shoo him away. So, on withered hands and bony knees, he scrubbed and shined each paving stone with the care a jeweler might take over a diamond. He had no candle but worked entirely by the light of the blue star shining through a narrow window.

An icy breath wafted beneath a certain door. The scrubber felt it and sat up slowly on his heels, every joint and bone creaking. He moistened his shriveled lips, which froze immediately after. Then he crawled closer to the door and put his ear against it. Closing his eyes, he listened.

He said, "Ah! There it is again."

In the chamber beyond the door, he heard the beat of horses' hooves.

Alistair rides in glorious hunt.

Out here, flying over the grounds of Gaheris beside the shining, twisting rush of River Hanna, the full wildness of spring bursting on every side, he is free. Here, the sun chases away all darkness, and he himself chases his prey. His dogs—sight hounds, scent hounds, and massive curs—streak before him, their voices raised in bloodthirsty chorus, singing out death warnings to the wolf.

This is what it means to be Master of Gaheris. To protect his people and their flocks. Danger sets upon the village, and who would ride out and subdue it? None other than the lord of the castle.

Flanked by his uncle's huntsmen, Alistair urges his horse onward, pursuing the trail of the lone wolf deeper into the wilds of Gaheris's estates, beyond the tilled fields and hamlets. His heart beats with a certainty that he never feels within the confines of the castle itself. He will be lord of this house; he will be protector.

And when the earls of the North Country offer Gaheris the crown, as surely they must, he will be king. He will hunt down the North Country's oppressors and put them to the blade even as he hunts down this wolf!

The sun goes black.

It does not vanish behind a cloud, nor even sink beneath the horizon. It simply blackens as completely as a blown candle.

Alistair stands in darkness. He feels it crawling up his skin, beneath his clothing, sliding down over his ramming heart. Where is his horse? Where are his dogs? Where are his uncle's huntsmen?

All gone. All devoured in the black.

He tries to take a step but cannot see whether or not he has succeeded. He tries another, then another.

A white light flickers in the distance. And he sees the shadowy silhouette of the child.

He screams.

The scrubber drew back from the door, putting a finger in his ear as though he could rub out the ringing sound of Alistair's scream. With a shiver, he turned around and went back to his work. Bending to the stone, he blew away invisible dirt. Then, dipping his soiled cloth in a bucket of soiled water, he wetted down the floor.

He muttered to no apparent listener, "His night terrors are getting worse."

Through the window above, the blue star winked twice.

"The time is near; that's what it means," the scrubber said in answer to a question no one heard spoken. Then he whispered, softly:

"Starlight, star bright, guide her footsteps through the night . . ."

The simple children's rhyme rolled from his tongue and danced its way down the dark, sleep-filled corridors of Gaheris Castle.

For possibly the hundredth time that hour, Alistair rubbed his eyes and watched again as the words on the page before him swam slowly back into focus. He could hear the Chronicler's voice droning in lecture. He knew he should be paying at least cursory attention to whatever was being said.

But his gaze kept sliding to the illumination on the opposite page of the day's selected reading. An unskilled artist's portrayal of Sir Akilun standing with the Asha lantern in his outstretched arm.

On the brink of a bottomless chasm.

"And you have heard not a single word I have said for the last quarter of an hour." The Chronicler snapped shut the book he had been reading. He inspected the young lord slouched over the table. There was nothing lordly in Alistair's bearing or demeanor that morning. His hair stood up in wild tufts as though he'd made no attempt to tame it, and his clothes, though finely made and trimmed in fur, were mismatched and buckled in odd places.

Worst of all was his face. It was so full of dumb dullness, it made the Chronicler want to slap him.

The Chronicler crossed the room and stood at Alistair's elbow. And still Alistair stared at the page before him, his eyes glazed over without a notion of what he was meant to be reading. "My lord?" said the Chronicler, and again more loudly, "My lord?"

Then he slapped his hand down on the page beneath Alistair's nose, startling his pupil upright. "Oh! Chronicler!" Alistair gasped, frowning and pinching the bridge of his nose. "I do apologize. My mind's simply not in the books today."

"As though it ever is," said the Chronicler, backing up and crossing his short arms. "What excuse do you have for me this time? Another pale-faced child? Or perhaps it was a whole crowd of them, eh?"

Used as he was to the Chronicler's sharp tongue, Alistair did not reward this remark with so much as a sour look. He leaned back in his chair and, assuming a dismissive expression, yawned. "I'm simply not interested," he said, which was both a truth and a falsehood. "I have . . . things on my mind."

The Chronicler opened his mouth but shut it again suddenly. He backed up, returned to his desk, and climbed up onto the high stool. This stool had been commissioned and built specifically for him so that he could sit at Raguel's tall desk. From this height, he was the equal of any man. He looked down his nose at Alistair.

"I'm sure contemplation of the forthcoming delights your impending marriage will bring is indeed a great strain on your intellectual capabilities," he said. "But if you could see fit to set these pleasant daydreams aside and concentrate on the lesson before you, I'm certain even Lady Leta herself would understand."

Alistair snorted. Beyond that, he could think of nothing to say, however, so he bowed his head, his fingers pressed to his throbbing temples, and tried yet again to make some sense of the lines scratched in umber ink across the vellum.

"*The elder brother, Asha in his hand, stepped into Death's—*"

The library door swung open.

"Just *what* do you think you are doing?" rang the voice of Lady Mintha.

Not once in all the years of Alistair's life had he compared his mother, even in his thoughts, to anything heavenly or ethereal. Yet he turned to her now with a smile one might very well bestow upon a rescuing angel, glad for any opportunity to escape the labor before him.

"Well met, Mother," he said with false cheer and stood to greet her with a kiss as she swept into the room. Mintha put up a hand and pushed his face away, rounding on him in a flurry of thick gowns, her veils settling over her like the heavy darkness of thunderclouds.

"Four months, Alistair!" she said. "Four months, and have I seen even the *slightest* effort on your part?"

Alistair shrugged and settled back into his chair. He leaned an elbow on the book's open pages and rested his head in his hand . . . an attitude that made the Chronicler, sitting on his stool in the shadow of Lady Mintha, writhe with scarcely suppressed fury as he considered the damage to the volume's spine.

"You know I always make an effort," Alistair said, grinning behind the hollows under his eyes. "Simply put a task before me and I'll jump to it."

"Don't be flippant with me," said Lady Mintha. "You know how important this is, and yet I find you here, hiding away behind these Lumé-forsaken books of yours."

"Well, they're not mine. They're Uncle's really, for all the pleasure he gets from them. Besides, Mother, I don't quite follow what's brought you here in such high dudgeon."

"Why must you pretend ignorance?" Mintha wrapped her arms so tightly about her body that she became a quivering pillar of indignation. "You've made no effort whatsoever with the girl, and don't think I haven't noticed."

"Oh." Alistair heaved a sigh. "Leta."

"Yes, Leta. Your bride-to-be. Granted," Lady Mintha continued in a slightly gentler tone, "she's an insipid little thing. I myself can scarcely get two words from her. But that in no way reduces the importance of your role, Alistair."

Her son shrugged and, mercifully, took his elbow off the book again. "Leta's a nice girl. Sweet."

"Is that all you can say?" Mintha cried. "She's been here four full months, and have you made any attempt to woo or win her?"

"Why bother?" Alistair replied, staring down at the illustrated lantern on the page. "The betrothal is set. The papers are signed. We wed next spring, come what may. She's a fine match, and I'll make her a good husband if I can." His finger traced the line of the chasm opening just behind the ugly figure of Akilun. "We simply have nothing to say to each other."

"Don't be overconfident," Lady Mintha said sharply, emphasizing her words by grabbing her son's shoulder. He started under her touch, but she did not let go. "If something goes awry . . . if that little chit sends word to her father that she's unhappy at Gaheris . . . what's to prevent him from coming to fetch his daughter?"

"If that should happen, so be it." Alistair felt his mother's anger build right through her fingertips. Just then, however, he was too tired to care.

Mintha growled. She let go of her son and backed away, moving to the window and gazing down into the courtyard below. Alistair could hear her heavy breathing as she collected herself. When she spoke again, her voice was calm but edged with an ice that was more dreadful than the fire of her wrath.

"This is not the attitude I expect from you. This marriage must take place. You *must* secure the alliance with Aiven to have any hope for the future crown."

There it was again. In the last ten years of his life, Alistair could not remember a single conversation with his mother that didn't revert to kingship. The Crown was the darling wish of her heart. He had been brought up with his gaze always turned to the future unity of the North Country. His uncle also talked of it with an air of grave certainty that made one almost believe it possible. For Lady Mintha, it was nothing short of a consuming passion.

But neither of them knew of his nightmares.

Alistair shuddered. Then he said heavily, "Let it be, Mother. If the earls were going to unite under a king, they would have stuck a crown on Uncle Ferox's head long ago."

Mintha turned from the window, narrowing her eyes at her son. The light from the day outside fell upon her, making her very pale beneath her dark veils. But her eyes were bright.

"The earls had reason enough for not crowning Ferox," she said, her voice low as though she feared being overheard. "There was talk of it for many years."

"Which came to nothing."

"Who would crown a sonless king?" Lady Mintha asked, her voice dismissive. Then it hardened into the sharp resolve it always held when she spoke on this subject. "You are their new hope. The hope of Gaheris. The hope of the North Country. And if you prove yourself a worthy successor to Ferox, you will see the earls kneeling at your feet soon enough. But you must secure alliances now. Earl Clios is behind you, and Ianthon and Sondmanus. Aiven is the key. You make certain this marriage takes place; you make certain you have Earl Aiven at your right hand, and kingship is only a matter of time."

Alistair glared at the illustration of Akilun but did not dare to glare at his mother. "It will be a matter of *some* time," he said. "Uncle Ferox isn't going to hand over Gaheris next week. We have years yet, and I'm not going to concern myself with a future too far away to consider."

"Your uncle will not live to the year's end."

A stone dropped.

Both Mintha and Alistair turned at the sound and watched the Chronicler's pumice roll across the floor to the edge of Mintha's long gown. The Chronicler, silent upon his stool, stared at it as though it were his own life rolling away from him. Ink from an overturned inkwell dribbled to the edge of the desk and began to drip into his lap.

"What are you doing here?" Lady Mintha's voice washed the room in frost.

The Chronicler, brought back to himself, put out a hand to catch the dripping ink, then fumbled for a blotting cloth, hastening to wipe up the mess. Busy with this task, he replied in his dry, quiet voice, "Allow me to remind you, my lady, that this is my library."

"*Your* library?" Mintha picked up the pumice stone, hefting it in her palm. "Is that what you think, Chronicler? Is that what you've been led to believe all these years? That anything within Castle Gaheris is yours?"

"Mother," said Alistair, rising and taking the stone from her, half afraid of what she might do with it. "The Chronicler was here already, as he always is. You intruded upon his privacy, not he on yours. Have a little courtesy."

"Courtesy? To a scribbler?" Lady Mintha gave the Chronicler a final look, a look he met with equal coolness. In that moment they were surprisingly alike, this tall, proud lady of the castle and the humble, misshapen servant. Alistair could easily believe that anyone who stepped between them would either turn into a pillar of ice or burst into flame.

He took his mother's arm and pulled her gently away. "We'll speak of this later," he said. "I am in the middle of my reading lesson, in accordance with Uncle Ferox's wishes." He led her to the library door and opened it.

And found Leta standing there.

Mintha and her son stared down at her, and she stared down at their feet. A long, silent moment hung between them, full of too many questions. How much had she heard? How long had she stood there?

Then Mintha exclaimed, "Gracious, child!" putting a hand to her heart. She masked her scowl behind a quick smile and stepped quickly out into the hall, drawing her son behind her. "You did give us quite a turn! What are you doing in this lonely quarter?"

Leta, still without looking, opened her mouth but said nothing. So Mintha continued to fill the silence. "Are you here to meet this handsome son of mine, perhaps?" She pinched Alistair's cheek winsomely and laughed. "Has he quite charmed you yet?"

"Oh no!" Lady Leta protested quickly. She glanced up at Alistair and turned a remarkable shade of red. "I wouldn't . . . I mean, Lord Alistair and I . . . I mean, I would never dream of—"

"Tut, don't rattle on so," said Mintha, her voice less bright than a moment before. "I'll leave the two of you to your little tryst, and no harm done." She began to move on, leaving a terrified Leta trembling before Alistair, who stood with his arms crossed, trying not to look at her.

Mintha paused before she had gone many paces and looked around.

"Leta, my dear, it just came to me: Are you come here to have the Chronicler write a letter to your father?"

Leta blinked. Then, as though ashamed that she had not had the idea herself, shook her head.

"Well, if you do," Mintha continued, her eyes shrewdly fixed upon the girl, "try not to mention my dear brother's health, will you, my pet? I think it best if your lordly father heard the news from Gaheris House first. All in due time, you understand."

"Earl Ferox is ill?" Leta asked.

Her voice was so full of innocent concern, one could almost believe she could be so ignorant. Mintha smiled grimly. "All in due time. There's a sweetness. You keep your letters full of wedding details. Tell your dear mother all about your new gown, yes?"

With that, Mintha chucked Leta under the chin, wrinkled her nose as though to a baby, and moved on down the hall, her heavy skirts dragging on the stones behind her.

Leta stood very still, her jaw clenched. If Alistair had not known better, he would have thought she was barely suppressing a boiling anger. But Leta lacked the passion for real anger, he felt certain. It was probably nothing more than timidity and nerves.

When at last she glanced up at him, she could not hold his gaze. "I'm sorry, my lord Alistair," she said in her small voice. "Am I interrupting your lesson?"

Alistair shook his head. "I believe I am through with reading for the day." He sighed then and asked with resignation, "Were you looking for me?"

"No!" she said, perhaps too hastily. Her small hands squeezed into fists at her sides, and he thought for a moment that she would say more. But in the end, she was silent.

He sighed again. "In that case, would you mind very much if I excused myself?"

"Not at all," she murmured, and Alistair beat a hasty retreat, leaving her standing at the library door.

She remained awhile, unable to move, her ears ringing with words she desperately wished she could un-hear. But she could not stay here forever, undecided and afraid. So at last, her head bowed, she slid into the dimness of the library.

The Chronicler sat as he always did, at his desk, wiping his stained fingers with a still-more-stained blotting rag. He did not seem to notice her entrance but stared at the page he had been copying before Alistair's lesson began, perhaps reading it, perhaps simply gazing at nothing.

Leta coughed. She wasn't good at this sort of cough. It was too obvious a ploy for attention, and attention was never Leta's realm of comfort. But she coughed anyway, and when the first one did not work, she tried a second, louder.

The Chronicler turned. For just a moment, she thought she saw his face light up with a glow brighter than the candle on his desk, brighter even than the afternoon sunlight streaming through the window.

But all warmth vanished the next moment, replaced by the Wall.

Leta had become all too familiar with the Wall over the last four months. It was not present at every lesson. No indeed! Many days when she came to the library, eager and embarrassed by her own eagerness, and took her place at this table, she could see equal enthusiasm in the Chronicler's face. She could hear the excitement in his voice when he told her the list of letters and words she was to learn that day. She would sit and copy these until the Chronicler told her she'd done enough, and then he would draw up his stool beside her and listen to her stumbling attempts to sound out the words.

On the days when the Wall was down, the Chronicler would exclaim, "Listen to you, m'lady! You read like a chronicler yourself!"

But such days were invariably followed by the Wall. The Chronicler would sit on his stool, surrounded in a silence as strong as all Gaheris's fortifications, retreated so deeply into himself that Leta wondered if he even knew who besieged him anymore.

He would speak, but only as necessary. A curt "Good" or a curter "Wrong." And scarcely a word of explanation in between.

On such days, Leta rarely read well, and she always left wondering if she had offended him somehow.

She saw the Wall go up now, blocking out that glimpse of warmth and, she dared believe, pleasure.

Pleasure? Her practical side scoffed. *Did you not hear them, you ninny? Insipid little creature, that's what you are!*

The Chronicler doesn't think so, her rebellious side replied stubbornly.

The Chronicler doesn't think anything of you, said her practical side. *You're nothing but a diversion, and not a very welcome one at that.*

Leta ground her teeth against that thought and forced a timid smile. "I'm here for my reading lesson, Chronicler," she said.

"So you are," said he. "Come and sit, m'lady."

He slid off his stool and cleared Alistair's place at the table. He muttered something unpleasant that Leta could not hear as he tested the strength of the spine on the volume from which Alistair had been reading. Satisfied that it wasn't permanently ruined, but no less irked, he replaced it on the shelf and searched for another book for his new pupil.

Leta took a seat in Alistair's chair and waited quietly with her hands folded until he placed the selected volume before her.

"Please turn to page ten," he said, returning to his stool.

"Um." Leta licked her lips nervously as she flipped to the appropriate passage. "Are you not having me copy?"

The Chronicler shook his head. "We are going to practice another side of the chronicler's art today."

He seemed to expect a reply. Leta nodded but kept her mouth shut.

"Can you not guess what that is?" the Chronicler asked, his voice a little sharp.

She shook her head.

"*Thinking.*" He punctuated the word with a pound of his fist upon his desk. "I want you to *think* today. You will read that piece before you and then, rather than copy it out, you will tell me its meaning."

They looked at each other across the dimness of the chamber. Warm afternoon light poured through the windows, falling on the Chronicler's hair and turning it gold, falling on Leta's face and turning it white beneath her barbet and veils.

The Chronicler said, "Do you understand?"

"I understand, Chronicler."

With a wave of his hand, he indicated for her to proceed. Leta picked up the parchment, frowning as she studied the words. Slowly, some of them came to her, like a camouflaged deer in a thicket becoming more visible as she stared. She recognized words here and there, then whole phrases. The rest she could fill in from memory, for she had known this simple rhyme from the time she was in her cradle.

She both read and recited:

> *"The king will find his way*
> *To the sword beneath the floor.*
> *The night will flame again*
> *When the Smallman finds the door.*
>
> *"The dark won't hide the Path*
> *When you near the House of Light.*
> *Sometimes you have to run away*
> *To win the final fight."*

Another silence. Leta glanced up at the Chronicler, wondering if he would scold her for reciting much of the piece rather than reading it. She knew he could tell the difference; he always spotted any faking or guesswork on her part. But he sat with his arms crossed, watching her, saying nothing, allowing the silence to dominate everything until Leta thought she might suffocate in it.

"Well?" he said at last.

"Well?" she replied quietly.

"What does it mean?"

Leta looked at the page again. "It doesn't mean anything. It's a nursery rhyme. For children."

"Why should that make it meaningless?"

She felt stupid. *Insipid little thing,* her inner voice whispered, and no rebellious counter offered itself. "It's just a story," she said. "About the Smallman, who they say will find the lost House of Lights and . . . and battle a great evil."

"And who is the Smallman?" asked the Chronicler.

"I don't know. Probably the child for whom this rhyme was originally written. Or someone from another tale I don't recall."

Another silence. Leta felt her limbs shaking with pent-up frustration, shame, anger she dared not express. She wanted to tear the page in two, to fling it from her, to run from the library and never return. She had never felt more foolish or useless. Daughter of an earl, intended for marriage to a man who scorned her, for childbirth, for death, for dullness worse than death. Tears stung her eyes, and her heart beat a furious pulse. She opened her mouth to say something she hadn't yet thought out, something cutting.

But the Chronicler's voice broke the silence. "What have they been telling you?"

Leta started and looked up at him, saw the expression on his face, and quickly looked away again. Her own anger melted in sudden trembling. "I beg your pardon?" she whispered.

"What have they been telling you?" he repeated.

"About what, Chronicler?"

"About yourself." His voice was like a wasp's sting, swift but leaving behind a lingering pain. "What have they convinced you that you are?"

Leta opened her mouth, but no words came. Her whole body felt colder than the river's icy flow.

"Let me guess," the Chronicler persisted. "They've told you that you have no mind. That you are less than a man because your body is not shaped like his."

A roaring blush spread up Leta's neck and flooded her face—a flush of embarrassment that he should dare mention a woman's body and of shame at the truth he spoke.

The Chronicler slid from his stool and slowly crossed the room. "They've told you that the outer shape of you determines the inner shape of your spirit. And you, foolish, *foolish* girl, have believed them! You make yourself less than you could be and hide instead."

He stood before her now, his head tilted to meet her gaze. She wanted to look away but dared not. How angry he was, with an anger that frightened her for she could not quite understand it. His frame shook with the potency of his feeling, and his hands were fists.

"You've believed them," he said, his voice an accusation. "You've let yourself be made into something you were never meant to be. Tell me— tell me, Leta!—have you not longed all your life to prove them wrong?"

"Our woman's lot," said the voice of her mother in her head.

"Insipid thing," Lady Mintha repeated.

But the Chronicler took her by the hand. Though his fingers were cold and ink stained, his grip was surprisingly strong. Leta tried to pull away, but he would not release her.

"Where is the maid who came to me," he said, "and dared me to believe she could learn anything a man could learn? Where is she?"

The Wall was gone. Leta saw suddenly the whole of the Chronicler's heart and life exposed in dangerous vulnerability. And she knew that he sought an answer not only for her but also for himself. Her spirit lurched with a pain she could not name, reaching out to what she saw in his eyes. Somehow she thought she could give him the answer he needed. But she did not know what that answer might be.

Frightened, Leta closed her eyes, her final shield against those things she could not fathom.

For a moment, the Chronicler held on, studying the bowed face of the girl before him. Then he let go her hands and stepped back a pace or two, folding his arms. "Tell me what the rhyme means, m'lady," he said.

She heard the return of the Wall. For the first time, its presence relieved her; she felt it cosseted her own spirit as much as his. But she also knew that it made for a restrictive fortress, more a prison cell than a protection.

She found her voice in little more than a breath. "I think it means that we will have a king. When Etanun's sword is found. When the House of Lights is opened once more."

"Good enough." The Chronicler's voice was as hard as his pumice stone, but it bore an edge of determination. "So who is the Smallman?"

Leta shook her head. It was heavy with unshed tears, but she knew now that she would not shed them. "Um. The Smallman is . . . is the future king. The one who will find the door to the House of Lights."

"And the House of Lights? What is that?"

"The House that Akilun and Etanun built," she said. "The last one, the one not burned by the Flame at Night."

Here the Chronicler shook his head and returned to his own desk. He climbed up onto the stool, faced about, and folded his arms again. "Have you ever heard the word *metaphor*, m'lady?"

Leta shook her head.

"Metaphor," said he, "is the use of a symbol to represent an idea. Do you follow?"

Though she hated to, Leta shook her head again.

"No." He grunted and shrugged his shoulders up to his ears, looking ceilingward. "Let me explain. The House of Lights doesn't exist. You understand that, don't you?"

Leta frowned but made no answer, so the Chronicler continued. "It is a symbol passed down through ages of oral tradition, via minstrels and songsters of generations past. A symbol of enlightenment, of understanding. The House of Lights is no literal house but a representation of the understanding humanity desires to attain in a dark and confusing universe.

"The Smallman, or Smallman King, as you have named him, is also a symbol. He is not a real person or, at least, not any *one* person. He represents mankind. Small-minded. Ignorant. Struggling to make sense of life. He is a figure created by bards long ago, searching always for this House of Lights, for enlightenment, and standing up to all foes who oppose him in this quest. When he succeeds at last, *'the night will flame again.'* The darkness of ignorance will be driven out by the light of understanding."

His voice was confident as he spoke. Here, in this realm of books and academic speculation, he held uncontested sway. Here he was stronger than any man of twice his height and double his breadth. Though the protective Wall remained firmly in place, a glimmer of light shone from beyond it, revealing the life that dwelled within.

"Do you see?" the Chronicler asked. "Even a child's nursery rhyme—so simple, so small—has much to offer those who will take the time to consider. Those willing to *think.*" He leaned forward on his stool now, and his face was eager, his eyes interested. "Now tell me, m'lady," he said, "beyond the simple Faerie tale, beyond the stories you've been taught, what do you think it means?"

Leta stared at the book, seeing words she could read where only months before she would have seen nothing more than scratches in dark ink. Those words, those doorways to other worlds, to other times, beckoned to her, and she felt her heart begin to race. How she longed to use her mind as she had never before used it! How she longed to run into places she had never believed possible for one such as herself!

"Are you afraid to answer?" the Chronicler asked.

Leta drew a deep breath. Then she nodded.

"Why?"

Even that was a dangerous question. Clutching the book in both hands, scarcely daring to raise her gaze from it, she said, "Because I don't think you'll like it."

He snorted. "What does that matter? Think something; think something on your own. Not what *they* tell you to think or what *I* tell you to think. You are Leta of Aiven. I want to hear *your* thoughts, for they are neither mine nor anyone else's. Only yours. This makes them interesting."

His words pierced the numbness she had felt since meeting Lady Mintha, since coming to Gaheris, since the moment her father had told her she would wed and did not consult her wishes on the matter. They pierced down to a warm, living part of her spirit that she had scarcely been aware existed.

Tell him what you think! her rebellious side cried. *Tell him!*

He'll believe you such a fool, her practical side rejoined.

Tell him anyway! Tell him!

So she said, "I think you're wrong."

Then she blushed and pressed a hand to her mouth. Never in her life had she dared to cross the will or opinions of anyone! The glory of freedom surged in her heart. Before she could stifle the words, she repeated, "I think you're wrong!"

The Chronicler laughed a genuine laugh, and the great stones of the Wall crumbled away in that sound. "Do you, now?" he said, his eyes sparkling with mirth and, wonderfully, interest. "Why is that?"

"I think . . ." Blood pounded so hard in Leta's head, she could scarcely get the words out. "I think the House of Lights is real. I think it stands somewhere in our own country, hidden until the time is ripe. I think the Smallman is a real person, and he will find Etanun's sword, and he will find the hidden door. He will open up the House of Lights so that we will hear the Sphere Songs again!"

"Silly superstition?" the Chronicler said, but it was less a rebuke than a suggestion for her to consider.

"Maybe," she replied. "Maybe not. But I believe it."

"What you believe cannot affect the truth of the matter."

"Cannot the same be said for unbelief?"

Their eyes met. She saw appreciation written across his face. More than that, she saw what she thought might be pride. Gazing upon her, the Chronicler saw only something that pleased, that inspired.

"A good point, m'lady, and a fair one," said he. "I will think on it."

Her heart beat faster still, and Leta thought she might explode with the sudden power she felt tingling through her body. Let Lady Mintha say what she will! Let Alistair ignore her existence! Let her father force her into a marriage and treat her like bargaining baggage! She knew now what none of them knew.

She was Leta. And she had a mind all her own.

"I disagree with you, you know," said the Chronicler, still smiling.

"And I disagree with you," Leta replied, full of the joy of contradiction.

4

*T*HE TWELVE ARRIVED SOON AFTER. *They are Cren Cru's servants, his slaves, perhaps his worshippers. They passed through our gates uninvited, breaking barriers that should have been impassable. But once the Mound appears, who can stop him or his work? His Twelve marched into our land, the tramping feet echoing on our unwalked streets, and the Sky People flew into their towers and hid from those blood-cold gazes. Each warrior carried with him—or her, for I saw females in their number—a sharp, bronze stone. They arranged these in a circle around the Mound. The stones glittered in the daylight until the sun himself must have shuddered at the sight.*

Cren Cru was come indeed. And when he made his demands, Etalpalli trembled.

Through the Wood Between walked a Faerie who wore the form of a cat and who didn't give a whisker's twitch whether anyone believed in his existence or not.

This was the prevailing attitude among fey folk, truth be known. Amid all their philosophical contemplations, many mortals overlooked the fact that Faeries, on the whole, were just as happy to be disbelieved in as believed in.

An attitude of disbelief was easy enough to encourage in this age, when men of letters were few and libraries sparse. Faeries were by and large dismissed as imaginative fancies brought on by deeply instilled superstition and possibly a bit of distilled spirits. And the cat was just as happy to encourage this sort of dismissal. On the whole, a healthy disbelief in Faerie and all the folk who lived there made his life easier.

He padded confidently, tail high and ears perked, down a certain Path in the Wood Between, which grew in the strange, predominantly timeless stretch of existence separating the Far World from the Near. Indeed, the more the cat trod the various byways beneath the trees' long shadows, the more he suspected the Wood was not really a wood at all, but itself a living consciousness, or possibly many consciousnesses all bundled into one. Some of those were pleasant enough sorts. More were cheeky devils, and the rest downright wicked.

The Wood would turn a person round and flip him inside out if given half a chance. This the cat knew for certain.

But as long as one walked a Path—a known, safe Path belonging to a known, safe master—there was little the Wood could do to interfere.

So the cat remained firmly upon his particular Path, scarcely looking to the right or to the left. The Wood was always shifting around him in any case, and he did not expect to see familiar landmarks, or at least not in familiar places. That boulder shaped like a rabbit's head, for instance, had been a good mile or two back up the way when he'd been here last. And that tree, which last time had been split right down the middle as though by a bolt of lightning, was mostly mended now, the trunk knitting itself back together with threads of green ivy and pins of stout branches.

Landmarks were of little use to the cat. He was interested only in the gates.

He approached one of these now. To any mortal eye, it would look like nothing more than a thick cluster of bamboo standing in the middle of a fir grove. The firs were newcomers; the bamboo, however, remained ever in place.

The cat sniffed at it, his pink nose twitching delicately. Then he put out a paw and touched one of the slender green stalks. It swayed under that slight pressure but sprang firmly back into place when the cat removed his paw.

"Good," said the cat. "Still locked."

Just as he'd expected it to be.

He continued on his way.

There were several hundred such gates to be checked on this patrol through the Wood Between; soft places, so to speak, in the fabric of reality. Places where those of the Far World could all too easily slip into the Near, wreaking havoc on mortal disbelief in Faerie tales and magic. Thus they must be locked, and those locks must be carefully guarded. So the cat followed the Path of his liege lord.

Sometimes it still surprised him.

For one thing, he'd never much cared for mortals and their problems. Immortal himself, he had spent countless ages of cheerful existence never once considering those who lived beyond the Between in the time-bound realm.

And yet here he was. A knight. A defender of the weak, as it were. A minister of truth, advocate of justice, and who knew what other nonsense no self-respecting cat ever wanted to be!

The cat shook his whiskers as he continued his trek. The Path opened up before him with each step, and the trees and ferns and underbrush drew back to make way. He tested another gate and another after that. All locked. All safe.

The fact was he could no longer claim to be entirely indifferent to mortals.

"Dragons blast it," he muttered. "I warned you, didn't I, Eanrin? Get involved, and you'll find yourself caring. Then there's no end to the mischief!" He flattened his ears at this thought. He could blame no one but himself for his present circumstances. He had chosen this lot. Or he thought he had. Often he felt a little unclear on that score.

Often he felt that knighthood had been chosen for him against all his best efforts.

A certain smell tugged at the cat's nose. Or rather, not a smell but an unknown sensation whispering to an unknown sense, earnest and quiet and dangerous.

At first the cat ignored it. But within a few more paces, it had strengthened until his nose twitched and his tail flicked and his whole cattish being could no longer deny what he was sensing. He could only hope he was mistaken.

"But when has *that* ever happened?" he asked himself with typical feline shortness of memory.

He turned and, stepping carefully, pursued a small Path that opened off his regular track. Very soon he found what he'd expected.

"Light of Lumé," he growled, then sighed heavily. "Not another one."

Before him lay a circle of white stones that shone out brightly against a bed of dark moss. Even a mortal might have recognized it for a Faerie Circle.

The cat recognized a new gate beginning to open.

From this position, he could not tell exactly where in the Near World it opened to. It could be anywhere. It wasn't completely formed yet, he knew that much for certain. And if precautions were taken, it might never fully form.

One way or another, it would have to be added to his regular patrol. An unguarded gate was dangerous.

"Where do you lead, I wonder?" the cat mused, sniffing each of the circling stones in turn. Then he hissed and drew back sharply, his nose filled with the aroma of caorann berries. They littered the ground around the Faerie Circle, dozens of them squashed and stamped flat among the stones so that the moss was stained with their juices. No caorann trees grew in this vicinity that the cat could recall. Which meant someone had carried the berries here.

Caorann trees were known for one chief quality: their ability to unravel enchantments.

The perfume of the berries was very light, but once it entered the nostrils, it didn't easily let go. The cat sat for a while, grooming his face as though he could somehow push the smell out of his nose with one white paw. As he groomed, he thought.

Someone had been working enchantments here. Someone whose smell was now hidden by the caorann. Everyone knew that Knights of the Farthest

Shore patrolled this particular stretch of the Wood, and someone wanted to disguise nefarious doings.

The cat finished grooming and sat quite still, his paws placed delicately before him, his plume of a tail sweeping gently back and forth. His eyes were mostly closed so that one might assume he dozed, but the thin membrane of his third eyelid remained open as he studied the setting from behind long, cattish lashes.

He came to a sudden decision and stood. Trotting back to his regular Path, he hurried on to the closest gate. This appeared to mortal eyes like a pair of young trees with unusually large and twisted roots twining together in vegetal affection.

With a slight shiver of his whiskers, the cat stepped between these two trees and into another world.

It was colder than he expected. And he stood in icy water.

"Dragon's teeth!" snarled the cat and leapt back, scrambling up from the river's edge into the brush lining the bank beyond. It had been some time since last he'd passed into this corner of the Near World. The river had been low in its bed then. Now it was swollen, the warmth of summer bringing rushing thaw down from the mountains.

The cat climbed into the shelter of a grove of aspen trees and gazed out across the river, catching his bearings. He recognized the stern face of Gaheris Castle above the tall cliff across the river. A likely enough focus for secret Faerie plots. But from this vantage, the cat could see no sign of a gate opening. He'd have to venture deeper.

Picking his way downriver, following its flow, the cat reached a place where large boulders offered a crossing. To most looking on, there would seem little point in taking this daring bridge, for the stone cliff on which Gaheris stood rose sheer and forbidding on the opposite shore.

But the cat had been this way once or twice, and he knew more than a few secrets. He sprang from boulder to boulder, surefooted even as the fur on his spine stood up like a crest for dread of the rushing water beneath him.

On the far side, nearly hidden behind a stone, was a cave entrance.

The cat slipped inside easily enough; his golden eyes flared with their own bright light, like two small suns in the damp darkness. Water from the river ran into the cave, not deep but still freezing. A convenient ledge provided the cat with a dry route for the first stretch of this journey, however, and only near the end was he obliged to spring down into the water.

A stone stairway rose into the darkness, cut from the cliff itself. Up this the cat ran, higher and higher until he left the cold of underground behind and entered the cold of man-laid stone. His sensitive nose caught the many smells of mortals going about their daily lives within the castle, unaware of his presence within the secret passage behind the walls.

It always surprised him how strongly mortals smelled of oncoming death. How strange it must be to live governed by so short a span of existence! But this stink of death was stronger than expected, and a suspicion began to form in the cat's mind.

He came at last to the top of the stair and faced a heavy, locked door. Not an iron lock, thank the Lights Above! He could not manipulate iron. But brass would bow to his will.

The cat took a different form and worked on the lock such influence as Faeries have. He heard the catch give way and carefully pushed the door aside.

The smell of near death nearly overwhelmed him.

A fire burned in the darkened room, casting all in reddish glow, for little daylight found its way through the east windows this late in the day. On the wall hung a heavy tapestry depicting a scene from the Legend of the Brothers Ashiun, complete with the House of Lights and the swirling fires of the dragon, though the dragon itself had been omitted. Equally heavy curtains embellished with flowers and vines and fantastical creatures surrounded an enormous, four-poster bed.

Behind the bed-curtains someone breathed raw, unwilling breaths.

The tapestry on the wall shifted, and the cat slinked out from behind it. The clunk of a door shutting was muffled by the heavy fabric, and no one was listening for it in any case. The cat crept quietly up to the bed, his pink nose delicately sniffing out the scents of mastery, of lordship, of strength swiftly slipping.

The lord of the castle was dying.

"Interesting," the cat whispered.

But it wasn't a complete explanation for what he sensed, so he hastened on his way, slipping quietly from Earl Ferox's sick chamber into the passage beyond. He moved through Gaheris as though he owned it, and neither servants nor members of the household questioned his right to be there. A lady in rich garments drew back her skirts a little at the sight of him but otherwise left him to his business.

He followed his nose, which was as good a guide as any, sniffing out anything atypical. In pursuit of one such scent he approached the door of what proved to be a library and glanced inside. He beheld the castle chronicler—a short fellow recognizable by his ink stains—sitting on a high stool drawn up beside the table, speaking guidance in a low voice to a pupil. A female pupil, the cat noted with some surprise.

He regarded the tableau a moment, his nose hard at work. He smelled anger on the Chronicler, which puzzled him a little. Still more puzzling was the other scent, a strong emotion closely akin to sorrow. Given time, it might very well overwhelm the anger. The cat smelled it, and he saw more in the Chronicler's stance: The care with which he guided his pupil, care that was nearer to fear than affection.

Then the cat caught a glance (so swift none but a cat's eyes would have seen it) the girl gave the Chronicler beside her. That glance told him all he needed to know about that little scene.

But none of this answered his question, so he moved on, leaving behind the library and continuing through the castle.

He stopped suddenly as a nasty funk, stronger even than the stink of mortality that pervaded the Near World, struck his senses. His hackles rose, and he growled in his throat, a sound that sent all rats and mice in the vicinity rushing for the safety of their holes. But the cat did not hunt them.

He turned and slipped quietly up a flight of stairs, led by a thin line of rankness in the air. It took him into a set of private chambers, and he crept quietly to the doorway of a young man's room.

The young man sat pale at his window, wrapped in fleeces though the sun shone fully upon his face. His face was pleasant enough but scored with dark circles beneath the eyes, which gazed unseeing upon the landscape of Gaheris's grounds.

He reeked of nightmares.

The cat padded into the room, his tail high and curled at the tip, though his nose urged flight from the stink. He rubbed against the young lord's leg, startling him so that he gave a small gasp.

"Oh. Hullo, cat," said Alistair, looking down and smiling wanly. "Is there a rat about? Find it if you can. I don't want it gnawing my boots in the night."

With that and a (the cat thought) condescending pat on the head, the young man rose and left the room, dropping his fleece on the floor as he went. The stink of nightmares dissipated.

"Well, that's no help," said the cat to himself. Gaheris was certainly ripe with enigma. But nothing yet confirmed a new gate opening from the Between.

The cat explored more rooms and passages. At last he moved on to the courtyard, pausing on the doorstep to look around. It was strangely quiet for the time of day. The only person in view was an old scrubber, who creaked on his hands and knees as he ran a damp, dirty rag over the marble doorstep of a magnificent mausoleum.

At sight of the mausoleum, the cat uttered a triumphant, "Ah yes!"

Stepping daintily down the steps, he hurried across the way and sat behind the scrubber, studying the closed doorway of the Gaheris family crypt. The scrubber, hitherto unaware of his presence, paused in his work and, frowning, looked around. He smiled then and dropped his rag to put out a hand, rubbing his fingers together in invitation. "Kitty kitty?"

The cat put his ears back, glaring at the scrubber. The scrubber's eyes smiled through their wrinkles, and he made coaxing chirrups. But the cat turned up his nose and darted back across the yard, disappearing back into the castle.

The scrubber sat awhile looking after him, his face as inscrutable as a walnut shell. Then he returned to wiping down the stone. He muttered to himself, and any who might have overheard him would have recognized the words:

> "Sometimes you have to run away
> To win the final fight."

"So there is a new gate trying to open on our watch, and I need you to keep an eye on it while I'm gone."

Dame Imraldera—Knight of the Farthest Shore, Lady of the Haven, and keeper of the greatest library in the known worlds—did not bother to look up from her work but went right on writing. She was copying a narrative prophecy from a disintegrating parchment into a sturdy bound tome, and it was an interesting piece involving a princess, a garden of thorns, and a sleeping enchantment. Having once fallen prey to a sleeping enchantment herself, Imraldera found the foretold fate of the princess in question quite engrossing.

"Very well. Safe travels," she called absently over her shoulder, dipped her quill, and prepared to start the next line.

A hand slapped down and blocked her page.

"Oh, have a care, Eanrin! Look, you've made me blotch it." Shooing the offending hand away, Imraldera grabbed a rag and did her best to soak up the damage. Too late. The stain, though not large, was definite, marring her careful, scrolling script.

Exasperated, Imraldera rubbed a hand down her face and turned to the man beside her. He flashed her a grin so brilliant, it would have dazzled the eyes of all but the most hardhearted observer. Imraldera, unfortunately, was far too used to that smile and the devilry it usually masked, to succumb to dazzlement. She scowled in return.

"So sorry, old girl," Eanrin said, carefully wiping a speck of ink from one of his long white fingers. "Didn't get the impression you were listening, and I wanted to be sure I had your ear."

"I was listening." Imraldera flipped the last few pages to see how far the damage had soaked. "You said something about something, and now I'm going to have to take the spine apart and remove at least three pages. All that work!"

"I most certainly did say something about something." The cat-man stepped out of her way as she slid from her stool and stormed past him to retrieve various book-binding tools from a nearby chest. "And you'd do well to heed me! I said there's a new gate opening up. A death-house gate, what's more, and probably dangerous."

Kneeling at her chest, Imraldera paused, the lid partially upraised. She looked around, and Eanrin could see her ire slowly giving way to curiosity. "A death-house gate? What is that? It sounds dreadful."

"Sounds worse than it is," Eanrin said, perching on her vacated stool, one leg bent, the other extending to balance himself. He moved with a feline grace as natural to his essence and being in this form as when he took the form of a cat. In place of a fur coat, he wore scarlet velvets and silks, a plumed and jaunty cap clutched in one hand, and a cloak secured with gold brooches swept back over his shoulder. He shrugged dismissively, though Imraldera could see he was eager to divulge what he knew.

"Sometimes in your mortal world," he said, putting an emphasis on the *your* that Imraldera did not entirely appreciate, "dark places develop. For instance . . ." He cast about for an example, and his eye lit upon the blotting rag she'd been using a moment ago. He held it up so that the light from the window nearby shone through it, making it appear as delicate as a spider web, save for the dark stains of ink. "Say these dark patches are places in your world where the dead are gathered. What do you call those?"

"Graveyards. Tombs." Imraldera shivered. "Houses of the dead."

"Exactly. Those places lie very close to the Netherworld, closer than most Faeries ever come. And it stains the fabric of the mortal realm so those death-houses are not quite like the rest anymore." Eanrin jabbed a finger at one of the ink spots. "During times of death, a gate can open, and a dangerous gate at that."

"And you say one is opening on our watch?" Imraldera dropped the lid of her chest and stood, crossing her arms as she faced Eanrin. "Where?"

"A little up the way, beyond the bamboo grove. A Faerie Circle's grown up that could lead, I do believe, to the North Country and Castle Gaheris. Nothing to worry about on its own; it might never come to anything. But," and the cat-man's bright face grew serious, however momentarily, "I think someone might be trying to force it open."

"Who?" said Imraldera.

Eanrin shrugged again. "Whoever it is, he left caorann berries all over the place, undoing whatever enchantments he might have used. I can't get a trace of him." He smiled again, swinging his leg back and forth until Imraldera thought the stool might tip right over. "I do say, my girl, that long face of yours could curdle milk! Didn't I tell you it's nothing to worry about?"

"You said it could be dangerous, Eanrin. A dangerous new gate opening on our watch."

"Could be. But won't be. We have to check it, and if it ever fully grows, make certain it stays locked." He hopped down from the stool then and approached Imraldera, who stared down at the floor, her brow deeply furrowed. He reached out and playfully tapped her chin. "Not to worry, little princess. You've certainly seen worse than Faerie Circles. You'll be fine while I'm gone."

Imraldera jerked her face away, rolling her eyes, though she had long since given up trying to convince her comrade-in-arms that she was no princess. Changing a cat's mind once it had fixed upon an idea was about as possible as changing the dance patterns of the stars. She watched Eanrin set his hat on his head at a rakish angle, but he was nearly to the door before she said, "Gone? Wait a moment, where are you going?"

"Ah, so you *weren't* listening." He paused at the door and grinned back at her. "I'm off to Rudiobus and the court of my good King Iubdan and fair Queen Bebo. I've not seen the Hall of Red and Green since we came to this Haven, and it's high time the Merry Folk heard the golden tones of my dulcet voice ringing once more through the mountain corridors!"

"But . . . but you can't just leave," Imraldera protested. Though she had received her knighthood and entered the service of the Farthest Shore at the same time as Eanrin, she had not lived in the Between or known the ways of the Far World for nearly as long, having been born a mortal. Ever since establishing her place in the Haven and this library, she had relied on her fellow knight and his cheeky confidence, not to mention his knowledge of those things that seemed so strange to her but were as natural to him as night and day. Indeed, she needed him (though she might well have died before admitting as much).

She stood now, her frown lost in an expression of openmouthed worry that she battled to disguise behind another frown. "You have a duty, Eanrin," she said. "A duty to the Farthest Shore, to the Lumil Eliasul. You cannot leave all this behind and return to Rudiobus!"

Eanrin continued to smile, though more gently now. "There, there. Is that what you fear? That I'd abandon you?" For a moment he almost recrossed the room to reach out to take her hand. It was a foolish moment, and he stopped himself by a firm grip on the doorpost. "I'll be gone only a short while. You'll not even notice I'm missing! I'm not giving up my knighthood or our work. But I am Iubdan's Chief Poet, and I can't ignore my duty to Rudiobus. Besides," and here his eyes twinkled with redoubled mischief, "I'm certain my Lady Gleamdren has come to miss me while I'm gone. You wouldn't want me to drop my suit now, would you?"

"Oh. Yes. Lady Gleamdren." Imraldera returned to her desk and picked up her quill with the same aggression with which she might have unsheathed a blade. "I wish you the best of luck in your wooing, Sir Eanrin, and will see to it that our watch is well tended in your absence."

Eanrin eyed her carefully, searching for something in that irked face of hers. Jealousy, perhaps, though he couldn't quite convince himself that he saw it. He sighed a little but waved nonchalantly. "Everything is locked and safe for the time being. Be sure to watch that new gate. Cheery-bye, old girl! Try to miss me a wee bit."

With that, he was gone.

Imraldera took her seat before her work and toyed with the quill in her hand. The Haven had been her home for some time now. (Quite how much time, she couldn't begin to guess, for time was an inconsistent element in the Between, timeless though most considered it.) And she was used to being on her own, having grown up solitary and silent with only her baby sister for company. Lumé above, how long ago that seemed now!

She sighed and opened the book again to see if the blotting was as bad as she'd thought. Possibly she'd only need to remove a single page after all, not several. Dragons take that cat and his games!

Intent upon her work, Imraldera almost missed the sound of footsteps until they drew quite near her library door. Surprised, she sat up and turned around. The light falling through the library window was so bright that it was difficult to see into the shadows by the doorway. But she knew who it must be. None but a Knight of the Farthest Shore could enter the Haven uninvited.

"So you're back already?" she said. "That was fast! Or did you forget something?"

"No, I don't think I've forgotten anything," said a strange voice. "And it's been a long while, actually."

Imraldera was off her stool and crouched behind the desk in a second, grabbing her penknife as her nearest weapon. Her heart ramming in her throat, she stared into those shadows, trying to force her eyes to see what they could not. She did not struggle long, however.

A hunched little man crept into the light from the window, heavily supporting himself on the handle of a mop.

"Beasts and devils!" Imraldera exclaimed, nearly dropping her penknife in surprise. "Who are you?"

The wrinkles on that withered face creased into a smile. "I'm sorry. I forgot we've not formally met. I'm called the Murderer by most these days, though I rather hope you'll call me friend."

PART TWO

HEIR

1

THE PARASITE DEMANDED THE FIRSTBORN CHILDREN *of every house-hold. From the youngest, newly hatched fledgling, to those who flew among the clouds but were not yet counted among the adults of our number. Only these Cren Cru wanted, or so the Twelve said as they marched through the streets of our city, proclaiming their master's will.*

Some who knew the workings of Cren Cru made no attempt to resist. They offered their children swiftly and stood by while those unfortunates were thrown by the Twelve through a strange, small doorway in the side of the Mound, never to be seen again.

I trembled as I stood in Omeztli beside my mother and my brother, Tlanextu. He was older than I, his wings broad and strong, green against the blue of the sky, purple in the light of evening fires. He was very like our father, King Citlalu, in face and bearing. I thought him lordly and strong.

But he was still counted a child. And he was firstborn.

"Will they take you, Tlanextu?" I asked him.

"Never," said he, and his voice was harder than I had ever before heard it.

I looked up at him, suddenly afraid. "Will you offer yourself?"

"No!" It was my mother who spoke. Queen Mahuizoa the Glorious, older than the foundations of Etalpalli. She stepped before us, blocking our view of the Mound, and her eyes were filled with her death to come. "Citlalu will not permit this. Nor will I. You will be safe, my son."

"But what of you, Mother?" Tlanextu asked. "What will become of you and Father if you resist the will of Cren Cru?"

She did not answer. But she knew.

Alistair stood at his bedroom window as evening spread across the sky, sweeping over the fields surrounding Gaheris Castle, the hamlets, the groves. Autumn was breaking up the warmth of summer early this year, drawing heavy rains inland from the ocean. Even now Alistair saw storm clouds gathering, blocking out the red light of the setting sun. He trembled where he stood. He was a brave man, this heir to Gaheris, strong in battle and courageous in the hunt. By the strength of his own arm, he had brought down boar, bear, and wolf.

But Alistair was afraid of the dark.

So he trembled as he watched the thunder-rolled evening sweep over the earldom, plunging the world into the deep shadows of night and nightmares. He had sent all his servants and waiting men from the room an hour before, keeping only a tallow candle and the blaze on his hearth. Their warmth comforted him now. But he knew that sometime in the night the fire would go out and the candle would gutter in a plume of black smoke.

No earl should stand with knees knocking and palms sweating before an unarmed foe. For nighttime was nothing more, Alistair told himself. Nothing but spooks and fancies playing the fool with his mind. Yet his heart turned to water as the last of daylight faded and evening's grasp tightened on his world.

The wind blew in Alistair's face, fresh and full of the distant sea, tasting of rain. A gentle caress at first. But then it swooshed into his room, dousing his fire, plucking his candle's flame, and hurling all into darkness.

He stood, hands at his sides, eyes wide and unseeing as the wind spat rain into his face.

"Light the candle," he said, and his voice was steady. He knew where it stood on the low table near his bed, the tinderbox beside it. "Light the candle," he repeated and turned slowly, proving to himself that he was undaunted as he took one step, then another.

The wind stops. As he knew it would.

All sound of the storm, all smell of the sea-blown rain vanishes in sudden heavy darkness. As he knew it would.

Drawing breath is agony, for it is drawing that darkness down into his own body. But Alistair forces himself to breathe and to take another step. He must find his candle. But he no longer feels floor rushes beneath his boots. Instead, his feet step on rough-hewn rock.

"Alistair!"

He turns to the voice that called his name. As he knew it would.

The child's face, lit by a white light. Pale and frightened, it stares at him with shadow-ringed blue eyes.

"You shouldn't be here!"

And Alistair's voice replies, though he did not himself speak: "I came to find you."

"You fool!" the child says. "Run away!"

"You must be king," Alistair hears himself say. "You must save Gaheris."

The child screams, and there are words in the scream. "Watch out! Behind you!"

Alistair whirls around and sees: Red eyes and the flash of blackened teeth in a mouth leaping for his face.

As he knew it would.

Morning dawned.

Alistair lay in his bed for some while, immobile, his jaw tense as though in death, staring at nothing. At last he rose and, his limbs trembling from more than mere cold, crossed the room to his water basin. He broke the thin film of ice with his elbow and splashed his face until it burned raw. Then, still trembling, he dressed himself and left the room.

He felt a need for horses and hunts. He often did on these mornings after night terrors. Somehow, he must prove to himself that he was not the coward the darkness told him he was.

Somehow, he must drive out the face of that child and the words still echoing in his ears.

Slinging a heavy cloak over his shoulders, he hastened down the stairs, ignoring covert glances from the servants already up and moving about their dawn tasks. He proceeded out to the inner courtyard and stood cursing when the heavens chose that very moment to open.

He'd not be able to ride now. But perhaps the smell of stables and the nearness of his horses would be some comfort. Still cursing, he hurried through the courtyard. Rain drove across the stone cobbles, soaking the edge of his cloak, but it wasn't as cold as he had expected, and he did not mind it.

In his haste, he ran into a scurrying little scrubber.

"I do apologize, your lordship!" the old man cried, though it was he who had been quite nearly knocked from his feet, saved only by Alistair's swiftly catching hold of his skinny arm.

"No, no, my fault," said Alistair quickly, making certain the scrubber was steady on his feet before letting him go. The old man, unsheltered from the rain, grinned damply up at him, water dripping through his white beard.

"I'm all right now," he said in a thin but cheerful voice. "A pleasant morning to you, my lord."

Alistair nodded and made to move on, but a gnarled hand gripped his arm. "Look ye there, fine sir," said the old man, pointing.

Alistair, surprised, looked up. There was a break in the clouds, an odd enough sight on such a heavy morning. But odder still, Alistair spied the gleam of a star in the sky above.

"The blue star!" the old scrubber said, his voice almost gleeful. "Do you see it? Ah, the clouds have covered it now. But did you see?"

"I saw," Alistair said, shaking the old man's hand away. "I saw it, grandfather."

"They say," the scrubber persisted, "that when the blue star shines at rainfall, it's a sign of change to come."

"Do they? Well, that's interesting of them," Alistair said, hurrying on before the daft little man could babble more nonsense.

He nodded to the guardsmen as he passed through the gate into the outer courtyard. It was quiet that morning without the usual market bustle beginning to arrive, for no one dared display wares or offer services in such grim weather. A few soggy page boys, scullery girls, and stable hands scurried about on various errands. Otherwise, only the luckless wall patrolmen were out. Everyone else remained hiding like rabbits in a warren until the rain should let up.

Alistair kept on toward the stable, set on reaching its shelter. But suddenly he stopped and turned. A shout disturbed the drone of pounding rain, drawing his attention to a disturbance at the outer gate.

"Etanun! Etanun!" a high, youthful voice shouted.

Alistair frowned. Of all names to hear cried in that tone of distress, this one from legend and children's tales was not the first he would expect. Curious, he changed his course and made for the gate, where he saw two guards standing menacingly at their posts. One of them was shouting.

"Get away, little rat! You're not welcome here."

Alistair drew closer and looked beyond the guards and fastened bars of the gate to see a ragged urchin kneeling in the mud of the road beyond, hands clasped, feet and head bare. The visible skin was brown as a nut, and the short, skull-plastered hair was black as a rook's wing. The poor little thing trembled with cold.

"What's going on?" Alistair said, and the guards turned and hastily saluted.

"We don't know, my lord," the first replied. "The creature doesn't speak our language. Keeps chattering on in some foreign tongue. Maybe an easterner, jumped ship at the ports?"

Alistair approached the bars for a closer look. The urchin stared up at him with wide black eyes, mouth open and filling with rainwater. "Um . . . *he* is freezing," Alistair said.

"Then he should return where he belongs," the other guard growled, shouting again at the stranger. "Be off with you! Go back to your own kind, and let this be a lesson to you not to abandon your ship!"

But Alistair, frowning, did not think the little person was a sailor. There was something altogether earthbound about the child. If it was a child.

On shaking limbs, the ragged person stood upright and took another step toward the gate. A stream of unknown talk fell from his tongue, ending with a question and the only word Alistair recognized. "Etanun?"

"He keeps asking that," said the first guard, puzzled. "Can't understand it. Does he think Etanun lives here or something? Daft foreigners."

Alistair studied the dark face before him: the delicate features, the great, soulful eyes. "Etanun?" the child repeated and put out a hand in supplication.

"Etanun is not here," Alistair said slowly, ignoring the looks the two guardsmen gave him. "Not for centuries. He vanished when the House of Lights was closed."

The urchin licked bloodless lips, swallowing rainwater. Quietly, he said once more, "Etanun?"

"You see, my lord," said the second guard. "An idiot. Can't understand right speaking. Shall I send him off with the butt of my lance?"

Alistair drew a long breath. "A child," he whispered.

But the child in his dream had blue eyes.

He shook himself sharply and grinned at the two guards. "He looks harmless enough. Why not let him through? He'll freeze out there for certain; he's obviously not accustomed to our northern climate. A spell by the kitchen fire will do him good, and perhaps Cook can find use for him."

The guards grumbled but Alistair was his uncle's heir. So they opened the gate, and the mouse of a child scrambled through, babbling in that strange language. It sounded like thanks, Alistair thought.

"Well, little mouse," he said, smiling down at the child. "Seems you're inside now. We'll try to find a place for you."

The urchin, still shivering, smiled back, displaying white teeth in a flash across that dark face. A frown quickly replaced the smile, however, and he ducked his head. "Etanun," he said firmly, then added something that sounded like, "Cé Imral." A skinny hand pointed up.

Alistair looked as indicated. To his surprise, he saw that the clouds were beginning to clear away and the rain was lessening. In a clear patch above, still gleaming faintly, was the blue star.

Alistair turned abruptly back to the child, who was gazing at him in earnest supplication. "Change to come, eh?" he said. Then he shrugged and laid a hand on the thin shoulder. "I don't know who you are or what you want, but I hardly think you're going to bring disaster upon Gaheris."

He ordered the guardsmen back to their posts, ignoring their feeble protests, and led the brown stranger across the courtyard and on to the scullery entrance. Down a flight of stairs, into the pungent warmth of Gaheris's kitchens they proceeded, where Cook reigned like a fat king over a kingdom of drudges and kitchen maids. All was noise and bustle and hurry as preparations were made for the coming day.

"Here, Cook!" Alistair called.

The huge man, red from standing over a spit, turned to him. "What can I do for you, my lord?" He made his lumbering way through the throng of workers to bow before his young master. "Have you eaten yet this morning?"

"No, I'm not hungry." Alistair drew the urchin forward. "I want you to give this child food and work."

Cook eyed the child. "A foreigner," he said and sneered. "I don't like the looks of that one. Too brown by half."

"I don't care," said Alistair coolly, his hand gripping the child's shoulder. "Give him a place in your kitchens until I say otherwise."

Growling but obedient, Cook reached out and took hold of the child's arm, dragging him away from Alistair and propelling him into the kitchen. "Wait," Alistair said, and Cook looked grudgingly back at him. "See to it that the kitchen boys leave . . . leave him alone. You understand me?"

Cook turned from Alistair to the child, giving him an up-and-down appraisal. Then he shrugged. "Whatever you wish, my lord."

The urchin, eyes round with terror, stared up at the burly cook. He pulled suddenly out of his grasp and pushed his way back to Alistair on the stairway, grabbing his hand and falling to his knees before him. "Etanun!" he cried. "Etanun!"

Alistair shook his head. "There is no Etanun," he said. "Not anymore." He bent and gently touched the urchin's wet head. "I've done what I can for you, little mouse. You'll be safe here."

With these words, he left. And the urchin remained kneeling upon the dirty kitchen floor.

———

Growling, Cook thumped back across the room and took the child roughly by the collar. "I have no need of another drudge," he growled. "But orders are orders, and the young master is bound to check on you at least once. What shall I do with you in the meanwhile?"

He looked around, ignoring the little person's struggles to escape his grasp. Inspiration struck, and he bellowed across the kitchen din: "Scrubber! Come here, scrubber!"

A bent man carrying a mop and bucket hobbled across the room and stood before the cook. "What can I do for you this fine day?" he asked.

"Take this *boy*," Cook snarled, shoving the child to the scrubber's side, "and give him food and work. He doesn't speak the language, but I'm sure you can make him understand scum scrubbing, eh?"

Smiling, the old scrubber put an arm around the boy's shoulder and gently guided him back through the room. Relieved to be out of the big cook's grasp, the child went without protest. The world was all strange smells and sounds, and his toes and ears smarted painfully as they warmed. The urchin swallowed hard, trying to force down tears that would brim despite his best efforts.

Suddenly the scrubber bent and whispered in his ear: "Did you follow the blue star?"

The urchin jumped, backing away and staring at the man. For he had understood the scrubber's question, spoken in his own language.

"Cé Imral!" he replied eagerly. "Yes! I followed the star, and it led me here, and I am trying to find Etanun and . . . and please, sir, are you he? The Silent Lady delivered your message, and she is even now captive in the dungeons below the Spire! If she is to be saved, I must bring the heir to Fireword! I must—"

"What is that foreign rodent babbling about?" Cook roared from his place by the fire.

The scrubber looked up mildly. "I haven't the faintest idea," he replied.

"Well, shut him up, will you?"

But there was no need. The child stared at the scrubber, his mouth open but still. Maybe he was mistaken. Maybe, in desperation, he had only imagined that he understood the old man's speech.

Maybe he was trapped in this dreadful, freezing world without a soul to help.

By evening, the storm had blown past, leaving a quiet, cold world behind. Stars filled the heavens like snowflakes, waiting to fall.

A lonely guardsman patrolled the wall overlooking the inner courtyard on one side and the drop to the river far below on the other. It was a useless watch, he always felt, for no one would invade Gaheris from this side, even were invasion imminent. But he must follow orders, and he must march while the rest of Gaheris fell into sleep and dreams.

Suddenly, rising from the darkness in the courtyard below, came a voice faint as a whisper.

Open the gate! Let us through!

The guard shivered and hurried along the wall. Sometimes the nights played dreadful games with a man's fancy.

2

So the Twelve came to the doors of Omeztli, *and their voices carried from the ground to our high perch above.*

"Cren Cru commands. Send us your firstborn."

I clutched Tlanextu's arm in terror. I could not bear to lose him! He took my hand and held me gently.

Then we saw a powerful form rising up from Itonatiu Tower. It was Citlalu, our father. He flew across the city, his wings like a roc's, blocking the sunlight from view they were so vast! He landed before us, and I shivered with fear and love at the sight of him, for he was King of Etalpalli, bound to the realm by his own blood, by the beat of his heart. He was strong as the nation itself . . . stronger, I thought. The pinions of his wings were like daggers, and he shouted down to the Twelve below:

"Begone to your master! You will take none of mine into that Mound, not while I have life yet coursing through my veins!"

His voice shook the foundations of Etalpalli. I thought the Twelve would scream with terror and flee the storm of his gaze.

*They did not. They merely turned and retraced their path to the Mound
and the circles of bronze.*

*But the next day, they returned. Once more they called up to the heights of
Omeztli: "Cren Cru commands. Send us your firstborn."*

Once more my father denied them.

Something about the smell of books made the library feel warm even
when it wasn't. A low fire burned on the hearth, and morning light began
to creep through the narrow windows. It felt, oddly enough, like home to
Leta. Indeed, it was more of a home to her than Aiven had been.

Now months into her covert education, Leta was still very much a
beginner. Nevertheless, the Chronicler sometimes requested her help with
the laborious task of cataloguing all the piled-up scrolls and loose parchments not yet copied into bindings. He asked her to sort them according
to scribe, which required not so much reading skill as ability to recognize
individual handwriting.

But sorting provided her ample opportunity to explore more deeply into
the written word. She suspected she was better at it than the Chronicler
let on. What's more, she suspected he was tremendously proud of her.

She glanced up at him from her place at the table where she sat sorting
through a small box of old documents. He was bowed over his usual work
of copying, having spent much of the morning mixing inks in a variety
of vivid hues. How intent his face was, his brow indented with furrows of
concentration. It was an intimidating face, truth be known, fierce somehow.

But Leta found, as she studied him quietly from that angle, that those
fierce lines had grown very . . . She paused, choosing her words carefully
even in her thoughts.

Dear, whispered the secret part of her. *The lines of his face are very dear
to you.*

Sentimental drivel, her practical side responded with a snort. *And inap-
propriate besides! Have you ever thought as much of your betrothed? Have
you ever tried?*

She frowned and focused once more upon her work. A bubbling well of frustration, which had become all too familiar in the last few months, threatened within her heart. It took a certain amount of resolution to force it back down. So much foolishness!

Shaking her head and selecting another document, she peered at it closely, then blinked, surprised. Up until this moment, she'd thought she knew the hands of all the scribes whose works were collected in Gaheris's library. The Chronicler's square script was familiar to her, of course, and the more rounded hand of Raguel, the former chronicler. These two between them had inscribed the bulk of the work to be found in this chamber, but there were other scraps of handwriting both spidery and elaborate, some with spelling more creative than she would have ever believed possible, some in foreign languages.

But this hand was entirely new to her.

"Chronicler," she said, frowning over the scrap of parchment. "Chronicler, who wrote this?"

He leaned back in his stool, able from that high vantage to read over her shoulder. Leta looked up and saw him frown. Then he slid down and came over to the table, taking the parchment from her hand for closer inspection. His head came up no higher than hers, though he stood and she was seated. It amazed her sometimes how quickly she had grown accustomed to his odd appearance. Remembering how startled she had been that first day back last spring was enough to make her blush!

The Chronicler was unlike any person she had ever seen before. But he was himself. Her instructor, her mentor, her—she hesitated even to think it, for it seemed wrong for a young woman to think such things of a young man several years her elder—her friend.

But she hated the Wall.

She watched now as the Chronicler inspected the piece of writing she'd found, and the silence extended too long between them. No expression revealed his thoughts. His face lost its concentrated lines and fell into a relaxed blank. Had the Wall risen yet again? Would he block her out for the rest of the day behind barriers she could not understand? She waited, hoping and dreading she knew not what.

But at last the Chronicler said quietly, "This piece was done by Earl Ferox's wife."

He handed the parchment back to Leta and returned to his stool. Relieved enough to breathe once more, Leta stared at the work, the elegant, unfamiliar hand, almost too elegant to be easily read. Now that the idea was in her mind, she could detect a feminine touch. She frowned a little. "I thought you said you'd never known a woman to read or write."

"I haven't," the Chronicler replied. "Lady Pero died before I was apprenticed to Raguel."

"But this is indeed her hand? She truly could read and write as well as any man?"

"That she could," the Chronicler said. "According to my predecessor, she was the cleverest woman in all the North Country. Delicate of body but strong of mind."

Leta felt warmth fill her at this thought, a bond to this woman she had never met. "What does it say?" she asked.

"It's a bit of nonsense," said the Chronicler, picking up his quill and pumice. "An older version of that nursery rhyme you know, the one about the Smallman and the House of Lights. This version must have been that one's forerunner. It's a better piece. Nonsense, but better nonsense."

"How would Lady Pero have come upon it? And why would she take the time to write it down?"

"Everything should be written down," he replied, "however unimportant it may seem. She must have heard significance in this piece when some wandering minstrel visited Gaheris and sang for her and the earl."

With that, he bowed again over his work, leaving Leta to study Lady Pero's writing on her own. She knew she should set it aside and go on with her cataloguing. But somehow she could not resist trying to make out the words, disguised as they were behind embellishments and curls. Her lips formed the sounds under her breath.

"Fling wide the doors of light, Smallman,
Though furied falls the Flame—"

The library door opened, and Lady Mintha stood looking down on them. Leta gasped and dropped the slip of writing, her body filled with the urge to flee. But she couldn't move.

Mintha looked at her as though she could not see her, her gaze unwilling to admit what she did not expect to find. She said, "What by Lumé's name are you doing here?"

"I . . . I'm sorry, my lady," Leta said, rising and curtsying, scrambling for something more to say. She had over the last several months prepared many explanations should she be caught at the books. But she had grown so used to being completely ignored by the members of Gaheris's household, especially Lady Mintha and her son, that the need for excuses had faded into obscurity.

Now, when need pressed, she found her tongue tied.

Lady Mintha studied her, taking in the ink stains on Leta's fingers and the pile of work surrounding her. Then her gaze flashed, however briefly, to the Chronicler, who had turned upon his stool and regarded her, his face a cool mask.

What conclusions Lady Mintha drew, Leta could not guess. She said only, "You should not be in this part of the keep unchaperoned. What would your good father say? Return to your chambers at once."

Leta did not try to protest. Years of ingrained subservience worked their own power on her limbs, and she dropped Lady Pero's writing and scurried from the room, her head bowed, her face hidden behind her veils. She paused once she gained the hall, however.

You should never eavesdrop, said her practical side. *Do what you're told and return to your rooms.*

She took a few more steps.

But why would Lady Mintha visit the Chronicler today? rebellious Leta wondered and froze her in place. *She has no interest in books.*

It's not your business. Go on, fool girl!

But Leta ground her teeth. Then, before she could change her mind, she slipped back to the door, hiding a little behind the wall and peering through the crack. Lady Mintha stood in such a way that her rich green robes filled most of Leta's view, blocking all sight of the Chronicler. Every word they spoke, however, rang clearly against the stone walls.

"All of them must know," Lady Mintha was saying. "Without delay. Urge them to make their way to Gaheris to bid their last respects. And make certain they know that, should they come, it will be seen as a pledge of loyalty to the new earl."

"Yes, my lady," said the Chronicler, his voice very soft and emotionless.

"You do understand the importance of this task?" Lady Mintha pressed. "Your wording must be clear, the intent unmistakable. My brother has trusted you these many years to hold the best interests of Gaheris dear to your heart. I would not like to think that trust misplaced."

"It is not misplaced, my lady," said the Chronicler.

Leta saw Lady Mintha draw herself up even taller than she was already. Even from this position, where she could not see her face, Leta could guess at the expression of command Mintha wore. It was an expression as much a part of the Gaheris family line as their coat of arms or insignia.

"You are loyal to Earl Ferox," Mintha said. "May you prove equally loyal to his heir."

She turned then toward the door, and Leta only just had time to dart into the shadows along the wall and crouch there, cowering, before Mintha swept past, her robes flowing behind her like battle standards. She did not look to the right or left but moved swiftly down the passage, as though, having accomplished her important deed, she now fled some evil goblin's den.

Leta waited until she was quite certain Mintha had gone before she crept back to the door. Her gaze went first to the desk, where she expected the Chronicler to be seated. He was not there, however, so she glanced about and found him instead standing by one of the windows, his small frame nearly hidden in the lower shadows. The afternoon light struck his pale face and his fair hair.

"Chronicler?" Leta said quietly, half afraid to be heard.

He turned. His face was now mostly hidden from the light, but she saw the curve of his cheek, half his mouth, and one eye. It was bright. Too bright and glassy.

"What is it?" Leta wanted to hasten across the room to him but did not dare. So she hung back in the doorway, helpless. "Are you unwell?"

His face was stricken and silence enveloped him. But it was not the Wall she had come to expect from him. This silence sparked with energy, like rubbed wool on a cold morning bites at an unwary hand.

"Please," Leta said, desperate to break the tension of that stillness. "Please, tell me."

He opened his mouth but remained unspeaking a frozen moment. Then he said, "Earl Ferox is dying."

Tears spilled over onto his cheeks.

Leta felt her heart stop, then begin to beat a wild rhythm in her breast. She said nothing aloud, but both sides of her mind, practical and rebellious, clamored at once in her head.

So that's who you are, Chronicler.

Every night, he heard the voices crying out from the crypt.

Open the gate! Let us out!

They were his ancestors, Earl Ferox thought as he lay and gasped for air upon his sickbed. The cold of autumn nights penetrated the heavy curtains of his great bed like icy, ghostly fingers pressing through to caress his gray cheeks. His breath steamed the air before his face no matter how high they piled the fur rugs across his wasted frame, no matter how bright his servant kept the blaze on his hearth. But while his face burned with cold, his insides burned with fire.

Let us out!

They would come for him, he thought. If any fool heeded their voices and opened the crypt door, all the spirits of the great lords who had mastered Gaheris earldom before him would pour from the darkness, sweep up the stone stairs of the castle, and come for him as he lay helpless upon his bed. They knew his sin. They would not be forgiving.

Open the gate!

The curtain near his head moved. The dying earl drew a strangled breath and struggled to push himself upright. He saw long, gnarled fingers grasping and pulling back the heavy brocade. "Who is it?" the earl cried, though his voice was so thin his own ears could scarcely hear it.

"No one at all," said the old scrubber, leaning over the earl's bed.

"Ah," said the earl as he fell back upon his pillows, his face sagging with weakness. But his eyes were relieved. "Ah, but you aren't no one, are you?" he said, shaking his head slowly.

"I am no one anymore." The scrubber sat on the edge of the bed, sighed, and bent over to rub his sore feet. "I've been no one for such a long time."

The earl coughed—small, spasmodic puffs from his once powerful chest. "Tell me," he said when at last the spasm passed. "When will the House of Lights be reopened?"

"When your son is king," the scrubber replied with a shrug.

The earl frowned, drawing several painful breaths before he could find more words. "I have no son," he said.

The scrubber shrugged again. Then he stood, creaking, and carefully rearranged the warm rugs across the earl's body, tucking them in about him as gently as any nursemaid might. "Too bad," he said with a sad smile. "In that case, I suppose the House of Lights will never be reopened."

3

SO FOLLOWED DAY AFTER DAY. *Always the Twelve returned to make Cren Cru's vicious demand. Always Citlalu, King of Etalpalli, refused to comply. Every morning I woke with dread, afraid that Tlanextu would disobey our parents, would go with the Twelve and vanish into the Mound like the hundreds upon hundreds of others I saw vanishing every day. This fear was so great that at first I did not see what was becoming of Citlalu and Mahuizoa. Not until near the end did I realize.*

They were dying. Every day, more life fled from their shining faces. Cren Cru clung to the ground of Etalpalli, and I could almost see the fingerlike roots clutching into the soil, draining the demesne of life. Draining my father, my mother.

Faerie lords and ladies are gifted with three lives. Twice they may be killed, and only a third death will send them down to the Final Water, never to return. But as I watched my parents deny Cren Cru, I saw all of their lives at once slowly drawn from their bodies.

The blue star shone above Gaheris Castle.

Mouse, the kitchen drudge, moved as quietly as his namesake across the inner courtyard, escaping the confines of the castle kitchens. The air was cold, and the cobblestones bruised his feet. The only shoes he had acquired were thin soled, and he might as well have been barefoot.

But he wasn't used to the cramped, closed-in spaces where he had worked this last frozen month. He was used to open vistas and warm, dry breezes. So he sought the courtyard and, under cover of evening shadows, climbed a narrow stairway to the top of the wall. He passed a sentry, but the man took little notice of a lowly scrubber boy, not even bothering to jostle him, though Mouse prepared for as much.

In recent weeks he had experienced more jostling and shoving and rough use than in all his prior life combined. The kitchen was an isolated world with its own masters and rules shouted in a language Mouse couldn't hope to understand. The quiet loneliness of the castle walls was by far preferable to a pallet by the kitchen hearth, however warm, surrounded by pale faces and foreign babble.

Mouse shivered uncontrollably, teeth chattering in his skull. But he sought the solitude of the wall in this hour before dawn, eager for what little privacy he could steal.

A scuffling sound drew Mouse's attention, and he looked down to the yard below. He saw his master, the scrubber, making for the old shed that stood on the opposite wall. The sight of him was enough to make Mouse's jaw clench. That old man could take the most menial tasks in the castle and find a way to make them more demeaning still. And these were the tasks he foisted off on Mouse. It was bad enough to empty chamber pots . . . but worse by far to be forced to scrub them out with nothing but a rag!

Mouse's stomach heaved at the memory he wished he could pass off as a mere nightmare. He turned away, moving to the other side of the wall overlooking the sheer drop down to Hanna River. The river was a black liquid snake twining about the base of rock on which Castle Gaheris stood.

"Hanna," Mouse whispered. The word was strange on his tongue. It had taken him some while to begin to pick out the names of things, for no one cared to teach him, and he scarcely cared to take the time to learn. But he did learn despite himself. Hanna. Gaheris. Ferox. Alistair.

"Etanun," Mouse growled, and his eyes flashed in the night. He tilted his head back, looking up from the river to the vaults of the sky above. To the blue star that seemed to gaze back down upon him.

"If I follow it any farther," he whispered to himself in his own tongue, "where will I end? The sea? This river must run to the sea eventually. And what then? Take a ship, journey out into that wild bigness?" His stomach heaved once more, this time with terror mingled with sorrow. "How long?" he muttered, shaking his head. "How long and how far? I will never find the heir in time!"

Footsteps coming along the wall startled Mouse, and he turned, pressing his back against the stone. A tall figure approached, and the moonlight and the starlight revealed little of his face and form. But then a voice spoke, and though Mouse could not understand the words, he recognized at once who it must be.

"If it isn't the Mouse," said Alistair, surprised but not displeased. He smiled, though the urchin could not see it. He drew closer, though not so close as to startle the boy, and also leaned against the stone wall, looking out upon the river and the cold winter world beyond. "You are, I must say, the last person I expected to meet here. What are you doing away from the kitchen fire? Aside from freezing, that is."

Mouse could hear a question asked but had no idea what it was or how to answer. He couldn't decide whether to scamper away or stay. It seemed to him, from the young lord's stance, that Alistair wished for company. So for the moment at least, he lingered, though his body was tensed to run.

"I couldn't sleep," Alistair said. "Never can much, you know. Sometimes it's better not to try, so I wander about. I'm sure the guardsmen think I'm quite daft! That, or they assume all earls and earls' heirs are a bit touched in the head. I try not to disturb them anyway."

He leaned his elbows on the stone, looking down at the river, then looking up, much as Mouse had done, to the crowded heavens. Mouse saw his teeth in a brief flash of a smile.

"We have a name for that star," Alistair said and pointed at the sky. He indicated the blue star, Mouse was certain of it. Although many bright lights gleamed in that inky sky, the blue star stood out like a torch.

"*Ceaneus*," Alistair said in the tone that meant he wanted Mouse to repeat it. Mouse sighed. He didn't like being treated like a trained parrot. "*Ceaneus*," Alistair said again, still pointing.

Mouse folded his skinny arms across his chest. "Cé," he replied. "Cé Imral."

Alistair dropped his pointing arm and rested it once more on the stone wall. "Cé . . . Imral," he said, though his accent was off. Still, it was an effort, and Mouse had to grin appreciation. The tall young lord ruined it, however, by rattling on in his own language immediately after.

"Is that your name for our star? I wonder what language that is. Perhaps you're from Corrilond. They're a dark-skinned folk but not so dark as you, I think, and their eyes are different. Hard to say for certain, but I don't think you quite fit the Corrilondian description. Probably just as well. Corrilonders killed my father, and while I don't bear a grudge for that—I mean, war is what war is—it's a bit awkward, you must agree."

Mouse stared at him. Concentrate though he might, he couldn't pick a single word from this stream of talk. It ran together in a rush of sounds, leaving Mouse's head spinning. When the young lord stopped for breath, Mouse could do nothing but offer a relieved smile. Alistair's return grin vanished after scarcely a moment of life.

He spoke again in an altogether different tone: "My uncle is sick. Earl Ferox."

Ferox. That name Mouse recognized. He nodded noncommittally, uncertain whether or not he wanted to encourage more babble from this pale stranger. But Alistair needed no encouragement. Scarcely aware of Mouse's existence, he talked to himself or to the stars or to no one. "He's dying, actually. Won't last the winter. And then I'll be Earl of Gaheris."

Gaheris. Another word Mouse knew. He nodded again, his brow puckered.

"They say the next Earl of Gaheris will be made king of all the North Country," Alistair said, and his voice was as cold as the night air. "But if I am that earl, how can this be? I know I will never be king."

He laughed, a bitter sound. "My mother is convinced I will be. As are my uncle and Earl Lebuin of Aiven and all the most powerful men of our land. They believe when they look at me that they see their future ruler. They're wrong. All of them."

He bowed his head into his hands, running white fingers through his red hair, which was dark under moonlight. Mouse pulled back, at a loss for what to do. What could possibly have upset this young man so badly? "Are you unwell?" he asked without hope of being understood.

"I'll never be king," Alistair whispered, "because I'm going to die. I know it. I've seen my death every night for the last three years. Can you imagine what that means, Mouse?"

Suddenly, pale eyes turned upon Mouse, who drew back, frightened by the power of that gaze. "Every night," said Alistair, "three years running, I see the same vision. I see the child lost and wandering in a dark place on the brink of a great chasm. I call out to him, telling him to save Gaheris, but I don't know what from! And then I am torn apart by a shadow with a red mouth."

The young lord's voice had dropped to a tremulous whisper. The sound of it was enough to freeze Mouse's heart even without understanding. But it also, strangely enough, made him want to reach out, to touch Alistair's bowed head, to speak some word of comfort, to offer some kindness in the face of such distress.

The moment passed. Alistair straightened and the fading moonlight illuminated his mouth, twisting it into an unnatural shape. "It's grin or perish, Mouse," he said. "It's smile or go mad. So I'll smile. Even when my uncle breathes his last breath, I'll smile, and they'll set the shield of Gaheris in my hand and talk of a crown and a throne. And I'll smile, because I know they're all fools."

Mouse shook his head, his eyes round and frightened. "I don't understand a word you are saying, sir," he said at last, his voice a little breathless. "I wish I could help you. But I can't even help myself, and I don't know what you are saying."

It was more than he could stand. The shivering boy turned heel and ran, unable to remain in the presence of that strange, tall lord. He ran along the wall, past the sentry once more, down the stairs.

Alistair watched Mouse's slight form as it flitted across the inner courtyard and on to the kitchen doors. He remained awhile on the wall and waited for the coming dawn.

Forty couriers rode out in all, twenty to the earls themselves, twenty more to the smaller baronies and lowland keeps of the North Country.

From her chamber windows, Leta watched them ride. The swiftness of their going made her own imprisonment more painful by far, but she kept her tears at bay and her face firmly turned from the questioning stares of her servants and waiting women.

"Your father will be here soon," her head lady said. "He'll come to pay last respects and to honor your future husband when they place the shield of Gaheris in his hand."

Leta made no reply.

For some days now, she had avoided the library. She was afraid somehow, knowing what she knew, or at least what she guessed. Her practical side whispered to her, *Stay out of it. It's not your business. Only trouble will come if you meddle.*

It was a strong argument, and her heart was not brave at the moment. "Our woman's lot," she whispered to herself.

But the memory of the Chronicler's face and what she had seen there haunted her. Even when she sat at table, listening to Lady Mintha's voice going over her head, watching her husband-to-be as he sat hollow eyed and unspeaking, she thought of the Chronicler. Lady Mintha's talk was all of preparations to receive the earls of the North Country within Gaheris. Alistair, when he spoke at all, remarked on the unusual coldness of that autumn.

And Leta wondered: *Do they know?*

Snow fell upon Gaheris Castle, and the river, reduced to a channel with ice lining its edges and swirling in frozen chunks along the dark eddies. Nevertheless, the ferry from Aiven made its slow way to the banks below Gaheris. Leta, wrapped up in furs and fleeces, went down to the shore along with Lady Mintha and Alistair to greet Earl Aiven.

Her father, whom she had not seen in nearly a year, scarcely looked her way. He bowed over Mintha's hand and addressed himself to Alistair, saying, "I came as soon as I could."

"You are welcome to my uncle's home during these sad times," said Alistair. His face was paler than usual, and his blue eyes were dark with lack of sleep. But he spoke with the cool confidence of a lord, and Leta could see that her father was favorably impressed by him.

Lord Aiven glanced her way at last. "You're looking well, girl," he said, and that was all. He offered his arm to Lady Mintha, and they made their way up from the river to Gaheris, Alistair leading the way, and Leta trailing far behind.

She wondered as she tramped through the crunching snow: *Does my father know?*

She sat unspeaking at dinner between her betrothed and her father. They spoke of lands and alliances, of wars long past and grudges all too present. They never spoke of the crown, but plenty of latent meaning lurked in the not speaking.

Leta could not eat. She picked at the bones of a small roasted fowl, feeding much of it to the dog under the table. Her gaze kept shifting to the great, heavy chair, its wood as delicately scrolled as any illuminated manuscript, filled with Earl Ferox's absence.

Suddenly Leta stood. Her father and Lord Alistair gave her swift glances but scarcely heard the excuses she murmured as she left the table and hastened from the room. She felt Lady Mintha's gaze like daggers between her shoulder blades, and it drove her swiftly out to the darkened, frozen passages beyond the warm light of the dining hall. She picked up her pace, all but running now, lifting her heavy skirts as she climbed the stairs.

The Chronicler sat at his desk, bowed over his work by the light of three tall candles. He turned when he heard the door open and sat up straight. "M'lady." He said nothing more, but Leta saw how quickly he covered his page with his blotting cloth. And she could feel the Wall surrounding him as though it were built of stone and mortar.

She closed the door and stood a moment, her face hidden in shadows. Her heart beat a dangerous rhythm in her breast, and she could feel the wellsprings of sorrow trying to rise up inside, to drown her. She forced them back.

"Chronicler." Her voice froze on her tongue, unable to say what she had come to say. So she wrapped her arms around herself, her hands buried in her fur-lined sleeves, and moved across the room to his desk. By rights, he should have climbed down from the stool and bowed to the future wife of his future earl.

But the Chronicler only drew a long breath and let it out in cloudy vapors. "What have you come about, m'lady?"

"I . . . I was wondering,"—her voice dropped almost to a whisper—"what it is you are copying."

His look was sharp. Slowly he removed the blotting cloth and allowed Leta to look at the vellum page. She saw there, in his firm hand, the nursery rhyme she had seen days ago in the hand of Lady Pero. Lady Pero's own fragile parchment lay to one side of the book, held in place by a stone weight.

"Foolishness," said the Chronicler. "More nursery rhymes. More tales of Faerie brothers and mystical houses full of lights and songs and truth. More deaths and prophecies of coming kings. Foolishness."

Practical Leta nearly cowed her into submission. *He doesn't want to see you now. Leave him be. Go back where you belong.*

But when Leta opened her mouth, though she could scarcely get the words out, she heard herself say, "Would you read it to me?"

He did not meet her gaze but sat staring at delicate lines of red ink, still drying, a little smeared from his attempt to hide them. The Wall around him was almost palpable. But there was a frailty to it. At the right provocation, it would crumble, leaving him unprotected.

He read:

> *"Fling wide the doors of light, Smallman,*
> *Though furied falls the Flame at Night.*
> *The heir to truth, blest blade of fire,*
> *He finds in shielded shadow light.*
>
> *"Not in vain the hope once borne*
> *When flees the king to farther fight—*
> *Dark and deepness hold no sway.*
> *The brother dies, the lantern lights."*

It was like the nursery rhyme of Leta's childhood, but quite different as well. A distant inspiration that had perhaps become twisted over time into the simple lines so familiar to her. This one was closer to the truth, she thought even as the last words died upon the frosty air.

"What does it mean?" Leta asked.

"What do you think it means?" he replied as she knew he would. Never willing to give an opinion for her, he forced her to form her own.

"I think it means," she replied quietly, "that though he flees, though he hides, the king will come to us one day. I think it means the true heir will be revealed in the end."

She felt his gaze upon her face. She felt him reading her thoughts. Drawing a sudden breath, she lifted her eyes and met his, and she thought with all the fury she dared not speak: *You want the Smallman to be true, to be truly true. Not a symbol. Not a metaphor. You want him to be real. But you're afraid.*

She could not know how bright her eyes flashed, how her face resembled that of her father, a strong and determined lord of men. But unlike Lord Aiven's, her eyes held kindness as well, and this made her face the stronger by far. In that brief span of time, she looked the woman she was born to be, not the creature she had been molded into.

How much the Chronicler understood in her eyes, no one could guess. But at last he whispered, "It is all Faerie stories. Men of old trying to make sense of a senseless world. Nothing more."

Leta swallowed and dropped her gaze. But the flash of rebellion had not quite gone from her spirit. She moved a little away from the book that now seemed dangerous, the written words full of power and desire.

She whispered, "My father has come to take final leave of Earl Ferox."

"I know."

"And then Alistair will be made Earl of Gaheris."

"I know."

She could not look at him. But she said, "What about you, Chronicler?"

"I am nothing," the Chronicler replied. "I do not matter in these great events."

"What about . . . what about me?"

The Wall redoubled with such tremendous force, Leta almost felt it slap her face. She took a step back, her arms tightening about her small frame, her gaze fixed upon the legs of the Chronicler's stool.

The Chronicler said, "You will marry Lord Alistair as you should. You will bind Aiven to Gaheris. And one day, m'lady, you will be queen. A great queen, able to read and to write. You will be stronger than these men can begin to guess, and you will serve the North Country as you rule by Alistair's side."

She could not believe it. He spoke of some other girl. Not Lord Aiven's useless daughter, fit only to sit quietly in her chambers. Fit only to bear children and pass them off to nursemaids while she stitched at tapestries and thought of nothing.

But that wasn't her anymore. Leta knew it deep down, even if she did not yet believe it. Worlds were open to her that no other could see, for she could read and she could think. She could travel to distant lands and glean the wisdom of ancient times and histories.

"You will be a great queen," said the Chronicler.

"Is that why you've taught me?" Leta said. She looked at the Chronicler then, full in the face, seeing every detail etched out in the glow of those three candles. "For the good of the North Country?"

Even in the candlelight, his cheeks drained of color. He was sinking back into that silent fortress he had built for himself from the time he was young, from the time he was first made to realize that he was different from other children, from other young men. The muscles in his cheek tightened, though otherwise he was still as stone.

At last he said, "I have work to do, m'lady. You should return to the hall and Alistair's side."

Leta's hand darted out. Her practical self didn't have time for a word, for she moved before thought. She dashed the books and papers from his desk, knocking them in a shower to the floor along with one candle, which snuffed out the moment it struck stone.

And she cried, "Why are you such a coward? You tell me that I make myself less than I could be, that I hide inside what people tell me I am! But how are you any different?"

Then, catching up with herself, she realized what she had done. She stared down at the mess on the floor beneath the Chronicler's high stool. He sat there quietly, looking at her with wide eyes.

"I'm sorry," she whispered.

The next moment she had fled the library, leaving the door standing wide behind her. She ran down the cold corridor, her slippered feet soundless on the stone. Tears froze on her burning face.

4

ONE FINAL DAY, THE TWELVE CAME TO OMEZTLI. *Citlalu and Mahuizoa were scarcely recognizable by then. Their feathered wings molted but did not replenish, and their limbs were gray and wasted. These were not the immortal rulers of a Faerie demesne! They were no better than mortals, unable even to fly. Broken creatures. I could not bear to look at them.*

But when the Twelve called up the tower, "Cren Cru commands. Send us your firstborn," my father and mother replied as if in one voice: "Not while we've yet life coursing through our veins!"

With those final words, they fell from the rooftop of Omeztli Tower. They fell and crashed upon the stones below, winged beings made flightless. Dead.

And Tlanextu became King of Etalpalli.

Other earls arrived, some by river, some by road, all wrapped in heavy furs with dustings of snow on their great shoulders. They came with large retinues, and Gaheris was filled to bursting. Soon even the fields beyond the castle walls were crowded with fine tents, and nighttime was full of campfires in the snow, like so many stars fallen to earth. Alistair stood wrapped in furs upon the walls of his uncle's keep and thought how like a siege it looked, all those tents, all those fires.

"They've come to honor you," his mother reminded him.

"They've come to bid farewell to my uncle," he snarled in response. But that wasn't the whole of it, and he felt the weight of coming mastery hanging above his head like a suspended sword, ready to drop.

The castle was full of feasting and the booming talk of men. Mouse ran his legs off on errands for both Cook and the scrubber, and he shied away from the gazes of those earls, wishing he could find a hole to crawl into and never emerge again. Alistair, always in the thick of it all, laughed and joked and spoke of North Country policies with those who were his uncle's allies. Leta, when obliged, sat at his side, testimony to the Earl of Aiven's link to Gaheris.

And the Chronicler sat in the silence of his library. In that silence, he could almost hear Earl Ferox struggling to breathe.

"You are wanted in the earl's room, my lady," said Lady Mintha's page, bowing in the doorway of Leta's chamber. Leta sat by the fire, wrapped in a fur cloak, her face red with cold. Even here in seclusion, she could hear the rumble of crowded life in the castle's great hall below. She wondered if Earl Ferox heard it in his sickroom and what he thought, if anything.

"Ferox must be near his end," said Leta's head lady, and she fetched a mourning veil from among Leta's things and fixed it to Leta's head, covering her hair and partially hiding her face. "Go now," she said, her voice stern.

Silent as a phantom, Leta followed the page from her chambers and down the darkened hall, which was not as cold as it might be, crowded as it was with the servants and retainers of all the various earls. They waited, their backs against the walls, their arms crossed over their chests, their faces sullen because they were not with their fellows in the feasting hall down below. They were made to wait outside Ferox's room, to wait and bring word to their lords the moment there was word to bring.

Leta passed beneath their gazes and on to the sickroom. Though a large chamber, it too was crowded. Ferox's closest allies stood along the walls, the light of the great fire flickering on them. A host of candles burned near the head of Ferox's bed but could cast no warmth upon his gray, strained face. Leta briefly wondered if he was already dead. Then she saw the rise and fall of his wasted chest and heard the labored scraping of his breath. He lived. Only just.

Alistair stood on the other side of the bed, his face white in the candlelight. He did not look at Leta as she entered, scarcely seemed aware of her. But Lady Mintha at his side beckoned her near. "He's not long for this world now," she whispered in Leta's ear. "You must be present at the end. Here, take my place beside my son, and offer what prayers you know for Ferox's passing."

Leta dared steal a glance at Mintha as she spoke. She saw no sorrow there, though Earl Ferox had always been a kind and true brother to her, giving her a place of precedence in his house and at his table. No, there was no sorrow in Mintha's gaze as she watched her younger brother struggle upon his deathbed.

Shuddering, Leta did as she was commanded and drew close to Alistair. In his expression, at least, she saw real pain. The pain of coming loss and . . . something else, she thought. Something that was akin to fear if not fear itself. She wondered if she was expected to do something to comfort him but could not think what. She hardly knew him, and she did not think a word or gesture from her would make any difference.

So she turned to Earl Ferox, his face worn so thin, his nightshirt folded back to reveal the hollows of his neck and collarbone. He sweated and shivered at once. There could be no comfort for him now save death.

What prayers did she know? She thought of all the little phrases she had been taught as a child, songs of olden days that according to the Chronicler were nothing but fanciful stories. Her heart plummeted at that thought. At a time like this, a man needed fancy to be truth. And if he could not believe it himself, he needed others to believe it for him.

She whispered softly the first of all the prayerful songs that entered her head:

"Beyond the Final Water falling,
The Songs of Spheres recalling.
When you hear my voice beyond the darkling veil,
Won't you return to me?"

She did not realize how loud her voice was until Lady Mintha reached out and pinched her arm. Instantly, Leta clamped her mouth shut, her face burning with embarrassment and the threat of oncoming tears.

But Earl Ferox opened his eyes.

They were clouded over with pain, shimmering with regret, and blind, Leta thought, to all those gathered near. She heard a collective gasp from those around her, and Alistair started forward, kneeling down by the dying man's side. "Uncle Ferox." His voice was rough yet gentle. "Can you hear me?"

The earl's throat constricted, and the muscles of his face tensed with pain. He croaked hoarsely, "Bring me . . ." His eyes closed. Was that a tear sliding down the grayness of his temple and vanishing into his thin white hair?

"Bring you what?" Alistair said. "What do you need, Uncle?"

Ferox's lips trembled, but his eyelids fluttered open again. "Bring me," he said, his voice a little stronger this time, "the dwarf."

Even the distant noise of the earls down in the great hall seemed to still. Leta stood, scarcely breathing, staring at the earl's tense expression, and she felt cold from the inside out. Alistair's mouth hung open, his brow wrinkled and puzzled. "Uncle?"

Mintha stepped forward and grabbed his shoulder. "He's raving," she said. "His mind is fled. Pay no attention to anything he says, my son. He's already as good as dead."

Alistair stood uncertainly, but the dying man repeated, "The dwarf. Bring me . . ."

Lady Mintha whirled upon the castle leech. "Have you a draught to give him, to make him sleep?"

"My lady," said the leech, bowing and scraping, "he ordered me to give him nothing at the end. He ordered me—"

"He can give no more orders," Mintha said. "My son is giving the orders now. Listen to him!"

"Mother," Alistair said, "I don't like to go against my uncle's wishes—"

Leta heard no more. She was already out of the room, slipping away like a thief on a wicked errand. She passed into the crowded passage, where retainers tried to grab her arm and whispers assailed her, asking, "Is there word? Is he dead?" She shook her head and pressed on through their midst to places where no torches were lit and shadows surrounded her like icy specters. She fled down the stairs, her black veil trailing behind her, on through ways she knew better than all the rest of Gaheris.

She came to the library door and burst through. "Chronicler!"

A single light burned at the desk. And there the Chronicler sat, pale and tense. She saw his eyes gleaming in the darkness. "M'lady," he said quietly.

She was across the room. Without thinking, she took hold of both his hands. She could scarcely draw breath enough to speak, for she had run all that way. "Earl Ferox is asking for you!"

Shadows cast by the candlelight played strangely across his features. She saw his eyes widen, his jaw clench. Then, without a word, he slid down off the stool. How like a child he seemed in the darkness, his head no higher than her heart. As fast as he could, he hastened from the library, and she followed him back through the cold passages, up the stairs, and on to the earl's death chamber. The retainers without muttered and pointed, but he ignored them all and passed into the room under the eyes of Gaheris's allies.

"What is he doing here?" Lady Mintha snarled and started to come around the bed. "Get him out!"

"Peace, Mother," Alistair said, grabbing her arm and holding her in place. "Or I will send you from the room."

So it was that the castle Chronicler approached his dying master unimpeded. He leaned over the bed, gazing on that wasted face, once so strong, so lordly, so commanding. There were tears in his voice when he spoke:

"I am come, my lord."

Earl Ferox's eyes slowly opened, and he turned to look upon the dwarf. Something like a smile pulled at his sagging mouth. "So you are, my son."

The scrubber stood in deep shadows, his back against the wall, feeling every contour of the cold stones pressed into his withered shoulders. He kept out of sight of the earls' retainers. His eyes, runny and clouded though they were, kept sharp lookout. He had seen the quiet maiden hastening behind the little man, and he nodded, grunting.

Turning about and hobbling down a quiet passage, he made his way to a window. Through the stone slit the blue star peered, watching eagerly. The scrubber, using his mop for support, hauled himself up to the window and put his head out into the night cold.

"Go tell Queen Bebo the time is come," he said. "She must send me aid."

The star twinkled brightly.

Then it vanished.

Down below, in the cold courtyard, the door of the crypt strained. Behind it, voices whispered: *Now! Now!*

5

*T*HERE WAS NO CORONATION. *None dared leave their high towers for fear of the Twelve and Cren Cru. But my brother took my hand and flew with me to Itonatiu, the Sun Tower, where the king's throne waited at the summit. He sat, his wings spreading on either side, his hands grasping the arms of the throne. His head bowed. He was so young, still a child by our people's standards. But when he sat on that throne, he became king indeed.*

I stood silently before him, weeping, for the image of our parents' fall was scored across my mind.

Suddenly Tlanextu looked up. I drew back, shuddering. "No!" I said. But I could not deny what I saw. For there was now death in his eyes as well. Our parents' sacrifice had been in vain. Cren Cru would drain him even as it had drained them.

"We must save Etalpalli," he said to me then. "At all cost!"

"What will you do?" I asked, afraid of the answer.

"There is little I can do," he said. "But I can hold him off, even as our parents did. And you, my sister, must leave."

"Please, brother," I cried, "don't make me abandon the City of Wings!"

"You must go," he said, "so that Etalpalli may be saved. Seek out the Brothers Ashiun, the Knights of the Farthest Shore. They may be persuaded to help us."

"How?" I asked.

"I do not know," Tlanextu replied. "It is said the brothers possess gifts, strange weapons forged in the fires of Lumé and filled with the light of Hymlumé. Perhaps these same weapons may be enough to drive Cren Cru from our demesne. You must go to them and plead our cause."

The idea filled me with dread. I had never before ventured beyond the Faerie Realm, never flown across the boundaries of Etalpalli, my beautiful home. I knew of the worlds that lay beyond our borders, the vast Wood Between, and the strange Near World, where people lived and died by the cruel hand of Time. The idea of journeying anywhere near that place was enough to make my blood run cold.

But Tlanextu asked me with death staring from his eyes. How could I refuse?

The Chronicler had a way of deflecting attention from himself, a skill honed to perfection over the course of his hidden life.

Nevertheless, standing now in the candlelit room, watching her teacher bend over the sickened earl, it was impossible, Leta thought, to miss the resemblance between them. Though Ferox was weakened to skeletal frailty, though the Chronicler was deformed in body, their faces were as like as ever were father and son. Save the Chronicler's features were softer with youth and, perhaps, with his mother's influence.

Leta saw it all. She did not know who else might. Mintha knew, but did Alistair, standing on the far side of the bed, looking on with eyes full of surprise and perhaps horror? Did her own father, lurking in the near shadows, know this great secret of his fellow earl?

"I have been no father to you," Ferox said, his voice so thin and quavering that Leta strained to discern the words. The Chronicler leaned closer, and his mouth worked as though struggling to form a reply.

"I've been no son to you," he said at last, scarcely above a whisper.

"I gave you a place," the earl continued. In desperation he tried to raise his head, but the effort was too great. His shaking hand slid across the heavy rugs of his bed, seeking the Chronicler. "I gave you a profession. I gave you a chance for power beyond that of other men, the power of words and pen."

The Chronicler drew his hand away from the earl's. But he said, "You . . . you have been good to me, my lord."

"No." The muscles in the earl's neck quivered as he shook his head. "I have not been good. I have been a coward."

"Enough of this," Lady Mintha said. "My dear brother must not be bothered at this time. Away with—"

"Be still," Alistair growled, and his mother lapsed into silence, her hands clenched into white-knuckled fists. Leta felt the tension in the earls surrounding her, heard the sharp breaths of her own father. But she did not turn her gaze from the scene playing out before her. Every sense in her body focused upon that isolated space of candlelight and death.

"You are like your mother," Ferox said. His eyes, clouded with memories, wandered across the room, seeking something he could not find. But he still spoke to the Chronicler. "Very like. She too was . . . clever. She wrote and she read. And she was small. Too small. Not so small as you, but too small. And she died. You lived. I thought I hated you."

Leta saw the tears on the Chronicler's cheeks. They were in a world apart, that father and son, a world that fit only the two of them, and she dared not draw near even had she wished to.

"A sonless earl can never be a king." Ferox's wandering eyes at last fell upon the face of his son. Slowly, as though lifting a mighty mace and chain, he raised his hand. The fingers trembled like dried leaves with the strain. "A cowardly earl can never be a man."

The Chronicler reached out. He took that trembling hand in his. For a moment his eyes were as fierce as ever the earl's had been. "You are strong," he said, and there was pride in his wounded voice. "You are the earl of Gaheris, the greatest man in the North Country."

"I will never be a great man," Ferox replied. "But before they inter me in the dark, I will be a *true* man."

With a gasp of pain, he lifted his arm up high so that all in the room could see how their hands were clasped. He raised his voice so that it was almost as loud as it had been in the fullness of his life. He said:

"This is Florien Ferox-son, my firstborn, my heir. Let him take up the shield of Gaheris and mastery of all his father's lands. I bid you honor him as once you honored me."

The silence was that of a crypt, and the earls and servants were specters in the dark. Lady Mintha's face filled with horror, and Alistair's was hidden in shadows. Leta felt her heart stop and then begin to race as a collision of thoughts battered her brain so hard that even the silence seemed cacophonous.

The earl's hand lowered once more. He drew his son closer, and with a painful rasp he spoke his last. "I have done you no service. They will try to kill you." He closed his eyes as though a knife were even now being driven into his skull. His final word came out in a struggling breath.

"Run."

The Chronicler got to his feet. The earl lay immobile upon his bed, his chest rising and falling with the labor of his final moments. All tears or traces of sorrow were gone from the face of his son so long denied, at last acknowledged. Every eye in the room fixed upon him, and none there could discern the workings of his mind.

He backed away: one step, then two. He turned and, passing Leta without a look, continued on to the door, through to the hall.

Leta, holding her breath, heard the sound of running footsteps fading down the passage.

No one moved. No one breathed but Earl Ferox. He drew a breath, and another. And then, with a final dry gasp, he was still.

Lady Mintha stepped forward. She put a finger to his pulse, rested her ear near his cold lips. Then she stood.

"The earl is dead. Long life to Alistair, Master of Gaheris!"

"Long life" came the murmured echo, cold as a broken oath, dark as a death sentence. Leta stared around at the faces of the earls, Ferox's onetime friends. She saw horror; she saw betrayal; she saw murder in every face. In her father's face. In Mintha's.

She turned and started for the door. But Lady Mintha leapt forward with the quickness of a cat and caught her by the arm. Without a word to Leta, she barked to those servants standing nearest, "Bring the dwarf to me."

"No!" Leta cried and tried to break free.

"Shut your mouth," Lady Mintha said. "Look carefully to your loyalties now."

Leta stared up at the strong woman holding her and saw the viciousness of a vixen. She turned to her father, but the Earl of Aiven was giving his own orders to his men. Desperate, she looked around for Alistair.

Her husband-to-be was gone.

Gaheris rang with the crashing footsteps of those who sought Earl Ferox's son.

Outside of Time there rests beneath a mountain a merry realm where yellow-headed little people dance and sing, and dance and sing some more. Their shadows, cast by brilliant torches, ring the stony hall of Ruaine-ann-Rudiobus, cavorting in the joy of song.

In their midst, singing loudest, dancing wildest, was scarlet-clad Eanrin. His bright voice rang above the throng, echoing in the highest vaults of the stone cavern hall of King Iubdan.

"Fair Gleamdrené, in splendor's vault thou art
Shining lone and sweet among the flow'rs of night!"

The poet sang with a hand on his heart to a lady seated on a humble stool before the great Queen Bebo. The lady refused to look his way or even to smile at the devotion painted across the poet's handsome face. But Bebo saw it and saw more besides, and she thought many thoughts that she kept to herself.

A star approached from the shadows.

Bebo turned, surprised at its coming. It wrapped itself in disguises so as not to frighten the Merry People dancing in that fey hall. But the queen saw this celestial being come to earth, shining and beautiful, its flanks tinged with blue light.

"Cé," she whispered in quiet greeting, not wishing to draw the attention of her subjects.

It bowed before her.

Fair Bebo, it said, *I come with word for you.*

"Tell me, shining one," said the queen.

Its voice was deep and far and full of multitudes singing when it replied. *The gates are unwatched. The Flame is building. And the Murderer has found his heir.*

"Ah," said Bebo, nodding. "So the time has come. Good. Very good indeed."

She turned and looked across the wild dance floor, watching the scarlet poet sing.

6

I LEFT *ETALPALLI, THE REALM OF MY BIRTH, flying with my back to the Sun and Moon Towers, my head turned away from the ugly, devouring Mound of Cren Cru. I do not know who saw me go. I wondered if the Twelve would try to stop me, but I wasn't a firstborn; perhaps they had no interest in my fate.*

However it was, I crossed through Cozamaloti Gate, the shimmering cascades of falling water that formed the boundary between our world and the Between. And behind me, Tlanextu placed a lock, a work of magic, some would say. Its substance was this: No one should pass through Cozamaloti again except for the sake of another. With this lock, he hoped to prevent any other evil from slipping into Etalpalli while the city was weakened by Cren Cru and his slaves.

Only I and the Brothers Ashiun, if they agreed to accompany me, should be able to enter.

The moment I passed into the Wood Between, I knew it was a terrible place. The trees grew so thick, so twined together, that there could be no flight for one of my size, though I was scarcely grown then to my full wingspan. I flew up from the mists of Cozamaloti and landed on the banks of a wide river I did not know.

From there, I was obliged to walk.

How can I express to you the pain of a winged creature forced to hobble along the dirt? My feet were tender; they bled as rocks and roots tore into them, and they soon throbbed as though with each step I trod upon hot coals. My wings I folded against my back, but branches reached out and snatched at them, tearing.

And there was no sight of the sky. The fate of Cren Cru's gaping void seemed preferable to me!

Dark halls, distant shouts, and the cold of biting winter.

The Chronicler fled, his senses ringing with bursting life made all too real in the pain of loss and the fear of pursuit. He ran, stumbling in the gloom, his hand pressed to the stone wall of a staircase to keep his balance, expecting men-at-arms to leap from the shadows any moment.

"You are not my father?" a tiny, malformed child had asked old Raguel, the former chronicler.

"No, thank the Lights Above," Raguel had responded with his habitual acidity. *"You have no father."*

It was true and untrue all at once. Impossible and all too possible. As an older child beginning to feel the bindings of his limited height, he soon guessed, though he never dared speak aloud his conclusions. He guessed that the man who visited the library every so often and asked after his progress was more than just the Earl of Gaheris. He guessed from glances; he guessed from curt words. Later, after Raguel died and his apprentice took over as castle chronicler, he guessed the truth when summoned to the earl's chambers to write out dictated letters. He guessed from tone of voice and turn of head. He guessed it all, and he understood, though his heart broke with hatred and love.

"You have no father," he whispered to himself as he fled. And now it was true indeed: His father was dead.

Loss that the Chronicler should not have allowed himself to feel swept over him, and he was almost glad for the fear to drive it out.

"I have done you no service," Earl Ferox had said. And this was the most painful truth of all. As castle chronicler, the diminutive, forsaken son might have spent a long life in solitude and quiet work. As declared heir, what life remained to him would be spent on the run.

For who would serve a dwarf lord?

In escape lay his only hope. Any moment now, Earl Ferox would breathe his last, and when that happened Alistair would send for him, he knew. Alistair, who had the support of the earls and who would not so easily give up mastery of Gaheris to his former teacher. So he must escape, steal a horse (was it stealing, after all, if Ferox had named him heir?), and ride into the wild lands. To the east and into the mountains? No, he would never pass over them. To the west, then, seaward? But what to do when he faced the wall of the sea? North, into colder climes? And freeze the blood in his veins! It must be south, then—

Foolishness, all foolishness. What good did any future plan accomplish if he could not so much as escape Gaheris's binding walls? The castle that stood in fierce defense against all comers was also a mighty prison.

It was all madness. All hopelessness. But he would not be taken like a lamb for slaughtering.

He could already hear the tramp of feet, whether real or imagined he could not guess. The pursuit would begin any moment, he was certain. But he passed no one as he fled through the keep and out the door into the inner courtyard. Round him were the high walls of Gaheris, and watch-men stood at their interval posts. Torches flickered in their iron holders, but their light was as nothing to the cold moon watching from above.

The Chronicler hastened across the stones, as yet unhailed by any searcher. But there were guards posted at the gates to the outer courtyard, and who could say if they would let him pass? His flight might end before it was well begun. But what else could he do? There was nowhere he might safely hide—

With a sharp curse, louder than he intended, the Chronicler crashed into someone in the dark and fell back hard upon the ground. A figure he could not discern stood above him, blending so perfectly into the darkness that he almost could not see it even now. Then it bent, and the light of the moon fell upon its face. A wrinkled, ugly, utterly old visage.

"Evening, Your Majesty," said the scrubber.

Snarling another curse, the Chronicler scrambled to his feet and tried to push past. But the scrubber put out his mop handle and impeded him. "Let me by, old fool!" the Chronicler said, grabbing the handle in both hands.

"I think not. Many apologies, Your Majesty," said the scrubber. With a flick of his skinny wrist and mop, he turned the Chronicler in the direction he wished him to go and, pushing between his shoulders with the soggy end of his tool, started him walking. "You need a place to hide. Word has already spread through the guards, and you'll not get past the gates. Best to keep your head down until further notice, don't you think?"

Though he wanted to fight, to lash out, the Chronicler found himself moving as directed. Strangely enough, he felt relieved. It was good to have all desperate choices taken from his hand. The scrubber propelled him across the courtyard opposite the old Gaheris crypt toward an old shed, a humble building the Chronicler had never noticed before. The scrubber unlatched and opened the door with many creakings.

"There we go," he said, pushing the Chronicler through. "No one will think to look for you here. But don't come out until you know it's time. Understand, Your Majesty?"

The Chronicler stumbled into the dankness of the shed. He whirled around to face the scrubber, saying, "Why do you call me that?"

"Call you what?"

"Majesty!"

"Why?" The scrubber scratched the back of his head, his cloudy eyes as wide and unblinking as an owl's. "Because you're the King of the North Country. Or you will be. Time is such a funny thing; it's all the same in the end."

"Daft fool," the Chronicler growled. "I'm not an earl, much less a king. By all the Dragon's brood, I'd be glad even to be counted quite a man!"

"Tut, so much fussing," the scrubber said, shaking his head and making a sour face. Then he leaned in, his crusty eyes close to the Chronicler's. "Look around you, Your Majesty. Tell me what you see."

Taking a step back—for the scrubber's breath was putrid—the Chronicler glanced from side to side. "An old, drafty shed," he growled, shivering.

"Pity," said the scrubber and shrugged. "Lie low. They'll not find you here. You'll know when it's time to emerge."

"But . . . wait!" the Chronicler began. The shed door slammed in his face. He stood in frozen darkness, hiding like a rat in a hole. He bowed his head, drawing a heavy breath. Never before had he felt so stripped of all manhood. In that moment, his desperation and sorrow too keen to bear, he almost wished they would find him.

Find him, and kill him quickly.

Alistair staggered in the darkness.

He felt as uneasy on his feet and in his mind as though he were inebriated, though he hadn't tasted drink all day. One does not drink when one's uncle is dying. One does not drink on the verge of being declared master of all one surveys. One does not drink on the day when the expectations of a lifetime are about to be fulfilled, when age passes away and youth steps into rightful forefront.

But one might possibly drink if one's future, title, prospects—entire life, when it came right down to it—were stripped away in the sudden blink of an eye.

A son! A *legitimate* son!

And yet, of all sons . . .

No wonder Ferox had kept it secret. No wonder he'd allowed everyone to assume the child died at birth. Alistair cursed as he staggered down a side passage, choosing byways of Gaheris Castle that were less traversed, hoping not to meet any of the North Country earls as he fled to . . . fled where? Where could he go?

Embarrassed, disinherited, bewildered, he wandered like a ghost in the nighttime corridors.

He should have seen the resemblance long ago. When the Chronicler knelt at the dying man's side, it was impossible not to see how he, for all his abnormal proportions, favored Earl Ferox. How could Alistair, through all those laborious hours of alphabets and finding words in scribbled ink, have missed the resemblance? But the Chronicler had such a way of hiding himself away. After all, one doesn't like to stare at those less fortunate; Alistair had made it a point not to look too closely at the little fellow who was his own age but the size of a child.

The little fellow who was now, by all legal rights, Earl of Gaheris. The little fellow who, in the course of a single moment, had taken everything Alistair possessed.

He didn't know where he would go. Somewhere he wouldn't have to face his mother. He knew how she would be. Even now, he could picture her taking aside various earls, planting words in their ears, plotting against Ferox's dying wishes before the man's body had quite gone cold. Of course there would be an uprising. And Alistair did not doubt that sufficient support would muster behind him to establish him in his uncle's seat. Even as he strode the dark passages, fury disorienting his brain, he knew that all was far from lost. He would still be Earl of Gaheris.

But to do so, he would have to go against his uncle's wishes. He would have to kill his cousin.

His cousin!

Unnerved, Alistair allowed himself to descend into a dark and dangerous brooding. And this brooding drove him outside, as was his wont on dark evenings. Out into the courtyard, making for the high wall overlooking Hanna and the northern sweep of Gaheris. If he saw two shadows scurry across the stones ahead of him, he did not notice. His head pounded with thoughts he could not quite think. Mastery and murder. Dreams and nightmares.

He hastened toward the narrow stairs leading up the wall, passing as he did so the marble doors of the family crypt. Moonlight shone upon the white doorposts of stone, carved with heavy embellishments and set with wrought-iron fastenings. Lady Mintha, he knew, had already arranged for the funeral. Even before her brother had taken to his bed, she had begun preparing for the interment. How eagerly she had awaited his death, the time of her son's ascension!

Now everything was in place. Ferox would be sent to his final rest in the morning, soon after sunrise. And according to Mintha's arrangements, the earls would then perform the ceremony to instate Alistair as one of their number, placing the shield of mastery in his hand and repeating the vows of brotherhood they had made to his uncle.

Alistair's mouth was dry as he stopped before that grim door. Tomorrow, his uncle would pass through. How many more decades until Alistair too would be laid to rest there? Beside his uncle, beside his father. A counterfeit earl, a murderer. A fraud.

"Lights Above," he whispered, "what are my life and death to be?"

Something scratched on the far side of the door.

Alistair stood and stared, telling himself he was imagining things. Things that sounded like claws or talons dragging from the top of the door to the bottom in a slow, deliberate stroke.

Then silence. Then . . .

Scratch!

Someone was picking at the wood with a fingernail, with a dagger point.

"Servants," Alistair whispered. "Mother's servants. Inside. Preparing for the funeral. Preparing his vault. That is all."

Then came a voice that was not a voice so much as a thought in his head:

Let us out.

Alistair's hand was at the door. There was no lock. Why lock away the dead? The dead do not rise.

Open the gate.

Alistair's fingers trembled. He forced himself to grip the door latch. He would open it and look. He would see that there were no ghosts waiting to judge him. Then he would shut the door and return to his rooms and let the future deal with itself as it must.

"I will die in the dark," he whispered, and his voice caught in his throat. "I will never be king."

The door was heavy. It did not want to answer to his touch.

Let us out.

He took hold with both hands and pulled. The door resisted, screaming on its hinges.

Open . . .

A crack in the darkness.

Suddenly an enormous hand gripping a dagger shot out from the opening. The blade flashed in light that was not moonlight. Alistair screamed as he felt the cold bite and then the fiery burn sink deep into his shoulder, a snake's bite full of poison. He fell back from the door upon the stone cobbles, and the knife pulled out with searing pain. His hand pressed to the wound. Blood seeped through his fingers, thick and warm.

The door pushed open. Alistair stared. He saw the looming figure standing there. He saw the dagger and the sword and the eyes like white moons.

"Oh no you don't. Not yet."

A withered hand, frail with mortality, reached out and shut the crypt door as gently as it might close the door to a nursery. A scream erupted from the far side, and a scraping and scratching like a thousand rats tearing at the heavy wood.

"Not yet," whispered the old scrubber again as he leaned heavily upon the handle of his mop. He looked down upon the tall young man fainted on the stones and shook his head. "Soon enough. Then we'll see what heroes rise to face the monsters."

"Eanrin! Bard Eanrin!"

The scarlet poet stopped midsong and whirled about upon the dance floor to face the upraised throne of his queen. He saw her hand beckoning him, and with a flashing smile and a great bound, he presented himself before her, bowing with a sweep of his cloak.

"Fairest Bebo!" he cried. "How may I serve you? Do you desire a verse sprung from the spontaneity of my heart? Or a turn upon the dance floor with the merriest of your children?"

Bebo smiled quietly. Though she was queen of all the Merry People, she was more solemn than they. "Neither suits my present need, poet mine," she said. "I have a question for your waiting ear."

"You need only ask it!"

And Bebo said to him: "Are the gates to the Near World watched?"

The smile fell from Eanrin's face. "Of course, my queen," he said. "I wouldn't leave them untended even to see bright Ruaine Hall once more. I know my duties, and I perform them well. Even now, though I am here before you, Dame Imraldera, my comrade-in-arms, watches over the gates to the Near World. No monster of Faerie will get past her to plague the mortal realm."

"But Imraldera has gone from the Haven," said Queen Bebo. "The stars have told me thus."

The poet's mouth opened. At first he could not speak. Then he cried out, "It can't be true! She would never leave the gates unguarded! Only great duress could force her to do so, and who would dare set upon Dame Imraldera?"

"The Murderer," Bebo replied. And even as all the color drained from the poet's face, she leaned close and whispered in his ear:

> *"Not in vain the hope once borne*
> *When flees the king to farther fight—*
> *Dark and deepness hold no sway.*
> *The brother dies, the lantern lights."*

7

MANY PATHS EXTENDED BEFORE ME. *Enchanted Paths belonging to enchanted beings, leading off into the vast reaches of the Wood. I did not know which to choose, but choose I must, or the Wood would choose for me. I felt the cruelty beneath my bleeding feet, felt the maliciousness in the shadows. Unseen forces reached out grasping fingers as though to snare me, to draw me down into the black places, and I cried out in my terror.*

Suddenly a strange voice sang in my mind. A voice I can scarcely recall now, though I know I heard it then. It was simple and small, but it held all hugeness inside it. And it whispered:

Won't you follow me?

I turned then and saw a new Path open up before me. I did not know where it might lead, and perhaps it was a trap. But I took it, desperate for any guidance in this world between worlds. I could not run, for my legs were too weak and my feet too wounded, but I stumbled along as fast as I could.

Soon I came upon the Haven of Ashiun, rising tall and strong and bright out of the shadows of the Wood.

I called out even as I approached. "Brothers! Hear my plea!"

I did not know if they would be within. Perhaps they were off in the hideous mortal world, aiding the dying ones. But somehow I believed that the voice I had heard while in the depths of the Wood would not lead me wrong. So I called again and fell upon the door, pounding with my fists. "Hear me, brothers! Hear me!"

The door opened. I collapsed into a pair of strong arms. I felt the encircling of strength and comfort. For a spell, I lay there, weeping and resting at once. Then I looked up.

It was the first I beheld the face of Sir Etanun of the Farthest Shore. He was the most beautiful being I had ever seen.

Mouse didn't have much of a bed.

He didn't like to sleep with the kitchen boys in the nook behind the kitchens. So he made a place for himself in a broom cupboard near the hearth where it was warm, if cramped. Every night, exhausted after being yelled at from sunup to sundown for not understanding a word spoken to him, he fell asleep instantly, without a thought for comfort. Without even a thought for the faraway home he doubted he would ever see again.

But not tonight. Though he did not understand all that was happening within the busy confines of Gaheris's walls, he felt the tension. The master of the house was dying, he had guessed. And the masters of surrounding lands had come to . . . to what? To take over rule? To fight for the right to sit in headship over these lands? He couldn't guess. But he could almost smell the coming bloodshed, and his fear would not let him sleep, though he curled into a ball in his cupboard, squeezing his eyes tight.

"Find Etanun. Find the heir."

He ground his teeth, trying to drive the voice from his memory. He was trying! In the name of the Fire, he was doing everything he could in this cold, dreadful land where everyone spoke gibberish and pale men of iron enclosed all life in their high stone walls!

"Fire burn," he whispered between his teeth. "Fire purify—aaaaaah!"

His scream was stifled as someone clamped a hand over his mouth. Grabbed by the back of his tunic, he was hauled from the cupboard and plopped unceremoniously on his feet, flailing ineffectually against some unknown attacker. But whoever had grabbed him let him go without a fight, and he whirled about, fists clenched.

And found himself facing the scrubber.

"Well, little Mouse," said his master with a grin, "you must come with me. The young lord has fallen ill."

Mouse stared, his mouth agape. Then he said, "You *do* speak my tongue! You *do* understand me!"

"So much fuss," said the scrubber with a shrug and, using his mop like a shepherd's crook, prodded Mouse in the stomach. "Hurry up now. We haven't much time."

With those words, he scuttled from the room, using his mop for support. Mouse trotted after, surprised at the speed of the old man, his voice hissing with excitement he could not suppress.

"I knew it! I knew I wasn't mistaken! You understand me. And you know where Etanun is, don't you?"

The old man's eyes were empty with senility when he turned his gaze upon the boy. Mouse found himself drawing back with disgust at the sight of such decrepitude. But the scrubber smiled, revealing his gums. "Come, child, faster."

Mouse followed.

The whole castle was in a state of quiet unrest. Mouse felt it as plainly as though his ears rang with the clash of mustering forces and brewing battles. Guards were patrolling, possibly searching. Earls and their retainers scurried hither and yon, muttering to each other, sometimes shouting. Ferox was dead, then, Mouse guessed. And what of Lord Alistair? Mouse recalled the face of the young man who had kindly let him through the gates and given him his position, however humble. He was to inherit, and he would be a good master. Why then the cruel looks and nasty words that shushed in the air of the castle passages? Why no mourning tears for the old master and no hearty wishes for the new?

Mouse shivered and hastened after the scrubber. Strange—though the castle was alive with bustle, wherever the old man went, he moved as though invisible. No one noticed him or Mouse as they progressed up to the wing where the earl's family dwelled.

The old man opened a heavy door, motioned to Mouse, and stepped inside. Mouse hurried in behind. He found himself in Lord Alistair's room.

And the young lord himself lay pale upon his bed, his face lit by a single smokeless candle.

Mouse gasped in horror at the dreadful wound staining Alistair's white shirt deep red and ghastly brown. It was like no wound he had ever before seen, open and, most dreadful of all, boiling.

Boiling! Even from across the room, Mouse could see bubbles of blood bursting and roiling. Vapors like steam rose from the gash. How could anyone live with such a wound as that? Yet Alistair's chest rose and fell with piteous moaning.

"What—" Mouse pressed both hands to his mouth, desperate to keep from vomiting. With a struggle, he forced the words out. "What has happened to him?"

"Aye, it's nasty," said the scrubber, grunting his way to the young lord's side. "He's been poisoned by a magic dagger. Would you believe it?"

Mouse scarcely heard. He drew back, pressing against the closed chamber door. "What can be done for him?"

"Oh, not a great deal yet," said the old man. "Was a time I might have helped. But not now. Someone's coming who will put a stay on the poison, and perhaps the Silent Lady will finish the job as soon as she has the chance." The scrubber gave Mouse a shrewd look. "Not that you'd be knowing anything about that, eh?"

Mouse felt the blood draining from his face. "The Silent Lady is . . . she's . . ."

The scrubber grinned, his eyes disappearing behind wrinkles. "I know, little mouseling. But you'll get her out in time. I have faith."

"Get her out?" Mouse cried. "How can—"

"Shhh." The scrubber put a finger to his lips. "You don't know yet, of course, and I don't expect you to. Tend to this young man now, and do as you think best come tomorrow. It'll come right in the end."

With those words, the old man started for the door. Mouse shied away from him, drawing back into the shadows. The scrubber chuckled at this and paused as he opened the chamber door. His eyes sought Mouse's in the darkness and did not seem to suffer for lack of light. And he said:

"You seek the dwarf, little one. He's the heir you need."

"The dwarf?" Mouse squeaked.

The scrubber clucked and shook his head. "Really, child, if you must go about in disguise, you should make some effort to remember it from time to time."

He shut the door.

Mouse stood alone with the earl's nephew and the ghastly stench of poisoned blood.

The fountain of misery welled up with such strength that it took all in Leta's will to force it back. She sat alone in her chamber, listening to the sounds of the hunt. Like a bunch of hounds running a fox to ground, that's what the men-at-arms, following the orders of Mintha and others, sounded like.

Leta hid her face in her hands. She must not weep. If once she began, how would she stop? This was not the time to be the ninny she'd been brought up to be! Now was the time to *think*!

Florien. It was odd; she had never even thought about his having a name. Not since she asked on that first day. And it hadn't mattered to her. Name or not, he was who he was, and she knew him, and she trusted him. Whom had he to trust now?

Maybe he would come to her. Had she not proven her friendship to him over many months? Maybe he would come to her for help. But there was nothing she could do, and Mintha would watch her like a hawk! No, it would be best if he fled, far and farther still, without a word to her, without a look, without a thought. How he would escape, she could not guess. Even the secret passage rang with the footsteps of soldiers. Mintha had taken the key from the earl's dead body and unlocked the heavy bolts of the door hidden behind a tapestry in Ferox's chamber. Leta had watched her do it and watched the soldiers march into the dark passage beyond.

Even now, she thought she could hear the pound of feet beyond her wall, and she shuddered as though they searched for her.

"Some of the earls might rally to him," she whispered to her own clenched hands. "Not all of them are like Father."

Not all of them wished to see the North Country united under a king. Some preferred to master their lands beholden to no authority. Those earls might support Ferox's son. They would see in him no threat of a future king as they might in Alistair. They might fight for his right to inherit his father's lands. They might—

"No," she told herself and relaxed her fists. "Don't be stupid."

After all, even if it were true, what kind of life would that be for the Chronicler?

A sudden pounding at her door startled Leta to her feet. Did those fool soldiers think she might hide her former teacher in her own chambers? Drawing herself to her full height, she strode to the door and flung it wide, demanding as she did so, "What cause have you to . . . oh."

A child, brown and wide-eyed, crouched before her, hands wringing. Leta could almost remember having seen this humble scrubber boy before, hard at work in various corners of the castle. "Lights Above!" she said, taking in the terror in that face. The boy looked as though he had seen a ghost. "What is the matter?"

"Allees-tar," the boy said, his eyes pleading to be understood.

Leta shook her head. "Say again?"

The boy chewed his lip, his eyes darting up and down the corridor. Then he reached out and took Leta's hand in both of his and spoke urgently. "Allees-tar."

"Alistair?"

The boy nodded.

A coldness took hold of Leta at the mention of her betrothed's name. "What about him?"

But the boy did not notice her icy voice or stance. He repeated the name and tugged at Leta, motioning and signing for her to follow. There was no understanding the child. Leta shook her head, her teeth grinding. "He must want me. A first time for everything under the sun!"

She grabbed her cloak, for it was far too cold to wander the castle corridors without one. Best to get the encounter over with as soon as possible, she decided. She followed the boy to Alistair's room. At the door, she pushed ahead and entered first so as not to seem dragged like a dog. She must retain at least some form of dignity.

Then she saw the state in which her betrothed lay.

"Alistair!" She hastened to his side, leaning over him on the bed. Her mouth gaped, and she grabbed the one candle and held it closer for a better look. She saw the boiling, smelled the poison.

One side of her mind said: *SCREAM!*

It's as well you aren't afraid of blood, her practical side responded.

RUN! roared the panicking Leta.

Someone's got to take care of this. And you want something to distract you. It might as well be you.

SCREAM, dragons eat you!

But as usual, practical Leta won the day.

She turned to Mouse. There was only a slight tremor in her voice when she spoke. "Fetch fresh water and some bandages." Then she shook her head. "How silly of me. You don't understand, do you? Stay with him, and I'll fetch them myself."

In the end, it probably took less time for her to get her own supplies. No one bothered with her. The castle remained in a quiet uproar of heated whispers and the occasional running messenger. The searching soldiers seemed to have finished their search and, baffled, started over again with a little less vim and a lot more thoroughness. She left her bedroom door wide open, welcoming them to enter and disturb what they liked. She had nothing to hide. She took some old petticoats, a pair of shears, and her washbasin back with her to Alistair's room, and found Mouse fidgeting over him like a frightened sparrow.

The wound was nastier even than she remembered. Several times Leta had to force herself not to vomit, and her head whirled sickeningly. But she got it clean even so, and succeeded in stopping the bleeding. Alistair remained unconscious, and a fever was developing.

Mouse stayed by her elbow, willing to fetch and carry, nervous as a young mother over a child. Leta found him a bit annoying but forced herself to speak soothingly even though she knew he would not understand.

"All will be well; all will be well," she repeated. "The night will pass. Morning will come. The Chronicler will escape. He is even now well on his way, far beyond their reach." Nothing she said had anything to do with the wounded lord beneath her ministering hand. But Mouse did not know, so what was the harm? "All will be well; all will be well," she whispered like a song.

"What is going on here?"

Lady Mintha's voice shot like an arrow through Leta's fragile senses. She turned and glared at the lady and said, "Peace!" Then she gulped. She had scarcely dared to speak two words in Mintha's presence before tonight, never dreamed of using so sharp a tone! What an upside-down existence life had become.

Mintha's face reddened with anger. She swept into the room, stopping short when she saw her son. Then she screamed. Mouse, on the other side of the bed, crouched into a ball, pressing his hands to his ears.

But Leta stood up, took four steps across the room, grabbed the lady by the shoulders, and gave her a hard shake. "Quiet! Do you want the earls to hear?"

Mintha's mouth clamped shut. Eyes round with fury, she turned her gaze from Leta down to her son. "What have you done to him?" she demanded in a tight whisper.

"Nothing. Don't be a fool," Leta growled, letting her go and returning to her work. She was cleaning away blood that had dried in Alistair's ginger hair. "His servant"—she nodded to Mouse—"brought me here to tend him."

"It's that dwarf," said Mintha.

"What?"

"That dwarf. That little blight of a wretch my daft brother claims as his son!"

A hot rush flooded Leta's body from head to heart. "Remember, Earl Ferox is dead," she said quietly.

"What does it matter? Dead or not, he's done enough to ruin the name of Gaheris!"

Leta pressed her lips together, afraid what she might say. Mintha sank onto the bed, clutching Alistair's hand. "Lights Above!" she swore, dropping it quickly. "He burns!"

"He has a fever."

"Come so suddenly? How did he get that wound?"

"I don't know," said Leta.

"It's that dwarf, I tell you," Lady Mintha snarled. "He must have come on him in a dark passage! Seeking to put an end to the true heir and steal the mastery!"

"The Chronicler would never do that," Leta whispered. She stared down at the dreadful gash in Alistair's shoulder, shuddering. "He wouldn't."

"Who else, then?" Mintha wrung her hands and paced across the room. Standing at the window, she cursed violently. "Dawn is coming."

Leta looked up. Sure enough, the sky outside was beginning to pale. At last, an end to this dreadful night! But what cruel fate would day bring?

Mintha, breathing hard, drew herself together. The house was full of all the earls of the North Country, a bloodthirsty crew ready to tear one another apart if they thought it might serve their own ends. Not one of them was sorry to see Earl Ferox, more powerful by far than any three of them, meet his end. They would not hesitate to stand against his chosen heir if opportunity arose.

But Alistair was no longer secure in his inheritance. As long as the son lived, who could say how much support the nephew could hope to have from the earls? And if they knew he lay helpless in his own rooms upstairs, what treachery might they invent even as they enjoyed the hospitality of Gaheris?

Mintha trembled like a rabbit that has discovered its own burrow to be a trap. But she was no coward.

"I'll be dragon-kissed before I let the earls know of this," she said, and her voice was like the old earl's come to life once more. Leta startled at the tone. "The funeral is in a few hours. As soon as the sun touches the weathervane, Ferox will be interred with his forefathers. We can invent some excuse to put off the ceremony of succession. My son is grieving the loss of his uncle, after all. Does not wish to be disturbed, the dignity due the dead, some such nonsense."

"What are you talking about?" Leta said. "Surely you don't think you can keep Alistair's condition a secret?"

"And why not?" Lady Mintha demanded, striding forward until she stood nose to nose with Leta. She was a good head taller than the girl, and her height was worthy of the House of Gaheris. "Don't tell me what I can do. Foolish little mincing ninny! Do you think the earls will stand idly by if they hear my son lies stricken upon his bed? They witnessed Ferox himself declare a freak his heir! They're already licking their chops. If they know Alistair is broken like this, they'll fall upon us like crows on a gibbet." She bared her teeth and growled. "My family has held this mastery for two hundred years. I will not see the House of Gaheris fall!"

Her hand bit cruelly into Leta's arm, and she dragged her away from the bed and toward the door. "Go! Get yourself ready for the funeral. Leave your page to serve my son; it will be enough for now. You must attend my brother's interment as though nothing were amiss. And if Earl Aiven hears a word of this, I will know whom to blame."

"Lady Mintha," Leta protested, trying to pull from the lady's grasp, "I can't leave Alistair now."

"Don't play games with me," Mintha snapped. "No one believes you love him. Now do as I say."

With those words, Mintha drove Leta from the chamber. Then she turned to Mouse, addressing him as though he could understand her. "Stay by your master. I'll return when I can."

The next moment, she was gone, slamming the door like that of a dungeon. Mouse sat in the near darkness beside the stricken lord. Beyond the window, the world turned from black to gray. Mouse huddled down into the space between the bed and the wall, near Alistair's prone form but hiding his head so as not to see it.

"This has nothing to do with me!" he whispered.

Ferox had never been more gloriously clad in the rich robes of Gaheris. Not that either gold or fur could bring him comfort in the darkness of his coffin as it was borne from the castle into the courtyard.

The Chronicler stood unseen in the shed, gazing through a crack in the door upon the gathered crowd. Ten earls of the North Country, ten of the strongest, stood with their entourages about them. Earl Lebuin of Aiven, majestic in his mourning garb, loomed over his daughter, who stood with hands folded and head bowed so that the Chronicler could not see her face.

Alistair was not among the company. Words were exchanged among the various earls, curious glances stolen. Someone whispered questions to Lady Mintha, but her stoic face gave the Chronicler no answers. And soon all of them were lost to his sight in the crowded courtyard.

Another solitary watcher observed the courtyard from a higher, more distant prospect. Mouse stood at the window of Alistair's chamber, gazing down at the gathered mourners like so many black crows in the yard. He shivered and turned to the fevered lord upon his bed. The wound in his shoulder was turning black around the edges.

Down below, the funeral service began. Mouse could not understand the words. Even those who spoke the language understood little of what was said. A cleric of uncertain order recited in rhythmic cadences old words he did not believe. But Leta, standing beside her father, picked out pieces here and there that were familiar to her:

> *"Beyond the Final Water falling,*
> *The Songs of Spheres recalling . . ."*

She searched the downcast faces of those around her. Did any of them recognize those words? Did any of them know the song from which it was taken? The Chronicler would know. Even if he did not believe, at least he would know.

But his face was not among the mourners. She was alone in the crowd beside the statue-like frame of her father.

The cleric, somber in sable robes, stood before the door of the Gaheris family crypt, the coffin of the earl before him. He sprinkled water that was supposed holy; he scattered spices that were deemed virtuous. He spoke prayers that were not prayers but empty words.

And behind his words, Leta heard another sound.

A *scritch-scratch* upon heavy wood.

Then a voice like a demon's whisper flowed from a dark place of echoes. *Open the gate.*

She ceased to breathe. The world stopped—all sounds, all movements, everything swallowed up in that voice.

Open the gate!

She felt the tension in her father's body. Dragging herself back into the cold present, she looked up at Earl Aiven and saw that his face was ashen, saw a straining vein in his neck and tightness under his eyes. Did he hear it too?

The cleric paused in his ritual. He stared out at the assembled crowd, and words failed him.

Open the gate.

Then it was gone, disappearing like spider webs caught upon a wind and borne far away. The cleric continued the ceremony, and the mourners breathed again.

But Leta thought, *There is something in that crypt.*

She opened her mouth to speak. Even as pallbearers lifted Ferox's coffin onto their shoulders; even as Lady Mintha, with great ceremony, nodded permission to Earl Clios; even as Clios's hands were on the latch, turning, pulling, Leta meant to scream, to warn them all: "Don't let them out!"

The latch turned.

And the ancient door exploded.

Earl Clios flew back through the air, knocking flat one of the pallbearers and landing in a broken pile atop his own son. The coffin, unbalanced, slipped from the other bearers' grasps and crashed to the stones amid the pieces of the door. Men and women alike screamed, and Leta realized her voice was among them. She heard the scrape of swords being drawn, heard the shouts of earls to their retainers. She saw Lady Mintha fall to her knees beside her brother's shattered coffin.

She saw the monster emerge from the darkness of the crypt.

"Where is the king of the mortals?" it cried.

8

ETANUN AND AKILUN, HIS BROTHER, *took me into their Haven. At first they did not ply me with questions, only fed me and tended my tattered wings and torn feet. They gave me sweet, clear water to drink, and I had not realized until I tasted it how parched I was. Only then, with my spirits beginning to rise, did I dare begin to tell them of my journey and why I had come.*

"Cren Cru," said Etanun, pounding fist to palm. "We have seen his work before."

"Seen it," Akilun agreed. "But never fought it. Never come to a demesne of his taking in time."

"Will you go to Etalpalli, then?" I asked. "Will you go to the service of my brother, King Tlanextu?"

"We will go to your service, dear lady," said Etanun, and though his voice was kind, his face was grim. "We will rid you of this evil."

And he went to retrieve his sword. A fine sword, wrought of sunlight and moonlight and shining equally as bright. Halisa it was called, and even I,

*sequestered away in Etalpalli as I had always been, had heard tell of its might,
the deeds it had performed both in the Far World and the Near.*

Halisa. Fireword.

Nearly seven feet tall, with skin like rock and a face some mixture of boar and man, the monster wore armor like stone slabs chiseled into a breastplate, pauldrons, and greaves, and the weapon he carried was stone as well.

He strode out of the crypt and stood in the new light of morning, so real and so terrible that everyone around him looked like mere breathless phantoms. He planted great feet above the wreckage of the door and the coffin, and gripped his stone sword in both hands. Lady Mintha lay nearest him, unable to move, while the pallbearers fell back among their brethren, shrieking and clutching at each other.

The monster, his gaze downcast upon the remains of the dead earl, spoke: "Where is the king of the mortals?"

His words swallowed the screams of the people, leaving silence in its wake. No one spoke. The monster's booming voice reverberated through their heads and about the stone courtyard, then died away. His lip curled, and he scraped his sword through the wooden fragments, lifting the edge of Earl Ferox's fine robe and inspecting it thoughtfully. Then he let it drop and strode across the wreckage, caring not whether he trod upon the earl's body. Now Lady Mintha was behind him, trying to raise herself up, frantic to get away from the gaping doorway of the crypt.

"Where is the mortal king?" the monster demanded again, still not looking at the crowd. No one answered. No one breathed.

He swung his sword, and the assembly drew back. Then shouts of command, and housecarls pressed through the crowd, falling upon the monster with battle cries. Leta hid her face but could not stop her ears to the screams and the sound of blows falling upon unprotected bodies.

"Is your king afraid to face me?" the monster bellowed, the stone sword now dripping red. "Is he afraid to stand up to Corgar of Arpiar?"

"The North Country needs no king!" shouted Earl Sondmanus. Taking a lance from one of his housecarls, he strode forward. The monster turned to him, leering down at the gray-bearded man who scarcely came up to his shoulder yet who spoke boldly. "A North Country man is king enough! We rule in our own right, and we drive out our own monsters!"

The monster growled. "Liar."

His sword swung. Earl Sondmanus's lance fell in two pieces, and the earl himself collapsed in a heap. With a roar of mingled pleasure and fury, the goblin swung around and fended off the blows of Sondmanus's enraged sons, killing with each stroke. The remaining warriors withdrew, their fine mourning garments dirtied with blood, and the goblin roared.

"Whom do you think you're protecting, people of dust? The Murderer told me all! He said if once we dared cross the borders into the Near World, the mortal king would drive us out. So answer me, maggots, where is this king? I shall spit him over my fire before I let him drive me back into Arpiar!"

He strode into the thick of the crowd; women fainted and men screamed. Blood spattered his face and armor. He was a nightmare made flesh and stone. "Shall I hack you all to the ground until I find him out?"

Leta, pressed into a throng of strangers so tightly that she could scarcely move, caught sight of her father. She saw the look in his eyes and knew what he was about to do. Earl Aiven, his sword drawn, stepped forward. His shoulders were thrown back, and his eyes flashed beneath his sandy brows.

"I am King of the North Country!" he cried. "I am whom you seek!"

The goblin turned on him like a predator preparing to spring. His jutting jaw slavered hungrily. "Are you?" he said.

The earl's sword lashed out. The goblin caught the blade and wrenched it from Aiven's grasp, hurling it away into the throng, which scattered to avoid being struck. Then the goblin's hand, large enough to crush a wolf's skull, took Aiven by the throat and wrenched him from his feet.

"Do you think," he said, "I cannot tell a king from a clod? Do you think I do not know the ties of blood that bind a man to his own demesne, the daily sacrifice of his heart and soul upon the altar of his kingdom? Do you think"—his voice rose to a shattering roar—"I am a fool?"

The earl's feet kicked the air. He could not speak, could not draw breath.

With another roar, the goblin brought him crashing to the stones, and Leta saw Earl Aiven's body break. This man who was her father and whom she had never thought she loved. She saw him break, yet light, defiant, still shone in his eyes. He struggled to raise himself up. The goblin's booted foot came down upon his chest, pressing him flat.

This man who was her father.

Leta fell to her hands and knees and crawled between the legs of those around her, forcing her way to that empty space in the center of the courtyard where the goblin stood. Even as the monster raised his weapon, her hands found the broken head of Sondmanus's lance. Tripping over her own long skirts, she scrambled to her feet and flung herself at the goblin from behind, driving the lance into the unprotected place behind his knee.

The lance point broke.

The goblin, diverted from his killing stroke, spun around and fixed Leta with the full force of his wide, white eyes. She felt blood and spittle fall upon her skin as he reached for her. She raised the broken lance in defense, but he paid it no heed even when she thrust it into his hand. It shattered, and his long fingers closed about her neck. The next moment, her head exploding with fear and pain, she was swung off her feet and dangling at the length of his arm.

"Where is the mortal king, little one?" the goblin demanded. "You know whom I mean, don't you? I can see it in your eyes. You know the king. Tell me where he is."

For the first time in her life Leta wished she was the fainting sort so she might escape this moment. But there was no escape. The moment must be faced. She must look into those dreadful eyes, into that face both animal and human.

"Wait! Wait, please!"

It wasn't a powerful voice of command that could inspire obedience or respect. It was small and desperate.

But it was the only voice that spoke up.

Corgar, his attention drawn from the dangling maid in his grasp, turned and looked over his shoulder. And when he did so, he swung Leta about, and she could see what he saw.

She saw a broken-down shed, great gaps in its boards, its door sagging on its hinges. Through that door stepped the Chronicler, his hands upraised in protest.

"Please!" he cried. "Put her down. I'm the one you seek. I . . . I am the Earl of Gaheris, future King of the North Country."

The goblin's eyes narrowed, disappearing beneath the deep furrow of his brow. He dropped Leta in a cloud of black skirts and strode across the courtyard. Fallen warriors scrambled out of his way, and he trod upon those that did not move in time. The Chronicler stood. His fists clenched, his mouth hung open, and his eyes were wide as sudden death, but he did not move even as the towering monster loomed above him, staring down into his face.

"King of the mortals?" said Corgar, his voice near a whisper. "You?"

The Chronicler nodded. "Yes," he said.

Corgar stared.

Then he said, "I believe you."

The next moment, his dreadful laughter filled the morning, shattering sunlight and driving darkness into every crevice of the old castle. His great claws closed upon the Chronicler's tunic front, and he lifted him from the ground, shaking him like a rag doll in front of all those assembled.

"Your king!" His laughter was like thunder. "Your king!" cried Corgar. "Foolish, pitiful mortals! Is this the best you can find? Is this the great leader who will drive me from your lands and save your sorry hides?"

The Chronicler, his small hands grasping at the great trunk of an arm that held him, shouted, "Your business is with me! Leave the rest in peace, and we'll discuss whatever you want. Or you can kill me now if you prefer. Only let them go."

"Let them go?" Corgar laughed still more. "I hardly think so."

Then he barked in a strange language none of them knew, a harsh language like a boar's roar or lion's snarl. Lady Mintha, lying near the crypt door, turned to the darkness. The tramp of many feet echoed up the stairway, and the howl of answering voices.

Goblins poured into the courtyard of Gaheris. Like ghosts rising from the Netherworld, they issued from the shadows, enormous creatures of stone and teeth and claws. They fell upon the people of Gaheris, pursuing them into the keep itself, grabbing women by the hair, killing those who stood to fight. Leta curled into a ball atop her fallen father as though to protect him. An enormous hand took hold of her, yanking the barbet and veil from her head so that her hair fell free down her back. She expected any moment to feel the sharp bite of a sword. Instead, she was dragged away from her father and did not know if he lived.

The Chronicler, writhing in Corgar's grasp, watched Leta vanish into the mob, watched the carnage and the madness filling the courtyard. A few housecarls put up a resistance, but he heard death screams that were distinctly human.

Corgar smiled and pulled the Chronicler close to his face. Breath like rotted meat filled the Chronicler's senses. "Well, little king," he said, "it looks as though it is I who will do the driving."

The golden cat streaked across the shadow-strewn floor of the Wood Between. The Chief Poet of Rudiobus chased his Path through the trees, through the darkness, with the desperation of a hunted beast, though it was he who hunted. Those lurking in the dark fled out of his way and watched him go with frightened eyes.

His pace never slowed, not though he ran a hundred miles. And when he neared the Haven of his Master, he redoubled his efforts. Smells pricked his nose, smells as deep as the shadows themselves.

"No, no, no!" he growled, unwilling to believe what he already knew was true. For Bebo had spoken, and Bebo was never wrong. He flew to the Haven, determined to reach it, determined that he could not be too late.

Another smell caught his nose, and he stopped, horror-stricken.

He stood with his ears pricked, and his great eyes turned in a direction slightly off his regular Path.

"Dragons eat you, Imraldera," he whispered in sudden terror.

Moving more carefully now, his body low, his tail catching leaves and twigs in its long fur, he crept down this new, narrow Path, one which he had only ever walked once before. Then he stopped and breathed another curse.

The Faerie Circle had grown. Stones taller than a man and silvery white gleamed before his eyes. And into that ring of stones, marching, marching, passed an army of goblins.

"Lights Above, mercy!" Eanrin growled.

He whipped about and rushed back to the nearest gate into the Near World.

9

AKILUN, WHO HAD REMAINED BY MY SIDE, *his deep eyes studying my face, rose suddenly and crossed to his brother. Though he spoke in a low voice, I strained my ears and caught his words.*

"Are you certain, Etanun?" he asked. "Is it wise for us to venture with her to Etalpalli?"

"Why do you ask?" Etanun said. "She and her people are desperate. And from what she has told us, can you doubt that it was our own Prince who guided her to us through the Wood?"

"True," Akilun replied, and I saw him bow his head and cast a swift glance my way. "But when I looked into her eyes, I saw death."

"You saw the mark of Cren Cru," Etanun said and his grip upon the sword tightened.

"No," Akilun said. "It is something else. Death in fire. Death in water. The death of thousands. Flame. And the fall of night."

I turned away from them, wrapping my arms and my wounded wings tightly about my body, for his soft words frightened me as neither Cren Cru nor the dreadful Wood had done. I could not explain it, and this made it worse by far.

But Etanun said, "My brother, man of insight, would you counsel me to rest my sword and allow the Parasite to destroy yet another demesne?"

I waited to hear Akilun's answer. It never came.

Instead, Etanun approached, his sword in hand, and when I looked, I saw that Akilun drew close behind, and he held the lantern Asha. When I saw its light, delicate and white, I found my heart rising. For the first time since the fall of my mighty parents, I began to hope.

Goblins filled Gaheris Castle.

From Alistair's window, Mouse saw the creature stride from the crypt. He saw the bloodshed in the courtyard, the crushed coffin, the dishonored form of the dead earl. He saw Leta flung around like a husk doll, and he saw the Chronicler held in the monster's grip.

"You seek the dwarf, little one."

"I seek the dwarf," Mouse whispered without knowing what he said.

Then goblins poured from that narrow doorway as though it were a portal from another world. They killed as they went, and Mouse could not see if they took prisoners.

"I'm not part of this," he whimpered.

In moments, they would be swarming every passage of the castle. In moments, they would find this chamber.

Mouse fled to the door, his hands trembling as they reached for the latch. He wanted to crawl under the bed and shiver into nothingness, to let the nightmare of monsters sweep over his head and be gone! But that could never be. He must escape this chamber now, before they filled the keep and he was trapped.

He opened the door and peered out. The corridor was empty, but all around were roars and screams.

If he could get to a lower level, perhaps he could escape out a window? He was small; he might fit through one of the narrow openings. Or if he could make it to the wall, perhaps he could jump? Not on the river side, of course; that would be suicide. But off the southern wall, would the ground below be soft enough? Was it worth the risk of a broken leg or worse?

He stepped out into the passage.

Alistair moaned.

It was a slight sound compared to the screams rising from outside, but Mouse started and looked back into the room. The young lord's eyes blinked blearily open, but they were glassy, unseeing. The wound at his shoulder was blackening fast, spreading ugly veins of poison across his chest, up his neck.

"They'll kill him." Mouse closed his eyes, and a curse choked him. "They'll kill him in his bed."

If he tried to help, the goblins would catch them both.

"There's nothing I can do," he told himself. "I am no part of this."

The next moment, the sounds of horror below ringing through the air and rattling Mouse's ears like the voice of insanity itself, the boy sprang back across the chamber. He took Alistair's limp arm and pulled it across his shoulders. "Dragons eat you," Alistair groaned vaguely, trying to push the boy away. But he was too weak and scarcely awake.

"Come on!" Mouse muttered, hoping the tone, if nothing else, would give Alistair the right idea. "You must help me, or I shan't be able to help you!"

His head lolling, Alistair sagged but somehow found his feet. He was much taller than Mouse and a great deal heavier. The boy cursed and knew even as he staggered under his burden back to the doorway that they would never make it out alive. Goblins would pour up the stairway, ripping, tearing, slaying as they went! They would run the young earl through and tear Mouse to pieces. How vividly his imagination painted it all, as though it had already happened.

Nevertheless, he supported Alistair into the corridor. He could scarcely balance, and he fell against the stone wall, bruising his shoulder, just managing to keep the tall young man upright.

The goblins were coming. Mouse saw their shadows along the wall at the end of the corridor. He froze, unable to find his heartbeat.

"Pssst! Look here, mouseling!"

Again Mouse started and turned. From the doorway a few paces down the passage, the scrubber's ugly old face peered out at them. He beckoned with the handle of his mop. "Inside, quick!"

Desperately, Mouse flung himself and his burden forward. They reached the open door and fell headlong into the chamber, but Mouse was up like a shot. He heard the bark of a goblin voice, thought he saw a shadow along the floor. His mouth open in a silent scream, he pushed the door shut and stared at the lock to which he had no key.

Any moment . . . any moment . . .

There was an inside bolt. He threw it just as a goblin hurled its weight against the door. One instant more would have been too late.

Mouse stood, his hands shaking, one finger dripping blood where the iron bolt had caught it. He turned around, crying, "Help me!" to the scrubber.

But the room was empty, save for the prone form of Alistair on the floor. Of the scrubber there was no sign.

"Come out. Come out, tender mortal!"

There was no time for wonder nor even for pain, only action. That bolt would not hold them forever. Fire coursing through his body, Mouse grabbed a nearby chest and, with strength he did not know he possessed, shoved it across the floor, blocking the door. Beasts and devils! If he could move it, so could those monsters.

"We'll have you in a trice anyway. Best come out and give us no fuss!"

He understood. Their dreadful voices rang through his head, and he understood each word as though it were spoken in his own tongue.

"Fire burn! Fire purify!" Mouse cried out and leapt back. There was a washbasin along the wall. It quickly joined the door and the chest. What else? What else? Their hands were at the latch!

Mouse turned about, searching the room. He realized—in a distant manner, for it scarcely mattered now—that he stood in the dead Ferox's own chamber.

There was a chair by the fire. He shoved it alongside the washbasin and the trunk. The earl's hunting knife and a ceremonial sword hung upon the wall. Mouse leapt for the sword, but he could not lift it from its place. So he took the knife, cutting himself in his frenzy, and stood with it clutched in his hands for half an instant.

But he did not know how to use a knife.

It dropped with a ringing clang to the floor. Mouse flew to the window, drew back the heavy curtains, and looked out. No use! The earl's room overlooked the inner courtyard. Even if it weren't three stories up, there would be no escape that way. The monster below stood in the center of a nightmarish horde. Men, women, and children were being dragged before him and forced to their knees.

Mouse let the curtain drop. He couldn't watch whatever horror was taking place outside.

"Come out, little mouse! Come out and play!"

The great door rattled on its hinges. The iron bolt buckled, ready to give.

The boy wheeled about and grabbed a tapestry down from the wall. Cumbersome though the dense fabric was, it could do no good against that assault. But Mouse could not stand there and do nothing, and there was little else he could lift in the room. Jumping over the prone Alistair, he added the tapestry to his pile.

He did not notice the heavy door the tapestry had covered. And he did not, above the din of the onslaught, hear the croak and groan of its hinges. He was aware of none of this until a voice he had never heard before spoke behind him.

"I say, Imraldera, old thing, what by Lumé's crown are you doing here? You let the Faerie Circle open! You let goblins into—"

Mouse screamed and swung about. An orange cat as large as a spaniel, tail raised in a questioning curl, stood in the dark doorway of the earl's secret passage. Golden eyes fixed upon the boy. They were not animal eyes. They were more sentient than those of most humans.

The cat drew back his lips, and it was a man's voice that fell from his mouth. "You're not Imraldera!" he growled, leaping into the room. "Who are you?"

The bolt broke.

The washbasin, chest, and tapestry flew across the room as the door burst open, knocking Mouse from his feet. He landed atop prone Lord Alistair, his eyes unseeing, his ears unhearing in the overwhelming rush of terror. He felt the reverberation of goblin footsteps upon the stone, smelled the stench of goblin breath and goblin death.

With a yeowl like a panther, the cat leapt forward, flinging himself at the goblins. Mouse scrambled up from the floor and pounced for the knife he'd dropped. His hands grasped the hilt, and he spun about, prepared to defend himself to the last. But he saw a man, a tall golden man dressed in scarlet. In his hand was a long knife, darting like claws. Unlike the blades of the housecarls in the courtyard, his weapon pierced the goblins' armor. Though they towered over him and must each have doubled his weight, he spun and darted, avoiding their stone swords and dealing wounds upon their rock hides. They screamed and Mouse heard one cry: "It's the knight! The gate guarder!"

They retreated, howling, and the golden man pursued them into the passage. For one moment, Mouse believed he had gone for good. But the next, he sprang back into the room, his eyes wide and his hair bristling. He slammed the door, though the bolt was broken and it could provide no fortification. Growling, he took hold of a tall wardrobe and, without any apparent strain, pulled it on its side across the doorway. It would provide pause against whatever force with which the goblins returned.

Then he turned on Mouse.

"Where is she?" he demanded.

Mouse fell to his knees. "Please, please, glorious one!" he cried. "You must help us!"

The stranger trod on Alistair's hand as he crossed the room. His knife upraised threateningly, he glared down at Mouse. "I am not glorious," he said, and then he sniffed, his nose wrinkling. "Where is Imraldera? I smell her on you."

Mouse cringed away like a cowering puppy before a lion. "Please!" he cried. "The Silent Lady is held prisoner beneath the Citadel of the Living Fire!"

"What?" Deftly sheathing the knife, the stranger grabbed Mouse by the shoulder of his tunic and dragged him to his feet. "I left her at the Haven to guard the gates in my absence, and I return to find goblins breaking through to the Near World, and you're going to gibber about some *citadel*?"

"She's there, sir! I swear!" Mouse cried. "She sent me to find Etanun of the Faerie folk! She sent me to bring back Etanun's heir!"

"Nonsense," Eanrin snarled. "Imraldera wouldn't leave the gates unguarded, and she hasn't—"

The door rattled, and the heavy wardrobe inched away, leaving a crack opening. A great goblin hand struggled through, tearing at the rock wall. "Come out, little knight!" one of them roared. "Come out and face our brothers!"

Mouse shrieked, straining against the stranger's hold. "Help me!" he cried. "Help me get out, and I will explain everything!"

The stranger cursed. Then he dropped the boy, and the two of them took Alistair's arms and hauled him upright. "Hurry," the stranger said as he slung Alistair across his shoulders. He was significantly stronger than he looked. "Into the passage."

Mouse obeyed, ducking into the darkness, which was soon all the darker when the stranger followed and pulled the door shut behind. Mouse heard him mutter something, presumably some locking or shielding enchantment, and only just in time, for the goblins burst through. Mouse, trembling in near blindness, heard their furious growls as they tore apart Earl Ferox's room, searching for their quarry.

"Move your feet!" the stranger hissed.

Mouse hastened down the passage as fast as he could go without seeing. The stairway was long, narrow, and steep, and dampness made each step slippery. He nearly fell several times, but the stranger caught him from behind. Beyond the stone walls were sounds of horror and battle. Were the goblins slaughtering all the pale dwellers of this land? Mouse shivered and wept and whispered, "I am no part of this!" But he believed it less every time he said it.

The walls gave way to uncut stone and deeper darkness and heavier dankness, as though fresh air never came to these parts. They were below the castle now, Mouse thought, winding down and down into the rocky out-cropping over the river on which it was built. The sounds of war diminished. Now he heard only the tramp of his own feet and the labored breathing of Alistair, still slung across the stranger's shoulders. The stranger himself moved with catlike stealth.

Suddenly Mouse's feet touched icy water. He cried out, clawed desper-ately at nothing in the darkness, and fell to his hands and knees, soaking himself through.

"Hush, mortal!" the stranger said. "We've reached the river; it's still high from autumn rains." His voice was grim, as though he spoke through clenched teeth. "I never come this way so early in the winter. Dragon-eaten dampness. You'd better have a good explanation for me at the end of this!"

Mouse, shivering and wet, got to his feet. "Go on," said the stranger with neither kindness nor sympathy. "It opens up eventually. You'll see light in another minute."

Mouse stumbled forward as ordered. It seemed like another hour, not a minute. But at last the cold gray of an overcast day gleamed at the end of the tunnel. Wading as fast as he could in the icy water, Mouse hurried forward. But the current became stronger, and he soon had to stop for fear of being dragged into the cold clutches of Hanna.

"Here," the stranger said and, looking around, Mouse saw that he had climbed up onto a wide ledge above the water and laid Alistair out upon it. He offered Mouse a hand, and soon the quivering child found himself pulled up beside the other two. He sat with his back against the wall, staring at his companion, whose face he could only just discern in this partial lighting.

The stranger was looking back up the tunnel, his fine long nose sniffing delicately. "I don't think they're following us. I'd smell them if they were," he said. Then he addressed his attention to Alistair, rolling the young man over to inspect his wound. "Great Lights above us!" he cried when he saw the blackened gash, which steamed in the cold tunnel. Then he bared his teeth, more animal than man in that moment. "I know whose blade did this. I've seen wounds of this kind before."

Mouse drew himself together, folding up his knees and wrapping them with his arms. He watched the golden stranger close his eyes and press long-fingered hands to Alistair's shoulder. The next moment, the lapping of river water below became accompaniment for a fey song, the like of which Mouse had never before heard. It was the oddest sound following the terror of that long night and longer morning. Though it was a song of peace and healing, Mouse shuddered.

When the stranger withdrew his hands, his face was drawn and tired. He frowned but nodded. Staring, Mouse breathed a quick prayer: "Fire burn!"

The black spidery lines of poison were faded to an ugly red, and the festering wound was now only a puckered white scar.

"It'll do," said the stranger. "Curse that dragon-blasted goblin! He killed more than a few of my people with that poison in the war with Arpiar. We should have done away with him when we had the chance."

He seemed to be talking to himself, not to Mouse, so the boy did not respond. His mind was numb, but a voice from his memory whispered: *"Someone is coming who can put a stay on the poison."*

And that same voice had said:

"You seek the dwarf, little one."

How could the scrubber have known? How could he have predicted such bizarre happenings? None of it made sense! But then, nothing had made sense since the moment Mouse had turned his face to follow the blue star.

The stranger, his shoulders arched and his eyes snapping fire, turned suddenly like a predator spotting its prey. Mouse shrank still more into himself, wishing he could hide from that gaze.

"All right," said the stranger, "tell me what's going on here, girl, before I lose what's left of my temper."

10

THEY JOURNEYED WITH ME through the Wood Between until we came at last to Cozamaloti. The lock placed upon it by my brother was strong; anyone with less need than I would have turned away, for Cozamaloti Gate had taken the form of an enormous waterfall thundering over a precipice. To pass into Etalpalli, we would have to jump into the churning mist below.

But the Brothers Ashiun never hesitated. Their strange gifts, sword and lantern, gripped in their hands, they stood on either side of me, and together we leapt.

It was like stepping through a door. No fall, no rush of wind. Merely a step, and we stood on the borders of my city. And though I strained my eyes, I saw no wings brushing the sky. There was nothing but the hush of Cren Cru's devouring and the call of his Twelve echoing faintly among the towers: "Send out your firstborn!"

Taking to the sky, I led the brothers swiftly through the winding streets to Itonatiu, where my brother waited. They climbed the winding stairs while I flew directly to the summit and found Tlanextu there.

Or rather, found what was left of him.

He still breathed, but only just. His was a body desiccated. I had never seen its like! The wrinkles on his hands, his neck, the sag of his cheeks, the shrunken hollows of his eyes, which were clouded and blind. His wings were nothing but broken stubs hanging from his shoulders. But he raised his head at the rustle of my approach.

"Is that you, sister?" he called.

I could not speak. I was too horrified by his appearance even to go to him, to tell him that I had done as he asked. I stood on the edge of Itonatiu's roof, my wings spread for flight, and I said nothing.

"I am glad you have come," Tlanextu said. With those words, he died, his final life drained away.

I was Queen of Etalpalli.

"I'm a boy," said Mouse.

The stranger blinked. "Right," he said. "And I'm the Queen of Etalpalli."

"No, really," said Mouse. "See? I . . . I cut my hair."

The stranger's wry expression deepened to one of incredulity. "Do you honestly think hair length is what makes the difference?"

Mouse blushed, gaze dropping. Then in a meek voice: "I, um. I bound myself up in certain . . . um, places."

"A valiant effort." The stranger sat down, and suddenly he was a cat, his ears flat and his eyes narrowed. "I am not the brightest light that ever shone in the vaults of heavenly inspiration," he said. "But I do know my boys from my girls, just as I know my mortals from my immortals. You, my dear young woman, are as mortal as they come. You also bear an uncanny resemblance to my comrade-in-arms Dame Imraldera. And you evidently know something of her and her whereabouts. I am, as the proverb says, all ears."

His fur-tufted ears cupped forward.

Mouse's mouth opened and shut. Then in a whisper: "All right. I am a girl."

Her disguise had been feeble at best. But she had clung to it in this foreign land of cold winds and unnatural speech, considering it the one shield between herself and all the fury this world could offer. Now, to be unexpectedly called out in a language not her own but which she understood, coming from the mouth of a creature that had a moment before been a man but was now most definitely feline, coming on top of nearly losing her life in a manner most violent to creatures more dreadful than her nightmares . . . it was too much.

She buried her face in her hands and burst into tears.

"Oh, dragon's tail and teeth!" The cat sat, his tail curled about his paws. "You mortals are such a weepy lot," he said and started grooming. "Let me know when you're quite through, will you?"

It felt like hours but was probably mere minutes later when Mouse wiped her eyes on her wet sleeve, sniffed, and sat up. While she was probably the safest she'd been in a long time, this place was gloomier than the most dreadful dungeon she'd ever seen. How was it possible for a person to be so cold?

And overhead she still heard, echoing faintly down, the pound of goblin feet.

The cat stopped grooming and nudged her with a paw. "Perhaps I should start," he said, his voice gentler than before. "My name is Eanrin. Sir Eanrin, Knight of the Farthest Shore. Bard and poet and brilliant songster." He angled an ear. "You've heard of me?"

She shook her head.

He sighed and his whiskers drooped a little. "Time enough to amend that later. But first, who are you?"

"Mouse," she said.

He sniffed. "What's your real name?"

"I cannot tell you."

"Why not?"

"Names bear too much power. The women of my order do not give their names freely to any who ask."

"Women of what order?"

"I am an acolyte," Mouse whispered as though afraid the watery passage would catch her voice and echo it to the worlds, "in the Citadel of the Living Fire, servant of the Sacred Flame."

Eanrin tilted his head, his pupils thin black slits. "And it's in your heathen temple, you say, that my Imraldera is held prisoner?"

Mouse did not like the way he spoke without reverence, with mockery. But then, no one she'd met since beginning her journey seemed to know or respect the Flame. What a strange, barbaric world lay beyond the Citadel walls! Coldly, she nodded.

"How can that be?" Eanrin demanded. "I left her safe in the Haven. She could not be taken against her will."

Mouse's face darkened. "The Silent Lady came of her own accord to the threshold of the Flame's abode. She came with a message for the goddess, but she was disrespectful of the goddess and punished by imprisonment."

The cat searched her face with eyes that, she felt, saw more than she cared to reveal.

"You said something about Etanun and his heir." The cat's tail twitched. "What has my lady Imraldera to do with that?"

Mouse dropped her gaze. "I don't know," she admitted. "I know only that she asked me to find Etanun before she is put to death."

The cat went still. Not so much as a whisker twitched on his face. At last he spoke in a voice as dark as the tunnel around them. "Etanun. The Murderer. Bebo said something about him. I myself have seen nothing of him in . . . centuries, I think, by the Near World's count! No one has seen him since he killed his brother and went into hiding. Why should Imraldera wish to send him a message?"

Mouse shook her head. "I know only what she told me. She said to find Etanun and Etanun's heir, and the heir is the dwarf, whom I must bring back to the Citadel."

"You do realize you're talking nonsense?" said the cat.

"Please, let me try to explain!" Mouse pleaded.

"Very well, tell me everything. And be quick about it."

Hardly knowing where to begin, Mouse said, "The Silent Lady came to the Citadel not two months ago—"

"Stop!" said the cat. "Why do you call her the Silent Lady? She was healed long ago and, believe me, I *know* she is not silent!"

"But . . ." Mouse frowned and rubbed her tired face. "It is her name. It is the name of our prophetess, the herald of our freedom, the forerunner of the goddess herself. It was she who, by the will of the goddess, rescued us from the grip of the Wolf Lord. She *is* the Silent Lady! To call her anything else would dishonor my tongue."

The cat growled. A dreadful shadow had crossed his heart as the girl spoke, a shadow of memories not too far gone. Memories of a wolf and hunt, of flames and stone-charred land.

"Who is this goddess of whom you speak?" he asked.

"The Flame," said Mouse, her voice reverent and low. "The bright and beautiful, the holy Flame at Night, who lights our way in darkness."

"The Flame at Night?" Eanrin closed his eyes. His tail twitched across the stone. "Imraldera is not going to like this. Not at all."

In Gaheris courtyard a fire burned, filling the castle with its fumes and shrouding all in thick, rank smoke. The mortals choked and gagged, their eyes watering, but the goblins welcomed it. In this world of mortal smells and sights, the smoke from their fire brought relief to their senses, shrouding the sun and disguising the strangeness of the realm they had invaded.

They bound their captives—young and old, male and female—in goblin chains of some stone unknown in the mortal world, so heavy that many of the prisoners could scarcely move. The goblins prodded them like naughty boys might goad a stray cat, laughing at whatever reaction they might get, be it fierce or frightened. Yet every last one of them suffered fear as keen as that of their prisoners. They might disguise it with bluster and roars and braggadocio, but each one looking into the eyes of his brother or sister saw the same dread hiding inside.

They had passed unlawfully through the gates. They had invaded the Near World against the Lumil Eliasul's command. What price would they pay for their disobedience?

Not one would suggest an early retreat, however. After all, to return to Arpiar meant facing Queen Vartera herself. They must burrow in, plant themselves as firmly as possible. They were an army, weren't they? They might yet stand a chance.

If their leader shared their fears, none could guess it. He had fastened a chain to the small mortal king's neck. This sight made many breathe a little easier. For prophecies may be undone, even at the last. The mortal king couldn't drive Corgar out while chained like a dog!

Corgar established himself in the earl's great hall, sitting in Earl Ferox's chair, which was hardly large enough for his bulk. He propped his feet on the table and barked orders to his men as he saw fit. Crouched in the shadows behind the chair, the Chronicler pulled at the collar on his neck. Corgar had secured the other end of its chain to his own belt.

The Chronicler's mind ached with a mixture of wrath and terror. What had possessed him to declare himself king before this monster? He bowed his head and tugged at his hair. While he lived, he must think. He must try! Sure, he was as good as a dead man here in the monster's presence. But did that mean he had the right to give up? Until Corgar dealt the final blow, he must strive.

But the chain was almost too heavy for him to lift his head. So he crouched, gagging at the smoke, and could not collect his wits.

Suddenly Corgar reached behind the chair and dragged the Chronicler forward, dropping him like a hunting trophy upon the table. "Well now, little king," he said, leaning back in Ferox's chair, his hands behind his ugly head. "I have a question. You look like the straightforward sort, and I think you and I might get along well. After all, I care for this chilly land of yours no more than you care to have me in it. So you tell me what I need, and our business might conclude faster than you think."

The Chronicler slowly stood upright despite the weight around his neck. He faced the monster, his eyes flashing defiance. But there was no point in fighting until he knew for what purpose he fought.

"Why are you here?" he asked.

"I need the House of Lights."

The Chronicler could find no words of his own as the monster's rolled around in his brain. At length he replied, "It doesn't exist."

Corgar had never encountered mortals before this day. He knew goblins who had found one of the little dirt creatures lost in the Wood Between. He'd been told they were great sport, loud squeakers when poked, fast runners when pursued. He'd also been told they were ignorant about the ways of the worlds, no better than mute beasts when it came right down to it.

He'd never expected them to be stupid.

"Don't toy with me." His right hand fell upon the great table, and his claws dug trenches into the wood. "I'm no fool, and I'll not be played as one. Tell me where the House of Lights is, I command you!"

The Chronicler shook his head. The heavy chain pulled him down until he bowed before the monster. "It does not exist. I cannot tell you where it is, for it is nowhere and has never been."

Corgar got to his feet. The Chronicler cringed away, expecting a strike, a deathblow even, but the goblin only shouted at his monstrous servants waiting at the other end of the great hall. "Bring in the slaves!"

A string of captive humans entered the room, staggering under the weight of their bindings. The Chronicler's heart nearly broke at the sight of their desperate faces. Among them were several earls, men who would have seen him murdered or used him as a puppet for their own ends. Even as the Chronicler looked no more than a child when compared to them, so they appeared like children under the heavy watch of the goblins.

Corgar, however, was given as much to cunning as to ferocity. Ignoring the slaves, he studied the diminutive king on the table before him, watching his face as each of the mortals came through the door.

Until he saw what he was looking for.

"Stop!" he growled to his servants. He strode out from behind the table, gazing at those slaves displayed before him. "Take these away," he said. "Except for that one."

And he reached out and snatched Leta by the arm.

"Unbind her," he commanded and a goblin hastened to obey. Corgar's grip was more than enough chain for any human maid. She could not bring herself to look upon that dreadful face again but gazed across the room.

"Chronicler!" she cried and reached out to him.

The goblin hauled her across the room with all the gentleness he might show a side of pork, flung her on the ground before the table, and caught her by the hair on top of her head, dragging her upright to expose her throat. He drew a stone dagger.

"This one," he said, addressing himself to the Chronicler. "This one means something to you. Something more than the others."

"No!" the Chronicler protested. "She means nothing."

"Shall I kill her, then?"

"No!" The Chronicler nearly fell from the table as he lunged. The chains dragged him down, but there was fierceness in his voice. "Don't touch her!"

Leta, unable to speak for terror, grabbed at the great hand wrenching her hair, then felt the chill of the stone blade against her throat.

"Where is the House of Lights?" Corgar demanded. "I know it is near. For many long ages I have watched the gates between the Far World and the Near. I have tested and I have tried. And when I found this one opening, I did everything I could to pry it, even under the very noses of the Knights of the Farthest Shore. Not until now, however, have I found it unwatched and unlocked to me. The moment is ripe. I will have the House of Lights, if I must decimate this entire land!"

"You have to believe me," the Chronicler said, his voice choked with urgency. "You *must* believe me. The House of Lights does not exist. Not in this world or anywhere else I know. It's . . . it's a story. Nothing but a story."

"And what about me?" Corgar demanded. "Am *I* a story?"

The Chronicler gazed at Leta, helpless in the goblin's grasp. Her eyes rolled like a crazed horse's, but at last she looked at him. How often in this past year had he repeated to her, "These things are merely the fancies of men trying to make sense of the world's emptiness. They are not real."

He had never, until now, wished so desperately to be wrong.

It's all right. Her eyes, though bloodshot with fear, nevertheless seemed to reassure him: *It's not your fault.*

But it was.

He struggled against his chains to stand upright. How heavy were the collar and the great stone links! Bracing himself, he stood like a man tensed for battle, though his short limbs were helplessly bound.

"I cannot tell you what you want," he said. "I cannot give vapors substance. But I offer you my life. Kill me. Leave the girl alone. She knows nothing, and her death will accomplish nothing."

"Neither will yours, little majesty," Corgar said. Even as the dwarf screamed at him to stop, he hauled the girl onto her feet and spun her about to face him, for he would look into her eyes as he sent her to the Netherworld.

And he saw that he held the girl from the courtyard.

He had scarcely noticed her then. She had merely been one of the many beasts fleeing like insects before his stomping feet. Yes, she had assaulted him, but why should he care for her ineffectual sting? Yet something stirred in his memory. He gazed into her ashen face and recognized a quality most would have missed.

Corgar had been a warrior for centuries as the mortals count them. He had marched to battle against kings and princes, against battalions of monsters far more terrible than he. He had lived; he had thrived. In his veins flowed the blood of war, the pulse of battle. His eyes were sharp, never missing a trick or chance.

Corgar knew a warrior when he saw one. Granted, so frail a creature could not lift the weapons he bore. Granted, she could not hope to prevail in a contest of strength. Yet he saw that she would stand before his onslaught and die with courage.

Corgar had been a warrior long enough to know that it was a warrior he held with a dagger beneath her ear.

The small king on the table was pleading, his voice rising and falling and desperate. There was a thump as he rolled to the ground and a clanking as he struggled to his feet, pulling himself up by the chain attached to Corgar's belt. But Corgar, caught up in the wide eyes of the mortal maiden, could not hear what the king said.

He realized that he was not going to kill her. And he hated himself for it.

"Let her go! I told you, I cannot give you what you ask!" the little king was shouting. A dull blow brought Corgar's attention down, and he saw that the creature was kicking him and pounding his leg with his chained hands.

With a roar, Corgar flung the girl to the ground. She crumpled, gasping but otherwise unmoving, as though she did not yet believe that she still lived. Her hands clutched her throat. Why was no blood flowing? Why did she still breathe? The Chronicler collapsed by her side, his heavy chains smacking the floor, and tried to touch her.

But Corgar caught up the length of chain, dragged him back, and forced the small man to face him.

"Listen to me, mortal king," the monster snarled. "Sooner or later, every warrior meets the blade's end. Her life is forfeit, and I will claim it when I am ready. Tell me where I may find the House of Lights if you wish to spare her."

The Chronicler wrung his hands, his face colorless. "I . . . I can't tell you what you ask. I do not know where it is."

Corgar roared, and goblins came running at his voice. "Take this wretch!" he cried, indicating Leta. "Bind her with the other slaves, and set them all to work. I will tear this castle apart brick by brick, stone by stone if I must. I *will* have Queen Vartera's prize!"

The goblin soldiers laid rough hands upon the girl, dragging her from the room. The Chronicler watched until she was beyond his sight. Then he bowed his head and cursed the day of his birth.

11

*H*OW CAN I EXPLAIN WHAT CAME OVER ME *in that moment? I had never known, never dreamed anything of the kind! My parents were Citlalu and Mahuizoa, ageless, immortal, never intended for death.*

I felt the pulse of my demesne. I felt the beat of its heart, the draw of its breath. I could sense the flutter of every pair of wings. Oh, my people! My kingdom. My world. I was more powerful then than I had ever believed possible. More powerful . . . and more bereft.

When the Brothers Ashiun reached the rooftop, they found me standing with my back to my dead brother, gazing out across the city to where the Mound had taken root.

"There," I told them. I did not try to explain the death of my brother, the sudden oncoming of dominion that filled me with physical potency. I merely pointed. "There he lies, and there he sucks at the blood of my demesne. Root him out!"

The child in the darkness.

Alistair saw it standing on the brink of the chasm, bathed as always in white light. Next, the monster from the darkness that bayed in the voice of a wolf would leap upon him and devour him.

And then he would wake. As he always did.

But this dream was deeper than ever before. He ran toward the child and the light, never drawing any nearer. There was a stench too that had never been there before: a rank, poisonous, rotten stench, like the breath of some dead thing come to life. His shoulder hurt like fire, but he ran anyway, pursuing the child and the death that must come.

For years now, he had experienced this same dream, sometimes for many nights running, sometimes not for months at a stretch. But it was the same dream, and he knew the pace of it and the violent end. He must reach that end before he could wake.

But he was running and not catching up. He would never reach the child. He would never reach the light. He would run in darkness forever, without death, without end.

"No!" he cried. "Come and kill me, monster! Kill me as you must!"

The baying of the dogs was too far away. The light was too distant.

"Help me!" he cried.

A golden voice sang. He turned to it as to a light, and the song became a Path at his feet. A new Path, one he had never before trod in this darkness of his subconscious. This wasn't how the dream was supposed to go, but he was desperate now. The voice sang, and he pursued it, changing course and running.

———

Suddenly his eyes opened and he looked upon uncut stone in a dimly lit tunnel, and the sound of flowing water filled his ears. And a voice. Not the golden voice he'd pursued. No, a chattering, swift, high voice, speaking unintelligibly.

This was not what Alistair last remembered of waking life.

He closed his eyes, and his throat constricted but was too dry to make a sound. Where was he supposed to be? What should he remember? He tried to lift his hand, and pain shot through his shoulder. He grimaced and was still. Why was he in this damp tunnel? Why was he so cold?

Why didn't that unseen person stop babbling?

The second time he tried to groan, he managed to make something close to a noise. More like a grating in his throat. He decided to risk opening his eyes again and still found himself looking at the stone and shadows.

His uncle was dead.

That memory crashed through his consciousness, dragging with it everything else. His uncle . . . his cousin . . . his lost future. He ground his teeth, and the groan this time was a little stronger. But there was something else he needed to remember, something on the edge but not quite within reach.

Why was his shoulder on fire?

A voice he felt he should recognize cried out in a burst of anger, interrupting the foreign babbler. "*What? Etanun is here?*"

The first speaker replied, sounding anxious. Alistair, after a battle of wills against his own body, turned his head. He saw Mouse, the scrubber urchin, dressed in rags and ill-fitting shoes, kneeling beside a large orange cat. The cat was listening and watching as though he understood.

Then the cat opened his mouth and the golden voice from Alistair's dream fell from his lips. "And he stood by and watched goblins march into the Near World? Let them break through the gate and come right in? Well, *that* goes to show—"

Alistair screamed.

The cat screamed and arched his back, spitting feline curses.

Mouse screamed and fell off the ledge into the running water below.

Perhaps, Alistair decided, he'd been a bit premature. Yes, he'd had a shock, and one couldn't expect a fellow to lie down and *take* a world that inflicted talking cats upon him. But then again, this could only be a continuation of his dream.

Suddenly relearning to move, he sat up straight and his hands clutched at the cold ground. A dripping Mouse climbed back onto the ledge, glaring daggers his way. The cat, tail slowly smoothing back to a respectable size, mirrored that expression. Then he sat, licked his chest and paws a few times to prove how unafraid he was, and said in the coolest tone:

"So you're awake. What have you to say for yourself in all this, eh?"

Alistair's shoulder throbbed, and he put his hand to it, feeling the distinct pucker of a scar. "A dream," he whispered. "It's all a dream."

"How metaphysical of you," said the cat. "But we're neither of us impressed."

Alistair looked up and down the tunnel and realized where he was, though he had never before been in his uncle's famous passage. He saw how it wound away into rock, how the water flowed through a gray-lit opening. The smell of smoke and death lingered from his dream.

"What is happening?" he asked.

"Oh, a great deal," replied the cat, making his silky way to Alistair's side and sitting down. "Gaheris has been attacked from the inside by goblins let through the death-house gate from their world into yours . . . possibly by a traitorous knight of my order, but I wouldn't like to be casting slurs on the Murderer just yet, you understand. My comrade-in-arms has been taken prisoner and, according to *this* person"—with a glance at Mouse—"it appears that everything comes down to our needing to rescue the Chronicler before it's too late. Isn't that right?" The cat addressed this last to Mouse, who nodded. The cat turned to Alistair again. "Caught up now, are we?"

Alistair stared. "Why does my shoulder hurt?"

"You were stabbed by Corgar, warlord of Vartera's horde. You're lucky you didn't lose your head."

"What's a Corgar?"

"A goblin."

"As in slavering jaws, gaping eyes, stone hides?"

"The same."

"They don't exist."

"Neither do talking cats."

Mouse, wet hair plastered and dripping, leaned forward, chattering again in that language Alistair could not understand. But the cat understood and responded, "Why do you think that matters?"

"Why does what matter?" Alistair demanded.

Cat twitched an ear at him. "I wasn't speaking to you."

"You were speaking to . . . him?"

"Yes."

"And, er, *he* understands you?"

"Yes."

"But so do I!" Alistair shook his head. "How can we both understand you? We don't speak the same language!"

"Proving yet again the superiority of immortal tongues," said the cat, smugly sinking his chin into the downy ruff of fur about his neck. "You'll understand anything I want you to, and nothing I don't. It's the way of it with Faerie."

Mouse looked from the cat to Alistair, then said, "Please, what are you telling him?"

"Nothing," the cat said, tucking his tail closer to his paws. "What did you think I was telling him?"

"You won't . . ." She glanced at the young lord again. "You won't tell him my secret, will you?"

"What secret?"

"That I'm . . . that I'm not what I seem."

The cat's ears went back. He turned to Alistair. This time when he spoke, Alistair understood him but the girl did not. "You do realize, don't you, that she's a girl?" he said.

"Of course I do." Alistair glared. "Do I look stupid?"

"Would you like me to answer that?"

"What did he say?" Mouse demanded. "What did you tell him?"

The cat shrugged and allowed her to understand his words. "I made certain your secret is as safe as it ever was."

She breathed a great sigh, relieved. "Now," she said, "will he help me rescue the dwarf?"

"Ah yes. The Chronicler," the cat said musingly. "He's not a dwarf, you know. He's a small man. There is a difference. I've met dwarves. They're ugly little brutes, nothing like him."

"What does it matter?" Mouse cried, ready to explode with anxiety. "Dwarf, man, he's Etanun's heir! I must bring him back to the Citadel, don't you see? I must bring him back, or the Silent Lady's life is forfeit!"

All traces of smugness vanished from the cat's face. His purr turned to a growl.

Alistair stood, a little shakily, putting a hand back to support himself against the stone wall. Some memories were beginning to leak back through, memories he had thought part of the nightmare. He recalled his uncle's empty chamber and Mouse struggling to pull a hunting knife down from the wall. He recalled the shouts of goblins, a rock-hard hand coming through the doorway.

"What did she say?" he asked. "Does she know something about all this?"

"About the goblins? No. Not directly, that is."

Alistair did not like to ask the next question but knew that he must. After all, the world was a twisted, upside-down place this morning, and anything was possible. "Did she bring them here?" His eyes strayed briefly to her, then away.

"What, her?" The cat shook his head. "I hardly think so. This is much more likely to be the Murderer's doing. But with the gates unwatched, Corgar could have pushed through without anyone's help."

"What gates?"

The cat did not answer. Although seated between them, he somehow seemed untouchably distant. Alistair could almost believe the creature had slid into another world entirely and that he and Mouse looked in from the outside, unable to join.

"Please," Mouse said. "Please, help me rescue the heir. It is the only hope." Her voice was so distressed, Alistair almost reached out to her, though he did not know what she said.

But the cat replied, "I have a better idea," and paced toward her. His posture was that of a tiger, though his size had not altered. Mouse scrambled away from him, but he kept coming until he had her backed up to the edge of the rocky ledge. "Why don't you take me to your little temple?"

"Without the heir?" Mouse gasped.

"*Now.*"

She shook her head. "I cannot return without him! The Silent Lady would be slain!"

"Not if I've rescued her first," said the cat. "Which will happen much more quickly if I'm not sidetracked by goblins and misproportioned mortals."

"No." Mouse's face set into hard lines unfamiliar to her young face. "I will not go without him."

"What's going on? What does she say?" Alistair demanded.

The cat's fur bristled, and his claws dug into the rock. "You will take me now, girl," he said.

She whispered, "I won't."

Suddenly the cat unfolded himself into a tall man in red with flashing eyes and a head full of fiery hair. He grabbed Mouse by the fabric on her shoulder and lifted her to her toes. His face was that of a wildcat, and his voice was a snarl.

"I haven't time to waste on fool's errands," he said. "Imraldera's life is at risk. I do not know where to find your pagan temple, but you *will* take me there and show me where my lady is being held, or so help me—"

His voice broke in a caterwaul as Alistair's hands descended on his shoulders and dragged him backward. He dropped his hold on the girl, who nearly unbalanced into the water again, and was himself tossed into a heap. But he was up again in a swirl of his red cape, his gaze fixed on Alistair, who was as tall as he and perhaps a little broader, and whose face was white as a sheet with terror. A grin flicked across the cat-man's face before he sprang and knocked the mortal man from his feet, pinning him to the ground.

"Don't interfere, mortal!" he growled. "I'm not a man to be—"

Again he broke off, this time spitting a curse as Mouse struck his face with her fist. His hand darted out, snatching her wrist and wrenching it until she fell to her knees. She winced but shouted, "She told me you were good! She told me you were her fellow knight! She said you would help us!"

The cat-man paused, his teeth bared, his breath caught. Mouse's black eyes fixed upon him in storm-like fury. "She never told me you were a monster!"

Still gripping her wrist, Eanrin looked from her down to Alistair, who was terrified and trying not to show it.

They were neither of them his enemies.

Eanrin released Mouse's wrist, got to his feet, and offered a hand to Alistair. "All right, boy," he said, hoping his voice sounded friendlier than he felt. "I'll not hurt you."

"Are you sure about that?" Alistair said, hesitating to accept the hand.

"Mostly sure," Eanrin growled. He assisted Alistair to his feet, then faced the trembling Mouse. Her dark skin wore a sickly pallor, and her drying hair stood out comically from her head. But her eyes were fierce, unwilling to release the anger.

She looked remarkably like another young mortal girl Eanrin had once met in a far dark forest.

Eanrin shook himself, stretching out his neck and swinging his arms to work out kinks. Then he brushed off his sleeves with all the care of a dandy. "Very well, girl," he said coolly, as though passing the time of day with an inferior. "We'll accede to the Murderer's demands if you insist."

Her voice was small but sharp. "They're not *my* demands. I care nothing for you or any of this. I am here only on behalf of the Silent Lady. I do not wish to see her condemned to death."

"Condemned by your own so-called goddess."

"Do not speak insolently of the Flame!" the girl said. "If the goddess demands the great sacrifice from any of us, we are glad to give it. Her knowledge is greater and her purity vaster than our comprehension. I am sure her prophetess would say the same!"

"I'm not," the cat-man growled.

"Then you do not know the Silent Lady."

"No," he said. "You're right. I do not know this *Silent Lady* of yours. But I do know Imraldera." He sighed then and flicked dried mud from the front of his red doublet. "And I know she would not have sent you without reason. I don't understand it, but I . . ." He grimaced. "I will have to trust it. Even as I must walk the Path of the Lumil Eliasul though I cannot see its end."

Neither Mouse nor Alistair understood his last words. Alistair had understood only the cat-man's side of the conversation anyway, and now his brain felt numb. Both he and the girl in boy's clothes stared at the red-gold creature before them and found him more frightening than ever now that his words were also strange to them. They looked to each other, the one tall and pale, the other short and dark, seeking comfort in this world that had gone all wrong. Lacking the bond of language, they at least shared the bond of mortality.

"Now," said Eanrin, coming to a sudden decision. He shook himself and was a cat again, crouched between the two humans, speaking so both could understand him. "We climb back to Gaheris and rescue the Chronicler."

"What?" Alistair said. "Why are we rescuing *him*? What about my mother? What about all the other folk of Gaheris?"

The cat gave him a flat-eared glare. "Sometimes I believe I spend my whole life giving explanations to humans. I shall inform you briefly, for we have little time available to us. My Lady Imraldera has been taken captive by *this* one's"—nod to Mouse—"people, and will not be released until the heir to Halisa is found."

"Halisa, the sword of Etanun?" Alistair asked, unbelieving.

"Good little mortal, keep up. Yes, Halisa, Etanun's sword. The Chronicler supposedly is his heir, your legendary Smallman. Surprise! We must nab him, take him south to fetch the sword, liberate my kidnapped comrade—"

"She's not kidnapped," said Mouse. "She offered herself."

"Whatever you say. We rescue her, and then our favorite little hero returns to drive Corgar back into the Far World, where he belongs. Understand?"

Alistair's mouth went dry. Insane. He had gone insane! That was the only explanation for any of this. But he heard himself saying, "We can never journey to . . . to wherever she's from and back in time to save my people."

"We can," said the cat-man, "if we use the Paths I know."

"But none of this—"

"Please don't tell me that none of this is true or that it can't be happening. I don't have time for it, and neither do you."

"But, the *Chronicler* is the Smallman?"

"Makes sense, doesn't it? He's small enough."

"That's a metaphor!"

"Well, don't you sound all mortal about it?" The cat yawned, showing long white teeth, then blinked as though bored with it all. "Do you never pay attention to prophecies, portentous tellings, and the like?"

"No."

"Can't say I blame you. I'm not overly fond of them myself."

12

*T*HUS I SPOKE MY FIRST COMMAND, *and thus was I obeyed. For Etanun and Akilun went at once down into the city, following the light of the lantern through the winding streets. I watched from above as the Twelve set upon them from all sides, desperate to bar their way. Each of these fell before the might of Halisa in Etanun's hand. Not even the four strongest, standing beside their four bronze stones, withstood his mighty arm, though all the hosts of Etalpalli had cowered before them.*

While Etanun stood over the slain, Akilun stepped forward to the Mound itself, to the very mouth of Cren Cru, the doorway through which the firstborn had vanished. I saw him fling wide the door; I saw him thrust the lantern into that darkness.

And Cren Cru fled. He did not try to fight, could not bear to have the brilliance of Asha enter his darkness. So he fled Etalpalli, and the Mound vanished, leaving only a raw, gaping wound in the ground.

Etanun and Akilun, their mighty gifts blazing, stood victorious.

In the tunnel far below Gaheris Castle, the three laid plans in dank darkness, and feeble plans they seemed to Alistair, though any plan was better than sitting dully in the dark. Only the cat's eyes glowed like fey lanterns.

At last the cat stood. "Come along, mortals," he said. "Night has fallen; not that it'll make much difference. Goblins see better at night than in daylight. But they may have grown more comfortable in the last few hours, let their guard relax. They won't expect much resistance here in the Near World."

He took his man's form, slid down into the water (growling at the wetness, for even as a man he was still a cat), and started sloshing back along the passage toward the long stone stair.

Mouse and Alistair hastened after, hating to slide from that ledge when they couldn't see the bottom. Knowing the drop was short didn't make it better. Icy water flowing in from the river filled Mouse's thin shoes and froze Alistair's bare feet.

"I must remember to grab some boots," he muttered as they tramped along behind the cat-man, whom they could not see, though his muttered complaints were easy enough to follow.

At first it was a relief to step from the chill water onto the steep, slippery stairs, bracing themselves against the walls as they climbed. But the ceiling was so low that Alistair was soon reduced to an upward crawl, using his frozen hands as much as his frozen feet, for he was too tall to stand upright.

"We cannot guarantee the creatures haven't discovered the passage," Eanrin said. He had taken cat form and was therefore making much swifter progress than the other two. He sat on a step above, and they climbed to reach the glow of his eyes. "It's never been much of a secret, not since I first came to guard the gates, and that's at least a hundred years ago."

"You're a hundred years old?" Mouse whispered in awe, her voice carrying up the stone passage.

"Oh no," said the cat with a chuckle. "Much older!"

"What's funny?" asked Alistair, bringing up the rear and feeling rather ill used. "What did she say?"

"She says your breathing is so loud, you might as well blow trumpets to herald our coming," said Eanrin. "So duck your head and keep your mouth shut, eh?"

Alistair muttered, but the echoing of their voices unnerved him, so he did as he was told. He crawled in darkness so close he could scarcely breathe, in the wake of a talking cat and a girl who thought she passed for a boy, attempting to infiltrate his own home filled to the brim with goblins. And for what?

To rescue his cousin.

They were nearing the level of the castle. Up here, the passage broadened and the ceiling was higher. Alistair could almost stand. "So what's our plan again?" he asked.

"Simple. Nab the Chronicler."

"What, stroll in, pick him up, and stroll back out?"

"I never said it was a master plan, did I?" the cat growled. "I'm a cat, little lordling. I'll improvise."

"What about us?"

The cat didn't bother to answer. Just then, they heard the stamp of feet above their heads. Something latched hold of Alistair's arm, and he nearly hollered before realizing it was Mouse reaching back in fearful blindness for comfort in a world full of hostile sounds. Alistair smiled despite the awfulness of their circumstances. She really had no notion how to play her part, had she? He wondered if she had ever been around boys in her life. He touched her hand with the tips of his fingers, and she drew back as though stung, realizing her mistake. They proceeded in silence broken only by the thumping feet above.

The cat stopped. "I'm going on ahead," he told them. "I'll find where they're keeping the Chronicler and see what is best done. You wait here and try not to be stupid."

With that, he was gone. The two mortals, blind as they were, could sense the sudden absence of superiority. Alistair, sighing, took a seat on a cold step and rubbed his numb feet with equally numb fingers. Mouse, a few steps above him, leaned her back against the wall, her arms crossed, her head bowed.

Goblins marched the floors above them.

Alistair had not seen them clearly. Only vague impressions lingered in his imagination. These were, if anything, worse than reality, and he wished he could face one here and now and know his enemy. A known enemy could be fought. An imagined one, however, carried every advantage.

"You're breathing too loudly," Mouse whispered.

"Don't speak, they'll hear you!" Alistair replied.

Since neither understood the other, they lapsed back into silence.

A silence cut short only moments later when a voice rumbled, sounding so near, Mouse could have believed it was in the passage with them. A handful of frozen heart beats later, she realized that it came from the other side of the wall against which she leaned.

"What do you think the master is going to do with the little maggot?"

It was a goblin. The voice painted an ugly picture in both their minds. Uglier still because the speaker was mirthful.

"I couldn't tell you, Ghoukas," his companion replied. This one's voice held a possible feminine lilt, heavily disguised behind chomping. Mouse realized this passage must run alongside the kitchen stores wherein the goblins now helped themselves. "I don't see why he doesn't crunch its head between his thumb and finger!"

"It's got pluck," the one called Ghoukas replied. "Pluckiest manling I've seen since we got here, though they're a miserable enough lot. That one, it's no bigger than a goblin pup, yet it had the cheek to stand up to Corgar! Were you there, in the great hall?"

"Nah, but I heard," the female goblin said with a snarl-like laugh. "Imagine, refusing to give Corgar what he asks! Doesn't it know it's refusing the queen's favorite?"

"Ah, but these little mortals don't know or recognize our queen Vartera, do they?" said Ghoukas. "I hear they believe theirs is the only world."

"What, this place?" The female laughed, sounding as if she'd bitten into something and now sprayed it across the room. "Such a notion! What a small-minded crew these mortals are."

Alistair stood slowly, his heart in his throat. He could see nothing but reached out to find Mouse. He touched her shoulder, and she gasped but allowed him to drag her back down the steps. She couldn't see him, so he could do nothing to reassure her, but at least she was quiet. He cursed the lack of the cat's interpretation.

"They're speaking of the Chronicler," he whispered.

"I think they're talking about the dwarf," Mouse whispered.

They both stopped, each wishing for some idea what the other had said.

"They've got him in the great hall," said Alistair.

"From what I understand, their leader has him captive in the feasting hall," said Mouse.

They stopped again.

"I think we should go rescue him at once," said Alistair as Mouse said, "We must wait here and tell the cat when he returns."

Another pause. Then Alistair took Mouse's hand and pulled gently.

"Wait! What are you doing?" she whispered frantically.

"Dragons eat it," he muttered. "I'd hoped we were thinking along the same lines. Look, we can sit here until we rot, waiting for that cat to come back, or we can act on the information we have. Always was more a man of action myself. Come on!"

Mouse, however reluctant, followed his tugging, and they crept on up the stairs, moving as quietly as they could past the goblins in the room beyond. The passage opened into his uncle's bedchamber, Alistair recalled. What he could not recall was whether or not they'd be able to get through that heavy door, which as he remembered it, was under lock and key. Were there other exits? Via the stables or some spy hole, perhaps?

He drew a sudden, hissing breath as Mouse's hands clamped down hard on his arm. "Listen!" she said in a strangled whisper, and he didn't need to understand her.

The sound of footsteps descending the stairway thudded in his ears. Heavy footsteps.

A goblin was in the passage.

"Back! Back!" Alistair whispered, and the two of them stumbled down the stairway, slipping as they went.

The thudding steps gained upon them, and a thick, gnarly voice growled, "I see you, blind little mortals! I see you in the dark!"

Mouse whimpered, lost her footing, and slid down the stairs, tripping Alistair. He caught himself, pressing his hands on either wall, preventing a plummet into darkness. He heard the goblin's breathing behind him, could feel before it happened strong fingers latching hold of his neck. The snap, the break . . .

Instead, there was a dreadful thud, a groan, and then Alistair was knocked from his feet as the goblin, inert, rolled down the stairs. Its great body wedged into the narrow space, providing just enough buffer to prevent Alistair from tumbling interminably to his doom.

"Didn't I tell you to wait for me?" Eanrin's voice snapped like sparks.

Alistair, his legs pinioned beneath the heavy goblin, felt around. His hand landed on Mouse's face, and both of them struggled not to scream. But the girl was all right, and her fumbling hands took hold of his arms and pulled, unable to free him of the goblin's weight.

Eanrin, who could see perfectly well, stood above them, his knife upraised. He shook his head and snapped his fingers. The knife began to glow softly, enough to allow the humans dim vision in the stairway. The light outlined the contours of the goblin's hideous face. Mouse pressed her hands to her mouth. A black trail of blood ran from the goblin's head.

"Is he dead?" Mouse demanded when she could find her voice. She turned stricken eyes to Eanrin. "Did you kill him?"

"Would it bother you?" asked the cat-man, descending the stairs and stepping over the prone body.

"Yes," she said, though she knew it was foolish. After all, the monster would have slaughtered both her and Alistair. Nevertheless, she repeated, "Yes, it would bother me."

"Then he's unconscious," said Eanrin, and Mouse never knew whether he lied. The cat-man tossed her something he'd held draped over one arm, and it fell over her head like a heavy net. She scrabbled to get it off while Eanrin helped Alistair to his feet.

"The great hall," Alistair said as he scrambled up and leaned against the wall. "We heard some of them talking. They've got the Chronicler in the great hall."

"I know," said the cat. "I found him. Here, help me strip down this goblin."

"What for?"

"We have a plan now."

"We do?"

"Yes indeed," said the cat-man with a grin. "You're a big enough chap. You'll pass for a small man of Arpiar."

"You expect me to disguise myself as a goblin?"

"Certainly do."

"And what about Mouse? Is she supposed to sit here while we risk our necks?"

"Oh, I have a different plan for her."

Mouse, who didn't understand the conversation taking place, turned her attention to the brocade Eanrin had thrown at her. She held it up for inspection.

It was a gown.

13

I WAS CROWNED WITH MAHUIZOA'S CROWN on the peak of Omeztli, the Moon Tower. Kings and queens, lords and ladies, Faerie masters of many far demesnes came for my coronation, and Cozamaloti permitted their passing. I was small on the throne of my mother, and the crown was heavy upon my head. But I felt the surge of Etalpalli itself inside me, and I knew I would see my city rebuilt to the glory it had known before Cren Cru's coming.

I saw the Brothers Ashiun standing quietly among the brilliant throng of fey folk, their weapons quiet at their sides. When the coronation feasting was at its height, they came to me and drew me aside.

"Reign long and well, Queen of Etalpalli," Akilun said, then kissed my hand and departed.

I turned to Etanun. "You are a great hero." The surge of power I had known seemed to vanish, and I felt small and weak beneath his gaze.

"As are you," he replied with a gentle smile that was strange and beautiful on his warlike face. "Reign long and well," he spoke in echo of his brother.

"Will you return one day?" I asked him as he turned to go.

"I will," he replied. "To see how you are getting on."
Then he left. With his promise soaring in my heart, I returned to the feasting.

"Are you sure this is a good idea?" Alistair whispered.

They stood in the earl's empty bedchamber, which was a disaster. The goblins had torn the room apart while searching for Mouse and Alistair. The heavy bed-curtains hung in tatters on the broken bedframe. Every piece of furniture from the flimsy screen to the heavy wardrobe had been gouged with stone weapons, and the wardrobe had also been partially burned.

The three invaders had slipped into the chamber from the passage, Eanrin working the locks from the outside without any apparent difficulty. Alistair wore goblin armor so heavy he could scarcely stand upright. The helmet, which was swiftly bringing on a headache, disguised his face, and the jagged visor muffled his voice. "They're not going to believe I'm one of them," he growled.

Mouse, huge skirts gathered in her arms, stepped from behind the earl's broken screen. Alistair and Eanrin both looked at her, and the cat gave a noncommittal nod. "Not bad," he said.

Mouse scowled and reached around to fumble with one of the many ties and braces. The light green gown was gorgeous with heavy embroidery. It must have belonged to one of the ladies of the castle and was entirely impractical. It was hardly possible to walk in the thing, much less run.

Alistair spoke behind his visor. "You look very pretty."

Mouse looked to Eanrin. "He sounds concerned. What did he say?"

"He said they're never going to believe you're a girl."

Mouse clamped her mouth shut but shot a swift glare Alistair's way. Alistair turned to Eanrin, attempting but failing to shove up the visor. "What did you tell her?"

"I told her you're afraid to face goblins."

"That's not true!"

"Then stop criticizing my brilliant scheme. If you can manage to humble yourself and follow an order, recite to me your part."

Giving up on the visor, Alistair let his gauntleted hand drop to his side. "I'm to march her through the castle like I've caught a prisoner, somehow drawing no attention to either of us."

"Good. And once you're in the great hall?"

"We're to fetch the Chronicler in the midst of the distraction you will have provided."

"Excellent."

"But won't he be chained?"

"Oh, he definitely is."

"How are we to manage that?"

"Find the key, I would imagine. This is *your* side of the rescue, my dear boy. You can't expect me to do everything."

"What if someone stops me on the way to the hall?" Alistair persisted. "They'll know as soon as I open my mouth that I'm not one of them."

"Then don't open your mouth. Grunt and growl; pretend you're too good for this world. Besides, I told you, I'm going on ahead. I'll take care of any in your way and give you a clear path."

Mouse, who had only understood Eanrin's side of the conversation anyway, stepped forward then. "What of that great goblin?" she asked. "What will you do about him?"

"I told you, I'll see to it," said the cat-man, his voice as smooth and calm as a summer stroll. "Your job is to rescue the Chronicler, understand?"

"But who will rescue us?"

Eanrin shrugged, sank to the floor in his cat form, and trotted to the cracked door. "I had rather hoped you'd rescue yourselves." And with a flick of his tail, he slipped out into the hall. "Remember," his voice called back to them, "we'll all meet in the inner courtyard!"

By the time they reached the doorway, the corridor beyond was empty.

This really was a dreadful world.

So Ghoukas thought as he staggered up the stairs from the kitchen into the keep. For one thing, it was much too cold. Not that Arpiar was a realm of balmy comfort. Icy winds blew across its broad plains, driving luckless goblins back into the warrens below, thankful for the warmth of close tunnels. But here the cold seeped into the bones. It crept through every crevice and cranny until a goblin felt he could never escape it.

Ghoukas growled as he stumbled along the corridor, laden with findings from the castle storerooms. Corgar had sent for food, and he would be disappointed in Ghoukas's feeble scavengings. Did mortals know what real food was? Did they know *anything*?

Well, they knew ale at least. Good, strong ale for quaffing after hunts, and Ghoukas and his friend had quaffed large quantities while inspecting the larder. Muttering and cursing, anticipating a beating for his failure to provide Corgar with exactly what he wanted when he wanted it, Ghoukas proceeded at a lagging pace, decidedly ale-sick.

A vague part of his brain noticed dimly that the passages were strangely deserted. Distantly he heard goblins shouting orders to human slaves laboring at tearing down the castle. The maggots were so puny, it would take them weeks to accomplish the task!

A rustle and thumping of booted feet drew Ghoukas's attention. Down the nearest staircase came one of the human females, prodded from behind by a goblin.

"Hey! Krikor!" Ghoukas called, his ale-dimmed eyes blinking blearily but able to recognize his friend's armor. "Hallo, brother!"

The goblin's violent start knocked his helmet askew, and in his haste to clamp it back down on his head, he dropped his spear. It was this dragon-blasted cold and the stink of mortality, Ghoukas thought. It got into a fellow's blood and made him jumpy.

"Krikor!" he said again, swaying his way to the foot of the staircase. "Remember me?" More than willing to put off his unpleasant duties, Ghoukas began climbing the stairs to meet them. "Look at the sorry piffle these mortals eat. Would you believe it? Want to try a bit? It's vile! Something to tell the folks back home about."

He reached out to slap his friend's shoulder, but the goblin dodged, and the little mortal female ducked away, pressing herself against the banister, her skirts gathered up in a bundle to her chest but still falling nearly to her feet. Ghoukas turned to her, looking her up and down. She was so little, she scarcely reached his breastplate! But unlike the pasty mortal womenfolk he'd seen all day, she was a nice brown and healthy looking.

Ghoukas tipped back his visor, revealing a hungry face. "Are you taking this morsel to Corgar? He's ordered all the mortals put to work, you know. A shame, really. A beastie like this might have other uses."

He leaned down. The girl tried to back up the steps but tripped over her skirts and sat down in a pile of petticoats and brocade. Ghoukas laughed. "Pretty!" he said. "I think she must be pretty. What do you think, Krikor?"

The goblin said nothing. Ghoukas turned to him, his huge eyes narrowing, his stony brow wrinkling into puzzled crevices. "I said, what do you think, Krikor?"

Silence—other than surprisingly light breathing from behind the helmet. Ghoukas frowned. "Wait a minute," he said, his addled brain slowly catching up. "Wait a minute, you're not—"

Suddenly he dropped the food, snatched the helmet away, and stared at the pale human face with the shock of bright red hair.

Then Mouse leapt on his back, managing despite her heavy skirts to get purchase on his shoulders and cling there. Ghoukas roared, surprised, and twisted about, trying to loosen her grip, but she clung with the tenacity of ivy, and Ghoukas could not reach her to pull her off.

Alistair, moving heavily in his armor, picked up the goblin spear. He breathed, timed his stroke, then swung the stone spearhead and struck Ghoukas such a blow across the face that the goblin stopped, his vision whirling.

"Jump!" Alistair cried to Mouse, and though she did not understand, she obeyed, sliding from the goblin's back and landing in a cushioned cloud of skirts. Alistair struck again, and the goblin, not so impervious to one of his own weapons as to those of mortals, tumbled down the stairs. He landed at the bottom, lost in a stupor.

Alistair assisted Mouse to her feet, and they both stared down at the hulking form of Ghoukas.

"Nicely done," Mouse said, grinning up at the young lord.

He understood her smile, if nothing else, and smiled back. Then he reclaimed his helmet. "We'd best hurry," he said, indicating the passage with his spear. "If the cat missed this one, we don't know how many others might have slipped his notice. I don't know that we can repeat this little performance."

Mouse took her place as the captured slave, and the two continued on toward the great hall. All was gloomy, lit only by the dimness of moonlight through the windows. The air was thick with things unseen.

The Chronicler crouched behind Corgar's chair, his senses dull. For hours, it seemed, Corgar had sat with his feet up, barking orders to goblins, sending them skittering about Gaheris at his whims. He had ignored the Chronicler's existence since Leta was dragged from the room, and for this the Chronicler was grateful.

His manacles were large and appeared too loose for his small hands. Yet, although the stone neither shrank nor expanded, they held him fast.

The chain piled up beside him on the floor. He studied every stone link leading from the mass beside him up to the ring on Corgar's great belt. Everything about the goblins was stone, it seemed—their chains, their armor, their weapons. Stone should not be stronger than the iron weapons of Gaheris, yet the Chronicler had seen swords crumble into clay when they met the goblin hewers. He had seen lances break upon the hides of goblin warriors.

He hung his head, cursing under his breath. What could he, with all his book learning and his short limbs, hope to accomplish if he slipped his bonds? It would take a rare man indeed to stand up against such fiends. A rare man . . . not a freak.

The room was dark with sinking shadows; the two lighted torches served only to cast the rest of the room into greater darkness. And in that darkness, a flicker of gold caught his eye.

The Chronicler turned, startled. Was his mind playing tricks on him? He could have sworn he'd seen eyes peering at him from under one of the lower tables. Then what might have been a shadow moved and vanished. Frowning, the Chronicler sat up and craned his neck, moving slowly to avoid drawing Corgar's attention.

"I hunger!" the great goblin bellowed, abruptly standing. The movement yanked his prisoner's chain, and the Chronicler just avoided being struck across the face by the swinging links. "I have not eaten since we marched from the Wood. Are you beggars holding out on me? Would you starve your future king?"

"No, no, my lord!" several goblin voices replied.

"Where is Ghoukas? Did he not go searching out the larder hours ago? Fetch him! Fetch him at once!"

Goblins scurried to obey. Another—a female, the Chronicler thought, only because she was a little smaller, not for any feminine grace on her part—stepped forward and offered Corgar a draught of wine. The Chronicler smelled the richness of Earl Ferox's finest and grimaced as the monster downed it in a single gulp and called for more.

Another flash of gold. The Chronicler moved into a crouching position, trying to gain a better view. He could have sworn he'd seen someone dart to the female goblin's side. He could have sworn he'd seen a deft hand slip something into the wine. Surely these goblins with their night vision would spot anything peculiar much sooner than he could!

Yet they continued about their business. Corgar downed his wine and continued barking for Ghoukas. His servants and slaves bustled about in the dark, but the Chronicler could not see well enough to know what they were doing.

He thought he heard a *thunk* and a muffled groan.

"What was that?" Corgar growled.

"What was what, my lord?" someone asked.

The warlord did not answer. The Chronicler heard the scrape of his claws digging into the tabletop.

Another thump in the dark—soft, almost inaudible, and unpleasant.

"There's someone here," said Corgar, his voice suddenly thick and surly.

"There's lots of us here, my lord" came a reply.

"No, no," said Corgar. The chain linked to his belt swayed along with his huge body as he rose. "There's someone . . . something . . . *else*."

This time one of the goblins gave a strangled gasp. Instantly, the others were on alert, drawing their weapons. But though Corgar fumbled for his, he could not seem to get his hand about the hilt. This enraged him and he roared, "Who's there? Who dares assault the company of Corgar at his hard-won table?"

"Aiiieee, he's—" The voice cut off sharply.

Every goblin strained to see in the darkness, as seemingly blind now as mortals. The Chronicler fell to his hands and knees and crawled into the darker space beneath the table. He felt his captor on the other end of the chain swaying like a drunkard, ready to topple. A goblin screamed as his brother, striking out at a flicker of nothing, caught him across the face. "Sorry, there!" the inadvertent attacker said, then roared when the fallen goblin kicked him in the knees. A full-fledged brawl would have broken out, but Corgar, his voice almost unrecognizably thick, bellowed:

"Look, you rat faces, he's there!"

All eyes, including the Chronicler's, turned at once. Standing in the doorway of the great hall was a figure all of them recognized instantly, a figure the Chronicler knew only from books and engravings, so old and so odd as to be discounted without a thought. Yet there he stood—in flesh or illusion—larger than life and unmistakable.

Eanrin, Chief Poet of Iubdan Tynan. The Bard of Rudiobus.

His eyes alone shone brighter than his golden hair. A world of sunshine seemed to surround him in the gloom, and his red jerkin glimmered with delicate threads. He raised his arms as though to greet all those assembled, and cried out in a voice merry with smiles:

"What-ho, Corgar, old chum! It's been some time since last we met. Come now, haven't you a word for an old friend?"

"It's the knight!" Corgar cried. "The gate guarder!" He lunged but lacked control over his own feet. Without a thought for their warlord, the goblins flung themselves after the brilliant figure, who darted from the room with the speed of fleeting summer. The goblins loped from the great hall like hounds after a stag.

"Catch him! Catch . . . him . . ." Corgar snarled, each word more muddled than the last. With a growling gurgle, he collapsed across the table, his arms outspread and his jaw slack. His eyes remained open, two luminous orbs of white in the darkness.

The moment Corgar fell, the Chronicler was on his feet, following the chain, hand over hand, until he reached Corgar's belt. But the lock there would not give.

"Hallo?" A timid voice whispered across the hall. "Chronicler?"

It was Alistair.

"Can't see a thing in this murk. Watch your step, Mouse! You all right? The room is empty, I believe."

Of all people, this was possibly the last the Chronicler would have expected. He remembered dimly that Alistair had been absent from Earl Ferox's funeral. Somehow he must have escaped the turmoil of the day. And now . . . what? It was too absurd! The whole affair was turning into some nightmarish hallucination!

But Corgar was asleep, and the goblins, for the moment, were led away. This might be his only chance.

"I'm here!" His voice, so little used for the last several hours, cracked. "I'm here, m'lord, by the earl's seat!"

"Chronicler?" Alistair, setting aside his goblin's spear and shedding the heavy breastplate, waded into the dark of the room, his hands out, leaving Mouse behind by the door. "No one else is here, I trust? It looks empty enough, but I can't see much."

"Their leader is here!" the Chronicler said.

"What?" Alistair froze midstep. "In *this* room?"

"He's unconscious." The Chronicler looked again at Corgar's slack face. Though the muscles were motionless, there was fierceness behind his eyes. "At least, he can't move. He seems to be under some sort of spell."

"Ah! The cat-man must have got him. Mouse, where are you?"

Mouse recognized her name and picked her way across the room, following the vague shadow Alistair cast by the dim torchlight. He reached out for her hand, but she ignored him and hastened past to the long table, freezing when she saw Corgar. But she had not endured the last weeks and the last dreadful day for nothing! Calling on reserves of courage she had never known she possessed, she hastened around to the other side of the table where the Chronicler stood, his head barely higher than the board.

"Who are you?" he demanded. Mouse spoke in her strange, fast language, her voice furtive. The Chronicler shook his head, at a loss.

Alistair joined them and said, "We're here to rescue you. Any ideas how?"

The Chronicler showed his manacled hands. "There must be a key," he said.

Mouse leapt to Corgar's side. Though her fingers flinched and her skin crawled at the prospect of touching the goblin—who seemed to be watching her from those luminous eyes—she plunged her hand into the narrow space between his breastplate and his dreadful rock hide. Sure enough, there was a key ring hidden there.

She tossed the key to Alistair, who could scarcely fit it into the lock, his big hands were shaking so hard. But then the manacles fell away, and the Chronicler nearly fell over in his eagerness to be liberated of them. His wrists were raw and bloodied from his efforts to escape, but he did not care. He was free!

The first words out of his mouth were: "We've got to find Lady Leta."

"Leta?" Alistair snorted, not unkindly. "Look, Chronicler, we've come to rescue you and propel you into some nonsensical prophecy fulfillment. We have no time to be heroes. We have to save the world!"

"We can't leave her to these monsters."

"We haven't a choice."

Mouse, her eyes straining in the dark, turned from one young man to the next as they exchanged hushed words. They were arguing. They were standing in the middle of a goblin-infested castle in front of a possibly conscious slavering monster *arguing*. This was why men were never permitted to speak in the Citadel of the Living Fire! She thought she would scream.

Then Corgar moved, and she did.

14

IMMORTALS NEITHER COUNT THEIR LIVES IN YEARS nor feel the passage of time. Yet somehow I felt the passing of days, and they were slow. I ruled my city with a firm hand. In the place where the Mound had clutched the ground, we built beautiful tombs and in them laid the remains of my father, mother, and brother. Etalpalli grew and prospered, and I made alliances with Faerie lords and ladies of other realms and sat in councils of both war and peace.

I waited for Etanun's return.

At last he came. Though I spent every day with the beat of his promise in my heart, I was surprised when I saw him climbing the long steps of Omeztli to my throne. I smiled to see him, rose, and offered him my hands.

"You have grown!" he said when he saw me, "and you are more beautiful even than when I saw you last, though I did not think it possible!"

I felt my face flush at the praise, but I quickly laughed it off. I walked with him through the city, folding my wings and stepping delicately upon the stones so that I could remain by his side as I showed all that had been done during his absence. He in turn told me of his doings, of the brilliant Houses of Lights that he and Akilun were building throughout the Near World.

"Mortals cannot hear the voices of Lumé and Hymlumé," he explained to me. "Not on their own. But when the doors of a House are opened, and the sun and the moon shine inside, even mortals may hear and know the truth of the Song Giver, the Lumil Eliasul."

Everything he said was wonderful to my ears. I rejoiced with him at his successes and boasted to him of my own. At the end of the day, he bowed and said to me, "I am pleased to see you so well, dear queen, and shall gladly bear word of you to my brother."

"Will you leave so soon?" I asked, startled.

"I must," he said. "I have duties elsewhere."

"But you will return, won't you?"

"I will," he replied.

So I found myself obliged to live upon another promise.

It was only a small movement. One hand scraped along the table. One eye twitched.

But it was enough.

"He's coming awake!" Mouse cried. "Run!"

Alistair took hold of her hand and leapt onto the table and over, dragging Mouse along. The Chronicler ducked underneath, took a few paces after them, then stopped and darted back. He took up the manacles chained to Corgar's belt and clamped them around the leg of the huge table.

A snarl, and Corgar's hand crashed down beside the Chronicler's ear. Trembling fingers tore away a chunk of the table board. The Chronicler looked up into white eyes as Corgar struggled to push himself upright, his sagging jaw working and his lips contorting.

"Idiot!"

That roar belonged to Alistair, who grabbed the Chronicler by the collar, hauled him off his feet, and hurtled across the great hall. They flew across the dark room even as Corgar, screaming animal rage, lunged from his high seat. But his belt, clamped to the table, dragged him back down, and he was still weak from whatever drug Eanrin had slipped him. His roar grew, and though there were no words, the sound carried throughout the castle.

By the time they reached the big doorway leading from the hall, the passage outside was crowded with oncoming goblins. There could be no escape that way. Without a choice, they slammed the door, threw the heavy bolt, and sped toward one of the servants' entrances, praying it would be empty. Corgar, straining at the chain, hurled a chair at them. Alistair narrowly missed a braining as it crashed into the wall beyond his head.

They raced down the servants' corridor, making for the inner courtyard. Goblins roared at their heels, and Mouse expected to feel the thrust of a stone lance through her rib cage. Alistair dragged the other two behind, his long legs making tremendous strides. The Chronicler would scarcely have made five paces before being overtaken, and Mouse, encumbered with skirts, could not have fared better.

This passage, like all others in the castle, was dark. But suddenly a rectangle of faint light appeared before them as the far door opened. Alistair redoubled his pace, his heart surging. To reach that opening was all that mattered in the tiny space of time that was now their whole existence.

A goblin loomed in their path, blocking out the faint light. Alistair yelled in rage. Nothing would keep him from his one, final goal! He dropped the hands of the other two. In three strides, he tore the helmet from his head and swung it like a club. By some luck or blessing, he struck aside the blade of the goblin's weapon, which clanged against the wall. He pushed into the goblin at full speed, and they both fell, landing in a tangle of limbs. Alistair lay stunned, his world exploding with bright, flashing lights. It didn't matter. They'd reached the goal. Let him die now, if he must; the doorway was gained, and he lay on the courtyard cobbles.

Hands grasped his neck. He felt himself raised up, smelled the stench of goblin breath.

"Can't be having any of that, now, can we?"

Eanrin's voice danced with the sparks in Alistair's brain just before he was squashed beneath an inert goblin form. The monster's face pressed against his cheek, one jutting tooth driving into his skin.

Mouse and the Chronicler fell through the doorway even as Eanrin clubbed Alistair's attacker. The Chronicler immediately turned and slammed the door, but the oncoming goblins fell against it, straining its hinges.

"It's no use!" Mouse cried as she dragged him away. She stared wildly about the courtyard, which in the moonlight seemed bright as midday after the gloom within. Goblins poured down from the castle walls, spilling like plague rats through the gates from the outer courtyard, from every doorway. "It's no use!"

Eanrin stood like a shining tower in the darkness, his face alight with a wicked smile. He helped the stunned Alistair to his feet, clapped him on the shoulder, then reached out and snatched the Chronicler by the shirtfront. "Are you the chosen one, heir to Halisa?" he demanded.

"What? No!" the Chronicler cried.

"Close enough." Eanrin spun about and, with a flash of his knife, knocked aside the descending club of a goblin. The thin blade should have broken under the heavy stone. Instead, the club split in half, and the goblin stood empty-handed, a dumbfounded expression on his face. Eanrin snarled at him, and the goblin backed away, staggering into one of his brothers coming up behind.

"This way, mortals!" Eanrin cried. He sank down into his cat form and darted across the courtyard. Somehow, where he ran, the goblins were not, as though he trod a Path they could not follow. The other three fell in behind him. They should have been slaughtered, hewn to pieces. . . .

Yet they arrived unscathed at the doorway to the Gaheris crypt.

Eanrin vanished inside in a flick of his tail. Mouse didn't hesitate to follow. But Alistair, his head still spinning, froze as though dragged to the mouth of hell itself.

It seemed to him that a voice in the darkness said: *Pursue this Path, young lord of mortals, and you pursue Death.*

The Chronicler, who had stopped when Alistair did, saw the goblins closing in, their faces twisted in fury, and among them the Chronicler saw Corgar.

He grabbed Alistair's sleeve. "Come, m'lord."

"You go," Alistair gasped. His face had gone white as a ghost's. "Go without me."

But the Chronicler wasn't one for impractical heroics, at least not in other people. He pulled. His strength was greater than his size indicated, and Alistair was weak and unbalanced. He staggered forward, and together they descended the stairs into the darkness where their ancestors slept.

At first, the stench of death surrounded them. As they pounded down the ancient stone steps, certain they felt the breath of goblins on their heels, neither could help wondering what use this mad flight might be. But the moment their feet touched the level ground, they realized they were not running on stone. The darkness, though thick, was not the blackness of a crypt. Another few paces and both realized the truth even as their senses rebelled against it.

Tall silvery stones stood in a circle around them. And beyond the stones, stretching as far as the eye could see in every direction, was a vast, unsearchable Wood.

Alistair's yell filled the whole of the near vicinity. "What in the dragon-blazing world is this?"

But a hand reached out and snatched his. He looked down into Mouse's strained face, and she said, "There's no time to explain! Run!"

Alistair's feet were moving before his brain realized what he'd heard. "Wait!" he cried. "I *understood* that!" Then he was running and had no breath to speak.

The cat darted ahead, his plume of tail like a beacon guiding them through the tangle of shadows and branches. All was dark—not the darkness of night but a heavy gloom cast by branches and foliage blocking all sunlight from the forest floor, which was nonetheless thick with briars and vines. They should not have been able to take more than two paces before becoming hopelessly tangled.

Yet where the cat ran, a Path seemed to emerge, just as it had through the crowd of goblins.

The goblins pursued them, roaring and cursing, crashing through the trees with hardly a pause. They evidently lacked the smooth Path Eanrin trod, yet their bulk served them well enough. The three mortals followed the cat deeper and deeper into this strange new world that had always existed behind the film of their fragile reality.

Suddenly Eanrin darted to one side, leapt into a thicket, and vanished. The mortals paused, stared at the snarl of brush, stared at one another. Then Mouse dove in after him, discovering to her relief that there was a Path still, though she had been unable to see it. It was so small that no human should have been able to follow, yet though her size did not alter, she found she could walk upright when she tried. After she vanished into the tangle of sticks and leaves, the young men had no choice but to follow. Alistair dove in headfirst.

The Chronicler looked back the way they had come. He could almost see the trees moving, drawing together to obscure their way. But that must have been the strange half-light playing tricks upon his eyes.

Then he heard a shout and saw the goblins approaching. Hating himself for fleeing yet again, the Chronicler pushed into the thicket after Alistair.

He gasped.

He stood in the doorway of a vast and shining hall of white and green stone.

15

ETANUN VISITED MANY TIMES over the long course of my reign. Every time I saw his face, it was like the first shining of the sun. And every time he left, it was like the setting of the moon and the fall of deepest night. But when I asked if he would come again, he said that he would. So I had hope.

The last time Etanun visited, I could scarcely enjoy our day together for the knowledge of its brevity. As the hour of his departure drew near, I reached out and took his hand in both of mine.

"Everyone I love leaves," I told him. "My father, my mother, my brother, all have gone down to the Final Water, while I remain behind."

"Your love for them keeps them close in your heart," he replied, and once again I marveled at how tender a warrior's voice might be. That tenderness gave me courage.

"But is my love enough to keep you close?" I cried, drawing his hand to my heart. "Is it enough, Etanun, for I cannot bear your departure again!"

For a breath I waited.

Then he withdrew his hand from mine, and his face was grave and sad.

"Dear queen," he began, and I felt as though a knife had been driven into my gut, for I knew what he would say. "Dear queen, I am a Knight of the Farthest Shore, servant of the Lumil Eliasul and the King Across the Final Water. My duty is always first in my heart, and it allows me to remain close to no woman."

I could not speak for fear of my voice shattering the stillness. But I managed to whisper: "Then tell me at least, my love, that you would stay with me if you could. That if you were free, you would be mine. I can live on that."

His eyes spoke his answer more eloquently than words. I stared at him, and I feared suddenly that he would feel the need to speak, to say aloud what I had already read upon his face.

I took to the air, flying from his presence as fast as I could drive my wings. My stomach burned, my heart broke, and I believed that all love was turned to hate inside me. There was no room to pretend anymore. No room to tell myself pretty lies. The truth was spoken with the merciless clarity of Halisa's own blade.

Etanun did not love me.

"What in the name of Lord Lumé—" the Chronicler began.

"Hush!" The cat appeared at his feet and stood up into the tall form of Bard Eanrin. The Chronicler's stomach turned at the sight, and his knees buckled so that he sat down hard on the marble floor beneath him. The legend stepped around the Chronicler to draw back a green-velvet curtain emblazoned with small white blossoms, and peered out.

Except—and the Chronicler knew he must be mad when he saw this— there was no curtain. There was only the branch of a hawthorn tree heavily laden with clustering blooms. But when the cat-man dropped it and stepped back, it was again rich fabric falling in folds.

"We've lost them," Eanrin said, crossing his arms as he addressed the three mortals. "They'll not find us here."

Alistair still lay on the floor, though he'd rolled onto his back and stared, openmouthed, at the vaulted ceiling above him. Mouse stood nearby, trying to disguise her own surprise at the sudden change in their surroundings. She looked more bedraggled and waif-like than ever in this setting.

She looked more familiar here too.

Eanrin gnashed his teeth at this thought. What a fool he'd been! But how could he have known? In all the time—such as Time could be measured here in the Between—they had worked together, Imraldera had never behaved so irrationally! She had never abandoned the Haven and left the gate unguarded, especially not when Eanrin was away.

He shouldn't have gone. That was the truth of the matter, though he could justify himself to the grave. Yes, he was Iubdan's Chief Poet. Yes, he had obligations to the King and Queen of Rudiobus. But he should never have left Imraldera alone.

"She shouldn't have done it," Eanrin muttered, blame shifting by force of ancient habit. "She should never have trusted the Murderer's word!"

How frail and foolish these mortals looked here in First Hall! By the standards of Faerie, the Haven's proportions were humble and reserved. But this was an immortal's abode, built by immortal hands at the direction of the Lumil Eliasul, who was neither mortal nor immortal but who stood in a place beyond either. Here, the little humans looked so imperfect in their Time-bound clay bodies.

Yet the frailest, most faulty of this lot was the heir to Halisa?

Goblin voices rang beyond the Haven walls, and the three humans looked sick with fear. Did they not realize they were safe here? No one and nothing could breach the Haven, for it belonged to the Lumil Eliasul.

"I tell you," one goblin said, "they took a turn back there. I swear, I saw the trail."

"Don't be a fool!" snarled another. "They came this way. I saw the little one take a dive into yonder thicket."

The Chronicler stepped away from the wall and curtain; Alistair and Mouse drew up behind him, and Mouse twisted the shreds of her gown between her hands. The goblins stomped and cursed and shouted at one another beyond the wall. Several even tried to penetrate the thicket, looming so near that the heavy velvet curtain of hawthorn wavered. But they could not get through.

"Corgar will kill us if we've lost the little one!" someone said.

"Don't be daft," said another. "Why should he care? It's not as though the beast was any good to him."

"It's the prophecy," said a third, and its voice was low and tremulous. "It's the prophecy, I tell you, and this is the first step to its fulfillment."

"What prophecy?"

"Didn't you hear? The Murderer came to Queen Vartera. He told her Corgar would break through to the Near World, just as he did!"

"So? Don't see what that has to do with anything."

"But there's more. The Murderer also said that, though Corgar would break through and assert his will over all the mortalings, the king of that country would drive him forevermore from the Near World. And Corgar believes the little one *is* that king."

"Yeah, that's all well and good. But did you get a look at the creature? He's tiny! Corgar could swallow him in one gulp and still be hungry after."

The goblins laughed at this and moved on. "Aye," they agreed among themselves, retreating back through the Wood, "not all prophecies are bound to be fulfilled."

Eanrin observed the Chronicler throughout this exchange. He saw how first a flush of red crept across his face, swiftly exchanged for a pallor like death.

Suddenly the Chronicler looked up and met Eanrin's gaze. For the first time, a sliver of doubt slid into the poet's assured mockery of the whole affair.

The last of the goblins departed and the mortals all sighed and sagged. Alistair sat down heavily, hiding his face in his hands. His head still rang from his contact with the goblin in the courtyard, and he suspected it would continue to ring for quite some time. Mouse withdrew from the others, embarrassed now.

But the Chronicler never broke Eanrin's gaze. "Where are we?" he demanded.

Eanrin snorted. "As if you didn't know."

The little man swallowed, his jaw clenching. "This . . . this is the Haven of the Lumil Eliasul. The Haven of the Prince of the Farthest Shore. Built by the Brothers Ashiun."

"Well done, Chronicler," said Eanrin. "You've done your research."

"I don't believe in this place."

"I don't see what your lack of belief has to do with anything."

"And you're Bard Eanrin."

"That I am."

"I don't believe in you either."

The cat-man smiled. "Be that as it may, you must admit that I did save your sorry skins when you yourselves were obviously unable to do so."

To this, the Chronicler had no answer. So he turned to Alistair and stopped in surprise. The young man had stripped off his remaining goblin armor, all but the boots, revealing the torn and bloodied shirt beneath, and the nasty pucker of his scarred-over wound. Its appearance had improved since morning, but here in the gentle light of the Haven it looked nastier than it might have elsewhere.

The Chronicler felt an unprecedented surge of concern and pity for his former pupil and recent rival. "My lord!" he cried. "What happened to you?"

Alistair felt his shoulder and grimaced wryly. "I couldn't tell you for certain," he said. "It appears I've had a rum go, but I can't remember much. A nasty sight, eh?"

"It's not as bad as it was," said Mouse softly from behind.

Alistair whirled about. "Why do I understand you?" he cried. Then he turned to Eanrin, pointing first at him and then back at Mouse behind him. "Why do I understand her?"

"Her?" Mouse's eyes went wide. "No, no! I'm a boy. Really, I am!" Then she saw the look exchanged between the Chronicler and Alistair, and her face flushed hot. Bowing her head and shrinking into herself, she said, "Oh. So you know?"

"I'm afraid so," Alistair said, rubbing the back of his head.

"But . . . I cut my hair."

"Yes, you did." Alistair nodded.

"And I . . . I bound myself up in . . . in places."

Now Alistair blushed. He couldn't look at the girl, so he turned to Eanrin again and repeated his question. "Tell me, cat-man, why can I understand her?"

"First," said Eanrin with a glower, "you will not call me 'cat-man' again. I am a knight, a poet, and a gentleman, and you will address me as *sir* or not address me at all."

"Yes, sir," said Alistair, undaunted. "Why can I understand her?"

"Because you are in the Wood Between. Spoken language matters here as little as time, or size, or any other of the restrictions to which you mortals are so well adjusted."

"Oh." Alistair rubbed his sore forehead again, wishing he could rub some sense back into life. He felt numb all over. What else, he wondered, had he always taken for granted that would, at any moment, be flipped upside down and proven complete twaddle?

"Well, now we've got the Chronicler," he said, "what's next?"

"We must hasten to my country," said Mouse, her voice still low and embarrassed but determined. "We must hasten there at once before it's too late!"

"What? Why?" demanded the Chronicler, stepping forward, his voice fierce. "Even now, the house of Earl Ferox is overrun. My people and many earls of the North Country are held captive. All because that creature wants the House of Lights. The House of Lights! As though we can pull nursery rhymes made real from our hats and present them to him on a silver platter! It's madness; it's insanity!"

"It's Faerie," said Eanrin, his voice a little gentler than before. He sighed and addressed Mouse. "They need to know," he said. "Tell them. Tell them everything you told me, and we'll see if we can't get a little prophecy fulfillment underway, shall we?"

Mouse hesitated but nodded. She felt as though choking hands gripped her by the throat. Yet she must speak. She must tell her tale, and she must get it right.

Fire burn! Fire purify! she prayed desperately.

Then she caught Alistair's eye. And she saw there . . . what? Encouragement? He was not her enemy at least, this man whom she had saved and who had saved her.

Don't think, she told herself. *If you begin to think, you'll never go through with it! Do as the Flame demands.*

"Well, girl?" said Eanrin. "In your own good time."

PART THREE

ACOLYTE

1

HOW MANY AGES WOULD MORTAL MEN *count my rule of Etalpalli? I do not know, but I know it was long. Longer after that final departure of Etanun. For he never returned. I heard rumor of his deeds from those who traveled to and from my court, and I shuddered each time I heard his name. Yet I drank in every word, for I thirsted for news of him. I thought then that the pain I felt was the sharpest I would ever know.*

But it was only the pain of embarrassment. I had not yet felt the fire of jealousy.

Then one day as I sat with my counselors discussing some treaty or policy, I heard a whisper among my ladies behind me. I would have disregarded them, save that I heard his name.

"They say Sir Etanun has fallen in love at last."

"No! I don't believe it possible. Not a Knight of the Farthest Shore!"

"Indeed, I heard it too. And with a mortal maid, no less! One of the frail beings he was sent to guard and protect."

"Impossible. How could anyone fall for such a creature?"

"I thought if he were to ever love anyone, it would have been our own fair queen."

I heard no more. Neither their babble nor the words of my counselors. I sat as one frozen, but my insides were turned to molten lava. I knew then what jealousy was. And once more, in desperation, my mind fed me false hopes.

It couldn't be true! No more than idle gossip!

They stank. That was the worst part about them.

Mouse, alone in her small chamber beside a blazing brazier, stared at the clothes. Boys' clothes. Slaves' clothes. And not the clothing of slaves that would dwell within the confines of the Citadel. These were far too poor, too ragged to grace the halls of the Living Flame.

They must have belonged to one of the Diggers.

Mouse shuddered, but the stars were already shining above; she must hurry. So she removed her outer garment, the rough-woven robe of black edged in red beadwork. Then she took long strips of cloth and wrapped them around her body, pulling the fabric as tight as she could to disguise all trace of feminine softness. With another grimace, she took up the tunic and pulled it over her head, feeling as though she clothed herself in rags of shame.

What would Granna say if she knew?

Granna had always encouraged her great-granddaughter to look away from the Citadel light. Back home on the mountain, high on the rocky goat paths that Mouse and her ancient great-grandmother had climbed every day, they had commanded a sweeping view of the land crossed by mighty rivers flowing from some unknown source.

The low country held such allure for Mouse, who disliked mountain life, with its cold winds blowing straight through her ragged gowns and its stink of goats. From her view above, the low country looked warm and the rivers so clean.

And from the low country rose the Citadel, with its ever-burning light at the topmost spire. As twilight fell on the mountains, that light became more vivid, beckoning to Mouse across the leagues. A speck no bigger than a star, but red and low to the earth.

"Stop looking at it," Granna would say sharply every time she saw Mouse's gaze wander that way.

"Why?" Mouse would demand. "It is beautiful and warm."

"It'll take you away from me and our mountain," Granna always replied. "It took your mother, and your fool father followed after her, besotted swain that he was. I don't want it to take you too."

"Maybe Mother was right?" Mouse would say quietly to herself later, sitting upon a rocky outcrop that afforded the best view of the low country and that far-off light. "Maybe it is better to look to distant things and seek a better life? Surely it is wrong for me to stay on this mountain among goats all my days."

But Granna always caught her and pinched her ear. "Silly girl!" she would scold. "Don't waste your time looking that way. Look up there instead."

Mouse always shivered at this, turning to where Granna's old hand indicated. Farther up the mountain, in a place inaccessible but plain to see, was a cave. A hideous cave that, when one looked at it cross-eyed, resembled the shape of a wolf's head. Mouse could have believed it was the gate to Death's own realm, it was so awful.

"One day," Granna would say then, her eyes fearful but determined, "the Silent Lady will return to us. She will step out of that cave, and she will see that we are delivered from evil again. Even as she did a hundred years ago. Even as she saved us from the Wolf Lord."

"The Silent Lady," Mouse repeated, but still she turned away from the cave mouth to gaze across to the distant light. "She must be dead long ago. While the Fire lives and burns."

"It burns all right," Granna would mutter. "And I suppose you could say that it lives."

Then she would pat Mouse's head, clucking to herself, and her faded old eyes would fill with tears. "Don't follow the path of your mother. If you go down to the temple, child, no one will ever know your true name, and you yourself will forget it."

Mouse sat now before her fire, clad in the stinking clothes of a slave boy, her stomach churning with disgust and dread. The brazier burned sweet incense, but it couldn't clear Mouse's nostrils of the stench of slavery.

Her next task was more heinous still, but she dared not shirk it. Taking up a knife, she grasped the long waves of her hair, pulled tight, and cut.

She nearly dropped the knife. She had not expected it to tear and hurt as it did! And across her hand lay a hank of black softness, her one great pride. Her glorious hair.

"Fire burn," she whispered, tears in her eyes. "Fire purify."

After all, pride was a sin. All pride must be purged from the body, through pain if necessary.

She adjusted her grip on the knife and resumed the task.

Her hair had been her great treasure from the time she was twelve years old. It had been difficult, of course, to keep neat, free of burs and bugs. But she hoped it might be beautiful, so she'd washed it carefully in a mountain stream and combed her fingers through it every night, freeing it of tangles and leaving it soft and shining.

"Your hair is like hers," Granna would say, watching across their humble fire.

"Like whose?" Mouse would ask.

Granna never responded. Mouse believed she must mean her mother; the mother who ran away, luring her father after. She liked to think she shared this one small link to that woman she had never known. And she would continue combing her hair.

Her hair that caught the eye of the temple women.

The summer of her twelfth year, women from the Citadel journeyed to Mouse's village to collect the temple tax. It was a hard journey, one not made every year. Four years had lapsed since the last time three red-clad women, tall, strong, and elegant, had climbed the mountain, flanked by silent bodyguards. Great woven wigs set with gold and uncut gems crowned their heads. Mouse, peering from the door of Granna's hut, thought them a wondrous sight.

"What are you looking at?" Granna had demanded and creaked up behind Mouse to see. Swearing, "Beasts and devils!" she gripped Mouse's shoulders with both hands. "You must go at once!" she said. "Take the goats up the mountain, and don't return until nightfall. Do you hear me?"

But though she pulled with all her strength, Granna was an old woman. Mouse twisted free with hardly a thought and, ignoring her grandmother's cries, darted into the village square to better see the beautiful women.

One of them spotted her. Dark kohl-rimmed eyes fixed upon Mouse with the intensity of a wildcat's. She pointed, speaking to her two equally beautiful sisters. "There," she said. "Look at that one with the fine hair."

"She is lovely indeed," one of the sisters agreed. "The Speaker said to look for a child of her likeness."

"She could not be better pleased with another," the third sister said.

They swooped down, surrounding Mouse in all their red-robed glory. "Would you like to journey to the Citadel of the Living Fire as your village's tax?" the first of the sisters asked her.

Mouse nodded, struck dumb with wonder.

"No!"

Granna burst from the little hut, and all the village stared in surprise and whispered together. No one denied the temple women what they required. Their guards placed themselves between the old woman and their mistresses, but Granna grabbed their spears in her withered hands and strained against them. "You cannot take her!" she cried. "She does not belong to you!"

"You have no say, old one," said the first temple sister, but her voice was not unkind. "If the Fire demands this child, the Fire will have its due."

She said no more. Mouse was given no chance to say good-bye, and in the heat of that moment she didn't care. She was free! Free of the village, free of goats! She was free of the mountains, bound for the lowlands and the great Citadel with its distant light!

The three red-robed sisters placed their hands upon her shoulders and head. "Fire burn. Fire purify," they chanted together, and Mouse thrilled at their words.

She stood now, her scalp sore and bereft of its black glory, her slender limbs hung with rags. Her smelly goat-girl's clothes had been finer than these. They at least had borne with them no shame.

A boy. She was dressed as a boy! What greater disgrace for a woman of the Citadel, an acolyte of the Living Fire? And yet, what choice did she have? It was either her own humiliation or . . .

But she could not think on that. She gazed out the tall window of her chamber, out upon a sky as dark as the fallen clippings of her hair.

There, high above, gleamed a blue star.

2

I HAD NOT VENTURED BEYOND the borders of Etalpalli for some time. But I left it now, under the storming protests of my counselors and ladies. I passed through Cozamaloti and found myself once more flightless in the Wood. I do not know how long I wandered there, for no true Path opened beneath my feet. I never saw the Haven or heard the voice of guidance calling in my head. I was too hot inside to hear anything.

Eventually, I stumbled from the Between into the Near World. I smelled the stench of mortality, and it brought back the memory of my wasted brother, my decayed father and mother. I was sick, and my legs trembled, for I still could not take to the air, not in that dreadful world.

I sought long and hard. I saw many Houses of Lights and heard how the sun and the moon sang through them. But their voices were cacophony in my ears, and I hated the sight of the mortals who danced and sang at the doors of those Houses. I thought how I would like to rend them to pieces!

Instead, I searched. On and on.

Until I found Etanun.

The journey down from the mountains had been a long one, longer still the trek across the lowlands. Always the light of the Citadel guided them, like a red star on the horizon. Other priestesses and their guards, other girls taken from poor villages as a tax to the Flame joined Mouse and her escorts as they crossed the wasteland surrounding the Citadel.

At last the Citadel itself came into view—the great red-stone Spire rising to pierce the heavens themselves, built atop a bedrock of equal redness. Around it spread the temple grounds, like a small city devoted to the Flame's service.

They passed through an arched red-stone gate and marched through the grounds to the central buildings surrounding the Spire. These buildings were pillared and open to the elements, for it was hot in the cloudless lowlands, and any breeze that might blow through to cool the inner sanctums was welcome.

The girls stood in a courtyard beneath the Spire, flanked on all sides by the temple guards—eunuchs all, Mouse was to learn later, and silent as statues. Priestesses filed from every part of the temple grounds, solemn and beautiful in red robes, their black wigs sparkling with gold. Behind them, lingering on the edges, were black-clad acolytes, hooded so that their faces were unseen, figures of mystery but not of majesty like their elder sisters.

And then the high priestess approached.

In Mouse's dreams of the goddess, of the Flame herself, she had envisioned something like this exquisite being: tall and strong with features almost too severe to be beautiful, full of power. She was clad in white doeskin stained brilliant hues of saffron, scarlet, and blue, the colors of fire. Her wig was more beautifully decorated than all the others, not in gold or gems, but in a crown of red starflowers, like the Silent Lady herself.

In her wake marched Stoneye. He was a powerful form indeed, bigger and handsomer and sadder than all the other eunuchs serving in the temple. Unlike many of them, he had offered himself freely into the temple's service, knowing full well the fate of any man who lived in the presence of the Flame. Now, mute and sorrowful, he was ever in the high priestess's company, her most devoted slave and bodyguard.

The priestess descended the temple steps, Stoneye close in her shadow. Her dark eyes studied the girls presented before her. Mouse had never felt more ragged and foolish than she did then, painfully aware of her humble clothes. She shivered though the day was meltingly hot. But her hair was lovely, and it flowed to her waist.

The high priestess's gaze fell upon her and stopped. Mouse felt her heartbeat in her throat.

"This girl," the high priestess said, her voice strangely cold in that blistering heat. "This girl will do. Send the others to the acolytes' house to be fitted out. I'll take this one into my personal service."

Unbelieving, scarcely breathing, Mouse was shuffled away between two eunuchs into the temple and her new life devoted to the Flame.

Now, she fled it.

Through the temple corridors she ran, a small, ragged phantom. This place that over the last four years had become familiar, if never truly comfortable, now seemed a world of dread. Her bare feet made no sound on the polished stone, and she avoided the torches and braziers burning at intervals.

Like a thief, she slipped from shadow to shadow, past the lower priestesses' living quarters, the acolytes' house, and the barren barracks, where the eunuch slaves slept at night. She met no one. At last she approached the arched gate. There two guards stood watch, and she knew they saw her coming.

Mouse hastened on without pausing. She saw one of them step forward. He opened the gate, pushing the heavy door aside, then slid into the shadows along the wall and turned his face away.

Neither guard acknowledged her. She passed through the gate and out to the open grounds beyond, hearing only her own panting breath and the thud of her running feet for several moments.

Then the clang of the gate shutting behind her.

The blue star glimmered high above. The blue star, and the fire blazing at the top of the Citadel Spire.

The fire was never permitted to go out. Throughout even the darkest, most storm-tossed nights it burned. And before dawn the high priestess would rise, prepare herself with ceremonial washings, and climb the long stairs to tend that blaze in the presence of the goddess.

It became Mouse's duty to help her in these morning preparations. She was unskilled at first, her goat-girl's fingers clumsy and unused to fine fastenings and delicate sashes. Often she wondered that the high priestess did not replace her with a more adept acolyte.

But the high priestess never spoke a word of either praise or complaint. She merely sat, her face quiet, and watched the fumbling girl clad in black robes as she fetched gems and sashes and always the circlet of woven star-flowers. Stoneye, arms folded, stood by the wall with his gaze downcast. Their silence unnerved Mouse, but she hastened about her duties and learned as quickly as she could.

A month into Mouse's life at the temple, the high priestess finally addressed her as she worked. As though Mouse had passed some sort of test and now deserved acknowledgment.

"I once had hair such as yours," the high priestess said.

Mouse paused while lifting the great black wig to her mistress's head. Beneath the wig the priestess was nearly bald, her scalp covered in burns. The high priestess reached up and touched that ragged baldness now, her face a little sad.

"I had fine hair," she said, "thick and shining." Her throat constricted as she swallowed, but her face was otherwise stoic. "Loss of beauty is but one price we pay for the sake of purification."

"You are beautiful, Speaker," Mouse said. *Speaker* was the official name by which all the sisters of the temple addressed their high priestess, for she alone spoke to and for the Flame.

The high priestess smiled gently. "I was beautiful," she said. "Now I am strong. Do you believe I am strong, Mouse?"

"I do," said Mouse. Though it was hard to say with sincerity after a month in the high priestess's service. Yes, the Speaker was strong in command, could order the lives and the deaths of all within the Citadel grounds or the sprawling lowlands beyond. But physically, she shuddered in a breath of wind, and her hands, arms, and neck were covered in burns. Another part of the rituals, of serving the Flame. But her face was like granite, unflinching in the service to which she had devoted herself. "You are strong, Speaker."

The high priestess again touched her burned scalp, then motioned for Mouse to adorn her with her wig. "We are all of us like clay," she said as Mouse worked. "Clay that must be put through the fire to achieve true strength. And even then, when dropped, we shatter."

She took the starflower wreath for herself and placed it atop her head. "Even as the Silent Lady underwent torments to fulfill the will of the goddess and save us from the Wolf Lord, so must we endure any pain to which the Flame calls us. For the good of our sisters. For the good of ourselves. Do you understand, Mouse?"

Mouse nodded.

"Now go about your duties, child," the Speaker said, patting Mouse gently on the head. "Go about your duties even as I go about mine."

With these words, the high priestess moved from her airy chamber, the train of her robes dragging behind her. Stoneye stepped from the shadows and followed, never sparing a glance Mouse's way.

So Mouse did as she was bidden and fetched the tools of her second daily task, lighting all the braziers in the lower south hall so that incense flooded that section of the higher temple before sunrise. She hastened there now, a lighting stick in one hand, a bucket of coals in the other, and a bag of powdered incense tucked under one arm.

The passage was open to all elements, and Mouse, warm inside her black robe, welcomed the cool breath of morning as she worked. One at a time she lowered a brazier by its chain, lit the coals, and poured in a handful of incense, letting off a strong, sweet smell that disguised all the pleasant scents of coming dawn. "Fire burn," Mouse whispered as she had been taught. "Fire purify."

The crack of a whip startled her so that she nearly dropped her lighting stick. Mouse strode to the edge of the open hall and looked down. Below her all was rock, the foundation on which the Citadel and the Spire were built. On all other sides, the temple city covered this rock, but here it was exposed and looked red and hot even by predawn light.

Another crack . . . and a cry. Mouse shivered at the sound of a man's voice. She had not heard a man speak since coming to the temple, and it seemed strange and terrible, especially laced with such pain. She saw torches now, approaching in a long line across the open countryside. Torches and shadows and the figures of men bound in chains being driven toward the Citadel. Their drivers, tall eunuchs in temple garb, urged them with whips, prodded them with spears.

So the procession made its way to the red rock beneath Mouse's feet. Shivering, she watched them approach, unable to tear away her gaze. To her surprise, rather than circling the side of the temple to enter by the gates, the eunuch guards drove the bound men straight to the wall.

They disappeared inside.

Craning her neck, Mouse could not see from this angle any opening or door where they had gone. Afraid of falling from that unprotected height, she set aside her tools, got to her hands and knees, and strained her neck further, trying to see.

"They've gone to the Diggings."

Mouse looked up, embarrassed to be caught in so undignified a pose. A tall girl, another acolyte, stood before Mouse. She was called Sparrow; Mouse did not know her true name. Each girl was given a new name upon entering service at the temple. Her true name was then forgotten, for only then could it be safe. So Mouse became Mouse, and this girl was Sparrow. She was older than Mouse and had been in temple service for three years.

"They've gone to the Diggings," she repeated as Mouse scrambled to her feet. "To be lost."

"Lost?" Mouse repeated.

Sparrow picked up the fallen lighting stick, which had gone out. "They are men from the mountains who have rebelled against the Flame. Their fate is to labor in her Diggings until they are lost."

"You mean dead?" Mouse asked, her voice trembling.

Sparrow shook her head. "I mean lost," she said. "Those who enter the Diggings beneath the temple without protection never come out again. In time all Diggers are lost." She handed the stick to Mouse, her disapproving face half hidden beneath its hood. "You shouldn't let your fire go out, you know."

Humbly, Mouse relit the stick in the last brazier. "What is in the Diggings?" she asked.

"Diggers," said Sparrow with a snort, looking back over Mouse's work. It was her morning duty to make certain the young acolyte performed her tasks up to standard. "What else?"

"No, I mean," Mouse said, "what do they dig for?"

"The chamber of Fireword."

"What is Fireword?"

"The demon sword that twice slew our goddess."

Mouse stared at the older girl. What blasphemy was this, spoken by an older sister, no less! For how could it be other than blasphemy? The goddess could not die! The Flame at Night was far too great to be extinguished by any sword!

"I . . . I don't believe you," Mouse said.

"What difference does it make what you believe?" Sparrow said sharply, turning from the brazier she was inspecting to fix Mouse with a stern glare. "The goddess was twice slain by Fireword, and she fears to be slain a third time. All this you will learn for yourself as you get older and are brought into deeper knowledge. Until then, know better than to speak back to your elders."

Mouse cowered, sliding her hood up over her head like a shield.

Sparrow, still frowning, moved on to the next brazier, lowered it on its chain, and indicated for Mouse to light it. Mouse obeyed silently, sprinkling the handful of incense and trying not to breathe in the thick scent.

"I was to have your place, you know," Sparrow said, looking across the hot coals at Mouse. "I was to be the Speaker's girl, to walk in her footsteps and care for her needs. I was being trained for it."

Mouse blinked. Her hand holding the bag of incense trembled.

"And then you come along," Sparrow continued, pulling the chain back into place, hand over hand. "You come out of some wild jungle mountain, all tattered and smelly. And the Speaker looks at you as though she's been waiting for you for years. All my work was for nothing."

Sparrow focused her attention on the swinging brazier as it settled back into place. Mouse, her mouth dry, didn't know what to say. "I . . . I'm sorry," she whispered.

"You are sorry," said Sparrow, moving on to the next brazier. "Sorry and small and ignorant. You are a mouse. And yet she favors you." Mouse followed, huddled up inside her robe. "It is the will of the Flame," the older girl continued with a shrug, though her voice was not so dismissive.

Somehow Mouse knew that only fear of severe punishment kept Sparrow from clawing her eyes out.

3

WHEN I FOUND ETANUN, he and his brother were hard at work building another of their Houses. This one overlooked a river in the cold north, and it was the grandest they had constructed yet. But when Etanun saw me, he abandoned the work and came down to me at once.

"What are you doing here?" he demanded, looking me over. I must have been a sight, ragged winged, hollow eyed. "Are you come alone? Is Etalpalli threatened?"

I shook my head. The sight of his face had driven from me all the fire inside. Though I wished to hate him, I could not but be glad to see him again.

"Dear queen," he said and took me by the shoulders, "tell me what is wrong!"

I spoke: "They say you're in love with a mortal maid."

His hands dropped away and he stepped back. Bowing his head, he whispered, "They say this?"

"Is it true?" I demanded.

He drew a long breath. For a moment I thought he would deny it.

But he said, "It is true. I do love her."

The blue star progressed in its arching path across the night sky, surrounded by its brethren. Mouse pursued it, watching the sky rather than her feet. There were no obstructions on this ground, the barren territory that surrounded the temple. The Flame and the Spire were at her back, and she drove her feet to hasten after that gentle light above, ever fearing the coming of dawn and the fading of her distant guide.

In the four years since her coming to the temple, she had never before left its confines.

Four years had fled so quickly, Mouse had scarcely felt their passing or noticed the change that came upon her body as she grew from girl to young woman. She served the Speaker, dressing her every morning for the ritual tending of the fire, undressing her every night before the high priestess stole a few precious hours of sleep, ever guarded by Stoneye. Mouse herself slept in a tiny chamber adjacent to her mistress's, separated from her only by a curtain.

Despite this proximity, she never felt close to this eldest of the temple sisters. There was something unknowable about the Speaker, as though she feared to be known. Yet Mouse grew to love her even as she feared her, and she served with all the zeal in her young body.

After the first year of labor, she, along with the other acolytes her age, entered into intensive studies under the priestesses, learning the rites and duties performed to the glory of the Flame. Some of these she knew already, for her mountain village celebrated the Days of Fire and the Breaking of Silence, and all the holy days of the year.

But within the temple every day was like a holy day, which meant grueling work for the sisters. Most days, Mouse was too tired even to think about rest, and most nights too exhausted to sleep. Yet she would never have exchanged that exhaustion for the easy life of the mountains. She learned reading and writing; she studied chants and histories. Life was as far removed from goat herding as it could be, and she reveled in the difference!

Then one dawn, everything changed.

She was in the lower south corridor, lighting her braziers as she did every morning at sunrise. This far into her service, she no longer needed Sparrow to oversee her work. Indeed, Sparrow, now a priestess in her own right, was far removed from Mouse's life, and for this Mouse was grateful.

She passed between the tall pillars, lowering and raising each brazier, filling the air with the thickness of sweet spices. It was late summer, and dawn came early, spreading light across the horizon. The southern mountains were hazy with distance but recognizable. The mountains that had been her home. For the first time in a long while, she thought of Granna. Crazy, ancient Granna, so withered, so stubborn, waiting for the return of a prophetess more ancient than she and scorning to look to the light of the Citadel.

Mouse shook her head and frowned. How was Granna getting on without her? she wondered. She did not doubt that the old woman still lived. Had she not already survived several generations? She was as old as the mountain itself, and she certainly had never needed Mouse.

But, Mouse thought, *perhaps I needed her.*

A dangerous path of thought. Mouse blocked it from her mind as best she could and resumed her work. One does not progress along the road to purification if one hesitates and looks back. Such was not the will of the Flame.

Suddenly the world went dark, as though Mouse and all around her had plunged into the depths of a moonless midnight. She froze, clutching the chain of a brazier in both hands, and though the morning was hot, she began to tremble.

Then, a light.

Mouse turned to it, surprise overcoming her fear. A stranger approached. Not one of the temple sisters. No, rather than the red of holy service, this woman wore green, save for a starflower tucked in her hair, the flower gleaming white rather than red as it would appear in daylight. It looked like a diamond in the thick blackness of that long hair.

Two enormous dogs flanked her, their eyes flaming red. But when Mouse blinked, sucking in a breath to scream, they were gone. Only the darkness remained.

The woman approached from the end of the passage. How had she penetrated the sacred Citadel grounds, her head uncovered, her feet unshod?

The guards should never have admitted her, and yet there she stood, a small, shining figure.

"Who are you?" Mouse cried, clutching the brazier chain like a weapon. "What are you doing in the halls of the Flame?"

The stranger frowned. Her face was beautiful but earnest. Then her eyes widened, and she stepped forward with a cry, arms extended. "Fairbird!"

Mouse leapt back, pulling the chain so that the burning brazier swung between them. "Stay back!" she cried.

The stranger withdrew her hands, her fingers curling into fists and her brow wrinkled. "Don't you know me?" she asked, her voice soft. "How long have I been away?"

"I don't know you!" Mouse cried. "You shouldn't be here! Get out!"

"You're not Fairbird." The stranger's voice was dull with sadness. She shook her head, and her face could have broken the stoniest heart. "I was mistaken. You're not Fairbird."

"I don't know any Fairbird!" Mouse said. Now that the stranger was closer, she appeared young, scarcely older than Mouse herself. But her voice was so old! And her eyes . . . they were the strangest thing of all.

Her eyes were like Granna's.

Mouse could scarcely find the voice to repeat, "Get out!"

The stranger folded her hands, and her sad voice became demure, her face unreadable. "I come on another's behalf," she said. "I would speak to the Dragonwitch."

Mouse stared at her. It was like looking upon a memory she hadn't known she possessed. More of an instinct than an actual thought. She felt sweat soaking her woolen robe in damp patches on her back.

"I don't know this Dragonwitch," she said. "You are come to the Citadel of the Living Fire, abode of the Great Goddess. And you are unwelcome here!"

The stranger tilted her head to one side, her lips compressed. Then she said, "I will not harm you. I know the Dragonwitch is near, and you must take me to her. Tell her I have come on behalf of one she knows: Etanun the Sword-bearer. I bring a message from him. He wishes to tell her where Halisa is buried."

The word *Halisa* rang through Mouse's brain. Somehow it rearranged itself, and Mouse heard it again, this time as a name she knew.

Fireword.

"The demon sword that twice slew our goddess."

Mouse could hardly breathe. "The goddess," she whispered, "searches for Fireword."

The stranger's calm mask broke into an expression of pity. "Poor little thing!" She raised her eyes to the dark sky that only moments ago had held dawn, and she cried out to no one Mouse could see: "Are my people always to live enslaved?"

Mouse lowered the brazier slowly until it rested on the floor. Pungent smoke drifted between her and the stranger. "Who are you?" she asked.

"I was called Starflower," said the stranger.

Mouse breathed, "Silent Lady!" and knew the name was true the moment she spoke it.

The Flame had purified this land and all the lands surrounding the Spire. Mouse felt the purification beneath her feet, the dryness of earth burned to cinders years ago. Even at night, with the star-filled sky above, the ground felt hot with the memory of that scorching.

The blue star moved across the sky, and Mouse followed it, changing direction as necessary. Her great fear was that it would set, leaving her exposed on this empty plain, still within sight of the Citadel. What she would do then, she could not guess.

How quickly the last few days had passed, leaving her dizzy and exhausted now as, in her awful disguise, she fled. Was it only yesterday that she had hastened up the long stair of the Spire as the rising sun dispelled at last the darkness of Midnight? She had come at last to the final door just as the high priestess, finished with her morning rituals, stepped through.

"Speaker!" Mouse, nearly beside herself, fell on her knees at her mistress's feet and grasped the hem of her red-stained robe.

It burned.

Mouse dropped it and withdrew, clutching her hand to her breast.

The high priestess stood a silent moment, regarding her. Then with a heavy sigh, she knelt, the black weaves of her wig swaying gently on either side of her face. "It is dangerous to draw near to the goddess's power unprepared," she said. "But I can forgive you this time. I see that you are greatly troubled, and not for your own sake. Tell me, little Mouse, what do you fear?"

"The Silent Lady," Mouse said at once. "The Silent Lady has returned!"

"Fire burn." The high priestess whispered the fervent prayer but without surprise. Indeed, her face was calm and accepting. "In good time too. The Flame will be pleased. Where is she?"

It was a dreadful procession back down the Spire staircase. Stoneye, armed with his spear, led the way as was his practice, and the high priestess followed, Mouse at her heels. Other priestesses and acolytes joined, and other eunuchs, armed and keen. But why should they need armed guards? There was no need for protection from the Silent Lady! She was the prophetess, the one who, at the bidding of the goddess, had delivered her people from the Wolf Lord and the terror of his inflicted silence! Why the need for weapons? Mouse shuddered, unable to think, and kept close to her mistress's shadow.

In the lower south passage, the Silent Lady waited between two pillars beneath a smoking brazier. By morning light she looked smaller than ever, little more than a girl, save for those old eyes.

Stoneye planted himself between her and the Speaker. But his lady stepped forward and, though he turned his head sharply, his face full of warning, she shook her head at him and drew near. Mouse watched, expecting to see the high priestess fall on her knees and make reverence before the chosen prophetess of the Flame.

Instead, the high priestess said: "Speak your purpose."

Her voice was sharp with command. It startled Mouse, who pressed a hand to her mouth. But the Silent Lady responded gently. "I am come with a message for the Dragonwitch."

"Neither dragon nor witch dwells within the Citadel of the Living Fire," the Speaker replied. "There is only the goddess."

"Then my message is for your goddess," said the Silent Lady. "From Etanun."

"I do not know this"—the high priestess hesitated over the strange name, pronouncing it with care—"this *Etanun*."

"My message is not for you."

"I am Speaker for the goddess. I am also her ears. Anything you wish to say to her must come first to me."

There was a long silence. Mouse shivered. She had never thought to see anyone more holy than the Speaker herself, who lived and served daily in the presence of the Flame, her own skin burning away with purification. But now to hear her speak to the prophetess in such a fashion . . . it was frightful! How could a priestess, no matter how holy, address an instrument of the gods so harshly?

The Silent Lady said, "Etanun has told me where to find Halisa's chamber. I will take you to it, if such is your will."

The high priestess recoiled as though struck. Stoneye hastily stepped forward, his hand outstretched. She bade him back away, but she swayed where she stood as though years of labor had come suddenly to an apex, yet even now she dared not hope for reprieve. Mouse could see the throb of a pulse in her throat.

"You will take me there," the Speaker said. "At once."

4

I LAUGHED. IT WAS THE FIRST TIME *I had laughed in many ages, and the sound startled me and, I could tell, frightened him. When the laughter eased, I said, "So I was not enough for you. Immortal Faerie that I am, glorious queen, beautiful beyond the description of poets and rhymes. I was not enough to keep you close, but you will love this woman of dust? You will love this decaying mortal?"*

He did not meet my eyes. But he said, "I love her."

"Why?" I demanded. "Why her? Why not me?"

"Because," he said in the gentlest, most tender voice I had ever heard, "when I look at her, I see the light of my home shining clear and bright in her eyes."

If I could have killed him then, I would have.

"What is her name?" I asked.

"Klara," he replied.

No sooner did the Speaker command than Stoneye stepped forward and took the Silent Lady roughly by the arm. There was no reverence or even gentleness in his action, and Mouse cried out in protest.

A protest unheard or unheeded by all those gathered. Stoneye led the way, marching the prophetess like a prisoner before him as the high priestess silently followed, the rest falling into step behind her. Mouse was caught up in the flowing tide of her sisters in red and black and the marching eunuchs around them.

Out of the open hall and around to a stair cut into the red foundation rock they filed down, following Stoneye and the strange woman to the ground below. For the first time, Mouse walked the low path where she had years ago seen the first throng of slaves driven, and many more since then. But she had never yet seen the door through which they were sent, the door into the Diggings.

It was little more than a crack in the red stone, jagged like a wolf's jaws. Darkness spilled from it and coldness as well. Mouse felt it even before they drew near, and she trembled with dread.

"Here," said a priestess beside her. Mouse turned and, to her surprise, recognized Sparrow, clad in red, adorned in a fine wig. "Take this."

Mouse felt something pressed into her hands, and looked down at a black cloth. Sparrow, still walking toward the crack in the stone, was tying a similar cloth about her face, shielding her eyes. "You must not see the darkness of the Diggings," she said, her voice calm. "If you do, you will be lost."

Sparrow finished securing her blindfold, then put out a hand. A eunuch, his eyes unshielded, stepped to her side and offered his arm, leading her to the gaping doorway through which the other priestesses and acolytes were flowing. Hating to follow but hating still more to be left behind, Mouse also blindfolded her eyes and felt a eunuch slip to her own side and tuck her hand under his arm. So she was guided into the swallowing darkness of the Diggings.

It was like the Midnight she had witnessed earlier, only deeper. With the blindfold on her face, she might have been drowning in the depths of a black ocean. Her only guide was the arm of the eunuch, to which she clung as a babe clings to its mother. The tramp of many feet ahead comforted her, but the silence, deeper than all other silences, flooded the world behind her, as if a thousand people cried out for help only to find their voices rendered mute.

So these were the Diggings into which those who rebelled against the Flame were sent to find the chamber of Fireword.

"Why does she want it?" Mouse whispered. The silence offered her no answer.

Onward they plunged, deeper and deeper. Sometimes Mouse thought she heard from a distance the ringing of hammers and picks, slaves hard at work. Their search for the chamber must have extended far into this subterranean world. How cold it was! Mouse was thankful for the woolen robes that had always seemed such a bother before. She should never doubt the will of the goddess.

It was difficult to say how far they progressed into those depths. Time meant little in that blind world. But sooner than Mouse expected, the procession halted and she heard the voice of the prophetess speaking clearly up ahead.

"Here. This is the place."

"Impossible" came the high priestess's reply. "We searched this entire quarter ages ago. There is nothing here. We must proceed."

"No," said the Silent Lady. "This is the place. Etanun's mark is on the wall."

Mouse released hold of the eunuch and, with trembling fingers, reached up and pulled the blindfold down. To her surprise, there was light all around her, the light of torches carried by the eunuchs, and the white light glowing from the starflower tucked in the prophetess's hair. The procession had halted at a crossroad where the main tunnel branched in two, a larger passage continuing to the right, a smaller to the left. It was an old part of the Diggings, carved out before the Speaker was even born.

None of the other acolytes had dared remove their blindfolds, but the high priestess, standing beside Stoneye at the head of the procession, looked upon the Silent Lady, and her eyes were bright even in that darkness.

"We would have seen it," the Speaker said, "long ere now."

"You could not," said the prophetess. "No matter how you searched. Etanun said his sword must sleep undisturbed. He did not wish it found until this time."

She took a step forward, but Stoneye clutched her arm. Mouse saw the pain shoot across her face. How could Stoneye treat her so? Did he not realize who she was? Or did he really believe she would try to escape in this awful labyrinth?

The high priestess spoke a soft command, and Stoneye unwillingly released his hold. The Silent Lady stood as though uncertain. Then, setting her jaw, she strode toward the ragged stone wall between the split passages. And suddenly everyone saw what had been hidden from mortal eyes for generations of enslaved Diggers, hidden until that moment.

In the place where the passages diverged was an arched doorway.

Only shadows had concealed it for all the lonely years of the Diggers' efforts. Only shadows more solid than any wall. When torchlight fell upon that spot, the shadows threw the light back and revealed none of their secrets. But when the starflower in the prisoner's hair gleamed, it shone upon a richly carved doorpost.

"Fire burn," the Speaker said. Then she leapt forward, ready to pass through the arch. But Stoneye put out his arm, preventing her. "Out of my way, man!" She spoke without malice, a dreamy haziness to her voice. "I must see it." And she breathed the name like a prayer: "Fireword."

Stoneye would not release her. He could not speak, but he indicated that she must let him go first. After all, who knew what lay beyond that doorway?

The high priestess stared up at him. For a moment, Mouse thought she would argue. But instead, she closed her eyes tightly, as though forcing her body to act against her own will. "Very well." She snatched a torch from one of the other slaves and pressed it into his hands. "Take this. And hurry!"

Stoneye approached the doorway. The shadows within thirstily drank up the light from his torch. The big slave hesitated on the threshold. He lifted the torch to study carved images of a story he did not know, perhaps of two brothers, one with a lantern, one with a sword. And he saw the one with the sword kill the first. It was a terrible tale, even in that momentary glimpse. A tale of murder.

The Silent Lady placed a hand upon his arm. He startled as though bitten and turned to her with a snarl. But her face was gentle, her eyes strangely calm.

"I will enter first," she said, taking the flower from her hair and cupping it in her hands. "Let me, please?"

The big man looked like a hungry dog ready to devour her. Then his face, cast harshly into relief by the glow of his torch, softened. He stepped back.

So the prisoner carried her little star into the chamber. It was a large chamber indeed, an enormous circular room with a domed ceiling. Unlike the tunnels and passages of the Diggings, it was well crafted, its smooth walls overlaid with fine encaustic tiles. The white light of the starflower revealed many colors of clay worked into delicate patterns in every tile, each one telling a different story. They were too many and too intricate for comprehension. The mind ached to see them, yet it was an ache of beauty not pain.

Centered in the room was a stone so ugly that it might have been chipped from the essence of darkness. More carefully carved was the likeness of a sword, hilt up, protruding from its top. A sword that was part of the stone itself.

"It's there!" Without a thought the high priestess plunged into the chamber, her hands outstretched, striving against the shadows, her eyes wide and hungry, even desperate.

"Wait!" cried the Silent Lady.

Heedless, the priestess pushed past the glow of the starflower, her robes flowing behind her, reaching for the stone, reaching for the sword.

There was a clatter as Stoneye's torch dropped and extinguished. The big slave caught the high priestess, lifted her off her feet, and dragged her back screaming and thrashing. It was the most horrible sight! Mouse wanted to cover her eyes, to avoid seeing her beautiful mistress so humiliated. Stoneye—a man who should not dare to breathe upon her—wrapped his strong arms around her rail-thin frame, holding her almost fiercely, his face full of fear.

The Silent Lady stepped forward, struggling to make herself heard above the inarticulate screams of the priestess. "Please!" she cried. "You mustn't touch it!"

"It belongs to the goddess," the high priestess shouted. "It is here beneath her temple, beneath the land she has made her own, and it is hers by right of conquest. I will, I *must* bring it to her."

"No," said the prophetess. "I have shown you the secret. I have led you to this place. Please trust me now when I say that you must not touch Etanun's sword. You must not touch Halisa."

The priestess became cold. Stoneye felt the resistance flow from her, and he set her down but kept hold of her shoulder. "Why not?" the Speaker demanded, her voice as black as that ugly stone.

"Only Etanun's heir may bear the sword from this chamber," the prisoner said. "See?" She hastened to the stone and knelt, holding her gleaming flower up to it. Mouse shouldered her way past priestesses and eunuchs to peer through the doorway. She saw what the flower revealed. She saw that the sword was indeed part of the stone itself. She could see where chisel and mallet had chipped its contours into the shape it now bore. And around the place where the stone blade seemingly entered the boulder were deeply carved letters. These were more elegantly depicted, if unreadable to those looking on.

Then, as Mouse watched, the characters suddenly shifted and moved, not on the stone itself, but inside her mind. She found herself not reading but seeing images that to her were unmistakable. They said as clearly as words:

> *Fling wide the doors of light, Smallman,*
> *Though furied falls the Flame at Night.*
> *The heir to truth, blest blade of fire,*
> *He finds in shielded shadow light.*

The high priestess saw it too. But she growled, shaking her head. "That is foolishness," she said. "Nothing will stand between the goddess and her prize, neither this Smallman nor any heir."

She tried to approach the boulder again, but Stoneye restrained her. She whirled on him, eyes flashing, and snarled, "Very well, if you are so set on protecting me! You pick it up. You carry it from this room and show everyone the power of the goddess over these old superstitions. The Fire will burn all else away, including shivering cowardice!"

Stoneye gazed upon her. And for the first time Mouse saw his rock-hard mask slip. She saw in his cold eyes a sudden warmth, a heat that shot pain through his whole body but surged inside him with power as well.

She realized with horror: *He loves her.*

Not the high priestess. No, for no one could truly love that tall, detached being. But *her*. The woman she was beneath the trappings of her office. Beneath the robes, the wigs, the woven crowns. Beneath the burns. When he looked at her, he saw the person not the priestess, and he knew her name, which all others had forgotten.

Mouse's heart broke. In that moment she might have wept for dreadful Stoneye, the eunuch who had sacrificed all to serve this hard shell of what had once been a woman.

"Do as I say!" the high priestess cried, her voice ringing shrill in the stillness of that otherworldly chamber.

Stoneye stepped around her, his head high, his shoulders back. Mouse saw the Silent Lady cast herself before him, heard her small voice protesting, "Don't! Please! As you value your life, leave it be!"

Stoneye pushed her aside, and she landed in a crumpled heap on the tile-paved floor. Her starflower flew from her hand, spun wildly through the air, and floated gently down to rest on the black stone. The Silent Lady pushed upright, her long hair tossed back, and cried again, "Don't!"

Stoneye's hand reached out. The starflower illuminated each finger as it closed upon the carved hilt.

There was a rush, a deep-throated groan.

Then a thud as the slave's huge body fell upon the stone.

How cold, how silent was this place beneath the world! In that moment, as Mouse watched death sweep through that fallen body, she felt as though it grabbed her as well, catching her heart, dragging her down. She was abandoned, alone, forsaken in this black universe of nothing.

The voice of the high priestess spoke like darkness itself:

"Stoneye, get up. I command you."

5

I LEFT ETANUN THEN. *For the first time since coming to that world, I took to the air and soared higher and higher. Perhaps I thought to fly into the hot embrace of Lumé himself and let him burn me away into nothing. But his brilliance was soon too great for me, and I was driven back to earth. I crashed upon a high mountain and lay with broken wings upon the stone. I hoped I was dead. My dreams were shattered, and life held no charm for me.*

"Greetings, child," someone spoke.

I did not have the strength to raise my head. It astonished me to hear someone in so high and remote a place. But the voice spoke into the churning fire in my gut.

"What a beauty you are," the someone said. I felt his approach, felt him kneel beside me, and when I opened my eyes, I looked upon the face of Death-in-Life.

The face of the Dragon.

She strode across the chamber, the soft, shushing noise of her robes the only sound in that stillness besides the crackling torches and the breathing of the stricken throng.

Stern, the high priestess stood over Stoneye. "Get up," she said.

Mouse, leaning heavily against the doorway, saw how the white flower shone on her mistress's face like starlight on ice.

"At once. Slave."

The woman did not seem to breathe. Her eyes were shadow-strewn pools of dark water. She nudged the fallen eunuch with her foot like one might prod a lazy dog. "Up. Up. Up." Each word was a small gasp.

Then her mouth opened in a black slash across her face. Without a sound, she fell to her knees, clutching at the dead man's head, clawing at his face, pulling at the sleeve of his tunic. Her voice returned in a sudden wail, an animal sound without words. It broke off in another eternal silence. Then she breathed again, and this time Mouse heard her crying, "Get up! Get *up*!"

Her voice was that of a child. She was, Mouse realized, weeping. Tears glistened like drops of fire on her face. Broken, she crumpled over the form of her dead slave.

And Mouse heard her moan, "Why did you do it? Why did you follow me?"

The Silent Lady moved. She picked the starflower up off the stone, casting the shadow of the carved sword across the floor. Mouse saw her face highlighted by the white light. Tears shimmered in her eyes as she knelt and touched the Speaker's arm.

The priestess hissed between clenched teeth. "Get up. . . ."

"I'm so sorry," the Silent Lady whispered. "I see how you loved him, though you yourself did not realize until now. Let that love guide you, dear woman, and leave the sword to sleep. The time of its return is not now, and your goddess will drive you only to death."

The high priestess drew a ragged breath and let it out in a sob. Then she gathered herself and rose with her arms wrapped tightly about her robe, the woven strands of her wig falling in her face.

Turning, she pointed to the nearest eunuch. "You," she said, in a voice as sharp and sure as a spear. "Bring me that sword."

The eunuch's face became that of a phantom in the torchlight. His eyes, lost in hollows of shadows, widened until the whites gleamed, and Mouse saw a spasm run through his body. Otherwise, he could not move.

The high priestess's hand lashed out and struck him across the face, sending him sprawling backward among his fellows. "Do as I say," she growled.

The other eunuchs pushed him, and he stumbled into the chamber. "No, stop!" the Silent Lady cried.

"Restrain her," said the high priestess, and two other slaves leapt forward and grabbed her, one by her hair, the other by the back of her robe, dragging her from the chamber. The luckless eunuch, compelled by his mistress, approached the stone as Stoneye had. Mouse heard him whimper, and she saw the sweat streaming down his face. She wished she could move, could run and spare herself the sight to come. But to run among the Diggings meant certain death, so she remained frozen, unable to tear her gaze away.

The eunuch reached out. With a moan, he gripped the hilt. Then he gasped and fell across Stoneye's prone body.

The sword remained unmoved.

"Enough!" the Silent Lady cried. "Enough of this! Don't you see you're murdering them?"

"You," said the Speaker, and collared another eunuch. "Bring me that sword. Bring it now!"

He recoiled from her grasp. With a wail, he turned and ran down one of the split passages, dropping his torch with a crash behind him. Its flame sputtered, then extinguished, but the sound of its rolling nearly drowned the sound of his footsteps as he lost himself in the deep black.

"Speaker!" cried one of the priestesses in protest.

But the high priestess whirled upon her. "Yes?" she demanded. "Have you something to say? Do you wish to volunteer, to serve your goddess to the last?"

The priestess shrank back, and the Speaker turned to yet another eunuch. "Bring me that sword!" she said.

The Silent Lady screamed and wrenched against the clutches of those holding her. "Stop this! Stop, I beg you!" she cried. "You'll kill them all, and you'll still not gain that sword! It's senseless; it's cruel!"

"They are my slaves," said the high priestess, turning upon the small woman. "They'll do as I say."

"You can drain this whole world dry, and Halisa will remain in its resting place until its time has come," the prophetess said, her face fierce.

"Why did you come here, then?" The Speaker took the Silent Lady by the front of her robe, hauling her up with surprising strength until she stood upon the tips of her toes. "Did you intend to kill my slaves? Is that it?"

"I came at the request of Halisa's former bearer to tell the Flame at Night where the sword might be found. That is all."

"That can't be all!" the high priestess cried, shaking the Silent Lady and slamming her against the stone doorway. Mouse, standing so near she might reach out and touch them both, shrank into herself, desperate not to be seen.

The Silent Lady, helpless in the priestess's powerful grip, shook her head, and her face was sad but defiant. "Only Etanun or his heir can safely bear the sword from its burial chamber."

"Where is this heir?" the Speaker demanded.

"I do not know."

Shrieking like a bird of prey, the high priestess flung the Silent Lady to the ground. She drew a long sacrificial knife from her belt and advanced as though to spill the young woman's blood as she would a goat's upon the altar.

Mouse screamed and jumped forward, flinging herself between the two.

After the fact, she wondered at herself. It was a rash, heat-rushing moment. She did not think; she merely acted. It didn't matter that the lady in question neither knew nor acknowledged the goddess. She was the Silent Lady; Mouse knew it with a completeness more real than rationality. So she stepped between the prophetess and the knife.

And the high priestess stopped.

She stared into the space beyond the acolyte's head, perhaps into the darkness of the chamber beyond. What she saw, no one watching could discern. Was it the sword, standing cold in its black stone? Did something else unseen amid those shadows stay her killing hand?

However it was, the high priestess withdrew, her mouth open and her eyes wide. Then she shook herself and spoke in a voice as crackled as an old woman's.

"What's this, little Mouse? Will you betray me for a stranger?"

The words cut Mouse to the heart. She bowed her head, ashamed, horrified. But she did not move.

The high priestess turned away. Slowly, unsteady on her feet, she passed through the throng, drawing her blindfold down over her face as she went. Tears dampened the dark fabric, but no one could see them.

The Silent Lady touched Mouse's shoulder. Catching her breath, the girl turned to look into those solemn eyes that were so dreadfully familiar. The stranger gave her a look of gratitude and also some sort of mysterious understanding.

The high priestess's voice came through the shadows. "I must consult the goddess," she said. "I must bring her word of what has transpired and learn her will. Let a guard be set over this doorway, and see that the prisoner is locked away."

She put out a hand then, searching for a strong arm on which to lean, a strong form to guide her through the Diggings. But Stoneye was not there.

Another eunuch hastened to her side, offering himself. She refused to acknowledge him. Instead, she removed the blindfold from her face and, open to the darkness around her, made her way up the long passage. Over her shoulder she called, "Bring the bodies of the slain!"

She spared not another backward glance. She was Speaker for the Flame; she would not mourn.

The world was swiftly falling into twilight when the procession emerged through the crack in the stone and climbed back up to the temple itself. The Silent Lady was dragged beyond Mouse's sight, away to the dungeons. Mouse wanted to follow, but her mistress spoke a sharp command, and she dared not disobey. She tailed behind the high priestess up to her chambers and there helped her prepare to stand before the goddess.

"I must tell her what has happened," the Speaker said, talking to herself, unaware, it seemed, of Mouse's presence. "She will know what to do. And then we can kill that wretch."

Mouse's blood ran cold. Kill the Silent Lady? She stared at the Speaker's face, and she saw murder there. Murder and vengeance.

The Speaker turned to Mouse suddenly, eyes flashing. "What?" she demanded. "Are you going to defend her again? Will you demonstrate your disloyalty even now?"

Mouse couldn't breathe. But the high priestess said no more. Mouse finished the usual preparations, and the Speaker, gorgeous in her ritual garb, left the room, making for the Spire and the presence of the Flame.

For several long heartbeats, Mouse stood alone in her mistress's chambers.

And the Silent Lady was imprisoned below.

No one noticed Mouse as she hastened down from the Speaker's chambers, along the quiet halls. She was a mouse; she was a shadow. She was as insignificant as a passing fancy. So she made her way down the steps of the tower, down and down farther still until she reached the dungeons themselves. Even here the guards paid her no heed, and she entered that stifling gloom unimpeded. Mouse snatched a torch from its holder and plunged down the passage dug beneath the lower temple grounds. After the darkness of the Diggings, the dungeons held no horrors for her. She ran lightly, her sandaled feet slapping on the cold stone.

"Who's there?" came a voice from a not-too-distant cell. "Who's there with that light?"

"It's . . . it's me." Mouse hurried toward that voice, then knelt down, looking through a stone grate.

In a tiny crawl space where she could neither stand nor sit upright, huddled the prophetess. She peered up through the grate, and Mouse saw her eyes glitter in the torchlight. One hand reached out and grabbed the stone barrier. "I hoped you would come," she said.

Now that she was here, Mouse hardly knew what to say or do. It was all too strange and terrible! "You are the Silent Lady," she whispered. "Please, tell me you are."

But the prisoner shook her head. "I cannot tell you what I do not know. Who is this Silent Lady?"

"The harbinger of our freedom," Mouse answered as she had been taught. "The forerunner of the Flame."

The prisoner's face was earnest but not frightened in the torchlight. "Tell me what she did," she said. "Why do you revere her so?"

"She killed the Wolf Lord," said Mouse.

The calm faded from the prisoner's face. She looked as though she had seen a ghost. Her hand dropped away from the stone bar and pressed into the too-close wall. But she said only, "Go on."

"The Flame at Night sent her to rescue us from the wolf," said Mouse. "Though she was unable to speak because of his evil curse, she was empowered by the Flame. And when she had killed him, her voice was freed, and she spread the word throughout the Land that we were delivered."

"No," the prisoner whispered. "Oh no."

"She is the prophetess," Mouse persisted. "She liberated us from slavery and prepared us to receive the goddess. She is the great servant of the Flame. And . . . and you are she, aren't you?" She was down on her hands and knees now, her face close to the stone barricade. "Aren't you?" she repeated.

"No," said the prisoner. "No, it isn't true."

Mouse thought she would burst with frustration. "Don't lie to me!" she cried. "I *know* you are! I don't know how I know, but I *know*!"

The prisoner's body tensed as though she wished to draw back, but there was nowhere for her to go. The close confines of the cell held her, and the most she could do was sit with her knees up to her chest, her head pressed into them; the stone grating above nearly touched her ear. But she still held the starflower gently in one hand, and it gleamed.

The prisoner said, "I saw to it that the Wolf Lord was slain."

"I knew it." Mouse breathed the words, overwhelmed by the sudden relief that flooded her. "The Flame sent you."

"No!" The prisoner's hands balled into fists. But there was deep sorrow etched on her face, and almost immediately she contradicted herself. "Yes. I came at the behest of the Flame at Night. I came because she wished vengeance upon her former lover. But it wasn't vengeance I meted out on Amarok! I did not come to do the Dragonwitch's dirty work."

Mouse sat up, pulling her face away from the cold stone. A weight dropped in her stomach, and her mind whirled. "The goddess would not take a lover," she said at last. "She is Flame. She is Fire. Fire cannot love."

"You are right," said the prisoner. "Fire cannot love."

"Fire is too holy to love!" Mouse insisted.

"There you are mistaken."

Mouse could not see the prisoner's face. But she saw the white light of the starflower shifting, casting the shadows of the stone bars in several directions. Then, turning her gaze up to the grate once more, the prisoner looked at Mouse.

"Only holiness," she said, "can truly love."

Blasphemy. Mouse had never heard it spoken before. Not out loud. Sometimes she had suspected her old grandmother of harboring thoughts unworthy of those who served the Flame. But Granna had never dared speak those thoughts.

Yet there lay the prisoner—the prophetess, the Silent Lady—speaking words that earned her nothing less than flaming death. Mouse could not speak. She sat staring down into eyes that were too familiar.

"Mouse is not your name. Is it?" said the prisoner after a long silence.

Mouse shook her head.

"I didn't think so," said the prisoner. "Your name is bigger than that. Your name is full of hope. Your name is—"

"No one knows my name!" Mouse snapped, though her voice was still scarcely more than a whisper. "The names of the Flame's servants are secret."

"I am sorry for you," said the prisoner. "The greatest tragedy is to never be known."

Tears welled up in Mouse's eyes. Unbidden, a picture of Granna flashed across her mind's eye. And with it came Granna's warning: *"If you go down to the temple, child, no one will ever know your true name, and you yourself will forget it."*

Had she forgotten it already? Was she becoming nothing more than Mouse? Would she someday be like the Speaker, her whole being caught up in her temple role?

Mouse bowed her head. At last she said in a low tone, hoping the dark echoes of the passage would not catch and carry her words:

"They're going to kill you, Silent Lady."

"I know."

"But you are the prophetess."

"I am not whom you have believed me to be. Nor are the worlds what you have been told they are."

Trembling so that she could scarcely get the words out, Mouse said, "Is there no one who can save you?"

Suddenly the prisoner's hand darted out between the slats and grabbed hold of Mouse's. "My life or death matters little now," said the prisoner. "What matters is that my mission here is not without purpose. I came to relay Etanun's message, and this I have done. It is up to him to see the rest of my Lord's purpose accomplished. But Etanun must know! He must know that I have told Hri Sora where Halisa rests. And he must name his heir."

"The heir," Mouse repeated. "The heir who can carry the sword from that chamber and not die?"

"Yes," said the prisoner. "The time is coming, the end of Halisa's sleep. The heir will take up the sword. And he will put an end to these chains that bind you. The heir will set free the captive names of my people!"

Mouse tried to draw her hand back, but those gentle fingers were stronger than they looked. "The goddess requires Fireword," Mouse said. "The goddess will use it for her great purpose."

"She will use it for no purpose other than vengeance," said the prisoner. "And when she is done, she will destroy it."

"It is an evil weapon," said Mouse. "I saw it kill Stoneye."

"The sword did not bring about his death," said the prisoner. "His misplaced loyalty was his undoing. His misplaced love."

"Love is a terrible thing," Mouse whispered.

"Only love gone astray," said the prisoner. "Only imperfect love."

Mouse tried once more, feebly, to shake off the prisoner's grip. "You frighten me."

"Oh, child!" said the prisoner. "The time has come you *should* be frightened. If fear will awaken you, be afraid! And then be courageous in your fear and act!"

"There's nothing I can do."

"You aren't the mouse they have made you be. You were meant for so much more!"

"The goddess has made us more," said Mouse. "She liberated us from the Wolf Lord, and she gave us back our voices. Now we are stronger even than the men, and we rule this land."

But the prisoner shook her head, and she squeezed Mouse's fingers. "You do not rule," she said. "You are more enslaved now than you ever were. And you know it."

Mouse bowed her head and did not say what she thought. But she whispered at last: "How can I help you, lady?"

There was a long silence. Then the prisoner said, "Bend down here so that I may see your face."

Mouse did not like to, but she could think of no excuse to refuse. She leaned down, her face once more close to the stone bars. The gleaming starflower shone in her eyes, but its light was mild. It reflected in the dark depths of the prisoner's eyes, which studied her and read things Mouse suspected she did not wish to show. She could not meet that gaze. She felt as though it could look down into the hidden places of her soul, and she feared what it would see there.

"Poor lost one," said the prisoner. "But my Master has always used the most unlikely to accomplish his ends. Perhaps, little mouse, you are bound for a greater destiny than this future of ashes before you."

Then the prisoner pressed her face as close to the stone as she could and spoke her next words in a hushed, hurried tone. "Listen now; listen carefully. I am going to ask you to do something quite dreadful. I know they have required things of you as well. I know they are driving you, like the Black Dogs themselves at your heels. But I am asking you to do this for my sake, not for theirs."

Mouse went cold as stone inside.

"Follow the blue star," said the prisoner. "You will see it in the north sky tonight. Follow the blue star, without turning to the right or left, walking straight and true after its course. It will lead you to Etanun, Halisa's former master. When you find him, tell him that I have done as he asked. And tell him that the rest is up to him."

Mouse's voice shook so that she could scarcely speak. "Will he know where to find the heir?"

"Ask him," said the prisoner. One hand reached up between the stone bars and touched Mouse's cheek. "Ask him," she said again, "but don't think you'll deceive him."

"Deceive him?" Mouse said. "What do you mean?"

"You will know what I mean soon enough."

Then she drew back into her cell, and the light of the starflower was hidden so that Mouse could no longer see her. "If you meet my comrade, Sir Eanrin the cat, he will help you. He is good and noble, though he may not at first seem so to you. Tell him of my fate, and he will help."

The prisoner's voice was low and strong despite the darkness into which she was now plunged. "Follow the blue star, child. Do what you must."

6

I WAS TOO WEAK TO FLEE. *The Dragon took my face in his hands and they burned me, yet somehow the burn felt right.*

"You are my kin," said he, the Dark Father. "You don't belong in this world or any world where Lumé and Hymlumé sing. They sing in praise of the One whom Etanun serves. Can you bear that?"

I shook my head even as he held it.

"No," he agreed. "You cannot. So let us make these worlds after our own fashion. Let us see what songs they will sing when fire rains from the sky."

I whispered, "Fire from the sky."

"Let me kiss you," he said.

"Kiss me, then," said I.

Mouse, dressed as a boy, slipped unseen from the Citadel of the Living Fire into the night. She scarcely believed it. It must all be a dream, a nightmare even. She was not one to run away, unless it was to hide. She was not one to step beyond the rules of life, to risk the anger of the Flame.

But here she was, clad in the rags of a slave boy, disgraceful attire for one of the Citadel's own. She dared not venture beyond the temple grounds as herself, however. She must be secret; she must be unseen; she must attract no watching eye.

So she passed between the guards at the gate and fled across the plain, and above her shone the blue star. She followed it as she had been told. The way was straight across the empty plain. She ran without turning until she reached a place where a deep gorge cut the dry plain.

Mouse stood upon the brink of that sharp drop, looking down at the rushing river below, and at the forest into which that river flowed and disappeared.

There could be no going around. The gorge stretched for miles in both directions, and the star led right over it.

To do as the Silent Lady asked, Mouse would have to climb down that rocky way, and she would have to cross not only the river, but also the forest.

Dawn was approaching. The blue star, having run its course across the sky all night, was fading away. In the half-lit gloom that was neither night nor day, Mouse scurried down the gorge. The river churned dark and swift, and she thought at first it was hungry for her, the white crests of rapids like a salivating mouth. But as she drew near, she thought instead that it was merely wary of her approach.

When she reached the bottom of the gorge, she found her feet on slick stone dampened by the river, which, this close, seemed more than ever to be a living entity, watching her as it flowed. Though she wanted to wash her gritty hands in the running water, she did not dare. Instead, she picked her way along the bank, keeping close to the gorge wall. The sun was rising. When she looked up, she could scarcely see the blue star.

The forest loomed large. The trees grew right down to the edge of the river, some plunging great, twisting roots into its rapids and clinging defiantly. Mouse trembled as she drew near. She did not like the looks of this forest, so different from the mountain jungles in which she had herded goats as a child. There, she'd had only to worry about wolves and panthers stalking in the shadows.

Here, she felt she must fear the shadows themselves.

"*Follow the blue star,*" the Silent Lady had said, "*without turning to the right or left.*"

Mouse looked up at the gorge wall and thought there was no way she would ever climb out again in any case. The river could not be crossed. There was no option left to her. She must do as she was told. She must deliver her message to Etanun, or she must perish in the attempt.

"Fire burn," she whispered. "Fire purify."

She stepped into the shadows of the trees.

Immediately she knew, without knowing how she knew, that she had stepped outside of her world. The river still ran close by, but she sensed that if she turned, she would not see the open gorge behind her. She felt the forest surrounding her, extending forever, unimpeded by gorge walls, overshadowing the river, wherever it flowed.

She was beyond her own world. And in this place of thick-woven tree branches, she could not see the blue star.

Mouse stood like a statue, not daring even to breathe. If she breathed, she would scream; and if she screamed, she would panic; and if she panicked, she would run and run and run and never stop.

She peered up, trying to see between the branches and leaves, and she couldn't help wondering if there even was a sky beyond them, much less any stars.

Should she go? Should she start walking, following the flow of the river, hoping the star, wherever it was, still led this way? "*Without turning to the right or left,*" the Silent Lady had said. But what about when the star was no longer visible? What hope or help was there for her then? Was she to sit here in the world beyond her own and . . . wait?

Mouse, standing undecided, suddenly saw a light, far away, almost hidden by the trees, so faint it might have been no more than a flickering candle. It grew steadily brighter and, she thought, drew nearer.

A whirring and shushing filled the air, as of trees speaking to one another in voices of leaves and bark and branches. Roots lifted from the soil and, grasping and coiling, pulled the trees away, parting them to create a path, and even the river itself seemed to rise up and alter its course. The ground beneath Mouse's feet shifted, though she herself remained where she stood, staring at that approach of light that was more than light, for it did not merely strike her eyes but penetrated down to places in her being that she had not known existed, perhaps that never had existed until now.

And suddenly the blue star stood before her.

In the shadows of the trees it stood, gleaming so brightly that it should have blinded her except that she did not see it with her eyes. It was not a being that could present itself in a mortal's view, so it presented itself in her heart, in the fantastical realm of her fancy, yet no less real. Its flanks were white but shone blue, and they were dappled like a starry night. A long, luxurious tail and a rich mane of light flowed like clouds behind it. Its eyes were like the depths of the sky, but also full of light and, more vividly, full of song made visible to the eyes of her heart.

Why are you following me? it said.

It spoke as though even when standing alone it still sang in unison with the whole starry host of the heavens. The sound of its voice sent her to her knees. But there were tears upon her cheeks because it was so beautiful and so good. And its body was fire from its dainty, cloven hooves to the tip of its graceful horn, which rose from the middle of its forehead like a battle standard.

I watched you, it said. *I watched you even as I danced across your mortal sky, and I lingered long after I should have pursued my brothers and sisters into the west. I watched you follow me. But you are no sailor, and you are no hero. So tell me why.*

She could not speak before such a being. Even in her wildest dreams of stepping into the presence of the Flame, Mouse had not imagined this feeling of utter insignificance that overwhelmed her now.

Those deep-as-night eyes blinked slowly, long lashes covering their depths for an instant. Then it spoke again.

Poor little thing. It has been so long since I spoke to a mortal. I forget how frail you are. Does this help?

Without any apparent change taking place, a different being stood before Mouse. It was still a strange, phenomenal creature, but not so terrible, not so overwhelming. Rather than moving and existing in a place beyond worlds, its form was solid and it stood upon the ground. It reminded Mouse, rather oddly, of nothing so much as a goat.

Not entirely a goat, of course. Perhaps a little of a deer as well, and of a much larger animal for which she had no name. The feet were cloven, prettily feathered, the legs delicate and thin. A beard wisped daintily from the end of its chin, and the tail was long and sweeping. Its face was much longer, much more noble than a goat's, and its ears were upright, oval, and soft as kitten fur. White lashes framed its black eyes, and the flanks, still dappled, were faintly blue.

It was a beautiful, frightening, wonderful creature. A desperate feeling, rather like love, rose in Mouse's breast, and she found herself exclaiming, "Oh! What are you? Please tell me!"

The beast looked down and around at itself and flicked its ears, rather like a shrug. When it spoke, its voice was singular, no longer the voice of millions, and she heard it with her ears, not her heart.

"I suppose, in this form, you would call me a unicorn," it said.

Mouse had heard of unicorns before. But she had always believed they were creatures of the water, for so her Granna had told her. This, however, was a creature unbound by water, fire, air, or stone. "You're lovely!" she said.

It bowed its head as though embarrassed. "I feel a little lost," it said, "without my brothers, my sisters. It's not often that I take on flesh. Stars don't, you know, especially not for mortals. I only do so now because you are a pure maiden. Would you like to touch me?"

How did it know that she was longing with all her heart to plunge her hands into the silky strands of its mane, to wrap her arms around that powerful neck? Though the thought frightened as much as thrilled, Mouse was on her feet in a second. It bowed its head, and she shied away from that sharp horn. Then, her fear stepping back to make room for her desire, she put out her hands and stroked the velvety nose and gently caressed the soft oval ears.

"I love you," she said without a thought.

It chuckled. "Little maid, you don't know what love means. But you will. Now tell me, what is your name?"

She told him. She had not told anyone her true name since she came to the Citadel, and she was certain no one but Granna remembered it. But she told the unicorn without a thought. And it nodded solemnly, accepting the knowledge with quiet grace. What a strange sensation to be known by name to a star!

"What is yours?" she asked then.

"You could not say my name," it said. "You do not speak the language of stars, nor have you or your kind heard our songs since the last House of Lights was closed. But you may call me Cé Imral, as the Faerie folk do."

She whispered it. The name was strange on her tongue, and she stumbled over it. The unicorn laughed, a sound at once like water and fire and springtime. "Close enough," it said. "But tell me, mortal, why are you following me?"

Her trust complete, and her fingers twined with white-blue strands of silk, Mouse told the star. She told it everything about the Silent Lady and the dungeon and the Diggings and the message for Etanun.

"Ah!" Cé Imral said when she spoke of Etanun and the sword. "Of course. I have sung this chorus and will sing it again, but for you the time has come. The Murderer will return, the Smallman will claim Fireword, and kingdoms will, for a breath, be established. This is much for you to understand, is it not?"

Mouse did not understand, but she didn't really care. "Can you help me?" she asked. "Can you lead me to Etanun?"

"Yes. But if I do, will you then fulfill what you have purposed in your heart?" Cé Imral asked.

Mouse bowed her head, wondering why she should suddenly feel ashamed. "I must . . . I must do as I am told. I am not a great lady, and I am not wise or strong. I must do as I am told."

"As must I," said the unicorn. It tossed its mane, and Mouse stepped away, though without fear now that she'd touched it. It could have run her through with that glorious horn, and she would not have made a sound.

"You stand in the Between," Cé Imral said. "On both sides of you are the Near World and the Far, all close and all more distant than you can imagine. I will lead you through the half-light and bring you to where Etanun awaits your coming. But once there, I will return to the heavens and you will be alone."

Mouse nodded. "I understand."

"No. You don't."

And the unicorn turned and started through the Wood. The trees backed away, bowing reverently after it, and the river laughed and waved as though pleased to see an old friend; for rivers, even the deadly ones, love the stars and feel close kinship with the sky. Mouse followed in the unicorn's wake. They did not move in Time, or not in a flow of Time familiar to Mouse. But she was not afraid, though perhaps she should have been. When she dared snatch a look away from the unicorn's streaming tail, she caught glimpses of vistas she had never imagined, waterfalls and forest glades and desolate shadows. Sometimes she even thought she peered into other worlds entirely, so strange and unearthly were the sights she saw.

At last the unicorn turned to her, and those deep eyes filled her vision, love driving out her fear.

"Here I leave you. Here you will find what you seek," Cé Imral said.

The next moment, it was gone.

Mouse found herself standing on the edge of a small, sparse copse. Dead leaves of autumn littered the ground, and a sudden biting wind blew through the branches. She was no longer in the vast Wood. She stood on the borders of low fields, gazing out across a winter-tinted landscape to a river, a rise, and a high stone castle, above which gleamed a shining blue star.

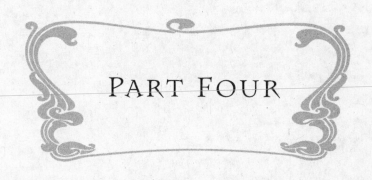

PART FOUR

GODDESS

1

Fire! Fire! Flame at Night!

Hri Sora, they called me, and they spoke rightly! My delicate feathers burned away, replaced by the mighty sweep of leathery dragon's wings, and the boiling of jealousy and rage inside me was replaced by a furnace that demolished my heart and pumped lava through my veins.

A woman's body cannot support such heat, so mine gave way into the scale-armored form of a vast dragon. I became that which had lurked deep inside me since I first drew breath.

"Sister. Child," the Dragon called me. "My beautiful firstborn."

The cat sat with his eyes half closed, his tail curled about his paws as it twitched slightly at the tip. Surrounding him was the Haven, a place of comfort, of familiarity, yet it was made strange now. Without Imraldera, it felt as foreign to him as the court of the Mherking.

He watched Mouse as she told her tale. He was not naturally intuitive, for cats tend to live in the moment, and the moment is focused on self. But he was more than a cat these days. He was a Knight of Farthest Shore, and as such he had begun to learn what it meant to put himself in another's shoes. Not like Imraldera. No one, he believed with something close to religious conviction, could possibly be as empathetic as she, able to weep at the death of monsters, able to look in the face of hell's hounds and see something to love!

But he was learning.

It wasn't love he felt for Mouse as he watched her, however, only deep suspicion. He flicked one ear when she told of the unicorn. In all the long ages of his immortal life, he had never seen one of Hymlumé's children come down from the heavens. Yet the girl's face was full of earnest honesty that he could not help believing. Who could invent a lie so fantastic?

The cat's tail lashed once, then wrapped tightly against his body. If only Imraldera were here! She would know what to believe and what not. Or would she?

After all, she'd believed the Murderer.

Mouse came to the end of her story. Other than when speaking of the unicorn, she'd kept her eyes downcast to her folded hands, as though afraid of seeing the Haven around her, of glimpsing too much of this strange half-light world.

Or she might be feeling the pressure of Alistair's gaze, which never once left her face.

"I think you know the rest," she said quietly. "Even after returning to the mortal world, I followed the star as the Silent Lady had told me, all the way to Gaheris. And there you, sir"—she flashed Alistair the briefest of looks, though she did not meet his gaze and hastily lowered her chin—"you let me through your gates and established me in the castle keep. So I began my search for Etanun."

Alistair nodded. "Did you find him?" he asked. It was a straightforward question, but Eanrin had to chuckle a little. Up until scarcely more than a few hours ago, Alistair had not believed Etanun existed outside fiction. But he was a straightforward individual, ready to believe much sooner than he was ready to doubt.

Especially if the girl is sweet, Eanrin thought, perhaps unfairly.

Aloud he said, "Of course she found him. Have you paid no attention to recent events? She found him, and in a dramatic twist of fate he told her the heir to the sword was your diminutive cousin. Not someone reasonable, no. Etanun couldn't be bothered to pick an heir one might actually *expect* to . . ."

He trailed off and looked about the hall, as did Alistair and Mouse. For the Chronicler was nowhere to be seen.

"Dragon's teeth and tail," Eanrin muttered. "Where has the imp got off to?"

The corridors of the Haven were wondrous indeed, more wondrous by far than any description the Chronicler had ever read or copied. And they were far away from the strange tale being told, a tale that felt to him like chains as solid as Corgar's clamping on his neck and weighing him down until he could scarcely move.

Smallman.

Flame at Night.

It was all too much, so he sought the soothing quiet of the halls, stately forests of shimmering green. Here sunlight touched the leaves and turned them golden, and sometimes they looked like colored-glass windowpanes. Not a single bird's song disturbed the silence.

He came at last to the library of Dame Imraldera. There he stood, his breath quite taken from his body, and stared.

For many years, by the Near World's count, the lady Knight of the Farthest Shore had been at work on this room. When she and Sir Eanrin, newly knighted, had made their way to the Haven of the Brothers Ashiun and rebuilt what had been left in ruin, they found the Wood encroached deeply on the once-solid structure. But the Haven was still there, beneath the growth, beneath the shadows.

So, Imraldera and Eanrin had set to work, binding back the trees gently, so as not to hurt them, but firmly, making clear that this was not their domain; it belonged to the Lumil Eliasul. The Wood had obeyed. Though Imraldera was no more than a slip of a mortal girl, the trees had backed away, drawing their shadows with them. Not even Eanrin, an immortal who had lived since before these trees put down their first tentative roots, could command their obedience as thoroughly as she did.

And so they reclaimed the Haven, and Imraldera built her library.

When she first entered the service of the Lumil Eliasul, she could neither read nor write in any known language. But she had quickly learned. "Records must be kept," she had told Eanrin. "We cannot have the worlds forgetting as they are so inclined to do. And since *you* can't be bothered to take time from your songster ways, I shall have to do it."

Now the great pillared room in which the Chronicler stood was filled with scroll after scroll of her hard labor. Prophecies both fulfilled and unfulfilled, legends of heroes and monsters, true stories, false stories, stories that were both. All could be found in this library, where Dame Imraldera could always be found at her work.

Except today. As the Chronicler entered into that solemn glory of written words, he felt the lack of the dame though he had never met her. The lady knight who lay curled up in a dungeon crawl space, lost in the darkness of mortality, lured away, perhaps, by the cunning petitions of the Murderer.

For how could anything this so-called Etanun said be true? If all else proved real, and there was a sword and a lost House of Lights and a twice-dead dragon alive for a third time . . . if all that was true, how could it be that he, the rejected son of a mortal earl, was the heir to Halisa?

It must be a lie. And the Murderer, Etanun, must be no more than a wicked trickster playing games with mortal lives.

The Chronicler approached Imraldera's desk with something close to reverence and fear. It was made of cherrywood, but the wood looked alive, a tree twined into the shape of a desk. The dame's work lay across it.

Written in Faerie letters was the same rhyme he had found copied in Lady Pero's hand.

> *The heir to truth, blest blade of fire*
> *He finds in shielded shadow light.*

"An impressive sight, eh, Chronicler?"

The Chronicler turned around, startled, and saw Eanrin sitting in cat form at the far end of the tall chamber. "Rivals your own library, doesn't it?"

Paling, the Chronicler stepped away from the desk. He glanced at the trove surrounding him. "I never thought to see so much captured in writing," he said. "How many scribes did it take to document all that I see here?"

"One," said the cat. "But she's an industrious little bee."

"It must have taken . . ." The Chronicler shook his head, staggered at the enormity of work surrounding him. "It must have taken decades!"

The cat shrugged, twitching both his tail and ears. "I couldn't say. We don't keep track of Time as such here in the Between. It might have been decades. It might have been minutes. Really, does it matter?"

"Perhaps not," the Chronicler said, glancing again at the wonders around him: the tall trees, the piled scrolls. He looked at the parchment on the desk, the rhyme with which he had become so familiar over the years, as though it haunted him. "Smallman," he whispered. A shudder passed through his frame. "So that is supposed to be . . . me."

"How should I know?" said the cat. "I didn't write that one. I've written much fine poetry in my day, I'll have you know, mostly romantic verse, all excellent quality, bound to make my name even in the Near World one day. But I don't write nursery rhymes."

"I don't believe in any of this," the Chronicler said, staring at the words on the page. As the speech of Faerie made itself understood, so did this fey writing. The characters seemed to rise off the page as he looked at them, rearranging themselves and playing through his mind like images, like tastes, like smells. It was the way music speaks without language but communicates more than words.

Yet the end result was the same. The end result was the nursery rhyme of his childhood.

The Chronicler drew a long breath. "I don't believe in chosen ones. In prophecies. In destinies."

Eanrin padded into the room. "Neither do I," he said mildly. "On principle, I'm against them. Inconvenient, nonsensical things, and a cat does like to be master of his own fate, you know?" Then he put his ears back and gave the Chronicler a pointed look. "But what I believe or don't believe has little to do with the truth of the matter."

The Chronicler ground his teeth. "I've fought against believing things I could not understand, and I laughed at those who clung to Faerie stories."

His voice was bitter as black tea. "Faerie stories are the last thing the likes of me needs to believe."

"Likes of you?" said the cat. "You mean, mortal?"

"I mean like *me*," the Chronicler snarled, fixing a glare upon the cat. "Malformed. Disfigured. An accident." His face was like the old earl's in that moment, the face of a warrior, but a defeated warrior who had fought a long, losing battle. A face all the more terrible for its youth.

The cat sat silent, his eyes slits, his ears quirked back as though he was offended. When at last he spoke, his voice was silky soft. "What is it with you mortals and your fixation on *size*? Do you think your stature has anything to do with anything?" Then he spoke like a knife. "Look at me!"

Suddenly he stood up, and his cat form dropped away into that of a man. The Chronicler, though he had seen the transformation once before, fell back against the desk, clutching at its legs for support.

"Take a good look at me!" the cat-man said, indicating his tall, straight, golden self, clad in brilliant red. But when he turned his head, he was a cat, small and furry. Just as the Haven was both a structure built of stone and mortar and a woodland glade of trees and moss, the cat was all cat, the man was all man, and both were simultaneously Eanrin.

"Look closer still," said the cat-man. "Do you know what I am? I am Eanrin of Rudiobus, Bard of Iubdan, one of the little people, one of the Merry Folk. Do you see?"

And the Chronicler saw what he had not seen before. Even as a man, Eanrin was unbound by size. He could be small enough to stand in the palm of a mortal's hand; he could be tall enough to speak eye to eye with the great centaurs. But he was still, no matter his size, Eanrin.

"Do you understand, mortal?" Eanrin said. "We Faerie know it's the spirit that counts, and all else is malleable. Beauty or ugliness; brawn or frailty; height or lack thereof—these appearances can be exchanged with scarcely a thought! But the truth . . . now, that's another issue. The truth of the thing, the person behind what you perceive with any of your paltry five senses . . . Creature of dust, it's the truth that counts! And you'll rarely find more truth than in Faerie tales."

With those words, the golden man dwindled into the golden cat, and try as he might, the Chronicler could perceive him as nothing else. But he was still Eanrin, and he smiled, pleased with himself.

"That wasn't a half-bad monologue. Do you find yourself inspired to new heights of ambition?"

The Chronicler passed a hand over his face, feeling both very young and very tired. "I can't believe the impossible," he whispered as though trying to convince himself against what he had just witnessed. "A man can't be big and small at once. He *can't* be a freak and a hero."

The cat glared. "Do you believe in justice?" he asked.

The Chronicler hesitated. Then, only once, he nodded.

"Do you believe in mercy?" pressed the cat.

"Yes."

"Ha!" Eanrin lashed his tail again. "What an impossible contradiction! Ha!"

Then his voice lowered and was, for him, gentle when he spoke. "But a man who can display both justice and mercy is the very reflection of the Lumil Eliasul, the reflection of the divine. In the divine, we find the satisfaction of contradictions. We find the wholeness of broken things and belief in the impossible." The cat shook his head. "Poor mortal! Your kind has not heard the Sphere Songs in so long, you've become deaf without realizing it."

The Chronicler said nothing.

"You must start believing the impossible," the cat persisted. "If you're to have any hope of 'saving the day,' as it were."

The Chronicler set his jaw. "So I'm to abandon my home to monsters, to travel across worlds to fetch some magic sword, all for a fool's errand?"

"Would you prefer to storm the castle gates and challenge Corgar to single combat as you are?" The cat snorted. "Now, *there's* a fool's errand!"

"I'm abandoning Gaheris." Too ashamed to speak loudly, he whispered, "I'm abandoning Leta."

The cat's whiskers twitched. His cupped ears picked up more than the words, and his sharp eyes saw more still. "Leta, eh?" he said. "Is she that pale little mortal maid I glimpsed in the library last summer? The one who's sweet on you?"

The Chronicler's look would have frozen the heart of any man not a cat. "Don't mock me," he growled.

"Who's mocking?" The cat's tail curled questioningly above his head. "I'm the Bard of Rudiobus, romantic poet of the ages, famed devotee of Lady Gleamdrené Gormlaith, and I know lovelorn when I see it. For instance, I can see that your cousin is head-over-heels-smitten with our dear Mouse, though I've made certain she doesn't realize it yet. Lumé love us, the last thing we need on this excursion is a romantic entanglement getting in the way!"

The Chronicler stared at the cat with more malice than he might have turned on a snake. "Alistair cannot love that girl," he said. "He is going to marry my lady Leta, and he is going to make her a good husband."

"You are a dense one, aren't you?" said the cat. "You've allowed this fixation on size and perceived beauties to blind you. And that, small man, is your true affliction."

With those words he stalked to the door like an actor quitting the stage. But before he quite got there, his skin shivered as though with an irritating itch. "Dragon's teeth!" he meowled, looking back at the young man once more. "One conversation! One simple, honest, true conversation, and all your questions would be answered, all your problems solved! Really, man, is that so difficult? Then you'd be free to fall into each other's arms and live your Happily Ever After. Why make it so *complicated*?"

The Chronicler gave no reply at first. It wasn't so simple; he knew that well. Even in the Faerie Realm he must recognize reality. Unlike the fey folk, he remained bound in his flawed mortal body. All he had left was his pride, a final bulwark of self-respect that prevented him from making himself a fool.

When the Chronicler spoke, his voice was almost lifeless.

"Very well, cat," he said. "I will attempt to believe the impossible. I will go seeking your Halisa. I will even believe myself a chosen one, a future king, or whatever you need me to believe so that I might hope to see the folk of Gaheris liberated from those ghastly creatures." He raised his gaze, fixing a dark glare on the cat. "But don't feed me false hopes. I will not live on dreams."

"No," said the cat. "You'd rather live on nightmares."

And with that, he left the room.

The scrubber stepped into the Wood.

It recognized him, and though it did not welcome his return, neither did it make any effort to reject him. He felt the more hostile trees withdrawing hurriedly, and he could almost hear the ripple of rumor spreading from root to root, leaf to leaf.

He hobbled, his back bent, his head low, but his pace quick, covering leagues in a stride.

Do you expect to die?

The scrubber did not startle at the voice, or voices, speaking suddenly from the empty space beside him. He did not turn. He did not wish to see, though he smiled at the welcomingly familiar presence.

"Good morrow to you, Cé," he said. "You have done a great service by me."

You mean in bringing the girl?

"Indeed," said the scrubber. "Among others. Everything is falling together rather nicely, don't you think?"

Are you afraid to answer me?

The scrubber shrugged. He looked frailer than ever, and his voice was thin when he spoke. "I'm afraid of very little anymore."

But you are afraid to see her again.

"Yes. Yes, I am. And I'm afraid of what I must do."

Then you do expect to die.

"No indeed," said the scrubber, chuckling to himself. "In fact, I rather hope to finally *live*."

The star, shining high in the vaults above, watched the old man until the Wood had quite swallowed him up.

2

I FOUND THE GIRL. *I had searched long and hard for her, following rumor, following whispers. I learned during that time to contain my fire and to walk in a form similar to my original. I wore a cloak to hide my featherless wings, which hung like a bat's at my back. No one knew what I was unless they smelled the sulfur on my breath.*

It was thus I found the girl. Was she a princess of mortals? Was she a beauty, a worthy rival to my queenly glory?

No indeed. She was a farmer's daughter, a creature of mud and labor. Her face and clothes were stained, her hands callused, and she stank of mortality.

But she sang as she worked, a simple, cheerful song of her own invention. And it was a reflection, imperfect yet lovely, of the Songs sung by the Spheres above. Her eyes shone with inner light, and despite her humble state, she was, I could see, lovely.

I hated her.

"Klara," I called.

She turned and saw me standing at the gate of her father's farm. "Good morrow," she called, her voice as charitable as it was sweet. "Do I know you?"

"No," I said.

"May I help you? Are you lost?" She approached me, her face open and kind. "I will share my supper and give you a place to lay your head, for you look weary."

They were the last words she spoke. I opened my mouth, and fire billowed forth.

I destroyed the entire farm that day, decimated that ground so that nothing should grow there evermore. Every living thing within miles fell under my flame.

Three somber figures stepped from the shelter of the Haven in the wake of the orange cat. They walked with heads bowed, as though afraid to see more of this strange Between than they must, and each face was bound up in unspoken thoughts.

Mouse's bare feet made no sound as she trod behind the cat, allowing him to choose their Path without question. After all, he knew better than she where to find her world. This journey was different from her journey with the star. Though they moved outside of Time, she still felt the presence of Time pressing in around them, and it seemed to her that the journey went on and on, though it may have been mere moments. Sometimes she thought she heard or glimpsed other beings in the surrounding shadows, beings for which she had no name.

"Fire burn," she whispered. Would all this dreadful experience serve for her purification? In the end, would the holiness achieved be worth the trial and terror?

Could she save the Silent Lady?

She felt the presence of Lord Alistair, a little to her side and behind her. She tried not to startle when he spoke.

"This Wood is something else, isn't it?"

She gave him a quick look. Although the words formed themselves into something comprehensible in her brain, the meaning escaped her. Something else? As in, something not a Wood? Well, perhaps. After all, it certainly didn't *feel* like the mountain forests of her childhood. Still, not liking to make a fool of herself, she opted not to answer.

"It gives you the feeling it's watching you," Alistair persisted, adjusting his long legs into a stride that matched hers. It was a rather lumbering gait, for she was quite short and he was obliged to keep amending his pace to stay beside her. Mouse glanced up and found him looking earnestly down at her, as though hoping for an answer. Having no answer to give, she offered a small smile. Then hastily looked at her feet again. Women of the Citadel did not smile at men. And men did not speak in a woman's presence.

"Ah, well," Alistair persisted, "perhaps you're used to it. You're quite the adventurer! Star follower, wood trekker. They could write legends about you without much trouble, couldn't they?"

Here Mouse smiled again, though she tried to stifle it. She, an adventurer? How the Citadel dwellers would laugh at the idea! Mouse the trembling, the hiding, the soft speaking . . . a legend! She rather liked the idea.

Suddenly, with more daring than she felt, she asked, "How long did you know?"

"Know what?"

Mouse licked her lips. "How long did you know that I was . . . that I wasn't . . ."

"That you weren't a boy?" There was a brightness to Alistair's voice, a cheerfulness close to a laugh that seemed strange indeed in this half-lit world between worlds. "Well," he said slowly, "if you must know, almost at once."

"What?" Her eyes widened.

"Yes," the young lord admitted, looking away bashfully. "Practically from the moment I saw you."

Mouse made herself blink. She felt a hot flush rising and hoped he wouldn't be able to see it. "I . . . I don't understand," she said. "I cut my hair."

He grinned again, rubbing the back of his neck. "It is a fine disguise," he said, and she could hear the lie in his voice despite its kindness. "You did your best, and you certainly are a ragged enough urchin."

She blushed again and couldn't look at him.

"But see here," he continued, "there are many more differences between boys and girls than . . . all that. You move like a girl. And from certain angles, you really are rather attractive."

She couldn't look at him. In fact, she wished the ground would open up and swallow her—or him—whole then and there. She could feel him watching her, and she wished he would stop.

"I thank you for your honesty," she managed. "Next time I'll be sure to . . . to take care of *certain* angles."

With that, she picked up her pace, chasing after the cat and leaving Alistair behind. He could have easily increased his stride and caught her, but his throat had gone strangely tight, and he thought maybe he'd like to be by himself for a while. Then he chuckled quietly, shaking his head. What a funny little creature that girl was!

It was the first time he'd laughed, he realized, in a long time.

This thought brought him up short. What was he doing? What was he becoming? He, the future Earl of Gaheris, destined to wed Aiven's daughter, bound to unite the earls under Gaheris's standard.

But really, what did it all matter? He bowed his head, watching his own tramping feet. How long had it been since the line between reality and dreams had blurred? How long since that same nightmare of the black path and the child and the red, gaping jaws had infiltrated his every living moment, both waking and sleeping?

"You'll never be king," he whispered.

He blinked.

And he opens his eyes to look upon the realm of his dream. He recognizes it at once, more clearly even than the haunts of his childhood. Every vivid detail: the jagged stone, the ghostly light, and the child ahead of him, turning, eyes wide with terror.

"Watch out!" the child cries, its voice bounding and rebounding in the blackness.

Then, the howling of the dogs.

He blinks again.

Alistair stood surrounded by the Wood. Ahead he saw Mouse behind Eanrin, her ragged, close-cropped head of hair held high. Beyond the cat, he saw the trees that seemed to move themselves out of their way, and he saw the deep green of forest gloom.

"My lord, are you quite well?"

The voice of the Chronicler startled him, and Alistair ground his teeth to keep down a cry as he looked around. His cousin stood behind him, watching him with concern in his eyes. "You look as though you've seen a ghost."

"You shouldn't call me that," Alistair said wearily. "I'm not your lord anymore, remember?"

The Chronicler bowed his head. "Old habits," he murmured. Then he shrugged. "Did you see something? I keep glimpsing things in the shadows myself. I don't think they can get at us as long as we're on this Path. At least I've not seen any try as yet. But we'd best not get too far behind the cat."

Alistair nodded. "Yes. Fine." And he set off with long-legged strides, making up the distance. Though his shoulder pained him where the goblin blade had bitten, he tramped on after the cat and the girl and the prophecy at the end of their journey.

And he thought to himself, *I'm going to die.*

The Chronicler stood watching the tall young lord put distance between them. His lips compressed into something between a frown and a smile. It was a wry, self-deprecating expression either way, and he sighed as he too set off to catch the others. His short legs could not bear him so fast, but he felt as though the Path itself carried him, and he knew he would not fall too far behind. Not so long as he kept moving.

There were many things in the Wood. Things he was not seeing but that rather he felt. Lining the edge of the Path, they watched him, bright eyes hidden in shade. So long as he didn't listen for them, he heard strange voices speaking in strange tongues, in words that made themselves understandable in his head.

"It's the dragon slayer!"

"Who? Who do you mean?"

"There, silly! It's the Opener of Doors!"

And someone sang like a chittering insect in a high, shrill voice:

> *"Fling wide the doors of light, Smallman,*
> *Though furied falls the Flame at Night."*

They all believed him to be some hero. They looked at him and his ungainly form, and they saw a legend! How strange, how dreadful, how wonderful it was.

Perhaps the world was bigger than he had realized. Perhaps he had always limited himself to things that could be perceived by his senses rather than realizing that his perceptions were nothing more than restraints. Perhaps there were worlds and ways and wonders beyond anything he had imagined.

But that didn't, in the end, make a difference.

The worlds may be bigger and grander, but he was still only himself. If anything, he realized now to a much greater extent his own insignificance. At least in the confines of Gaheris he'd had his realm: the library, the books; and he'd had his weapon: his ability to read and write. He could keep himself separate and see himself as superior despite his deficiencies.

Now he saw that even those things he had clung to—his wits, his talents, his hard-earned abilities—were nothing. They were no more useful than his paltry limbs. Here, in these new worlds, he was dwarfed in spirit as well as in height.

He should have stayed behind. He should have made some daring, foolish, useless gesture and been killed. Then he wouldn't have to keep on living. He wouldn't have to watch himself try and, inevitably, fail.

The Path beneath his feet was no longer mossy or leaf strewn. The Chronicler realized this slowly, then stopped and looked around, surprised. He stood on white rock, but rock harder than chalk. Above him, the trees had retreated and the half-light had given way to the full light of day. He was obliged to shield his eyes. Where were the others? He couldn't see them for the light, and he wondered if he should call out to them.

He took a step. And he found that he stood on the edge of a precipice.

The Chronicler's head whirled with a sudden dizzying sensation of height that was so much more than height, he could scarcely take it in. He saw clouds drifting below his feet, far away, like tufts of sheep's wool tossing on a breeze.

Beneath the clouds, he saw the North Country.

How he knew this, he could not say. It was not like the maps in the Gaheris library, which were flat, indistinct, and often inaccurate. Every detail, color, shadow, valley, and crest presented itself with a precision the

Chronicler's eyes should not have been able to perceive, which dazzled and frightened him all at once. He could see Gaheris, every stone of the castle, though the distance between him and it was beyond his ability to reckon. He could see Hanna winding, every ripple and wavelet. He saw Aiven, which he had never before seen in person but which he recognized with a lurch of familiarity, like a father seeing his child's face after a long absence, unfamiliar and yet dearly familiar at once. Every earldom, every fief, every hamlet and village and port . . . they presented themselves beneath the Chronicler's vision, and he knew that he loved them. He loved the North Country with a love that was painful and vital and true.

And Gaheris he loved most of all.

But Gaheris was overrun. Even at this distance the Chronicler saw the cloud of smoke and dust, clear signs of the goblins' desolating work.

"Fear not, small man," said a voice behind him. "You will see your people free."

The Chronicler whirled in place. A tall man stood behind him, but his height was all he could discern, for he could not see him clearly. The light in this place was much too bright.

"Who are you?" the Chronicler demanded.

"I am the one who chose you."

"Etanun?" the Chronicler said. "The Murderer?"

But he knew even as he said it that this was wrong. The voice was not that of a murderer.

"No," said the stranger. "Etanun did not choose you. He merely found you. Much is given and revealed to my servant, but it is not for him to choose his course or that of another. He has not the clarity of vision."

"And you have? You have the right to choose destinies, to direct lives?"

There was a smile in the voice that replied. "I, who have named the stars and given them the patterns of their dance across the sky, also named you and gave you the pattern of the dance that is your life. I have the right. I am the right."

The Chronicler wanted to back away, but there was only the precipice behind him and the great expanse of the North Country beneath his feet. He whispered a name he had seen only once or twice in the oldest, most-forgotten documents, but which was in his heart, ready to be spoken.

"Lumil Eliasul."

"And you," said the stranger, "are Florien Ferox-son. Smallman, sword bearer, dragon slayer. Future king."

The Chronicler could not breathe. He felt as though the depths behind him threatened to drag him down, and he was afraid.

"Why did you choose me?" He could scarcely speak. "I am nothing. Unacknowledged by my own father. I am the last person anyone would choose! I am the least."

"And in you my might will be made visible to all people," the stranger replied in a voice more golden than sunlight, more silver than moonlight, more varied than all the starry host. "When the people of the Near World see your triumph over the dragon and the goblin, they will know it was through my doing. And they will hear the Sphere Songs once again."

But the Chronicler shook his head. "Alistair. He's your hero. He was chosen ahead of me, and the earls will choose him still."

"I did not choose Alistair to walk your path," said the stranger. "His life and his death are not your business. Your business is to do the task for which you have been called, to become the man you were born to be."

"I was born an accident," the Chronicler said.

"You were born for a purpose," the stranger replied, "and in the best form to fulfill that purpose."

Suddenly the Chronicler felt hands upon his shoulders, and his gaze was fixed by a pair of eyes—eyes of no color and all colors, deeper than the drop behind him. He thought he could fall into those eyes and lose himself and be better for the loss.

"The time is near," said the voice, which rang in the air around him, the wholeness of all voices joined into one. As though created by that voice, an image formed within the Chronicler's mind. An image of a black stone, beneath which roared the waters of many conjoined rivers.

Protruding from that stone, a carved sword.

Halisa.

As familiar to the Chronicler as his own two hands and as rightly a part of himself. He longed to reach out and take it, to latch hold of the completeness his life had lacked, though he had scarcely admitted it to himself.

But it was only a vision. And, a bitter part of his mind tried to insist, that was all it ever would be.

Then the voice of the stranger crashed through his brain, and all else was forgotten:

"The flame of the Dragonwitch draws to its end. Twice she has been killed in fire, in hatred, in the heat of furious passion. The third death she will die in water, in the sweeping of true life, which the death-in-life she knows cannot resist.

"Call up the rivers, Smallman King. Call them up from the deep places and overwhelm the fire with living water."

As that voice spoke, the words turned to water themselves, and they swept down upon the Chronicler, catching him up and bearing him over the precipice. He screamed and felt the thrill of a fall that never came. For the water carried him up, higher and higher, into the light that sang a song he had always known but never before heard.

Then he was standing on a small boulder, surrounded by trees and the stunned silence of the watching Wood Between.

The Chronicler gasped and teetered for a moment before he fell from the stone and landed in the tall green ferns below. He picked himself up, his limbs shaking, brushing bracken from his sleeves. Water dripped down his face. He wiped it away, then stood a moment, staring at the drops that gathered in the palm of his hand. They gleamed as though touched by sunlight, but there was no sunlight this deep in the Wood.

"Ah! There you are, fool mortal!"

The Chronicler clenched his fist, hiding the water, and turned to face the wrath of Sir Eanrin. The knight wore his man's form, but his face was that of a snarling moggy.

"Have you *any* idea how dangerous it is to walk the Wood without a Path? Do you have the *slightest* notion how quickly you could be sucked away like a duckling into rapids, never to be seen or heard from again?"

The Chronicler offered no explanation but stood staring at the cat-man, whose quick eyes suddenly picked up details his ire had nearly missed.

Eanrin frowned. "You're all . . . wet. Did you fall in a stream or find yourself a thundershower?"

The Chronicler shook his head. Drops of water fell from the ends of his hair, spattering the ferns beneath his feet.

Eanrin regarded him uneasily. Then he put out a swift hand and grasped him by the shoulder, propelling him back the way he had come. "Stay on the Path," he said, "and don't wander off on your own. I might not be able to find you next time."

Trotting to keep up, the Chronicler stole a glance into his hand, uncurling his fingers. The sparkling water still rested there, like a quiet pool. As he looked at it, he thought he heard a voice in the depths of his heart saying:

"*Call up the rivers, Smallman King.*"

3

I SET UPON THE REST OF THE NEAR WORLD with a fury it had never before seen. Fire from the sky rained upon mortal heads. Across the nations I flew, and wherever I saw the glow of Asha shining through the open doors of a House of Lights, I flamed. My fire burned and consumed those lofty Houses, leaving smoldering rubble in my wake. Nothing could stop me. No one would dare.

Until Etanun found me.

Gaheris rang with the sound of stone on stone, and the air was thick with dust and destruction. Slaves linked together in long lines broke their fingers and bruised their arms as noble and serf alike tore apart the walls of the castle and carted them, stone by stone, through the gates and across the meadowlands. There they tossed them in unsightly heaps down to the riverbank below.

Leta, her mourning gown tattered, her hair straggling down to her waist, worked with the others. Her body had long since stopped shrinking at the crack of goblin whips, so often did she hear them, followed by the cries of men and women. Keeping her head down, she gathered into a rough-woven sack the broken stones men tossed down from the walls and hauled it over her shoulder to the river drop.

Two days ago she had wondered: *Why? Why would they do this? Why would they tear apart Gaheris?*

She no longer wondered. Her mind was too dulled with dust, with lack of food or water. Her muscles screamed; her bones strained. It was the third day, and all her questions had vanished. There was nothing but stone, dirt, grit, and the aches of slavery hitherto unknown.

Sometimes she heard the goblins talking among themselves.

"The Murderer misled our captain. He misled our queen."

"If that's true, we're not the ones to tell them. Drive the mortals and keep your mouth shut!"

"They'll never find the House of Lights in this place. Maybe it never existed?"

"Do you want Corgar to send your head rolling?"

Corgar.

The name was enough to make Leta's blood run cold. Sometimes she saw him, the dreadful goblin leader, standing on the walls above and looking down. She remembered all too clearly the close proximity of his ugly face, the cold of his blade against her neck. She hoped those searching eyes of his did not fall upon her. If once they did, he might remember his vow to the Chronicler, his vow to take her life when he was ready.

And she wondered: *Does the Chronicler live?*

Winter's iron-gray sky loomed above Gaheris, and chill winds blew in from the distant sea. The goblins with their thick hides did not seem to notice it. But Leta trembled, and her fingers were so numb she could scarcely feel the bite of the sharp stones as she gathered them into her sack. She looked about sometimes for her father in the crowd. Once or twice she glimpsed him and was pleased, though she could hardly say why, to know that he was not dead.

Lady Mintha, mute and bedraggled as any scullery drudge, worked in chains not four feet from Leta herself.

Sometimes that great lady wept and cursed as she worked; her back was scored by several lashes of goblin whips. Leta tried to be sorry for her. But she remembered the look on Mintha's face when, standing over Ferox's deathbed, she had given the command, *"Bring the dwarf to me."*

When she thought of that, all sympathy fled Leta's heart.

But now, on the third day, she hadn't the strength left for resentment or pity. Indeed, Leta began to wonder if she would ever feel anything again.

"Where is it?"

The voice rumbled above her head. Leta looked up. On top of the wall under which she worked, mortal men cowered, their tools of destruction clutched close as Corgar strode through their midst, his face a dreadful sight to behold.

"Where is it?" he growled, his voice louder this time. Others around Leta stopped their work, staring up at that towering form. He paced like a caged animal, his knife in his hand.

He turned suddenly to the nearest goblin, snatching the brute by the throat and dragging him up to his own face. *"Where is it?"* he bellowed.

"We're driving the beasts as fast as we can!" the goblin cried. "We'll find it, captain, I swear, if it can be found!"

"It *must* be found!" With a snarl, Corgar threw the goblin from him. The poor creature scrambled on the edge of the wall and nearly plummeted down to Hanna, flowing far below. Even that fall might not have hurt his stone hide, but he clutched the balustrade, his eyes so wide they might have dropped from his head as he turned to his ranting master.

"It *must* be found!" Corgar repeated, slashing the air with his knife. "Do you realize what will happen if it is not? If Queen Vartera does not receive her prize? Do you think *I* am going to take the fall for this failure? Eh?"

The luckless goblin had no answer. Corgar tore a piece of the wall out with his bare hands and hurled it into the inner courtyard. It smashed on the rock below, and shards struck the nearest slaves. Their pathetic wails seemed to calm him a little. He was, after all, still master here.

"There must be another way." His voice was almost despairing. Leta stood with her back to the wall beneath the scaffolding on which he stood, her heart racing, hoping he would not somehow sense her presence. "They must know something more that they aren't telling us," he persisted. "They're useless maggots, but they can't have forgotten their own heritage so quickly!"

The poor goblin still clinging to the balustrade spoke hesitantly. "They have a library."

"What?" Corgar said. "What did you say?"

"They have a library," said the unfortunate goblin, wishing to heaven he was down below with the other slave drivers. Dragon's flame, he'd be happy to be hauling rubble with the slaves rather than endure a moment more of Corgar's stare! "Where they keep records of deaths and births and the like. We found it two days back, and it's more writing than we've ever seen."

"And?" Corgar demanded. "Do they have records of the House of Lights?"

"Perhaps," said the goblin. "There were pictures that looked likely. But—"

"But what?"

"None of us can read the mortal writing."

Leta believed Corgar would take his stone knife and hack the goblin's face in two. The monster turned, however, and looked out into the inner courtyard once more, his teeth grinding like mortar and pestle. He gazed upon the little people crawling below him, and he hated the sight of them, hated the smell of them.

"Who among you can read?" he cried. His voice overwhelmed the shouts of the slave drivers, the thick thudding of stone chains, and the growl of breaking rock. All eyes turned to where he stood above.

"I need a mortal who can discern the scratchings of your language," he said. "Stand forth, any of you who can read for me!"

Pale faces exchanged glances. Leta, her heart beating a furious pace in her breast, crouched down into a ball.

Some daring soul whispered, "The Chronicler?" But the whisper swiftly hushed. Throats and lungs thick with dust, none dared speak out.

"So he must be dead," Leta whispered, her lips forming the words, though she made no sound. "He must be dead, or they would have him read."

Her heart sank like a dead weight.

Corgar surveyed the blank dullness below him. Suddenly he leapt from the wall, falling like a bolt from the sky and landing with a crash upon the stone below, which broke beneath the impact. He crouched, recovering himself, then strode forward and grabbed the nearest mortal to him. Leta, her eyes flying wide, saw who it was he grabbed, and her heart bounded into a frightful pace.

Corgar lifted his knife and, swinging Lady Mintha off her feet, held her suspended before all those gathered. "I'll gut you all," he cried, "one by one, beginning with this one. That, or you can tell me who among you reads!"

Keep your mouth shut, her practical side begged. *Keep it shut, fool girl!*

But her other side responded, *And watch him kill Alistair's mother before your eyes?*

Leta fell forward, dragging her chains behind. She could make only a few paces, but it was enough movement to catch Corgar's eye. He turned to her, and she saw the recognition on his face.

"I can read," she said. "Please, let the lady go."

Corgar stared at her. "Of course," he said. He dropped Mintha, who fell at his feet, shuddering and scrabbling uselessly at broken stones. "Of course. It must be you."

Goblins stepped forward on either side of Leta. One of them grabbed her arm while another began fumbling with her heavy chains. She stood frozen beneath Corgar's gaze, wishing to break free but unable to do so. It wasn't until the goblin holding her arm dragged her away that she felt herself liberated of those stone-hard eyes.

Someone grabbed her other hand.

She turned. For an instant she saw Lady Mintha. For an instant she saw urgency in that once-beautiful face. A coldness was pressed into her hand, and her fingers closed about it instinctively.

Then the instant passed, and Leta was dragged from the cold inner courtyard into the frozen keep. Up the stairs they led her and down a passage she knew well but which had grown unfamiliar and now stank of goblins. She hadn't the time even to look at what Mintha had given her. But she knew. She felt its contours in her hand.

It was a key.

4

*H*E STRODE INTO MY VISION ONE NIGHT *even as I reveled in the destruction of yet another House, high on a cold mountain. I sat amid the debris, fountaining my flame to the sky, when I heard that voice I knew so well calling to me.*

"Dragon!"

I turned. I saw Etanun standing there with his sword upraised.

"Dragon," he bellowed, and there was a fury of passion in his voice. "You will die for the death you have dealt!"

"And who will see to that?" I asked.

"I!" he replied. "I shall kill you now!"

"Kill me, then," I replied, letting my fire spill forth.

We fought there on the scene of that destruction. And though my flame had never been hotter, it could not prevail against the brilliance of Halisa. I was foolish and I was angry, and I gave him an opening. Driven by rage, by vengeance, he drove that sword into my heart.

It was no more pain than I had already experienced twice at his hand. I
scarcely cared even as I fell, crashing into the ruins of the House.
I died my first death.

Mouse and Alistair stood where Eanrin had left them beneath the shelter
of an oak tree, which the cat-man had told them was "kindly enough, but
don't tease it."

With this warning, he had vanished, and the two of them stood, not
speaking and carefully not looking at each other. They could feel shadows
creeping along the forest floor, sliding smoothly over moss and stump and
twig, reaching out to them. Not necessarily malicious, but curious like
sniffing puppies, ready to growl or wag a tail at a moment's notice.

Alistair glanced toward the girl, who stood with her hands folded—an
attitude of prayer, perhaps. Of all the otherworldly things surrounding
him, he somehow felt that she was the most otherworldly of all, though
she was as mortal as he.

He wondered suddenly if he would live long enough to know her.

The young lord clenched his teeth, his fine face suddenly vicious. Just
then he would have liked to take up his sword and hurl himself into an
enemy, any enemy, be it real or imaginary, so he could feel that he was
alive, so he could feel that there was yet some purpose in his being.

He turned to Mouse, and though she did not look at him, the muscles
in her cheek tightened and she was aware of his gaze.

"I know," Alistair said, "I probably shouldn't say this."

She did not turn or move.

"After all, it's hardly the time," Alistair continued, "what with my family
home overrun with monsters, my mother captured, possibly dead, and us
wandering through other worlds that shouldn't exist. . . ."

His voice trailed away. He thought of the smoke above Gaheris. He
thought of Lady Mintha, the last he'd seen her, her face pale with fury as
she watched her dream for her child snatched away at a dying man's whim.
He thought of the earls, his shame, and the face of his strange, small cousin.

He thought of his dream.

Mouse, stealing a glance, found that Alistair no longer looked at her but stared instead at his own feet. The scar beneath his torn shirt looked white and dreadful in the half-light.

"Yes, well," Alistair finished at last, "when I think about it, it's not the time at all. Forget I said anything."

The next moment, Eanrin came storming back, the Chronicler following, shamefaced. "Well, now that our fine little king has had a lovely stroll through the dulcet forest glades, shall we continue?" the cat-man snarled and stalked ahead, looking more like an affronted tom than ever, despite his human shape.

"Where did you go?" Mouse asked the Chronicler as the three of them fell into step behind Eanrin. She noted the dampness on his clothes and the water clinging to his hair.

He answered only with a shrug and a dismissive, "I fell behind."

With this and no other excuse offered, the three mortals proceeded in silence.

Mouse kept her gazed fixed upon the small form of the Chronicler, determined he should not wander off again. She noticed how even in the midst of this company he kept himself aloof, as if he believed that he moved in his own separate world where none of the others could reach him. It was a false attitude. For all the outward show of armor, Mouse thought it covered little more than a tender heart, easily battered, easily broken.

She frowned. Had the scrubber misled her? Had she been wrong to believe that wizened, smelly old man to be the fabled Etanun? She thought of powerful Stoneye, reaching out to the great sword one moment, lying dead the next. And this little man, weak as a child, was supposed to do what Stoneye could not? He was supposed to carry the sword from the chamber, to bear it into the presence of the goddess? He would scarcely be able to budge it from the stone! It was too much.

But he was all the hope she had.

The Land Behind the Mountains was separated from the Between and the realms of Faerie by the many rivers that cut across its territory. The last time he was there, Eanrin had recognized the magical quality of those rivers—a protective barrier set in place by someone concerned for the mortals dwelling within. But of course, there were always ways to get around such protections.

Now Eanrin felt the Near World close at hand.

He stopped and waited for the mortals to catch up. When they hesitated, he beckoned impatiently. "Come closer, little ones," he said. "Nothing to be afraid of."

"Well, there's you," said Alistair, folding his arms and scowling at the cat-man.

Eanrin didn't respond. He turned to Mouse. "We're close to your world," he said. "Do you see the gate?"

Mouse looked around. She saw nothing but Wood and more Wood. There was no sign of a break in the trees, no sign of a gorge. "There was a river where I came in," she said.

"That's nice," said Eanrin.

"No, I mean, shouldn't we be looking for a river now?" she persisted.

"Maybe," the cat-man replied, shrugging. "This is the Between. A river might not always look like a river to you. I can smell your world, and I feel the barriers. But I cannot get us through, nor will I even be able to see the gate. That's part of the protection on your realm. Only one from the inside can lead folk of the Wood in. Otherwise, none of us will get past the rivers. Quite the effective deadbolt, when you think about it."

"But . . . shouldn't we be looking for a river, then?"

Eanrin bit down hard on his tongue. He wasn't generally one to restrain his words. After all, he was a poet. But he drew a long breath and reminded himself that she was, after all, young, scarcely alive yet by immortal standards. "Look closely," he said between his teeth. "Maybe you'll see your river."

Mouse turned, as did the other two, searching the solemn gloom of the trees. Nearby was a place where green bracken grew knee-high. Anything could hide there, anything at all. Even . . .

Mouse darted forward. "Wait!" Alistair cried and started after her, but Eanrin put out a restraining hand. "No, let her be. She's safe enough, and it's up to her."

Mouse waded into the ferns, stepping through the lacy green fronds. And suddenly she said, "I've found it. I've found the river!"

The others hastened to her side and looked where she parted the ferns, pointing. A small rivulet passed this way, dampening the ground as it flowed, silent as a stalking snake.

"Well done," said Eanrin. "Quickly now. Lead the way."

Mouse hastened along against the flow of the little stream, pushing aside ferns. The others followed, noticing how it seemed that the ferns moved with a gentle, flowing rhythm, though there was no breeze. Then they thought how remarkably the ferns, flowing together in indecipherable patterns along the forest floor, resembled water.

The next moment, without any apparent change taking place, they walked along the edge of a wide river. There was a break in the trees up ahead.

"Typical," Eanrin said dismissively, though the others stared in surprise. "Rivers are all such crafty creatures; you never quite know where you stand with them." He backed away from the water, keeping close behind Mouse.

Then they stood at the edge of the Wood, gazing out into the gorge but keeping to the shadows. For though the Wood was the stuff of other worlds, it felt familiar by comparison. Both Alistair and the Chronicler, come from a North Country winter, were struck with a wave of sultry heat, and the light of the sun overhead was dazzling after the gloom of the Between.

"There!" Mouse cried, pointing up the wall. "There is the path I followed down! It's narrow but not impossible, and I'm sure we can make our way up again."

Alistair and the Chronicler exchanged glances, then turned to Eanrin, who was once more in cat form. "What did she say?" Alistair asked.

They had stepped from the Between into the Near World. Once more the barrier of language separated them as effectively as any wall.

"She says you have the ears of a monkey," the cat said, and trotted after the girl, who was scrambling over river-splashed rocks in glad haste. "Hurry up, lads!"

So they climbed from the gorge. The heat of midday beat down upon them, and both Alistair and the Chronicler found the going hard. The Chronicler perhaps made better time, however, for the narrow path was better suited to his short stature than to Alistair's long limbs. The cat sped ahead of all of them, slinking between their feet and hastening to the top, where he sat like a sentinel, looking out across the tablelands.

He remembered this country over which Amarok, the Wolf Lord, had pursued him. He recognized the line of mountains, hazy in the distance, which he knew ringed this land, trapping those within like so many rabbits in a snare. A mortal land, yet the sort of place that would draw malicious Faerie kind with irrepressible attraction. Fortunate for the mortals that the rivers had been set in place, cutting them off from the Far World as effectively as the mountains cut them off from their own kind.

But the Flame at Night had gotten through, and Eanrin could already see the scars of her work. The land on which he sat was dry as bone.

Mouse scrambled the last few feet out of the gorge and stood panting beside the cat, covered from head to toe in dust. "Look!" she said, pointing. "Do you see the Citadel Spire? Do you see the glow of the Flame?"

Like a lighthouse in the distance, a red fire burned above the horizon.

"Tell me, little Mouse," Eanrin said quietly, "what has your goddess done to this land?"

Mouse swallowed with difficulty, for dust clogged her throat. "She has purified it," she said at last, her voice full of conviction.

"Has she?" Eanrin had only ever been one place before that was burned so badly. He hated to say, even to think it. But it was true nonetheless. "I could believe I stood once more in Etalpalli."

But Mouse did not know that name. She turned as first the Chronicler and then Alistair completed the long climb and stood panting, bent over, runnels of sweat cutting through the caked dirt on their faces.

"Well," said the Chronicler when at last he'd caught his breath, "here we are. What now?"

Mouse couldn't understand him, so she turned to the cat instead. "Come, we must hurry." And she started across the plain, her gaze fixed upon the red light of the tower as firmly as it had ever fixed upon the gleam of Cé Imral.

The cat hesitated. "Stay close to me," he said to the other two. "We'll keep after her for the moment, but don't get out of my sight, do you hear?"

"What a dreadful place," Alistair said, gazing with disgust at the plain around them. "How can anyone live here?"

"They can't," said the cat. "They die here."

The Chronicler shaded his eyes against the sun, staring in the direction Mouse was hastening. "Is that a storm cloud?" he asked.

The other two looked.

Then Eanrin screamed.

Such a sound cannot be made in the throat of a man or even of a cat, but only by a strange blend of the two. Fear and rage and animal instinct combined.

"Back! Back, back!" he cried, taking his man's form and grabbing both Alistair and the Chronicler by their shoulders. "Back down, into the Wood!"

The darkness swept across the sky. "Mouse!" Alistair cried, shaking free of Eanrin's grasp even as the cat-man dragged them toward the edge of the gorge. "She's too far ahead; she can't hear you!"

"It doesn't matter! Get back, hurry!"

But Alistair paid no heed. He darted out across the plain, hurrying after Mouse, shouting her name. "Dragon-eaten fool," Eanrin snarled.

"What is it?" The Chronicler, his face white, struggled to turn, to see.

"It's the Midnight," said Eanrin. "The Midnight of the Black Dogs. She sent them for us!"

5

I AM A FAERIE QUEEN; *it matters not that I gave up that title and that name. Though I reject it, queenship does not reject me. So I am gifted with three lives.*

I woke in a dark place, deep in my new Father's realm. The Netherworld, the kingdom of Death-in-Life, my true Father. He sat upon a skeletal throne and watched as I struggled to breathe and felt the flame of my inner furnace course into my limbs once more.

"Well done, daughter," he said. "You nearly killed that little knight. But not quite. Your rending claws succeeded in filling him with poison, but not enough to end his life. See if you can't do a better job of it this time. I need both him and his brother dead."

"So will they be, Father!" I replied, and I returned to the Near World.

It looked like an oncoming storm rolling in from the sea. But there was no wind, Alistair noticed as he hurtled after Mouse, who was a good distance ahead of him. The air was thick and sluggish, without movement. He heard Eanrin's shouting behind him, but he didn't turn.

"Mouse!" he cried. Though he was certain she heard him, she did not turn, but her pace slowed and then stopped. She stood stock-still, her head tilted to the sky as the darkness rushed down upon them. Alistair put on a burst of speed and drew alongside her. "Mouse, we've got to take shelter!" he said, though he knew she wouldn't understand him.

In the quickly fading light, he saw her face. It had gone chalky, and her lips moved in that familiar prayer of hers.

"Fire burn!"

He whirled about, gazing up into the darkness; there were no clouds to be seen in all the vast stretch. It was the darkness of night that slapped down hard upon this world, nearly knocking him from his feet with its suddenness.

Howling filled the air. Mouse screamed, but the sound was lost in dissonance, in the haunting cry of the hunt. Alistair, thrown so swiftly from daylight into darkness, was blinded.

But in his blindness, he saw.

The Dogs.

The darkness.

Where was the child?

No! Don't look for the child! This was no dream! Where was Mouse?

He lashed out, both striking at the dark and searching for her. He screamed her name, but nothing could be heard above that demonic din of voices born of wind and fire and emptiness. He thought he felt Mouse's fingers brush his.

Then red eyes blazed through the dark. Four red eyes, and two great red mouths that howled darkness and flame, creatures bigger than horses, bearing down upon the two helpless mortals on the plain. There was only Death and Midnight and the hollow, empty longing of the Black Dogs baying across the worlds.

———

Then they were gone.

Alistair lay prostrate in the dirt, his mouth full of grit, his face pouring sweat. At first he was afraid to open his eyes, to discover that he was dead.

But when at last he did, blinking against the swirl of dust that threatened to blind him all over again, he lay upon the plain, and it was empty, and daylight had returned.

He sat up, coughing. Dimly he became aware of shouting behind him, someone calling his name; the cat, most likely. He looked around.

"Dragons blast and eat and blast again!" Eanrin swore as he skidded to a halt beside Alistair, grabbed him by the shoulder, and dragged him to his feet.

Alistair, bewildered, could only ask feebly, "Where's Mouse?"

"Where's *Mouse?*" the cat-man cried. He released his hold, allowing Alistair to drop, weak-kneed, to the dirt once more. "At a time like this, all you can ask is where the pretty little wench got off to? Egg-headed, dragon-blasted *mortal!*"

Alistair shook his head, trying to clear it of the ringing din of howls that remained. He realized suddenly that his cousin was missing. "The Chronicler," he said, turning to look back to the edge of the gorge.

"That's what I'm trying to tell you!" growled Eanrin. "They took him! They took the girl too! *She* sent them after us, and they took both the heir and our guide." He cursed again and kicked in futile frustration at the dirt. "The Black Dogs always catch what they are sent for. Dragons eat them!"

Alistair's mind whirled. He knew tales of the Black Dogs, of course. Death's hounds, spawn of monsters that dragged the souls of the dead into the Netherworld. "Are they dead?" he asked, almost afraid to voice the question. "Did the Black Dogs kill them?"

Eanrin, like a spooked cat trying to settle his upraised fur, took off his red cap and smoothed down his shock of bright hair. He shook his head, and his voice was a little calmer when he spoke. "I don't think so. I don't believe the Dogs were sent by Death this time."

"Who, then? Who else can command the Black Dogs?" Alistair asked.

"Their mother," said Eanrin, and his lips curled into a grimace. He stared across the plain, seeing, as the dust settled, the distant light gleaming once more from the Spire tip. A suspicion was growing in his mind. An ugly suspicion, but one he should have considered.

"Who is their mother?" Alistair asked. "Where are Mouse and the Chronicler? What . . . what are we supposed to do?"

"I don't know," Eanrin whispered. His hands clenched into fists. "Something. But I don't know."

"You could try waiting."

The cat-man whirled about, his cap flying from his head, and Alistair, still collapsed upon the ground, turned. The swirling dust parted like a curtain, revealing a lone figure—a small, hunched, tottering figure with a withered face like a cracked walnut.

"If there's one thing I've learned in the centuries of my existence," he said in a voice as dry as the dusty air, "it's that answers often come to him who will wait long enough to see them."

Eanrin's lips drew back in a teeth-baring snarl. *"Etanun!"*

The Chronicler came to himself with a start and realized that he wasn't dead.

His head rang with the echoes of the Black Dogs' snarls. He lay stunned, unseeing and unfeeling for the moment, aware only of the pounding of his head and the certainty that he did still breathe. Then he opened his eyes.

He lay upon his back on hard, hot stone, staring up at an arched ceiling, also of stone, blistered red but polished bright as gemstones and carved in reliefs of feathers and wings. He glimpsed pillars of the same red stone supporting the roof. Save for the dreadful heat, he would have thought it beautiful.

Then two pairs of hands grabbed him, hauling him upright and off his feet. There he dangled, his feet kicking in midair, his arms aching where powerful fingers dug into his skin. He heard harsh but human voices speaking—women's voices, not men's, although two big men held him. He did not understand the language.

Twisting in the grasp of his captors, he tried to catch a glimpse of those speaking. He saw two women, one tall, one short, both clad in red garments that looked like cured and dyed animal hides. Their arms were bare and brown, and their hair was long, black as night, adorned with uncut gems. Neither was beautiful; their faces were much too hard.

There was no sign of the Black Dogs.

"Take him," one of the women commanded, and though the Chronicler did not understand her words, he guessed her meaning by her gesture. The great men bore him easily down the pillared hall. They were naked to the waist, belted and armed, and their faces were stern and nearly inhuman. These were men who had never been shown mercy and would show no mercy themselves.

Doors at the end of the hall were opened, and the Chronicler was carried through into a great tower and the foot of a staircase. Straining his neck, he saw that there were no floors to break up the dreadful height of this tower, merely landings, almost like perches in a falconry mews.

They carried him up, higher and higher, his legs swinging, and the Chronicler thought he might shame himself and faint. He tried closing his eyes, but that was worse, so he forced them to remain open, refusing to look down. One of the priestesses went before, the short one. Behind there were others; how many he could not guess, but he heard the tramp of their feet.

They did not climb to the crest of the tower. Instead, they stopped at one of the final broad landings. There still was no barrier between a false step and the long fall to the floor below, but it was large enough to fit a crowd of fifty or more comfortably. In the center was a high-backed wooden chair covered with animal hides stained the same red as the robes of the priestesses. It took a moment before the Chronicler realized someone sat upon it: a tall, solemn woman whose face might have been handsome had it not been heavily scarred with sorrow and cruelty.

The high priestess, he guessed. The Speaker.

The Chronicler's head whirled with vertigo when the slaves threw him facedown before that red throne. He saw the priestess withdraw her feet in apparent disgust. Then she spoke sharply. He could guess what she said.

"Is *this* the one? Is *this* the heir to Fireword?"

One of the priestesses answered in a deep voice what seemed to be a tentative confirmation.

"It is what was brought, Speaker. They never fail in their hunt."

The Chronicler raised his head and met the eyes of the high priestess. She blinked once, then shook her head and looked away with something between repugnance and . . . could it be embarrassment?

He grimaced and pushed himself upright. They hadn't bothered to bind him. What was the need? He looked around and saw that a large crowd had gathered, most of them women, but slave men stood on the edges, their faces implacable as stone.

The high priestess spoke again, and though there was doubt in her tone, the Chronicler thought she was agreeing.

"If *they* brought him, he must be the one." Then, after a pause, "Where is the girl?"

The crowd parted. The Chronicler looked around and saw Mouse, more ragged than ever amid the sober grandeur of the priestesses. Another priestess, the short one the Chronicler had glimpsed earlier, walked behind her, a hand upon her shoulder. And yet, he thought, Mouse did not look like a prisoner somehow. Not quite.

"Come to me, Mouse," said the Speaker, holding out a hand.

Mouse went, passing the Chronicler without a glance. She fell upon her knees and face before the high priestess, her hands pressed to her chest in a manner of complete subservience. The Speaker leaned down and cupped her by the chin, lifting her gently upright. Even then Mouse could not raise her eyes to meet those of her mistress.

The Speaker said: "Well done, child. You have served the Flame with utmost courage and devotion. You shall have your reward."

The Chronicler stared. The words passed without meaning through his ears, but the tone was unmistakable.

"You betrayed us," he said. His voice was cold as ice in that hot realm.

Mouse started and spun around to face him. Her face was stricken, for she too understood his tone.

"You betrayed us," he said, struggling to his feet. "You led us here to hand us over to them. And what became of the cat-man, eh? What became of Alistair?" She winced at his cousin's name, which she recognized. But he did not hold back, only raised his voice in an angry shout. "Are they dead, then? Are they killed?"

"Take him away," said the Speaker quietly. The two slave guards stepped forward, and though the Chronicler struck out in his fury, he could do nothing against them. They once more lifted him from his feet, and he burned with humiliation and wrath. Writhing in their grasp even as they passed through the crowd, he shouted over his shoulder:

"You're not a mouse, do you hear me? You're not a mouse; you're a rat! A dirty, gnawing rat!"

Mouse, still kneeling, her mouth open, watched him disappear into the throng and heard him shouting in his barbarous tongue as they bore him back down the winding stair. She tried to swallow, but her mouth had gone as dry as the world beyond the tower.

The Speaker placed a hand upon her head. "We will clean you and make you presentable," she said. "Then you will have what many long for and never achieve. You will look upon the face of your goddess."

I will look upon the face of holiness, Mouse thought. *And then I will be cleansed of my sin.*

Down the long stair, and the descent did not stop. Another long stair opened itself like a mouth below the Chronicler, and he was dragged down farther still, out of the light, out of the heat, into the close, stifling dark of the Citadel's dungeons. They flung him unchained into a cell, and he heard the slam of iron on stone. Footsteps retreated. He was alone in the dark.

He lay for he couldn't guess how long, unable to move, uncertain of his own limbs. Above him was a stone grate. He reached up, just able to grasp it and, with a grunt, hauled himself up. He could see nothing. All was pitch-black. So he let go and stood in silence, unable to think. It was too dark to think. It was too dark to feel.

And then there was light.

It was faint, reflecting on the ceiling above. The Chronicler looked up at it like a lost sailor looking to the pole star. A gentle voice spoke in a language he understood, though it was not his.

"Who are you?"

He ground his teeth, then shrugged. "I am the castle chronicler of Gaheris."

A quiet moment, not quite silent. Then: "I am Dame Imraldera, Knight of the Farthest Shore. Are you Etanun's heir?"

"Supposedly," he replied. "According to some."

"You don't believe you are?"

"It's hard to believe much of anything in this place, isn't it?"

The light—perhaps from the starflower Mouse had mentioned in her tale—faded a little. Then Imraldera said, "It's as well that what you believe cannot affect the truth."

The Chronicler cursed and closed his eyes to avoid seeing that light. "If I survive this," he said, more to himself than to the prisoner, "I swear I will find Leta and retract everything I ever said about truth and belief!"

"Who is Leta?" asked Dame Imraldera.

He could not answer. He told himself that he was not weeping, for no one could weep in this place. It was far too dreadful an end to merit tears.

After a silence that lasted forever, the prisoner across the way whispered, "Perhaps I should not have trusted Etanun after all."

6

I SET UPON THE HOUSES OF LIGHTS AGAIN, picking them out as they shone at night and pouring flame down on them from above. So the gleam of Asha was extinguished across that world, and the voices of Lumé and Hymlumé were stilled.

Once more Etanun found me. Upon the Green of Corrilond we fought, and our battle extended for miles, decimating the land. I tore him with my claws, burned him with my fire, but Halisa protected him from death, and he dealt me many blows.

At last the sword found its way home and once more plunged into my breast. "Die, cursed devil!" Etanun cried. "And this time, stay dead!"

"But don't you know?" I replied with my last breaths. "I am a queen. I will return."

And with that, I took my original form. I was once more the woman he had known, suspended on the end of his weapon. I saw his eyes widen, his mouth open. I thought his lips formed the words, "Dear queen!"

But I was probably mistaken in that.

Darkness clouded out my fire. Once more I died.

"Lights Above us!" Alistair stared at the old man. "Aren't you the kitchen man? The pot scourer?"

The scrubber touched his thin forelock respectfully. "My lord," he said.

A snarl sliced the air. "You're behind this, aren't you? Traitor! *Murderer!*"

Alistair ducked his head as, much to his surprise, Eanrin flew over him, leaping like a cat, though still wearing his man's form, at the scrubber's throat. For an instant, Alistair believed Eanrin would break the old man in two.

But the scrubber, his scrawny limbs moving so quickly that Alistair almost missed the action, turned, caught Eanrin by the arm and the back of the neck, and twisted him so that he was down on his knees and unable to move, though he spat and snarled and kicked. He even tried to take cat form, but the old man kept his grip on his scruff and pressed all his weight into Eanrin's body.

"Steady now, kitty cat," said the scrubber. "No use hissing at me like that."

Eanrin, a man once more, knelt panting in the dirt, his red clothes dusted over and his immortal face smeared and dirty. But he calmed his struggles and only spat again, "Murderer!"

"Call me more names, why don't you?" the scrubber said mildly. "Call me all the names you like. But shall we have done with the physical violence, at least for the moment? It unbalances the humors."

Eanrin's voice dropped into indecipherable mutters, and Alistair took the opportunity to scramble to his feet. "What are you doing here?" he demanded. "Did you follow us? How did you escape Gaheris? Have you word from the castle?"

The scrubber looked up at Alistair, his face so wrinkled that its expression was impossible to determine. "Stop asking questions for the moment, my boy," he said. "Wait. Wait a little."

He loosened his hold on Eanrin, and the cat-man was up in a trice, backed away and braced for battle. Though he was taller by far than the ancient scrubber, and his limbs were well-formed and strong compared to the other's aged frailty, there was fear in his eyes. "What did you do to Imraldera?" he growled. "How did you force her to obey you?"

The old man chuckled. "When have you ever known Dame Imraldera to be compelled beyond her will? Remember, we speak of the same maid who fought Amarok and won."

"The Wolf Lord possessed nowhere near your cunning, Etanun Ashiun," Eanrin said. "Your manipulations are shrewd indeed, but do you really think you can convince the worlds to believe you anymore? Imraldera doesn't know. She wasn't there when you killed your brother and broke faith with the Lumil Eliasul."

"Neither," said the old man, "were you."

"I saw what happened! I saw the Near World tumble back into darkness, cut off from the Sphere Songs. I saw the Flame at Night ravage nations unchecked; I saw Etalpalli burned to ruins. I saw the results of your evil."

"So did our Lord," Etanun replied.

He said no more, made no defense or argument. And yet, to Alistair's surprise, Eanrin opened his mouth to speak, then swallowed back his words and turned away with a bitter curse. He refused to look at the old man again.

So it was to Alistair that the scrubber addressed himself next. "Mouse will be along shortly," he said. "When she arrives, you must do as she says. She knows more than she thinks she knows, and she will help you. All is coming together as it must, so try to be forgiving"—he glanced at Eanrin—"if you can."

With those words he began walking, bowed over and tottering, his face set toward the distant tower and the red light. "Wait!" Alistair cried, taking a step after him.

"That's right," the old man said over his shoulder. "Wait. Wait a little. You will see in time."

"But where are you going?" Alistair glanced at Eanrin, but the cat-man's head was bowed, his eyes closed, his face grimacing as though with pain. There would be no help from that quarter. "What do you intend to do?"

But the old man gave no answer. He continued on his slow, painful way, as though every step sent searing pain through his joints, along his veins. Then, as suddenly as the blink of an eye, he vanished. There was nowhere for him to hide, not on this wide, blank desolation. He was simply and utterly gone, like an interrupted dream, leaving only the faintest and most confused memories in his wake.

Alistair stared at the empty space. "Where did he go?" he cried, whirling upon Eanrin.

The poet straightened slowly, adjusting his clothes and wiping his face. He looked at the dirt that came off on his fingers and shuddered. Then he fixed Alistair with the intensity of his golden-eyed glare. "This land is crossed over with Faerie Paths," he said. "Secret ways, most of them unsafe, by which immortal kind may travel. He has taken one of those." Again he shuddered, and his throat constricted as though he was trying to keep from being sick. "Not one I would take."

"And what are we to do?" Alistair cried. "He said Mouse would return, but you told me the Black Dogs took her!"

Eanrin bit out his words as though they tasted foul. "I have no answers for you, mortal. For once, I find myself as ignorant as you." He drew a long breath and spoke with reluctance. "We will have to . . . wait."

Alistair stared across the wide and lonely plain to where the tower slashed at the horizon. A red light flickered faintly.

Nothing could be done about her shaggy, cropped hair. After multiple washings and peelings away of the grime and dirt in which Mouse had lived for the last many weeks, the Speaker finally declared that it was the best that could be expected. She ordered the other acolytes to dress Mouse in a red robe like those of a priestess, but they covered her head with the black hood of an acolyte to disguise the damage the shears had done.

"Are you ready?" the Speaker asked when Mouse, shivering and clean, was presented before her. "To look upon the face of the goddess is an honor even priestesses are rarely given. You have served the Flame with a willing heart, proving your devotion even to the point of risking your own life. The Flame is pleased."

The Flame should be pleased, Mouse thought with little reverence. After all, she had done as she was told.

"Follow the blue star, child," the Silent Lady had said. *"Do what you must."*

All those months ago, Mouse had withdrawn from the dungeons and made her way back up the long stairs to the temple above. Waiting at the top of that stair had been the high priestess.

"Well done, little Mouse," the Speaker had said. "Tell me, what did you learn from our prisoner?"

Mouse had told her. What else could she have done? She'd told her everything, including her promise to find Etanun and his heir.

"The Flame is pleased," the high priestess had said even then. "You will go. You will do as you have promised. And when you have discovered Etanun's heir, you will bring him back to us. Do you understand?"

"If I do," Mouse had whispered, surprised at her own daring, "will the Silent Lady be spared?"

The Speaker had smiled in reply a smile that did not reach her eyes. "If you succeed, small one, you will look upon the face of the goddess and plead for her life yourself."

So Mouse had gone. She had followed the blue star. She had risked her life in a cold nation where she did not understand the language. She had been nearly gutted by goblins.

And she had betrayed those who were her friends.

The Speaker's eyes now bored into the shadows beneath Mouse's hood. Mouse wondered, could she read her mind? She ducked her head, ashamed of her own thoughts. She hoped her attitude appeared merely humble.

The Speaker stepped back and made a final sign of blessing over the girl. Then she said, "Take care you do not undo all your good work. Take care you do not displease your goddess."

Mouse trembled so much that she feared at every step she might fall as, led by the Speaker and flanked by other priestesses of high rank, she climbed the long stair of the Spire. She had never before stepped beyond the door at the top of the stair. She knew only that the altar burned above and that the goddess lived behind the altar.

The goddess whose face she was about to see. The dreadful holiness so near.

"Fire burn," she whispered as she climbed. "Fire purify."

At last they reached the end of their climb, and the Speaker opened the final doorway. A blast of wind, full of heat even at this height, struck Mouse in the face as she hastened after her mistress out upon a flat rooftop, the tower's crest. No balustrade or barrier guarded against a fall to the dry plain below. The rooftop was bare except for the altar, which was red stone like the rest of the temple. On it burned the everlasting flame that must never die. And beyond the heat and smoke of that fire, the thin Spire itself, like a knife, pierced the sky.

In it was a curtained doorway.

The Speaker stepped forward and tossed a handful of black leaves into the fire. A billow of smoke rose up, and with it a strange smell. Mouse wanted to recoil but felt the presence of the priestesses behind her and did not dare.

"Come," said the Speaker, beckoning, and Mouse had no choice but to approach. The high priestess put a hand on her shoulder and directed her toward the doorway. "Beyond lies the near abode of the goddess. Enter on your knees, and may your righteous heart guard you."

As instructed, Mouse went down on her hands and knees, her eyes fixed upon the flat stone rooftop. She crawled, pushing through the heavy curtain, and her heart hammered like death tolls in her throat.

She entered a dark, small chamber that smelled heavily of incense, an incense that failed to disguise another scent Mouse could not at first recognize. Scattered about with no apparent order, little braziers gave off the dull red glow of dying embers. Otherwise, the room was empty, save for another red curtain, partially blackened by smoke and burned along the edges, which hung at its far end.

Beyond it, Mouse sensed a presence. A powerful, burning presence. The presence of Fire deified.

Sweat poured down her face, dampening her robes, dripping through the ratty ends of her hair. "Fire burn," she whispered, then realized she had not spoken loud enough. Still on her hands and knees, knocking her forehead to the stone, she said in a loud, trembling voice, "Fire burn! Fire purify! Make us worthy in your eyes and let us see your face!"

She wasn't certain if it was the right prayer for this occasion. No one had prepared her for what to say when she approached the goddess.

A voice emerged from the darkness beyond the braziers.

"Who is there? What do you want?"

It was like the hiss and spit of dying flame. It sounded as though it pained the throat and mouth of the one who spoke. Agony dripped from the words.

"I am . . . I am your humble servant," Mouse said, afraid even to speak her name. "I have gone into the world beyond the mountains, and I have sought for he who might deliver Fireword into your hands."

"Fireword?"

A low, hushed, horrible sound. The word itself was poison in the ear.

Mouse swallowed. She rose upright, her knees still on the stone, and made the signs of reverence due the goddess, the same signs she had made every time she lit the evening torches, again hoping this was right. "I have brought him to the Citadel," she said, "as you commanded. And now I beg that you would spare the life of the Silent Lady, your great prophetess."

She saw a hand. It crept out from behind the curtain and took hold. A large hand, gray even in the red light of the braziers. It fumbled, then gripped the curtain tightly and drew it back.

Mouse looked upon the face of her goddess.

Her goddess who was blind.

Her skin was gray ash, flaking from her body in a continuous cloud of dust. Her fingers were like bits of black charcoal, and she dug them into her own face, leaving black streaks. Her hair, as colorless as the rest of her, sizzled on the ends, red embers burning, and broke and fell away, but there was always more. Her form was like a woman's but also not, for there was no femininity left in her.

But her eyes were the worst of all. They were like two small lumps of burning coal, red and crackling with heat. They saw nothing yet revealed her soul. They revealed her inner fire.

She opened her mouth, and glowing red and smoke billowed up from inside.

"The heir?" the Flame at Night said. "They have got the heir?"

"Yes," Mouse gasped. "He's in the dungeons even now. So please, please, spare the life of the Silent Lady!"

The Flame laughed. It was a hot, roiling sound that swept over Mouse and knocked her to the ground, her forehead pressed against the stone that was suddenly hot and painful to the touch. She saw sparks land and break upon the ground, and still the goddess laughed. Then there were words in the sound, and they were dreadful as well.

"At last! Send him, send him at once!" The voice rose to a manic frenzy. "Send him to the Diggings and bring me Etanun's sword! I have waited too long for this. Bring me Halisa!"

Afraid she would be incinerated in the Flame's eager joy, Mouse backed out, catching and stumbling over the long red robe as she went, trying to cover her face with her arms, forgetting all her prayers and all her signs in her haste. She felt the curtain behind her, turned, and fell through it, landing headlong upon the rooftop, which felt cool compared to the lair from which she had emerged.

There was no time for thought. The Speaker was kneeling beside her, lifting her to her feet. "Did you see the goddess?" she asked.

Mouse, coughing and hacking, could only nod.

"And she desires that we bring her the sword?"

Again a nod.

The Speaker released Mouse's shoulders, letting the girl fall back to her knees. She strode around the altar, calling orders. "Prepare for the descent!" she cried. "We journey into the dark once more! The goddess has commanded."

But Mouse, bent double, her stomach heaving, closed her eyes and forced back the scream, the sob that wanted desperately to escape. For she knew now. She knew the truth.

There was no goddess.

There was only the Dragonwitch.

As he lay in the dark, every sound was amplified to the Chronicler's straining ears. He heard his fellow prisoner's breathing, however light it was. Once or twice, he thought he heard her whisper, and even caught hints of words.

"Beyond the Final Water falling . . ."

He could not tell the passing of time in this place any more than he had in the Wood Between. All was darkness. A darkness cold and distant, even as the cell walls were close and pressing. He had to be careful not to let himself think. As soon as he did, his imagination would take over. It told him that the walls, already so close, were closer still. That they slowly compressed on all sides, ready to squeeze the life out of him.

He realized that his fist was clenched so tightly that it hurt. Slowly he unclenched it, and something gleamed in the dark.

Wondering, the Chronicler peered into a handful of sparkling water. Water that should long since have dripped away and evaporated, but which lay in his palm, a tiny pool of light.

Then, for an instant, the Chronicler thought he held rushing rivers in his hand.

The pound of approaching steps overhead. The Chronicler closed his fist, blocking out the light and the vision, and sat in darkness, straining his ears. He heard the thud of a procession making its way down the stairs. In another minute, there was the glimmer of a torch, and he turned to it as a moth to the flame, realizing that it might mean his death but desiring the warmth, the glow.

"Chronicler of Gaheris" came Imraldera's voice, nearly lost in the approaching pound of feet, "if the sword is yours, you cannot give it to the Dragonwitch. Do you understand?"

He didn't. Not the way she wished him to.

Slaves washed in torchlight flung open the grate above him, and he was dragged out by his arms, once more suspended between them. They carried him from the darkness of the dungeons, far from Imraldera's voice, which called after him desperately, "Do you understand? Chronicler!"

Up the stairs they went and on out of the temple, outside into the blistering light of day that stung the Chronicler's eyes like a thousand wasps. They carried him down the red stair cut in the foundation stone. By the time they neared the bottom, he could see, though blearily, the host gathered below. The high priestess, glorious in her wig and wreaths, stood at the head of the procession, her face shielded in a thick blindfold.

Beyond her was the crack in the red stone. From it poured the stench of Death.

"No," the Chronicler said. Then he screamed and pulled and struggled, but there was no escape from the strong arms holding him. Another slave stepped forward and bound his hands with a thick cord that bit into his wrists. Still he would not have relented, save that a big man picked him up by the back of his shirt, lifting him like a helpless kitten dangling in its mother's jaws. The humiliation overwhelmed him, and though he kicked feebly, he had no heart to continue the struggle.

The high priestess stepped before him, her mouth hard beneath the black blindfold. She spoke and he understood nothing she said. But he thought—and the thought surprised him, especially in this shameful moment suspended before the door of Death—that there was heartbreak in her voice.

He heard the name, "Halisa," and knew what they were about to make him do.

The next moment he was plunged, without the protection of a blindfold, into the darkness of the Diggings.

The slave carried him for the first several paces, then put him down and let him walk, led like a lamb to the knife and the fire. He had listened incredulously when Mouse told her bizarre tale. Unicorns and temples and underground passages . . . none of it fit within the range of belief he had always known. He scarcely believed it now as he set one foot down before the other, following the slave and the high priestess, lost in the midst of the procession.

He was thankful in that moment to be so small and so surrounded by his enemies. Their shadows and their long robes provided a shield against the darkness beyond them. The Diggings were vast, and the footsteps of the priestesses and slaves echoed forever. The passage they followed was broad and descended quickly into a great cavern, a cavern that could not be seen for its vastness no matter how many torches were held aloft. Other passages branched off from this, twining away like snakes.

If the Chronicler allowed himself to hear anything beyond the tramp of feet and the breath of his captors, he could have heard the voices of the lost crying out from the depths.

His stomach jolted with the pain of realization. This place, where slave miners had spent the short span of their lives in search of a legend, rested in the Between. Just as the Wood itself stood between worlds, so this realm stood between the world of life and that of death.

He could deny belief in magic swords. He could rebel against the very idea of chosen destinies, of kingship, of stars come to earth or doors opened.

But this much was true beyond doubt: There was life, and there was death, and no one could survive between.

Suddenly there was a loud crash and clatter. A horrible sound in that darkness, a sound that must draw all the phantoms of the lost teeming to this place where the living dared walk. The Chronicler startled, for it was the slave beside him who had fallen suddenly, his torch clattering from his hands.

It was like the burst of a storm. The acolytes screamed, and the priestesses cursed them ineffectually to silence. Eunuchs rushed to the fallen one, and weapons were drawn, and frightened faces, many of them blindfolded, swam before the Chronicler's vision.

Then he was faced by a pair of black eyes that he knew.

Mouse drew a knife from the sleeve of her dark robe and cut the cord binding his wrists.

"Run," she said, and in this darkened realm, he understood her. The next moment, she was gone, vanished into the crowd of screams and curses.

Life and death swam before the Chronicler's eyes. He felt the pull of the Netherworld, the lure that must have driven a hundred or more miners to madness. For the space of a breath, he resisted.

Then he was running. Ducking under arms, dashing between pressing bodies, and he knew that even if they were aware, they would not catch him. The pull of the Netherworld was too strong. He would enter it.

And he would be lost.

7

W HEN I WOKE AGAIN, I was filled with fire, brighter than life, brighter than death, brighter than the sun or the moon. I stood there in the darkness of my Dark Father's realm and turned to face him on his throne.

"Look at me!" I cried, raising my wings. "Look at my fire! Look at my power! Am I not glorious beyond description?"

"You're bright enough," Death-in-life replied through flame-wreathed teeth. "But don't forget your place. You are my child and you will do as I say. You will kill the Brothers Ashiun."

The heady marvel of the strength I felt was more than anything I had ever known. Greater than when I had stood before my brother's dead body and felt the sudden surge of queenship inside me. Greater than when I first took the Dragon's kiss and destroyed that mortal maid. I was a force like the wind, like hurricanes, like earthquakes.

"I am Hri Sora!" I proclaimed. "I am the Flame at Night! All the worlds will tremble before me, for never has there been such a fire as mine!"

"Whom do you serve?" the Dragon asked me.

"None but myself!" I cried.

The goblins flung open the library door and tossed Leta in. She stumbled across the room, tripping over the tatters of her skirt, and fell against the Chronicler's desk. Her hand overturned an inkwell and knocked a stack of parchments to the floor. Red-brown ink pooled like blood across the stone.

The door slammed and she was alone.

She stood clutching the desk with one hand, her other clenched tightly around the key. How long this solitude would last, she could not guess, and she must use it, must think. Why had Mintha given her this key? What secret might it unlock that Mintha could not access herself?

Footsteps outside pounded in Leta's ear. She hastily dropped the key down the front of her dress, shivering as its coldness slid against her skin.

The door opened. Corgar ducked his head inside.

Leta turned about, her back pressed into the Chronicler's desk, and stared up at her captor. She thought she'd never find breath to breathe again.

"I need to know the location of the House of Lights," Corgar said.

Leta's mouth hung open. She could hear the Chronicler saying, *A symbol of enlightenment, of understanding. The House of Lights is no literal house.*

And her reply: *"I think you're wrong."*

She tried to form words now, her lips moving without sound until finally she managed to gasp, "I don't know where it is."

"I didn't think you would," said the goblin. He crossed the room in two great strides, and she shrank from his towering presence. He reached out and took a book from a shelf, his claws gouging the fine leather binding. He shoved it at her, and Leta grabbed it close to her chest as though to somehow protect it. "I need you to search these documents," said Corgar. "Read them all, every line, and tell me what you find. Perhaps hidden in this room is the secret to what I seek."

Leta turned staring eyes from him to the shelves of books and scrolls and loose pages, many of them still indecipherable to her unpracticed eye.

"Do you understand me, mortal?" the goblin demanded.

Her throat was too dry to swallow, and her voice croaked from her mouth. "Where is the Chronicler?" she asked.

Corgar's white eyes narrowed as he looked down upon her. "Do you mean the little king?" His voice was harsh and almost bitter. "Why should you care? Your task is before you. Open that book."

Her fingers trembling so that she feared she would drop it, Leta spun the book around and laid its spine across her arm, supporting its weight as she spread the cover. The pages, full of the Chronicler's familiar writing, blurred before her tear-filled eyes. She forced herself to study the passage she'd opened to. It was one she knew quite well, which was good, because otherwise Corgar's heavy breathing would have frightened her too much to make it out.

"Speak up," Corgar demanded. "What does it say?"

Trying once more to swallow, Leta read:

> *"The king will find his way*
> *To the sword beneath the floor.*
> *The night will flame again*
> *When the Smallman finds the door.*
>
> *"The dark won't hide the Path*
> *When you near the House of Lights—"*

"That's it!" Corgar cried, and one long finger came down hard upon the open page. "That's it! The House of Lights! That's what I need! Tell me, where is it?"

But Leta shook her head. "I . . . I'm sorry. That's all it says. Just the rhyme. The House itself was lost long ago. If it ever existed."

"If it ever existed?"

Corgar's arm came down hard, tearing the book from Leta's hand, shredding the open pages and scattering them at his feet. She retreated behind the desk, pressing her back to the wall, and watched as the great goblin turned and swept a shelf free of scrolls and loose paper that flew like large snowflakes in the air. Leta wanted to cower, to flee.

Instead, she yelled.

"What do you think you're doing?"

Corgar, startled at the ferocity in her voice, turned and saw her eyes flash fire. And she, watching all the long labor of the Chronicler swirling in destruction, strode through it, her hands clenched into fists.

"If you want me to search these documents, you'll oblige me by not destroying them first! What if you just shredded your precious secret? Do you expect me to pick up all those little bits and piece them back together? Do you?"

The next moment his hand was on her throat, and her back was against the wall behind, her feet kicking the air. She gagged, unable to draw a breath, and tore at his arm. His eyes were close to hers, his gaze coldly intense. For a strangled moment she believed for the hundredth time in the last few days that her end had come.

Then, slowly, Corgar loosened his hold, and Leta slid down until her feet touched the floor. Her back remained against the wall, and he loomed over her, his ugly face leering down.

"You're not afraid of me," he growled.

"You're mistaken," she said and wondered how much longer her knees would support her. "I'm terrified of you."

"Do you mock me?"

She shook her head hastily, her eyes wide.

His lips closed over his jagged teeth, and for an instant his face looked almost human. "Hmm," he grunted, then stepped back, apparently no longer angry. He gestured at the desk, took a heavy volume from a nearby table, and tossed it her way. Leta caught it against her stomach, nearly dropping it but managing to keep hold.

"Start reading," Corgar said and took a place in the dark corner by the door.

Leta spent the whole of the next three days poring over books and scrolls, sleeping only when she dropped from exhaustion. Corgar had quickly realized that she wasn't a particularly skilled reader, and she half wondered if he would kill her when he found out. But he didn't. In fact, when she confessed her lack of experience, he said nothing, only shrugged and indicated she should continue.

Now her eyes burned and the lighting was poor, for no candles were lit and the sky outside the window was thickly overcast with a winter storm rolling in. She could not guess the hour. It might be morning or late afternoon. She felt caught in a half-lit world without time.

And always below her in the courtyard were the ringing of demolished stone and the cracking of whips.

Groaning, she lowered her forehead onto the page over which she labored, a chronicle of taxes collected three decades ago and written in old Raguel's hand, which was far more difficult to decipher than the Chronicler's.

Weary, her head heavy with unshed tears, she looked across the desk at a piece of torn parchment, one of the scrolls Corgar had damaged in his rage that first day. It was nothing of significance, another nursery rhyme written as an afterthought and stored away. But she pulled it closer now and read with some relief.

"Starlight, star bright, guide her footsteps through the night."

She smiled and traced the familiar shape of the Chronicler's handwriting. Even if he was dead and gone, at least part of him would live on through this labor to which he had devoted himself: the chronicling of life, from taxes to nursery rhymes.

She shivered suddenly, for the room was bitterly cold. It had taken her most of a day to convince the goblins, who didn't feel the winter's bite, that she needed candles to see by and a fire to keep her limbs from numbing. Even now, with a small blaze on the hearth across the room, she felt cold through and through, and not even the Chronicler's writing could warm her.

Inside her bodice, down near the waistband of her tattered gown, rested Mintha's key. Leta placed a hand over her stomach, feeling the secret contours of that object. Why had Lady Mintha given it to her?

"I don't get it, Ghoukas."

The voice sent a chill down Leta's spine. It was one of the two guards posted outside the library door. The library itself had no lock to keep her imprisoned, so Corgar posted a constant watch. For the most part they were so quiet that Leta could forget they were there. But every now and then they spoke to each other in their growling voices.

"I don't get it. Is it pretty?"

The other guard, the one called Ghoukas, snorted. "I haven't regarded pretty or ugly in a hundred years. What does it matter?"

But the first one was dissatisfied with this. "Why else would Corgar value it so?"

They must be speaking of the House of Lights, Leta thought, still fingering the shape of the key inside her gown.

"Corgar doesn't care about pretty, no more than any of us," Ghoukas responded.

"Then there must be something else," said the first one, sounding truly mystified. "I've never seen our captain become enamored of anything, not treasures, not gems, not even our own queen. Why would he take it into his head to fancy a mortal girl?"

A weight dropped like a stone in the pit of Leta's stomach.

Hardly aware of what she did, she slid from the Chronicler's stool, stumbling across the floor into the deeper recesses of the library. There was nowhere to hide in this small chamber. But she fumbled for the spiral stairway leading to the loft and climbed partway before her knees gave out and she sat down hard.

You should probably dissolve into a lump of panic, one side of her mind whispered, and Leta, for once, had difficulty deciding if it was her practical or rebellious side speaking.

No! her other side snarled, and she shook her head. *You're not giving in. He's waiting for you to collapse! But you're not what they've told you that you are.*

"Think, Leta. Think," she whispered. It probably wasn't true, what the goblins were saying outside. Probably nothing more than confused gossip. "But you can't stay here and let him destroy you," she told herself. "You've got to act. You've got to do something."

Her hands, pressed against her roiling stomach, felt the key.

An idea came to her mind.

Moving on trembling limbs, she climbed back down the stairs, digging into her bodice for the key with one hand. She remembered hearing rumors about the secret passage of Gaheris Castle, a secret to which Lady Mintha would certainly be privy.

In an unlit corner beyond the fireplace, a musty old tapestry hung. Leta pulled this back and gasped in relief to find a door there in the stone wall. An old, brass-fastened door that led nowhere as far as she knew.

It was difficult to see anything in the dimness, but she felt out the lock of the door and, with a little fumbling, inserted the key. It fit perfectly.

Her fingers trembling, Leta tried to turn it. The lock, unused in many generations, resisted. Grinding her teeth, she applied the force of both hands, straining.

"Greetings, captain" came the voice of Ghoukas from beyond the library door.

Leta looked over her shoulder, her face draining of all color. She hesitated. But no, they would see the open door and pursue and catch her if she tried to escape now.

Yanking the key from the lock and letting the tapestry fall, she had only just dropped the key back into hiding when the door opened, admitting Corgar. His gaze went first to her accustomed place at the Chronicler's desk, then swiftly found her standing in the shadows.

"Are you hiding from me?" Corgar asked.

Leta, her heart racing but her face a mask, stepped out of the alcove beneath the stairs and paced quietly to the table where more volumes were stacked high. She selected one and carried it to the desk, taking her seat right under Corgar's nose. Yet she did not open it.

"Why are you not reading?" he asked.

Afraid of what her face might reveal, Leta lowered her forehead into her hand, hiding her eyes. "I need a rest," she said. "I'll go blind otherwise in this gloom."

"Is that true?"

She shrugged. "Quite possibly."

Corgar made no further protest. He stepped away from the desk to one of the windows and looked to the courtyard below, crawling with his slaves. Leta watched him from behind her hand. He was so awful and so powerful. But in his face was something else, something close to desperation.

She surprised herself by suddenly asking out loud, "Why?"

"Why what?" said Corgar.

"Why are you doing this?" Leta lowered her hand, staring at the monster, her brow wrinkled. "You seem to have no interest in or liking for our world. Your minions creep about like frightened rats though they're twice the size of any man here and our weapons cannot touch them. They hate it, and you hate it. So why are you here?"

Her own daring amazed Leta, and she waited for her practical side to step in and shut her mouth. It said nothing, however, and neither did the goblin, so she found her tongue running on unchecked. "Why don't you go away and leave us alone?"

"Because I need the House of Lights," Corgar replied.

"Yes, I know; that's what you keep saying." Leta grimaced at the snap in her own voice. She was terribly tired, and her pale hair, which she had tried to tie back in braids, had all come undone. Ugly circles underscored her eyes. She scarcely felt human anymore. "Why do you need it so badly?"

To her surprise and horror, Corgar laughed a rumbling chuckle, like a dog's growl but more dreadful for its mirth. Then he spoke, turning toward her as he did so. "It's not for me. It's for my queen, Vartera. The woman—or monster, as you might say—whom I am bound to marry."

Leta blinked owl eyed up at him, suddenly wishing she'd kept her questions to herself. He stood a pace or two from her now. The shadows were surprisingly gentle on his face, disguising the more hideous crags, smoothing out the rock-hardened skin. His eyes were bright with laughter as he looked down on her.

"I could kill you," he said.

"I . . . I am well aware of that," Leta said.

"But you're not afraid of me."

She couldn't find breath to answer.

"You faced me in the courtyard," he continued. "I remember. A little prick behind my knee, and there you were, fallen flat, a broken lance head in your hand. A comic sight, worthy of the songs of Rudiobus! And you weren't afraid of me then either. You are brave, little warrior."

One ugly hand reached out, and she thought he meant to slay her then and there. Instead, she felt the coldness of his talon slide down the curve of her cheek.

"Are you beautiful?" Corgar asked.

Leta's heart nearly burst in her throat as that one claw traced under her chin and rested there, tilting her face up to the monster's.

"I don't know what beauty is, and I have never cared. That was always Vartera's obsession. I wish her much joy with it!"

His voice was gentle. Yet with a flick of his wrist, he could cut her throat.

"Even so I can't help but wonder, looking at you," the goblin said, and the shadows could not disguise the gleam of his sharp teeth, "are you beautiful? Are you what that word means?"

She wanted to fall off the stool and crawl away. Instead, she spoke in a dry, crackling voice, "I'm very plain indeed."

"That," Corgar whispered, "is the first lie you have told me. The first of many to come, I trust."

"I have no reason to lie to you," she said.

To her unending relief, he narrowed his eyes and stepped back, removing his hand from her face. "Continue your work," he said as he turned to the door.

Would he go? Would he leave her alone even for a few moments? Long enough for a key to slip into a lock, for an old door to creak open and shut? What did it matter if she was lost in the darkness? What did it matter if she escaped to barren countryside in the depths of winter with no provisions? If only she could get away! If only she could escape this chamber, once her sanctuary, now her prison!

Corgar's hand was on the latch. He stopped. He looked around.

"Give it to me," he said.

"Give you what?" Leta asked.

He was back across the room, towering over her, and no gentleness remained in his voice. "Give me what you're hiding," he demanded. "Don't think you can keep it from me. If you do not place it in my hand, I will tear it from you myself."

There was no way he could know about the key! And yet, looking into those dreadful eyes, Leta dared not protest, not even to herself.

She put her hand into her bodice, withdrew Mintha's furtive gift, and dropped it into Corgar's outstretched palm. It disappeared behind the curl of his claws.

"Get back to work," the goblin said.

8

WITH THAT DEFIANT CRY, I TOOK TO THE AIR. *The Netherworld could not contain me. Nor could the Near World or the Far. I flew beyond them all to the heavens themselves, into the presence of Lady Hymlumé. I would devour the moon! I would end her song! Then all would know my might, and all would tremble at the name of Hri Sora! And the strength I felt then would ease my pain.*

Even as I neared the gardens of the moon, even as I saw Hymlumé's face turn to me in fear, the Dark Father drew up beside me. The blast of his breath sent me tumbling away, and I suddenly realized my mistake. I was the most powerful of all my Father's children, the firstborn among all dragons.

But I was not Death-in-Life.

"You fool! You wretch!" the Dark Father cried, his voice a wave of fire. "You will not shout this defiance in my face! You will not flaunt this strength that I gave you!"

His great claws reached out. With a stroke, he tore my dragon wings from my shoulders.

So the decision was made. She was a traitor twice over.

Mouse, jostled in the midst of the frightened crowd, pulled the blindfold back over her face. Now the jostling was worse. But she shouted like the others, and it was she who began the cry, "The heir? Where is the heir?"

It was taken up. Priestesses barked orders to silent slaves, and once more Mouse found herself knocked about. She fell to her knees on the stone and put her hands over her head in a feeble attempt to protect herself, still shouting, "Where is the heir?"

Someone grabbed her by the shoulder, dragged her to her feet, and tore her blindfold away. By the flicker of torchlight, she stared into the face of Sparrow.

"I saw what you did!" said the priestess, her onetime sister acolyte.

Mouse shook her head. "I did nothing—"

"Silence!" Sparrow snarled. "I saw what you did, traitor! It's time the Speaker knew what you really are!"

She dragged Mouse through the milling throng to where the high priestess stood like a stone, listening to the sounds of panic, her eyes still shielded.

"Speaker!" Sparrow cried, and the high priestess turned at the sound of her voice. "I saw it! I saw what happened! This one"—flinging Mouse on her knees—"cut the heir loose! She let him escape into the Diggings!"

The high priestess's face was unreadable behind her blindfold. Mouse, crouching on the stone, could scarcely see anything for the wild careening of the lights around them.

The Speaker raised both arms. "Stop!" she cried.

Immediate silence fell upon the throng. Still blindfolded, the high priestess turned to those nearest her. "The heir?" she demanded.

"Gone," a priestess replied. "Vanished into the dark."

"I told you, Speaker! It was this Mouse who let him go!" Sparrow cried.

How calm the high priestess was even as her world fell apart around her. In that moment Mouse's heart beat with the adoring admiration it had first felt for this woman, years before.

But the second beat was a cold bump, and she thought, *She knows! She knows what the Flame is, and yet she does what she does!*

"Stand up, Mouse," the Speaker said.

Mouse hastened to obey. *Now she'll kill me,* she thought. *Now she'll command the eunuchs to run me through.*

Instead, the Speaker wrapped her arm around Mouse's shoulders and drew her close. Then she turned to Sparrow, and the lower half of her face contorted into an ugly expression. "Seize her," she said.

"What? No!" Sparrow cried as two slaves stepped forward and grabbed her by the arms. "Speaker! I am not the traitor! This girl you favor so blindly, it was she who loosed the heir, she who has turned her back on the goddess!"

"You have always resented Mouse," said the Speaker, her voice as cold as the shadows around them. "Mouse, to whom I have shown favor that you believed due yourself. Don't think I have not noticed. I'll hear no more of your slander." She addressed the eunuchs. "Take her away."

Mouse shuddered as she watched Sparrow dragged screaming into the darkness. The Speaker's hand remained comfortingly on her shoulder. She turned to the silent cluster of priestesses and slaves around her. "Have you found the heir?" she asked.

"No, Speaker," a priestess replied.

"Fire burn!" the Speaker snarled, and it was a curse not a prayer. But she did not release her hold on Mouse.

"We will send the slaves after him," someone said. "They will track him down! They will find him!"

"No," said the Speaker. "No, they'll never find him. They will only become as lost as he is. There is only one way to catch him now."

The high priestess never loosened her hold on Mouse as the company retreated through the darkness of the Diggings, climbing to the world above. They emerged into sunlight that was dreadful to see, ascended the red stairs carved into the stone, and on through the lower temple. Mouse, her robe firmly gripped in the high priestess's fist, was dragged to the Spire itself, and then the long, long climb, up and up.

What would be done to her? Would she be brought before the Dragonwitch? Did the Speaker, despite her words to Sparrow, know the truth? Or would one look at Mouse's face reveal the betrayal?

But even as they neared the final turn of the stairway approaching the door that led out onto the roof, the high priestess said, "You did well, child. Many, addled by darkness, would not have noticed his disappearance. I heard you give the alarm. Thanks to you, we may act quickly and, I hope, not lose much time."

Then the door was opened, and Mouse followed the Speaker out upon the rooftop. The sun was setting, burning the sky so that it looked as though the fire upon the altar itself blazed into the heavens. To Mouse's surprise and horror, she saw through the smoke and heat-shimmered air that the curtain was flung back from the doorway beyond the altar.

The Dragonwitch stood framed by fire and silence. Her blind eyes burned.

"Where is it?" Sparks fell from her tongue. "Where is Halisa?"

Only then did the Speaker release her hold on Mouse's shoulder and fall on her knees before the altar. The Dragonwitch was taller, Mouse thought, than when she had seen her earlier. Or perhaps she merely seemed so out here on the rooftop, her hair disintegrating into the breeze.

"Where is it?" she cried and leaned forward over the altar itself, her hands grabbing hold of the burning brands, clutching them as though she clutched Fireword itself.

"Flame at Night, holy goddess!" the Speaker said, unable to raise herself up. How frail and pathetic she looked to Mouse now. Gone was the powerful woman she had always appeared. Mouse saw her now for what she truly was: A child playing foolish games of strength, toying with death.

Mouse cowered into the shadows by the door. Though her knees trembled, she could not make herself kneel, and she hoped the Dragonwitch would not turn those coal eyes upon her and blast her to oblivion.

"Tell me!" the Dragonwitch cried, crawling onto the altar and dispersing the bonfire, which should have caught upon her flaking skin and set her hair ablaze but seemed instead to recoil from her presence. She crouched upon the altar stone, her hands clasping embers and coals, shuddering with pain. "Tell me!"

"The heir escaped," the Speaker said. "We were betrayed by one of our own, and he was released into the Diggings."

From the look on that tortured, broken face, Mouse expected the

Dragonwitch to burst with fire, to consume the high priestess in her agonized frustration. Instead, she stood, and the smoke from her hair and skin was black as it rose to the darkening sky. Without another word to the priestess, without a look, she raised her arms and cried out in a pain-filled voice, for it hurt her to speak at all.

"*Yaotl! Eztli!*"

The blaze of sunset vanished. Howling Midnight fell upon the world as the noise of War and Blood rose up from where they had hidden themselves and appeared in dark-bound flesh.

Mouse screamed and fell to her hands and knees, but her voice was unheard in the din. She saw the Black Dogs, beasts she had glimpsed only twice before, when they brought the Silent Lady to the temple and when they swept down upon the Chronicler. Creatures of nightmares made real, they stood one on either side of the altar, and they could not be told one from the other. Even when they closed their great gaping mouths and swallowed their baying, the echoes rang through the Midnight, and Mouse scarcely could hear the voice of the Dragonwitch saying:

"He's escaped! The heir has fled into the darkness. Find him! Fetch him back to me!"

First one, then the other raised its ugly head and howled a joyous, bloodthirsty howl, the deadly song of the hunt. Then eyes like meteors streaked past Mouse. Though neither Dog could possibly fit through that narrow doorway, they vanished, dragging their Midnight behind, disappearing down and down, mad for their quarry.

The remnants of Midnight lingered. The bonfire itself had expired, and only the light of the Dragonwitch's eyes shone through the gloom. Any moment now she would turn to either Mouse or her high priestess and doom would fall upon them.

But then a voice spoke from the doorway.

"That was an unnecessary bit of dramatics."

It was a voice Mouse knew well.

She spun about where she crouched and saw the tottering figure emerge from the stairway to stand before the altar of the Flame at Night. A figure who leaned upon his mop handle as a magician of yore might lean upon his staff, though with perhaps less dignity.

"But then again, dear queen, you always were one for a bit of drama, weren't you?"

The Dragonwitch shrank back, nearly tripping over her own feet, and her flaming eyes narrowed. She could not see, so great was the fire burning her from the inside out. But she stood, her head to one side, listening to the echoes of a voice she knew. Her shriveled nose sniffed, and a long forked tongue slid between her teeth as though to taste something on the air.

Then she spoke, and her agonized voice caught and tore at her throat.

"So," she said. "You have returned to me at last."

The Chronicler fled.

How long ago had he escaped the procession and dashed down a narrow passage so small that it must have been dug by children? A fortunate discovery; he'd had no difficulty slipping through its opening, his fingers feeling the shadows ahead, unable to take precautions in his haste to slip away. He didn't think the eunuchs would fit through, but he must hurry, for other passages might connect to this. He must lose himself, and fast, if he hoped to escape the clutches of the Citadel folk.

The passage ended, opening into a wide cavern. His every footstep echoed, and somewhere far away water dripped. He still heard the indistinct shouts of his captors, and when he looked back along the passage, his blind eyes played tricks enough on him that he believed he saw torches gleaming. But no one could have pursued him. For once in his life, he thanked whatever fate had seen fit to let him be born malformed.

He turned toward the empty cavern, half wondering if another step or two would bring him to an endless chasm, so great were the echoes, so complete was the darkness. But what choice had he now? He could not go back, not that way. They would force him to take the sword, should it exist, and as soon as he had delivered it to their wretched goddess, they would kill him.

If he must die, he wanted to die on his terms. If he must die, he would die a man not a mistake.

So he stepped forward and heard the ghosts whispering.

They surrounded him, though unaware of his presence. In the deepness of the Netherworld, they were lost to all but themselves. And yet he heard them weeping, wailing, sighing for dreams dashed and dreams achieved, calling out the names of those they had once loved or hated.

One whispered close to his ear in a voice of tortured agony, "Starflower, my love!"

The Chronicler turned.

He could see nothing in the darkness, but the voice revealed all. A wolf. The Chronicler smelled the stench of fresh blood, and his mind saw blood-matted fur, felt the brokenness of spirit.

Then the creature was gone, moved on its blind, wandering way. But the Chronicler, horrified, sensed the nearness of many more straying souls.

"I have earned the right!"

The Chronicler whirled about to face that voice and thought he saw (though he couldn't have seen) the staring eyes of a warrior going to her death. But though her face was turned to him with an intensity of desperation, she did not see him. She moved toward him, her hands outstretched, each clutching brutal weapons. "The honor is mine! Open the door!"

Her powerful form overwhelmed the Chronicler, and he thought she would slay him. But she passed through him with a coldness like bitter winter. For a moment he felt the beat of her sorrowing heart, and when she had gone, disappearing into the shadow realm, he wept for her though he did not know why. All around him, the voices of the lost ones cried.

Then suddenly another sound echoed down from the realm above. It must have been a great noise indeed to sound so loud even here in the Diggings. The baying of the Black Dogs.

They were on the hunt.

Somehow the Chronicler knew they were coming for him.

9

*I*N THE BODY OF A WOMAN *I* FELL, *wingless, upon a cloud. I lay in hideous pain, uncertain what had happened. The fire still roiled within me, but my dragon form had vanished, and without it the furnace inside was too hot! I could not support such pain! Even now, though I have lived with this burning for generations of mortals, it hurts me more than you can know. It hurts like first love rejected. It hurts like jealousy eating me away from the inside out.*

So I lay in the presence of Hymlumé. When at last I dared raise my face, I found her looking down upon me, shining and luminous. And she said to me:

"Poor thing."

I cast myself from the cloud. I fell all that long, long way, streaking like a comet to earth, trailing fire in my wake. I hoped it would burn this frail woman's form to ashes and that I would die my final death, more painfully even than in the blaze of Halisa. I would die and then I would burn no more.

"I will kill you," the Dragonwitch said to the scrubber. Fire spilled from her lips, so keen was her hunger. "I will kill you at last."

"Maybe," the scrubber replied. "But you want my sword to do it, don't you?"

She could not answer. Her mouth contorted and fire bellied up from her throat, but she gnashed her teeth and would not let it spill forth. Slithering down from the altar, more snakelike than womanly in that moment, she crawled to the scrubber. In a sinuous movement, she stood up, towering above him.

"I will have your sword!" said she.

The scrubber grinned up at her, his cloudy eyes foolish. But his voice was sharp. "You've lost my heir," he said. "Not a good start to your plan."

"I will recover him. I have sent my children."

"So I saw," said the scrubber. He leaned more heavily on his mop, which was leaving a wet patch on the rooftop. "But you know," he continued, "they won't stand a chance of finding him. Not against the bonds of kinship."

"What?" The Dragonwitch stared down at him, spraying sparks in his face when she spoke. "What do you say?"

"The bonds of kinship. Surely you know what I mean. There was a time you felt those bonds yourself, Hri Sora. Before you took the flame."

She said nothing. So the scrubber, waving smoke from under his nose, persisted. "The bonds of kinship are never stronger than in the Netherworld. If my heir's own kin goes searching for him in the dark, even your Black Dogs will find it difficult to catch him first."

Suddenly that ancient face turned, and Mouse, lying near the rooftop door, was caught in the gaze of the old man who had taught her the scouring of pots and floors. It was a gaze far deeper, far older, and—oddly enough—far younger than she had ever dared imagine, and she gasped at the potency of it.

He was telling her, she realized, what she must do.

But her limbs were weak as water. For the moment, at least, she could not move.

"Your own Father," the scrubber continued, turning back to the Dragonwitch, "was unable to call me to the darkest place once my brother had set out to hunt me down. There is power in blood ties. Power you would do well to recall."

The Dragonwitch's face convulsed. What memories coursed through her brain just then to cause her such torment? But when she spoke, her tongue was a whip. "No hunter, no matter how skilled, is a match for my children!"

"He doesn't have to be a match," said the scrubber. "Not for this task. You know that well enough."

He leaned his mop handle away and stepped around it to approach the burning creature before him. And she, though she could have broken him in two, stepped back, avoiding his touch.

"You cannot count on my heir to bear Halisa up from the darkness to you," the scrubber said. "Prophecies and chosen ones can hardly be trusted in any case." He sighed heavily and passed a hand across his brow. "Indeed, dear queen, there is only one thing to do."

"What is that, Murderer?" the Dragonwitch hissed.

"I shall have to fetch it for you."

Waiting was not among Eanrin's more developed skills.

As a cat, of course, he had a certain amount of experience sitting before the mouse hole, every sense keen even as his eyes seemed to glaze over with disinterest. But though a cat at a mouse hole might look as lazy as a tub of lard, he was no less alert, no less purposeful.

This was different. This was waiting without apparent purpose. This waiting required patience. Eanrin was rarely game for patience.

He sat in cat form on the edge of the gorge, his outer eyelids mostly closed, but his third eyelids still open so that he might observe the world without the world being quite aware of his observation. He particularly observed Alistair. The poor young lord had paced himself to the point of exhaustion and now lay on his back, staring up at the sky. It was a fixed stare, not the vague gazing into nowhere one might expect. Curious despite himself, Eanrin glanced up to see what so fascinated the young lord of Gaheris.

Above them gleamed the blue star.

"Starlight, star bright, guide her footsteps through the night," Eanrin chanted, but his voice was acidic. "Don't put too much hope in those old nursery rhymes, mortal man. They mean little in the end."

"Maybe." Alistair shrugged without looking around. "Or maybe they have meaning beyond your knowledge." Perhaps he didn't intend to be heard, but Eanrin's pricked ears picked up every word.

Irked, the cat stood and trotted a little along the gorge, looking out across the long plain to where the fire of the temple burned. He had seen the second gathering of the Midnight in the distance and wondered what poor soul now had the Black Dogs on his trail. Could it be Etanun himself, fleeing along his chosen Path?

Could it be Imraldera?

Eanrin, as merry a man as ever sprang from the gardens of Rudiobus, growled bitterly. "This dragon-blasted waiting is more than I can stand," he muttered. But he must stand it. Until some guidance or grace was given him, he must sit here on the edge of the Dragonwitch's poisoned realm and do nothing, and it was the hardest task he had ever been given.

The evening passed. Alistair slept at last, the cat noticed and was glad of it. Who knew what the following day would bring? Possibly danger, possibly death. So let the lad sleep while he may. The blue star had danced its measure and descended below the horizon with its brethren, and the sun was beginning to rise. Otherwise, the world was still and hot, only to get hotter. And they must wait.

Then suddenly, there was Mouse.

The cat, dulled by the labor of doing nothing, didn't see her at first. Then he realized that the little figure on the edge of his vision, moving with the mind-numbing plod of mortality, was familiar. He leapt to his feet, meowling, "Get up, Alistair! It's the girl!" Away he streaked across the dust toward that distant image.

Disguised once more in her slave boy's rags, Mouse hastened along, head down, her mind full of the things she had seen and learned. Her ears were ever strained for the sound of pursuit, and though it never came, she expected it nevertheless.

The high priestess may have allowed herself to be deceived once. But she surely would not blind herself to Mouse's treachery a second time.

So Mouse fled, her one thought to reach the gorge and, if the cat-man and Alistair waited there, to tell them all she knew. Perhaps in this small way she might undo some of the evil she had worked.

When she at last saw the cat swiftly approaching, she stopped and her face went slack, almost dead. Eanrin saw enough in that expression to confirm his worst suspicions. Even so, as he halted at her feet, his ears back and his tail lashing, he asked, "How did you escape the Black Dogs?"

"I didn't," said Mouse.

The cat growled. Then he was a man towering over her, his hands clenched into fists. "You were sent by the high priestess, weren't you, to find Etanun's heir. Not by my lady Imraldera."

Still she did not avert her eyes, though her face was pale beneath the layer of gray dust. "I betrayed you all," she said. "I was sent to retrieve the heir to Fireword for the Flame at Night, and that is what I have done."

By this time Alistair was approaching. "Mouse!" he cried, but the girl did not shift her gaze from Eanrin's furious face.

"I betrayed you for the sake of my goddess," she said. "But my goddess does not exist. There is nothing but a dragon."

"Learned that a bit late, didn't you?" said Eanrin.

Her breath came in a shudder. "I freed the heir. He has fled into the Diggings. Lost. She cannot use him to retrieve the sword."

Alistair reached them and stood panting, his face, unlike the cat-man's, full of a surprised smile. "Mouse, you're alive! You're alive and whole, and I thought for sure you'd had it! How'd you get here? How did you—"

Mouse, who could not understand him anyway, interrupted. "Tell him," she said to Eanrin. "Tell him what I did. Tell him what I am."

Eanrin licked his dry lips slowly, his eyes narrowed. Then he turned to Alistair. "She's a traitor. She brought us here so that the Black Dogs could snatch your cousin for the Dragonwitch."

All trace of a smile fell from Alistair's face. He wiped dust from his eyes with a quick, annoyed gesture, turning away as he did so. Then, his head low like an angry dog's, he looked at Mouse again. This time she felt the force of his gaze and felt herself obliged to meet it. Her eyes swam, and she hated herself for allowing any trace of emotion to show.

"Is it true?" Alistair asked.

She did not need to understand his language to know his meaning. She said, "It's true," and he understood her as well.

"Dragon's teeth," he growled, and turned his back on her and the cat. She addressed herself to Eanrin, hoping she would be able to suppress the sob in her throat before it broke.

"The Chronicler is gone," she said, "down into the Diggings. The Dragonwitch sent the Black Dogs after him, but I don't know if they'll catch him. I don't know if it even matters."

"What are you doing here?" Eanrin demanded. "Why have you come? If you have some brilliant little scheme to save the day up your sleeve, do you really think we're going to listen to you a second time?"

"I don't, but that doesn't mean I won't try," she replied, her resolve much firmer than her voice. "Etanun came to the Dragonwitch. He has offered himself in his heir's place, to go down to the chamber and retrieve the sword. Tomorrow night, he said."

"Traitors abound," Eanrin said. "And what, pray tell, is an honest man to do?"

"What is she saying?" Alistair demanded.

Mouse persisted. "We must find the Chronicler. We must find him and get him to take the sword before Etanun can."

"The Black Dogs have been sent for him." Eanrin sighed heavily and shook his head. "They always catch their prey. We'll never find him."

"That's not what Etanun said."

"Really?" Eanrin ground his teeth. "Go on, turncoat. I'll hear you out. But make it fast."

Mouse quickly related the conversation she had overheard on the rooftop—the power of blood ties that even the Dragonwitch could not deny. And she expressed that she believed Etanun was telling them how to prevent the disaster about to fall.

"I don't believe it," Eanrin said. "Not from the Murderer."

"Alistair is the Chronicler's cousin," Mouse said. Alistair, who had understood none of their conversation, half turned to her at the sound of his name, then looked away again. "If anyone is to find the heir in the Diggings, it would be him."

"Yes," Eanrin acknowledged grudgingly. "I know about kinship bonds.

So what are you suggesting? That we sneak our redheaded hero into the Diggings right under the noses of your priestesses?"

Mouse shook her head. "The opening to the Diggings is too heavily watched. You as a cat might be able to slip through, but I could not get Alistair even within the temple limits."

"It would seem a hopeless business, then, wouldn't it?"

Here Mouse bit her lips, afraid of the reaction to what she was about to say. After all, why should they trust her? She scarcely trusted herself anymore.

"I know another way into the Diggings," she said.

10

*D*EATH WAS NOT TO BE MY FATE, HOWEVER. *After that dread fall, I landed in the Near World upon the crest of a high, green mountain. The explosion of my landing shook that world, and fire shot high like a volcano's eruption and burned all within the vicinity.*

Thus they call that place Bald Mountain to this day, for nothing will ever grow upon its slopes again.

The old woman sat in the cold, but she was too old by now to feel it. Only a few years ago, the biting winds of the mountain had been enough to set her reeling. Now she sat wrapped in her thin shawl, looking down from the barren heights to the lowlands far below. To the place where the red light of the temple flickered and where black smoke gathered above the horizon.

She felt the gaping mouth of the cave at her back, but she did not turn to it. She had been promised, yes, and she believed the promise. But now she found her gaze drawn to the temple, that horror to which her granddaughter and great-granddaughter both had run with open arms.

"Won't you return to me?" she whispered.

What tricks life played upon folks, especially if they lived long enough. She shuddered and drew her shawl closer. Goats wandered the rocks below her, nibbling grasses and yanking up vines by their roots, but she had no attention to give them.

They were coming.

The old woman stood slowly, giving her tired limbs the time they needed to unfold and brace against a world that would beat them back down. Behind her the wolf's-head cave leered, but she ignored it and watched the valley, the woods stretching across the mountain slopes below her. Someone came, and quickly too. Even as Starflower had fled the Land a hundred years ago. Even as the Wolf Lord had pursued her, every loping stride taking in miles. So they approached using secret Paths unknown to mortals, following a guide nearly forgotten by those of the Near World.

She spoke aloud, crying, "Is that you?"

"Granna?"

From the forest below, where the tree line gave way to the barren rock of the higher slopes, a small form appeared. The old woman, though tears of disappointment stained her face, smiled a toothless smile.

"My little child!"

She hoped the girl would run to her, would seek her embrace as she once had. But no. Mouse was a woman now or close enough. She climbed the stony Path, followed by two companions Granna could not see well. She could make out only the sad mortality of one and the shining but equally sad immortality of the other.

"Faerie," Granna muttered. She disliked seeing one of their kind returned to her world, yet her heart fluttered . . . not the flutter of weakness she had lived with for years. Rather, the flutter of an imprisoned bird that has just seen that the cage door is ajar.

"Well, child," she said as Mouse drew near. "You've returned."

"Granna," said Mouse and hesitated. She wanted to fling her arms around the woman who had been more than a mother to her since her own mother had left. But she dared not. She was a disgrace. She was a traitor. "I hoped I'd find you here."

"Yup," said the old woman, folding her bone-thin arms and shrugging. "Still here. Not dead, not moved. The old billy died, though. Got a young one from the village, and he gets a bit high and mighty more often than I like."

Alistair and Eanrin drew up behind Mouse, and now that they were near Granna could better see their faces. She liked the looks of the redheaded lad despite his freckles. His hands were a bit too soft for a man's, but his face told her that he wouldn't mind hard work. And when he bowed to her, she thought she might like him enough to kiss him.

"Greetings, good mother," he said, and his words were foreign but pretty in her ear.

"Lights Above us, what have you brought home, girl?" Granna said, raising the grizzle of her remaining eyebrows. "Please don't tell me you've gone and married this pasty white thing. And if you haven't, you'd better explain why not!"

"Oh no, Granna," Mouse hastily broke in. "It's nothing like that." She stood licking her lips, wondering how under heaven she was supposed to explain.

But Eanrin stepped forward then, took Granna's hand, and kissed it gallantly. Unable to ignore him and his immortality anymore, Granna turned at last to him. She found his gaze far clearer and deeper than she had seen in a long time. A gaze older than her own, though simultaneously younger. How like he was to the old Faerie lord she had once served! Yet unlike. There was kindness in this face, however grudging.

And he, looking on her, found it suddenly difficult to breathe. He knew her face, though it was harshly scored by Time.

"I'm here to rescue Starflower," he said.

"Good," said she. "Bring her to see me when you've done. I've been promised, you know."

"We must enter the Netherworld first," said he. "There are prophecies afoot. She's at the heart of it."

"I'm not surprised," said Granna. "She always had a way of getting to the heart of things."

"Mouse tells us you know another entrance to the Netherworld. An entrance of which the priestesses are unaware."

"I might."

"His kinsman is lost in the Dark," Eanrin said, indicating Alistair with a wave of his hand. "He must find him before it's too late. Can you tell us where the gate is?"

Granna looked into those ancient golden eyes and saw love shining there. A strange, young love for the age of that face. A love that was only beginning to understand what love meant. Very different from Starflower. Starflower had been born loving.

She turned to Alistair and gave him an up-and-down appraisal. "Does he know what he's doing?"

"No," said Eanrin.

"Probably as well. Why does he want to find this kinsman of his? Is it for his own sake?"

"Hardly," said Eanrin. "If he succeeds, his kinsman will take from him everything he has ever thought he wanted."

"Which can be the best thing for a man upon occasion. Wouldn't you agree, Faerie?"

Eanrin shrugged and his look darkened. "I'm not so well acquainted with your mortal ways as all that."

"What has mortality to do with it?" Granna reached out then and snatched hold of Alistair's wrist. He startled but did not draw back, offering what was probably meant to be a friendly grin. It was a bit condescending, but Granna shrugged it off. "Come here, lad," she said, though she could see that he did not understand her. She tugged gently. "Come, all of you. I'll show you the way."

She led them up the short incline. The wind grew harsher within a few paces, warning of danger and darkness. She felt hesitancy, even fear, running up and down Alistair's arm. But he was a good boy, she thought, for he did not resist her. She liked those she didn't have to battle, especially these days.

The open mouth of the cave awaited them. But it would not reveal itself even to the Faerie until Granna stood before it. "Look!" she said, pointing one gnarled finger.

They looked. They saw. Alistair drew a hissing breath, and Eanrin said, "Lights Above! So it's true!"

The cave like the head of a wolf yawned before them, and the breath of the Netherworld eased to and from its mouth. Mouse, who had seen it before, nevertheless hung back, and even Eanrin, who had walked the Paths of the Netherworld, felt the hair on his neck bristle.

But Alistair gently freed himself from Granna's grip and stepped forward, gazing into the darkness. "So," he said, "I'm to venture in there and find the Chronicler."

Eanrin nodded. "Try to anyway."

"And all I have to do is walk in and look? No guide? No map? No . . . no light?"

Eanrin stepped up alongside the young man and folded his arms across his chest. "I can't promise you anything," he said. "I know only what I've heard. Blood calls to blood. Kinfolk know kinfolk, in the dark better than anywhere. If you're meant to have a light, light will be provided. If you're meant to walk in the dark, then in darkness you'll walk."

"But I'll find the Chronicler?"

"I hope so," said Eanrin. And suddenly he turned and placed a hand on Alistair's shoulder. "I wish you well, mortal. You've demonstrated courage in all of this, and I think . . . I think you might have done your uncle proud had you inherited Gaheris."

"Too bad for that, then, eh?" said Alistair, and his voice was bitter. Then he shook himself as though he could shake away all the thoughts crowding his head. "What will you do?" he asked. "You'll not venture into this dark with me?"

"No," said Eanrin. "I would not be able to help you in any case. This is a matter of kinship and blood ties, and has nothing to do with me. Mouse and I will return to the Citadel. I have my comrade to free, and Mouse must try to rejoin the ranks of the priestesses. If they haven't found her out already, we might be able to infiltrate their number and possibly prevent Etanun from cursing the world yet again."

Alistair nodded. "Very well," he said, "it's a plan. I'm not saying it's a good one. But it's a plan."

He squared his shoulders and moved toward the cave mouth.

He looked into the dark of his nightmare.

He recognized the smell and felt the fingers of shadows reaching to touch his face. He strained his ears, expecting even now to hear the Dogs baying. He heard nothing more than heavy silence. That didn't matter, though. He would hear them soon enough.

"So it's not a child after all," he whispered. "It's the Chronicler I'll find. Before I die."

He had known this was coming. Yes, he could protest. He could tell Eanrin his fears, and he did not doubt that the cat-man, for all his sharp tongue, would tell him not to bother, to back away, to let them invent some other scheme.

He took a step.

Then he stopped and looked around.

Mouse stood in the shadows apart from the others, her arms wrapped around her small body.

Alistair drew a long breath. Then, despite Eanrin's muttered protest, he strode down the incline, and Mouse's face tilted back farther and farther as he approached, for he was much taller than she.

"I have something I want to say to you."

She didn't understand him. But she prepared for the tirade about to fall. After the kindness he had demonstrated to the bedraggled urchin begging at the gates, after the courageous way he had faced the goblins of Gaheris by her side . . . after all that, and after what she had done, she deserved whatever he gave her.

"I didn't want to say anything earlier," he said.

Though she knew none of the words, she heard anger, frustration. She forced herself to meet his gaze, though she feared she would embarrass herself with tears.

"All the while we were following the cat up here," said Alistair, "I told myself I wouldn't breathe a word. I told myself to let it go, to let the past be what it was, to think no more of it. After all, we're probably all of us going to die. Me now; you, soon enough."

She heard his voice shake. She could guess at every word that rained down upon her head, and she wanted to cower. At a command from him she might have flung herself from the mountain, so deep was her shame!

Traitor. Liar. Demon's minion. Nothing he could call her was as bad as what she called herself.

"I'm going into that dark," Alistair said, "and I know what end I'll meet. You're off on a death march yourself after all those dragon-eaten priestesses. And I think to myself, this is it. This is where heroes either declare themselves or go home. Well, I'm not going home."

His fists clenched and she wondered if he would strike her and if she would have the gall to ward off his blow.

"Look," he said, "you can't understand me, so I'm going to say this the simplest way I know how."

The next moment he took her by the shoulders. Because she could not help wincing away, the first kiss he gave her landed awkwardly on the side of her mouth, causing him to catch her face and shift her into a better angle. Her limbs went to stone and her heart stopped beating.

Then he was looking down at her. He blinked once and let her go. "I don't want to hear anything you have to say."

Before she could draw breath, he was climbing back up to the cave and soon would be swallowed.

"Why did you do that?" Mouse cried and nearly fell over herself scrambling after him. "Why didn't you hit me?"

He was at the cave mouth now. He was inside. The red of his hair gleamed in the sunlight and then vanished. Mouse fell on her hands and knees, cutting her palms, but was up again in a moment, standing on the brink of that darkness and shouting, "You had no right to do that, you pale-faced dog of a bullying man!"

Eanrin, leaning with his shoulder against the rock of the cave opening, called down into the dark, "She says your kisses are like drops of summer rain on a parched and thirsty land."

Alistair's voice carried up. "I don't want to hear!"

"Cat! Cat!" Mouse cried, turning to Eanrin. "Tell him I hope he trips in the dark and breaks that stupid face of his! I'd like to see him try to kiss me again!"

"She says," Eanrin called into the black, "she'd like to see you try to kiss her again."

"I'm not listening" came Alistair's voice, faint from the shadows.

"Tell him I hate the sight of him!"

"And she loves you."

There was no answer. Alistair was gone.

Mouse stood breathing hard, tears brimming in her eyes. She pressed a hand to her heart. Why did it beat so fast? Fury, most likely.

"Did you tell him, cat?" She gulped, anxious to disguise the tremor in her voice. "Did you tell him right?"

"I told him, girl," Eanrin said with a cattish smile. "I told him better than you could yourself."

11

I DO NOT WELL REMEMBER WHAT TRANSPIRED AFTER THAT. I lay for a time exposed and mindless upon that mountain. I did not know myself, and when Amarok the Wolf Lord came to me, I did not know him either. He told me I was a mortal, and I believed him. He told me that he loved me, that I loved him in return, and I believed this as well.

He, a mere Faerie-shifter, not a king, not a lord! Master of a stolen demesne carved from the mortals' world and peopled with slaves who called him "god." And I believed him a god as well, and I worshipped him, and I bore his monstrous children.

Twins. Dogs.

She could almost believe she was alone in the world, so quiet was Gaheris Castle at night. Even the breaking of stone below was stilled, and the crack of the whips as the slaves were shuffled off to sleeping quarters to steal a few precious hours.

Not Leta. She lit the few candles provided for her and continued search-ing the documents. It felt hopeless, but better to work than to sit in the darkness and be afraid. So she lit candle after candle, her eyes burning as she searched the various books and scrolls.

Four days had passed since she'd been imprisoned in the library. Every day Corgar returned and asked her what she had found. Every day, when she could tell him nothing, she expected his wrath to fall upon her. Instead, he would stand quietly and watch her work. Then he would leave, and she would find the ability to breathe once more.

"You've read everything," she muttered that night, shivering, crouched over her small candle flame. "You've read everything in this room! There's nothing here."

So he'll kill you, said her practical side.

Rebellious Leta had only the energy to shrug. "Let him kill me, then," she muttered. "I still have nothing."

She turned slowly on the stool, scanning the shadow-filled room. Her eyes lingered on the tapestry and the hidden door. But that was no use. Not without the key. She had inserted every quill knife and bit of broken kindling she could find into that lock; nothing would make it give.

Suddenly she frowned, her attention caught by something that had somehow escaped her notice. She hopped down from the stool, took up her candle, and hastened across the chamber.

How silly of her not to think of this before! In her mind, the library loft was the Chronicler's private space, a haven she dared not enter.

But the Chronicler was gone. And she was here. And she was bound to die come dawn, when she confessed to Corgar that the library docu-ments held nothing of interest to him. Before she gave in, she might as well thoroughly examine this room that had become her prison.

Her candle casting long shadows, she climbed the spiral stair to the humble space where she found, as she'd expected, the Chronicler's sleeping pallet and, naturally, even more piled scrolls and documents.

"Silly girl," she scolded herself, kneeling by the nearest pile haphazardly tossed in a corner. "You should have guessed. Who knows what you might find in here?"

Her spirits higher, if only a little, she set down her candle, took up the nearest scroll, and unrolled it across the floor, pinning it in place with her knee. Looking at it, she frowned. The handwriting was familiar, but she wasn't entirely certain why. It wasn't the Chronicler's, and it wasn't old Raguel's. Chewing the inside of her cheek, she leaned down and read:

> *I carry the future in my womb. I carry the king who will open the House of Lights. My only sorrow is that I shall never meet him, that he will never know how I loved him.*
>
> *Be bold, Smallman! Claim your right and live as you were meant to live.*

Leta stared. She read it again and a third time, hardly believing what she saw. Then she sat back, pushing her straggling hair out of her face.

"You knew," she whispered to the darkness. "You knew all along."

The hand was Lady Pero's. She recognized it now from the poem she had read earlier that year, the poem which the Chronicler had so meticulously copied.

Leta's fingers shook as she rolled up that scroll and reached for the next one. It too was in the ornate, difficult-to-read hand of Earl Ferox's dead wife. Leta read:

> *I have heard the Spheres singing. I have seen the House of Lights. What I know I cannot share with others; I write it here now for your eyes, my child. It is near, nearer than you think. And you will see it one day. You will open the doors. But you must see for yourself. I cannot show you.*
>
> *I wish I was there with you now to guide you. But I know, from the failing in my own body, that I shall not live to meet you face-to-face. My last request to my lord is for him to see to it that you are brought up with letters. One day you will read these words of mine, and I pray they will guide you.*

All this, hidden away in the Chronicler's alcove.

"You *knew*," Leta said aloud this time as she let the second scroll snap back into its comfortable roll. "You *are* the Smallman King! Why have you denied it? Are you really so afraid?"

Then she shook her head, her forehead wrinkling. "He's dead. The goblins killed him. How can he ever be king?"

Though the little chamber above the library was cold as ice, Leta felt sweat forming on her upper lip. Wiping her face, she reached for a third scroll. On this was inscribed only:

Ceaneus told me. Look to Ceaneus.

This was the most enigmatic by far of all Lady Pero's writings. Leta stared at it, whispering the name to herself. "Ceaneus. The blue star."

Taking the third scroll, she went back downstairs, set aside her candle, and approached one of the narrow windows to gaze upon the cold world below, at the broken walls and piles of rubble, the ruins that Gaheris was swiftly becoming under Corgar's direction.

The sky was overcast. But Leta thought she saw faint light, like moonlight, gleaming through the heavy clouds overhead.

Then, rather suddenly, there was a break. Rather than the moon Leta saw a single star, the blue star. Ceaneus, as the North People called it. It was bigger by far than she remembered it being, shining down upon the mortal world with an intensity like magic.

"Ceaneus told me," Leta muttered, clutching Lady Pero's scroll. Then, feeling more than half a fool, she called out in a meek voice, "Will you tell me too?"

There was no answer. Not that she expected one as such. Nevertheless Leta waited, her ears straining.

You're going mad, her practical side said. *Lady Pero went mad before she died. That's why she wrote these things. She went mad, and now you are too.*

"Be still!" Leta growled, and her practical side was shocked into silence. A silence that lingered under starlight, wrapped in the coldness of winter.

The courtyard was in ruins. The walls of the guest house extending from the keep looked as though some monstrous insects had been eating away at the stone. Even the mausoleum was broken, its fine marble scored with deep gouges, the door to the crypt hanging on its hinges.

But one structure, Leta noticed with mild curiosity, had not yet been touched by the goblins and their mortal slaves.

One lone, humble building.

Leta gasped.

She stumbled back from the window, dropping Lady Pero's scroll, and stood in near darkness. Suddenly she whirled about, hurling herself at the pile of books on the long table, books she had scoured again and again, and dug through them until she came to a volume near the bottom. A familiar volume. The first she had seen when she stepped into the library all those months ago.

It fell open to the familiar page: the nursery song of the Smallman, with its bold illumination of the House of Lights. The vellum was torn by Corgar's claws, but in the glow of her candle, the colored ink on that page still shimmered like liquid gold pouring from those carefully sketched windows.

Leta stared, hardly believing what she was seeing.

"I've found the House of Lights," she said.

The grating squeal of door hinges startled Leta into dropping the book. She whirled about as Corgar entered the library.

12

BUT EVENTUALLY MY MIND RETURNED. Amarok could not deceive me forever. I began to recall myself, my flame, my voice. I began to recall the power I'd been reborn to, the power of dragons. Though I could not again take my dragon form, I found my fire and blazed brightly. I could not kill Amarok in his self-made demesne, but I escaped him with our children.

And later, when opportunity arose, I saw to it that he was slain.

Two guards stood at the outer gate of the Citadel of the Living Fire. The younger kept glancing up at the sky. The elder fixed his eyes upon some distant point on the horizon that never came any closer, unwilling to see what the younger saw: the churning smoke, dark even against the night sky, blotting out stars. And the occasional flash of red flame.

The goddess was angry. Or glad. It scarcely mattered which.

Something was brewing, the young guard thought. True, the Flame was temperamental, and he'd seen firestorms before, some worse than this. But this evening the air held a tension he could not begin to describe—tension flowing from the top of the Spire down into the temple grounds and on even here, to the edge of the holy ground. He wondered if his comrade felt it and might have liked to ask. But he had long since forgotten how to speak. Perhaps he had been cursed or poisoned. Perhaps he had merely been forbidden to let a word cross his lips. Either way, he was as mute as if they'd cut out his tongue.

Men of the Citadel were less than animals. They were also loyal unto death.

Still, he could not help wondering what life might have been had he not been taken for his village's temple tax all those years ago, dragged from his mother's arms, presented before cold-faced priestesses, shamed and degraded. . . .

"What-ho, young fellow, got any Time?"

The guard turned to see his comrade drop like a stone under some unseen blow. His mouth fell open, and he raised his spear, but someone tapped his shoulder from behind. He whirled about to face a pair of bright eyes gleaming in the gloom.

Then he too fell senseless as Eanrin's blow struck his forehead.

Eanrin stood over the two fallen guards, his eyes narrowed. "Come out and help me, girl," he said. "We can't leave them lying here."

Mouse emerged from the shadows along the wall, hastened to Eanrin's side, and helped him drag the guards away from the gate into a hollow where they would be less visible from the inside. "They'll change watch eventually, but no need to draw attention before then," Eanrin said.

Mouse, shaking too hard to answer, eyed the same churning smoke and fire that had bothered the guard, and felt her stomach heave. Walking the Faerie Path in Eanrin's wake had so completely thrown off her sense of time and space that she thought her head might explode. Mortals weren't intended to walk such Paths, of this she was certain. Was it only a few hours since she had stood on the slopes of the mountain beside Granna? Since Alistair had vanished into the darkness?

Or had weeks gone by and the Dragonwitch already achieved her goal?

"What are you staring at, girl?" Eanrin growled. "Nightfall won't await our convenience, and we need to be well inside before we lose the last of this twilight. With any luck, they won't have noticed you're gone yet."

Mouse shuddered but followed Eanrin through the gate without a word. He wore his cat form, a better disguise in this land of black hair and eyes. He stopped in the middle of the road, his tail upraised, his pink nose sniffing uncertainly. She knew he hated to admit any deficiency of knowledge, so she took the lead, still without speaking.

Then it was the long trek through the city temple, which had become more familiar to her than the mountain of her childhood, but which was, she saw now, far more treacherous. Every shadow was a threat where dragons or ghosts or Black Dogs might lurk, and she felt the presence of the Netherworld beneath her feet.

"Dragon's teeth!" Eanrin swore quietly as they climbed the road toward the Citadel. "I know that building. It looks just like the towers of Etalpalli!" His tail lashed uneasily. "That settles it for sure."

Mouse did not understand what he meant by this, so she made no answer. She didn't like leading Eanrin through the broad front entrance of the lower temple, but she knew it would be the safest way, especially this time of night. The big entrance doors stood open, as always. Mouse clung to the shadows along the wall as she and the cat slipped inside.

To her surprise the cat scampered ahead, tail high, nose twitching. It was too dark to see anything of him save the faint gleam of his white paws and chest. He came to a stop, one paw upraised, then looped around back to her.

"I smell her," he said in a low voice. "I smell Imraldera. She came this way, did she not?"

Mouse nodded, afraid to speak. The cat's voice seemed to echo around the pillars, but that might have been her imagination.

"Which way to the dungeons?" Eanrin demanded.

Mouse shook her head vigorously. "Not yet. If you draw attention now, I'll never reach my chambers."

The cat's ears flattened, and his eyes glinted with their own light. "You do what you must, little girl," he said. "Infiltrate their ranks as you infiltrated ours. Follow Etanun to the Netherworld and see if you can push back the tide of prophetic events. I, however, will find my comrade, with or without your help."

With those words, he slinked away, vanishing into the heavy shadows of the pillared hall.

Never before had Mouse felt quite so alone.

"There's no one to tell you what to do now," she whispered to herself, forcing her feet to move. "You're on your own. Time to start making decisions for yourself!"

So she crept like a thief through the temple that was her home and succeeded in gaining the privacy of her room without being seen. Or so she fervently hoped.

Mouse entered the Speaker's chambers as she had always done, before the last of the sun's glow had quite vanished beyond the horizon, and prepared the braziers for evening incense. As she knelt to her task, her hands shaking with fear and exhaustion, she didn't hear the rustle of the high priestess's robes and remained unaware of the Speaker's presence until she felt the clasp of a hand on her shoulder from behind.

"There you are, child," said the Speaker, her voice cold but not ungentle. "I was beginning to worry."

With an effort Mouse kept a hold on her brand. She turned and made the sign of blessing and reverence but did not trust herself to speak. She had slipped into her acolyte robes, discarded her disguise, and hastened about her daily tasks as though everything was as usual.

But one look in the Speaker's eyes told her that everything, in fact, was not as usual, and no one was deceived otherwise.

She's going to kill me, Mouse thought and dropped her gaze again.

"I sent for you this morning," the Speaker said, the pressure of her hand still firm on Mouse's shoulder. "I thought you might need comforting after the experiences you underwent yesterday. The near presence of the Flame can be distressing even to the holiest among us."

Mouse couldn't speak. Her mouth was as dry as the land beyond the temple grounds.

"Though they searched, no one could find you to bring you to me." How stonelike was the Speaker's voice. Like those of the goblins who had taken Gaheris, Mouse thought. Only the goblins' voices were of volcanic rock, ready at any moment to burst into heat and danger. The Speaker's, by contrast, was a voice of marble.

The tall woman released her hold on Mouse and stepped back, her arms folded, the sleeves of her robe draping down her front. She wore her evening wig, woven ornately with gold, lacking its usual crown of star-flowers. Her robe was the finest, softest, most vibrant in her collection. Bangles decorated her arms but could not hide the burns. Some of these were fresh burns, Mouse realized, and wondered what agonies the high priestess had suffered under the Dragonwitch's passionate flames last night.

Yet the Speaker served, and if she questioned the rightness of her service, she never did so out loud. She was, Mouse realized, a woman who could never be wrong. No matter the evidence to the contrary, she would cling to the rightness she had first decided to grasp. It was this more than anything that bound her in chains.

"Poor child," the Speaker said. "You went into hiding, didn't you?"

Despite herself, Mouse's gaze flickered up to meet that of her mistress.

"Didn't you?" the Speaker repeated, and her eyes searched Mouse's face, revealing nothing in turn.

"I—" Mouse faltered, then stopped.

"You did," said the Speaker, as though deciding the shape of the universe once and for all; let no god or goddess try to contradict her. "You hid. But you are here now. And you are my loyal little Mouse, and you will serve me now, at the end."

Then the Speaker turned from Mouse and gave a sharp word of command. Slaves came forward and scurrying acolytes, none of whom looked Mouse's way. "Come, child," said the high priestess without looking around. "Take up my train. The time of Fireword's waking has come at last. I want you beside me."

So Mouse took up her mistress's train as commanded and progressed from the high priestess's rooms out to the pillared hall where all the priestesses and their slaves had gathered with unlit torches, gaudy in their finery. Even the eunuchs, their weapons polished, wore finer clothing than Mouse had ever seen them in.

Then she saw the scrubber.

He stood in the center of it all, humble and slouching, ugly in his servant's garb amid the splendor of the Citadel worshippers. He kept his face lowered, and at first Mouse wondered if he had the grace to be ashamed. Then she saw—though she wondered later if she had seen it right—that his head was bent because, of all things, he was trying to disguise a smile.

The Speaker approached, towing Mouse in her wake.

"The time has come," she said. Of the two, the Speaker and Etanun, it was she who appeared immortal. She was so tall and so beautiful, and one had to look closely to see the scars of burns on her dark skin. The scrubber, by contrast, was as dirtbound as a man could be.

He looked up at the Speaker, and his eyes twinkled. "So it would seem," he said.

To Mouse's surprise, he spoke her language. Not the Faerie language she was growing accustomed to hearing translate in her head. No, he spoke the language of her people as naturally as though he had been born and raised in this country.

It was the first time in she could not guess how long that she had heard her own speech pass the lips of a man.

The Speaker recoiled, offense etching her face. "It is now two hundred years, Murderer, since you earned yourself that title."

The scrubber shrugged. "So glad I got here at last. Wouldn't want to miss an event such as this!"

Mouse thought the Speaker would slap the old man. Her face revealed a struggle. Instead, she turned, the gold-edged braids of her wig swinging about her shoulders. "The will of the goddess!" she cried to the assembly. "The will of the Fire. We go into the Dark to retrieve the Light."

"The will of the Fire!" replied her loyal cohorts as one voice, and the silent eunuchs raised their spears.

Mouse felt a chill down her spine, as though something dreadful reached out to her from behind, drawing her attention. Holding up the end of her mistress's train, she looked back over her shoulder at the scrubber, her former master, and his foolish old face.

Their eyes locked.

And suddenly, without a word passing between them, Mouse knew what she must do.

The moment Alistair crossed the cave's threshold, shadows pressed in around him, thick and palpable. This was a different darkness than even the dank air of the secret passage. This was much more like the family crypt of Gaheris castle.

Alistair descended, taking firm strides to disguise to himself how his heart quaked with dread. He would not think of Mouse. He would not think of the sword, or kingship, or even of the Chronicler. He must concentrate entirely on making himself take each step.

Blood calls to blood, so the legends say, especially on the Path to Death, where the ties of kinship are all that yet link the dead to the living.

"Well," Alistair whispered, his voice catching in his throat, "let's hope the legends know what they're talking about."

The first few minutes seemed more horrible to him than blindness or death. But this was the world where the dead and living meet, and a confused half-light filled Alistair's eyes. Somehow, this was worse than utter darkness. He could almost see but not quite, and that bewildered him. Sometimes he felt his feet descending a steep, slippery slope, and he heard the skittering of loose pebbles as he kicked them free.

But sometimes he thought his feet trod a firm stairway, each step carefully formed to match its brothers. His going was easier then.

Blood calls to blood.

The thought went round in his head. How? he wondered. It would be one thing if, like the Brothers Ashiun, he felt some real sense of kinship with the man who was his cousin. But he didn't. The Chronicler was his teacher, his antagonist, a dry and disapproving entity whom Alistair had always ignored when he could. He scarcely knew him, when it came down to it.

And Alistair had more reason than any other living person to resent him.

Yet here he was, wandering in the half-light, realizing with every step he took that the gloom around him was far bigger, far broader than a subterranean cavern. It was a whole world.

A world peopled with its own inhabitants.

He could neither see nor hear them. But he felt them: lost souls, near and far at once, wandering all around him. Did they seek an escape back to the world above? Did they search for the Final Water and freedom from this tormented roving? He did not know. He could not understand them.

But he felt his heart breaking for them.

Alistair stopped suddenly when he realized that the Path he followed had leveled out under his feet. No more descent then. He had arrived in the very pit of the Netherworld.

"Blood calls to blood," he whispered, and his voice sounded foreign in his own ears. He drew a long breath and felt the invisible wraiths around him drawing theirs as well. The air was cold down here. Then, shaking his head and telling himself he was fearless, he shouted:

"Chronicler! Are you here?"

The wraiths fled. His voice was too much for them, and he sensed their swift withdrawal to the hidden-most places of their realm. Alistair stood, breathless, and listened to his own voice being swallowed up as it chased after the frightened ghosts.

There was no answer.

Fear inched up his spine, willing him to give way. It whispered in his ear. *You haven't forgotten your dream, have you?*

With a crash of memory, images stormed his brain. Alistair nearly fell to his knees at the power of them. Images of the darkness, of the ravening dogs, and of death.

"Dreams aren't real," he muttered. "They're only illusions."

But only illusions can live here, his fear responded.

Alistair started walking. It was that or stand and listen, which he could not do. He had made his choice: He had descended the dark way, and he would let no whispers or half-truths misguide him now!

"Blood calls to blood," he muttered. Well, he had called, hadn't he? He'd called as loud as he could, and he felt even now that his voice continued to wing its way into every far corner of this realm. But it was useless. He could not find his cousin like this.

Suddenly he stopped again. "Fool that you are," he growled, striking his temple with the heel of his hand. "Blood calls to blood! You know better than that."

Then he bowed his head and closed his eyes and recalled as best he could that moment at the bedside of his dying uncle.

"*Florien,*" Earl Ferox had said.

"Florien," Alistair whispered. Not Chronicler. Florien.

Cousin. Heir.

Kinsman.

The displaced young lord raised his chin and threw his shoulders back like a warrior ready to do battle with anything this realm might throw at him. And he called out once more in a loud voice:

"Florien! I'm coming for you!"

At first nothing happened. Alistair stood, breathing hard, listening to the fleeing echoes.

How long had that light been there?

Blinking, Alistair found he could not remember. He hadn't noticed it until now. Yet it had been shining bright as a star in the night, always present if not always seen.

Like a sailor guided on wild oceans, Alistair pursued the glow. At first he thought it must be a great light indeed. But the closer he drew, the smaller he realized it was, until at last he found himself approaching a humble gravestone, atop which sat a small lantern of delicate silver-filigree work, rendered unnoticeable by the beauty of the pure light it contained.

Alistair knew it and named it without hesitation.

"Asha," he said. "Gift of Akilun."

Akilun, who had once descended into the Netherworld himself in pursuit of his brother. Blood calling to blood. Kinsman pursuing kinsman.

Even unto death.

Alistair reached out and took hold of Asha's handle, lifting it from the gravestone.

13

I RETURNED TO ETALPALLI for the first time since my departure. And I saw my subjects, the Sky People, winging through the air while I myself remained earthbound, for the Dark Father had taken my wings.

I killed them all. Cren Cru himself could not have meted out the destruction I gave my own demesne. I killed the Sky People and I burned Etalpalli into blackened ruin.

So shall I burn all who oppose me.

Eanrin considered himself a cat of many talents. He could steal the attention of everyone in a crowded hall without raising his voice. He could entertain Faerie lords and ladies of any demesne beyond the Wood Between, and he charmed smiles from rocks and snakes if he felt the need.

But he was also remarkably good at lurking.

He lurked in the deepest crevices of the Citadel. Even as night fell and the priestesses gathered; even as he watched the Murderer, hands and limbs bound, brought to the center of the hall; even as the high priestess, Mouse standing in her shadow, rallied her slaves about her, Eanrin lurked and watched and waited.

When they had gone, he slipped down to the dungeons.

It was an easy enough feat getting past the dungeon guards. He kept to his cat form, and they never saw or suspected his presence. Following his nose, he proceeded down the long stairs, catching snatches here and there of a familiar scent.

"Imraldera?" he called, keeping his voice low in case there were more guards than he realized. "Are you around, my dear?"

He tested the air for her scent once more. But here below the Spire, the Netherworld was far too close, and it overwhelmed his senses. Cursing, he called again, "Imraldera?"

"Eanrin? Is that you?"

It was like the sudden easing of a pain grown so constant that he scarcely recognized its presence anymore. And the relief flooding in was sharper by far than the pain itself. Eanrin took on man form, but his body trembled so that he was obliged to lean against the wall for support. Then he was running down the dark passage, his eyes gleaming like two lanterns.

"Eanrin!"

Her voice called to him from down low. He dropped to his knees and peered into the cell. He could not see her face; even his cat's eyes struggled to find enough light to see by in this place, and her starflower had withered away. He reached his hand through the bars.

"Oh!" came her voice, irked and exhausted. "That was my nose you just grabbed. Have a care, cat!"

"Sorry, old girl," he replied, withdrawing his hand. His throat thickened and he could barely speak. "Well," he managed, his voice disguising a tremor, "this is a fine mess you've gotten yourself into, isn't it? If someone had told me that Dame Imraldera, Lady of the Haven, gate guarder and knight, would take the word of Etanun at face value and scamper off into the dangerous unknown without a second—"

"Have done," she growled and her hand, reaching through the bars, grabbed hold of his. How thin and weak it had become during her imprisonment! "Can you free me?"

"It would take more than a lock worked by mortal hands to stop me," said Eanrin and, with sudden gallantry, pressed her hand to his lips. Of course he had to laugh and pass it off as foolishness, and she pulled away from him quickly.

"Get me out, then," she said.

He felt around until he found the lock. It was more complicated than he had expected, but it was still nothing more than a mortal lock.

"They took the heir to the Diggings," Imraldera said as he worked.

"I know. But our little Mouse freed him," Eanrin replied. "So the Murderer showed up and offered to do the deed himself."

"Etanun?"

"They don't need the heir to fetch the sword as long as the master is willing." Eanrin's tone was merry, but his face was grim in the darkness.

"Don't be silly!" Imraldera snapped, and it warmed his heart to hear her sound like herself despite everything. "Do you really think our Lord would trust his will to an untrustworthy man?"

"I'm not saying anything against our Lord," Eanrin muttered, "when I say I don't trust his servant. Etanun is a sly dog—and I do mean *dog*, my girl, you may believe me! Do you know that because you were lured away from the gates, Corgar of Arpiar broke through into the Near World and is even now having his way with a whole host of pale Northerners? Tell me that's part of our Lord's plan, why don't you?"

Imraldera said nothing at first, and Eanrin congratulated himself on having talked her into agreement, however grudging her silence. But then she said, "His ways are beyond our understanding. That doesn't mean they aren't right."

"You are a trusting little mite, aren't you?" With a click, the lock swung free. "Behold! Am I not a wizard?" Eanrin smirked and took Imraldera's hands to haul her up and out. She could scarcely stand at first, for her limbs were too numb after that cramped imprisonment. Eanrin longed suddenly to draw her to his side . . . under the guise of comforting her, of course, though it was he who needed the comfort. But he couldn't quite bring himself to it. A cat does have his pride to consider.

So she stood on her own, leaning only slightly on his hands as the blood flowed back into her legs and shoulders. He heard her soft groans, but she did not complain. At last he felt her squeeze his fingers, and she turned to him in the darkness.

"I knew you'd come for me," she said. "Thank you."

He opened his mouth a few times, but words choked him. So he shrugged and flashed a careless smile to hide what his bright eyes might reveal. "It's not as though I can keep the watch by myself, now, can I? I need my comrade-in-arms all in one piece, thank you much."

Imraldera smiled softly, perhaps because she thought he could not see it; though of course he saw much better in the dark than she could. When she spoke again, however, her voice hardened and all trace of softness fled. "We must prevent the Dragonwitch from gaining Halisa."

"Oh, I wouldn't worry too much," Eanrin said cheerily, though he frowned as she took her hands from his. "There are great prophecies at work, you know; mighty deeds to be done as foretold by the stars."

"Don't be daft," Imraldera said, and it was so good to feel the world falling back into its normal patterns. "Prophecies don't come true on their own. We must do our part!"

She started up the dungeon passage, and he quickly fell into place behind her. "Wait, old girl," he said, reaching out but missing her shoulder in the shadows. "Don't get ahead of me; I don't want to lose you so soon after I've found you! You have a habit of doing stupid things, you know. Drinking from Faerie rivers, making bargains with monsters—"

"In that case, you'd better keep up!" said she.

The Diggings went on forever.

Sometimes the Chronicler believed he still walked in mortal-dug tunnels on rough paths hewn by mortal tools. But if he dared look too closely, the tunnels disappeared, leaving him wandering a flat plain, half lit by no visible light.

Always behind him, he heard the howls of the Black Dogs.

His feet fell into a never-ending rhythm of flight—one, two, one, two—on and on through the byways of the Netherworld.

"Find the sword," he muttered. "Find Halisa."

If he looked over his shoulder, he saw the blackness of Midnight approaching. The Dogs would catch him eventually. They must! If all these other Faerie tales were proving themselves true, why should he now doubt the tale of the Black Dogs, who always caught their prey. And he knew beyond doubt that this was his role now. A rabbit on the run, pursued through the tunnels of its warren without hope.

One, two, one, two. The steady slap of his feet upon stone was as unreal a sound in his ears as the baying of the hunt.

"Find Halisa," he whispered, but he knew that he never could.

"Fear not, small man. You will see your people free."

The Chronicler's pace slowed as the voice of memory filled his head. A promise, a prophecy. But how could it be true? How could anything be true in the dark? It didn't matter what he believed, because nothing he believed was real! No heroics, no chosen destinies, and no final moments of truth, because the only final moments could be revelations of falsehood. And that was—

The Chronicler screamed, his arms making circles in the air to catch his balance. He reeled on the edge of a precipice, a drop into nothingness that not even the half-light could penetrate. By some miracle, he caught himself and stepped back, unable to tear his gaze away from that line where the plunge began. An overwhelming sweep of coldness rose up from the depths, replaced a moment later with a blast of heat.

The howls increased. They were close behind him now.

Choose my darkness, spoke a voice from below. A voice like ever-consuming fire.

The Chronicler felt the lure of it more keenly than he had felt the barb of his father's rejection, the pain of Leta's expression when she first saw his ungainly limbs, the agony of disrespect and usurpation under which he had always lived and moved and breathed. Here was the end, the choice to leave all that behind and, in so doing, to clasp it more firmly than ever to his heart.

The Black Dogs drew near.

The Chronicler took a step. It was either that plunge of his own choosing, or the jaws of those monsters clamping down upon him. Whether they dragged him to death or back to life and the Dragonwitch's will, what did it matter? What did he matter?

Choose my darkness, said the voice from the pit.

It seemed the right choice. The only choice.

"Florien!"

At first hearing, the Chronicler did not recognize the sound of his own name. But it froze him in place, immobilizing his limbs. He could not take the next step to the edge.

"Florien!"

Don't listen to that, said the voice from the pit. *You have no name.*

Yet the Chronicler stood like stone. With an effort of superhuman will, he managed to turn his head to one side. He saw, coming toward him with great speed, a light. A pure, white light filled with colors within the whiteness. It was the light of nursery rhymes. The light of Faerie tales.

It was the light of Asha. And Alistair's voice called to him.

"Florien!"

"Alistair!"

Once upon a time, blood called to blood on the edge of darkness. Once upon a time, a choice was made and brother died for brother, and the light from beyond the Final Water shone its brightest in the realm of Death.

Both the Chronicler and Alistair knew the story. They turned to each other now, and the voice from the pit was stilled as the light filled the gap between them. The Chronicler saw the face of the one who had taken his inheritance; Alistair saw the face of the one who would take that inheritance back again.

But the light revealed more, and each saw the face of his cousin. His brother. His kin by blood.

Nothing else mattered.

Midnight fell. The Black Dogs closed in. They ran together, their heads low, their mouths open, and fire streamed from their eyes. They howled a ravenous hunting cry, as keen as hatred.

But Alistair was between the Chronicler and the Dogs now, his long legs bounding as he followed the light of the lantern. It was a mad race, a fool's race, but as his heart pounded in his throat, he knew he would reach the Chronicler first.

"You shouldn't be here!" the Chronicler yelled. He saw the Black Dogs, their red eyes tearing the darkness beyond Alistair's tall form. The dissonance of their voices was enough to slay all the senses at once.

"I came to find you," Alistair said, scarcely able to draw breath as he ran. But he knew what he must say. He had dreamed it too many times to forget.

"You fool!" the Chronicler cried. "Run away!"

But Alistair did not turn and run, even as the Black Dogs neared. He stopped before his cousin, heaving for breath. "You must be king," he said. "You must save Gaheris."

It was all clear now: his dream, his doom. His purpose, which was not kingship nor power.

The Chronicler screamed. "Watch out! Behind you!"

He did not hesitate. Though he knew what he would see, he spun on his heel. And as the first of the Black Dogs, racing ahead of its brother, leapt at the Chronicler, Alistair let go of the lantern and leapt as well. He wrapped his long arms around the neck and chest of that monster, and they stood, poised upon the brink of the precipice, the Dog snarling in surprise and horror.

"Alistair!" cried the Chronicler.

The tearing of his flesh.

The burn of flaming teeth.

With a final wrench, Alistair turned. It was the most he could do, this last act before he died. He had not seen it in his dreams. He had seen nothing beyond the pain that now shot through his body as the Black Dog ripped into him. But he turned and he pulled, and his strong arms held fast.

They teetered on the edge.

Then Alistair and the Black Dog fell into the swallowing chasm.

———

There was no Time in this place. The Chronicler might have stood for hours, for years, on the brink of that drop, searching the blindness into which his cousin—his cousin, whom he had despised all his life—had fallen.

The howl of the second Black Dog rang in his ears. The Chronicler turned and found the monster bearing down upon him, its mouth red and ravenous. The Chronicler hurled himself to one side and landed hard upon the strange stone of the Netherworld.

Asha gleamed by his hand, lying where Alistair had dropped it.

The Chronicler, unaware of the tears staining his face, grabbed the lantern handle. Then he was up and running back through the darkness through which he had stumbled, this time following the light of Asha.

The Black Dog pursued, hot on his heels.

14

*S*O I SHALL BURN YOU, *even as I plunge the blade that twice killed me deep into your heart.*

"I do not rest at night as you mortals do," Corgar said, closing the library door. "In darkness my people come alive. But mortals are so blind and helpless."

Leta felt the weight of the book on her foot, but she dared not look at it, dared not draw attention its way. She stepped away from the table, away from her flickering candle. But she knew the shadows could not shield her from Corgar's eyes, which gleamed as he moved across the room.

"You," he said, "do not sleep tonight. I saw your candle from below. You are still about your work."

If she spoke, what might her voice betray? Had she the skill to disguise it? She did not trust herself, so she remained silent. Corgar inspected the various papers littering her desk, his claw gently shifting them about, studying the marks he did not know. It was a relief to feel his gaze averted. Leta managed to draw a breath, light as moth wings.

"Do you know," Corgar said, still without looking her way, "that I will be a king?"

He waited so long, Leta knew she would have to answer. Her voice broke in her throat at the first attempt, but she forced it out on a second. "No, sir."

He cast her a quick glance, his eyes flashing in the candlelight. "King of Arpiar," he said. "King of the goblins." His voice was strangely bitter. "My queen, Vartera, has promised to make me her husband if I bring her the light hidden within your fabled House. A small favor but sufficient to make me worthy in her eyes. I am of humble stock, you understand, not the stuff of kings."

Though she dared not look at it, Leta was desperately aware of the book lying facedown on the floor a few paces from her. What if he should see it? What if he should pick it up, and the page was open, the secret exposed? But no. He couldn't possibly guess. Ceaneus would not reveal such a sight to his dreadful eyes!

But she dared not chance it, so she stood like a statue, her gaze fixed anywhere but on the floor.

And Corgar, his voice rumbling deep as the night, continued. "I've always thought I should like to be king. Who would not wish to sit upon a throne? I did myself proud in the war with Rudiobus and caught the queen's eye. *Now's my chance!* I told myself."

He turned to her suddenly, his eyes narrowed and shrewd. "You're quiet this night," he said, "small warrior."

Leta took another few paces back, hardly realizing she did so. She felt the heat of the library hearth behind her, warm on her feet though the fire was low. The rest of her was as cold as the winter-locked stones of Gaheris. "I have been working much," she said.

"Where have all your questions gone?" he persisted, still standing by her desk, where the candlelight caught the sharp edges of his face, casting the rest into masklike shadow. "Where is the fighting spirit?"

She shook her head. "I have none," she said. "I am tired."

"If you have no questions yourself, do you think you might answer one?"

For a crazed moment, Leta wished she could step back and be consumed by that feeble hearth fire. He would ask! He would ask what she knew, and he would know if she lied. Had he not guessed the secret of the hidden key? Somehow he had read her face, had wrested her secret and taken it without a thought.

"Please," she said, "leave me alone. Until morning at least. I am tired."

"Not too tired, I think, to answer me this," Corgar said. His one hand pressed into the desktop, and she saw how his claws tore into the pages lying there. "Tell me, little maid, why should Vartera have all the beauty?"

The words circled round Leta's mind. It took several moments before she realized what he had asked. Then she shook her head and looked down at her feet.

"She takes it all for herself," Corgar said. "Feeds everything into that enchanted pot of hers, boiling it down so that she may drink the brew. Witch that she is! She's drained all Arpiar. Drained it of everything that you, with your mortal eyes, might once have thought fine. Drained all of us, her people, of any graceful proportion, any fair feature we might once have boasted. Now she alone of all the goblin folk may be considered beautiful. But it won't last! No, it will fade, and she will need more fair things to feed her pot. Things like the Flowing Gold of Rudiobus, which we failed to obtain in the war. Things like the light of the last House, which you mortals cannot hope to defend."

Leta listened but understood none of what he said. She was aware only of his great bulk across from her, as yet unmoving. But his chest rose and fell with increasing breath, as though he prepared for battle. She trembled where she stood but could retreat no farther.

"When the Murderer came to Arpiar," Corgar said, "and told her that we should be able to breach the Near World on a certain dawn—the dawn of a nobleman's death—Vartera took my hand and said: 'If you bring back this prize for my pot, I will make you king. How do you like that?' And I said that I would like it well. Fool that I am!"

His hand clenched into a fist, crumpling parchments, tearing paper. "A sip from a brew made from the light of Asha will cause Vartera to shine like Hymlumé herself!" He snarled. "But why should she have all, and we none? Why may I not take a little beauty for myself?"

Leta reached one hand back, grasping the fireplace mantel. Using it as support, she slid around to the other side, behind the bulk of the chimney, wishing to hide and knowing she could not. Corgar's eyes followed her movements. Darkness offered no protection from him.

"I have been thinking," he said, "as I stood down below and saw your candle in the window." He seemed to realize what his fist was clutching and let the crumpled parchment fall to the desk and roll to the floor below. "I have been considering the question of beauty." His eyes flashed. "What is your opinion, mortal? Do I deserve some beauty, goblin though I am?"

Leta pictured the Chronicler earnestly urging her: *"You've let yourself be made into something you were never meant to be. Tell me, have you not longed all your life to prove them wrong?"*

If she did not answer, she feared what Corgar might do. So, though she clung to the cold stones of the chimney, Leta whispered, "We are never obliged to be only what they have told us we are. Not if we were meant to be more."

"Meant to be?" Corgar repeated. "And what was I meant to be? More than a warrior? More than a destroyer? More than a slave to my queen's every whim? Was I *meant* to be more than these?"

"I don't know," said Leta.

"And what of you?" persisted the monster. "Do you know what you were meant to be?"

Say nothing, practical Leta commanded at once. *You'll give away everything if you speak!*

But before she could catch up with herself, her mouth opened and she heard herself saying, "I'll tell you what, I *wasn't* meant to be bandied about like some sort of tool, not by my father, not by my future husband, and certainly not by you! Perhaps you don't see me as much more than a useful nothing with which to accomplish deeds in the name of your wretched queen. But do you know something? You can't read any of these documents without me. Not another breathing soul in Gaheris can do what I'm doing for you, which means, if you kill me, then all this is over. You'll have to go back to your foolish, blind search. So there you have it!"

She stepped from the shadows, her words emboldening her more than they should have, momentarily driving out the crushing fear. "Kill me if you like," she said. "You can bash me on stone like a hammer and chisel. Only my body will break. Because underneath all the usefulness, I am more than a tool. I am me."

She hesitated, telling herself she would regret the next words that sprang forward to be spoken. But rebel Leta was in full control, hotheaded and angry. "And you're you, Corgar of Arpiar. You're only your queen's instrument so long as you allow yourself to be. And maybe she'll kill you if you stop doing her dirty work, but is that really so dreadful a price? When it's a question of death or life-in-death, which is to be preferred?"

"You're quite the philosopher," said the monster dryly.

The rumble of his voice brought practical Leta back to her senses, and she shrank into herself, ducking her head and wondering what nonsense she had just spouted. "Not at all," she replied. "I ask questions, but I have no answers."

"Is that not the way of the philosopher?" Corgar asked. "I have always preferred sword and club to the wanderings of the mind. But here in your world, the air is different. Thinner, sharper. It is difficult for me to breathe, and I hunger for more. More air. More life. More beauty, perhaps, if I only knew what beauty was."

"Beauty is more than any one person can tell you," Leta said.

"What about love?" he asked.

It was a strange question spoken through snarling lips and ragged teeth set in a face from childhood nightmares. Leta could not speak. So he continued. "Love is the final, greatest beauty, am I right?"

"I suppose so," she whispered.

"I do not love Vartera," Corgar said. "Though I slave for her sake, though I will marry her if she will have me, I do not love her. I hate her."

"I'm sorry," Leta said. She could not look at him.

"Don't be. It's not your fault." There was a pause that lasted far too long. Then Corgar said, "Whom do you love, Leta? Whom *can* you love?"

She said nothing.

"Is it only possible for you," he continued, "to love beautiful things? Perfect, well-formed, admirable things?"

The light from the candle slid over his face and vanished as he moved across the floor. Leta wanted to retreat into the corner behind the chimney.

But she couldn't find the will to move. "Is it possible," Corgar said, drawing nearer, "for a creature like you—a creature of beauty—to love someone who is not beautiful? Someone who is marred. Can you see worth in what others would turn from in disgust?"

He stood before her now, towering and cold as the rock he was hewn from. She could see nothing but the light shining in his white eyes, which was far too dreadful to behold. She turned away, and her gaze landed on the discarded book lying facedown on the floor.

Corgar drew a hissing breath. "You have a secret," he said.

"No." Leta dragged her eyes back to his face. It was the most difficult thing she had ever done, but she stood and met his gaze.

"You lie," said Corgar. "You lie to me again."

"I'm frightened," she replied. This, at least, was true.

He put out a hand. She feared he would touch her, and her body recoiled. But his hand froze in the space above her shoulder, and those white eyes narrowed to slits. "I don't want to frighten you."

She shook her head and said, "Now you lie."

Corgar drew back as though stung. His heavy footsteps retreated, and the bulk of his great form blocked the candlelight. Leta stood in darkness until Corgar reached the door and turned back to look at her once more.

"Well, little mortal," he said, "we are at an impasse. Until now I do not believe I have ever seen you truly frightened. But you'll regain your courage, won't you?"

He opened the door and stood framed in the doorway. "Sunlight never fails to raise the spirits of you dying creatures. I'll give you until dawn, and then you must regain your courage and tell me this secret of yours."

He ducked his head and left the room.

The door shut, its iron latch having the final word in the odd exchange. Leta, hardly knowing what had just transpired, stood for a good while, unable to move.

Then she flew to the window and grasped the stone frame, wondering if she could somehow fit through that opening. But no, though she was slight, the slit was too narrow, and the drop below far too great. Even should she succeed in wriggling through, she would smash on the broken paving below.

"I cannot let him know," she whispered, and for once neither her practical nor rebellious side offered a counterargument. "I cannot let him discover what I have learned." Perhaps a fall to the paving stones was the only answer. Then her secret would die with her.

The clouds above churned like a coming storm. Once again they parted suddenly, and Leta gazed up at the shining light of Ceaneus, the blue star. Her eyes filled with desperate tears. If only the House of Lights was opened! If only she could hear the Songs of the Spheres as did the mortals of long ago! She might then be able to call upon their aid, for surely they would look with pity on the plight of those imprisoned in Gaheris.

Involuntarily, her lips formed the words of the old nursery rhyme: "*Starlight, star bright, guide her footsteps through the night.*"

The words vanished with a vaporous breath into the cold darkness. The star above shimmered.

Then it turned and looked at Leta.

How may I serve you? it said.

Leta fell over backward, landing with a thump on the library floor.

15

FOR THIS PURPOSE, I HAVE RETURNED to this land of my former enslavement. I have harnessed the power of mortal devotion, even as Amarok once did. And they worship me and serve me, and they would die for me.

They will die for me.

They will bring me Halisa, and all will be made right in my eyes.

The high priestess's train might as well have been links of chain, so effectually did it bind Mouse to her.

Mouse walked blindfolded, keeping careful pace with the Speaker in front of her, never allowing herself to walk too fast or too slow, as she had been trained from the day she came to the temple. Around her, she heard the murmured chants of the priestesses, the answering whispers of frightened acolytes, and the marching tread of the warriors' heavy feet.

The scrubber she could not sense at all, save for a strange, uneasy feeling that he watched her from behind.

Well, she knew what she must do. She couldn't guarantee it was right, and she was absolutely certain it was not smart. But she would do it, and she would hope, if hope could be found in the winding ways of the Diggings.

She would make certain the Dragonwitch, who had deceived her and all her people, did not gain that for which she had enslaved this world.

"Here," said the Speaker at last, and the company came to a halt. "Remove your coverings."

With one hand Mouse released the high priestess's train and slid her blindfold down around her neck. She blinked, for she had not expected the torchlight to be so bright. The Speaker met her gaze, her black eyes revealing nothing. Mouse looked away and found herself facing the old scrubber, who grinned and nodded knowingly.

The entrance to Halisa's chamber reflected back its shadows even when the eunuchs approached with their torches. It was difficult to believe there was or ever had been a doorway. But when the high priestess strode forward, trailing Mouse behind, the edge of the carved stone accepted the light and revealed itself in sharp contours, all the fine carvings of dreadful things.

And within lay the black stone from which Fireword protruded.

So the Smallman hadn't found it. Mouse felt her heart turn to shivering ice in her breast. She hadn't expected him to succeed, not really. He was lost in the Diggings, like the slave Diggers before him. He would not return. Some prophecies are not meant for fulfillment.

The ice of Mouse's heart hardened to iron resolve, and her fists clenched the edge of her mistress's train. Failed prophecies be devil taken! The Dragonwitch would not carry this day.

The Speaker passed under the arch, and Mouse was obliged to scurry after her. She had no desire to approach either stone or sword, but she had no choice, for her mistress walked right up and stood gazing down upon them. Mouse looked too . . . and was surprised.

The first time she glimpsed the weapon, it had seemed nothing more than an ugly object of violence chipped from the black stone itself. Now she saw, or thought she saw, the gleam of silver. A glimmer truer than firelight.

It's a gift.

The thought slipped into her mind and rested there, growing by the moment. Mouse's eyes widened with wonder.

This sword can slay dragons.

At that moment, Mouse first noticed a sound she hadn't heard the time they came with the Silent Lady—a rumbling like the snarl of a monster awakened from a long sleep. But it couldn't be that. This growl was far more alive than anything Mouse had ever heard before. Alive with power—deep, flowing power.

She looked down at her feet, down at the solid rock on which she stood. And she knew suddenly what voice made that growl.

It was the rivers. All the enchanted rivers of the Hidden Land, flowing beneath them.

Although she could not know if this was true, she believed it nonetheless. And for some reason she could not name, believing gave her hope.

"Come closer, sword-bearer," said the Speaker, turning to the chamber door, where the scrubber stood between his two guards. They led him in, and the other warriors followed, though the priestesses and acolytes remained without, clutching torches and staring into the darkness surrounding them.

"Behold your weapon," said the Speaker as the scrubber was brought before her. With a sweep of her hand, she indicated Halisa.

The scrubber regarded it mildly. "Yup. That's my sword," he said.

"This, the blade with which you twice slew the Flame at Night," said the Speaker. Her tone was incredulous, almost questioning, as she gazed from the stone-chipped sword to the wizened little beggar. "This, the blade with which you quenched her flame."

"Same one," said he, looking up at her. "Mind you, I was a bit spryer! There's been a lot of water under the stone since then."

"With this sword, you will meet your doom at the hand of the Flame," said the Speaker. "Now take it up, old one, and bear your death to her hands."

The scrubber cracked his knuckles, each one giving off a sharp snap. As nonchalant as though Cook had just asked him to fetch an iron ladle, he stepped up to the stone, reached out, and let his gnarled hand hover over the hilt. And as he reached for it, a strange thing happened. The stone flaked away in dry flecks of dust and debris. The nearer his skin came to touching the hilt, the brighter it grew, until it was no longer carved stone at all but wrought silver. Engraved with images of the sun and the moon and the stars, it shone as bright as any of the heavenly host.

Mouse could not breathe. She could scarcely bear to look away from that brilliance, from that glory come down from the sky and hidden here in the darkness beneath the worlds. But when at last she turned to study the faces of those around her, she saw only dullness in their eyes. Could they not see the change that had come upon Halisa?

"Wait." The scrubber, his hand poised in the air, turned suddenly and fixed Mouse with a slant-eyed glare. "What's she doing here?"

The Speaker looked at Mouse, who met her eye only briefly before looking away. *She knows,* Mouse thought desperately. *She knows what I'm going to do!*

But the Speaker said only, "She is my servant. Faithful and brave."

"Send her out," said he. "I don't want her in here."

Mouse turned to her mistress, hands trembling as she clutched the end of the red robe. The Speaker looked down at her coldly. "Go, Mouse," she said. "Wait for me outside. Our labor here is almost done."

Dropping the train, Mouse hastened to obey. Her heart beat wildly as she passed between the eunuchs and escaped through the doorway arch into the coldness of the Diggings. The priestesses and acolytes around her were like so many red-tinted ghosts in the torchlight, black hollows where their eyes should be.

Halisa glowed upon the stone.

The rivers beneath the floor roared in distant protest.

"Take the sword," said the Speaker.

Ancient fingers closed upon the still more ancient hilt. Though his arm was too skinny to support such a weapon, the scrubber lifted Halisa from its bed. It slid from the black stone as simply as it might slide from its sheath. Rising, it shone brighter, brighter even than the ever-burning flame atop the Spire.

The scrubber stepped back. Halisa was far too heavy for him, and after shivering for a moment in the air, the sword came to a ringing crash upon the floor, breaking tiles beneath its blade. But the old man kept his hold on the hilt. Heaving, he lifted the weapon upright again and, tottering with each step, made his way to the door.

The eunuchs parted to give him room. The Speaker drew up behind him, her head higher than the hunch of his shoulders. Mouse saw her face, full of joyless triumph.

The scrubber stood beneath the arch. "You know," he said, "I put a guard on this door. If anyone other than me or my heir tried to take Halisa from here, they should die. A harsh protection, I'll grant you, but didn't I just know people like you'd come poking around down here? I've won myself a number of enemies and lost a number of friends over the years. A man can't be too careful."

"Enough," said the Speaker. "We must hurry. My goddess awaits."

"Yes, she does, doesn't she?" the scrubber muttered.

One foot passed over the threshold. Then the other.

And suddenly, there was a rip, a roar, and a crash. Mouse screamed and fell back, her voice lost in the screams of the other priestesses and acolytes, of the Netherworld spirits around them. For the doorway to the chamber had broken, and the carved stone fell, dragging chunks of the wall with it. The cacophony was too loud for the cries of the eunuchs and the high priestess buried within to be heard.

Mouse, fallen to her hands and knees, was kicked and stepped on as the women fled, their torches flashing and vanishing in the panic. Soon she would be lost in utter darkness, alone in the Netherworld. All her plans to grab Halisa and flee into the Diggings were for nothing! Had it too been buried under the broken doorway? Would the Dragonwitch, disappointed again, send more slaves to die as they dug it out once more?

"There you are, Mousy. I thought you'd be close."

Mouse startled as the familiar stench of the old scrubber's breath filled her nostrils. She felt her hand grasped and something pressed into it. Something heavy, with a leather grip, that she recognized immediately even though she had never before held its like.

"Fireword!"

"Take it," said the scrubber. "Take it and run. Find the Smallman, for though he is lost, he still has a purpose to fulfill."

Mouse gripped the sword in both hands, feeling she must keel over from the weight of it. A silver light ran faintly along its blade, revealing the eyes of the old man. And in that light, other things became suddenly clear as well.

Mouse turned to the wreckage of the doorway, the pile of rubble. "Are they alive?" she cried.

"They're inside," said the scrubber. "As alive as they've ever been."

"I must get them out!"

"No, child," said the scrubber. His voice was firm but sad. "You must find the Smallman. Do you hear me?"

By the light of the sword, Mouse stared at broken stone. High priestess! She wanted to scream at the pile, to drive the sword into it, to tear it down. Mistress! Was she there, did she still breathe?

"Mother," she whispered.

The scrubber's hand touched her shoulder. "They're not dead," he said. "They're living the same death of a life they've embraced since the beginning. But you cannot stay here. Live, child. Live as you have never lived before. Take the sword to my heir and see your people freed!"

"What about you?" Tears clogged Mouse's throat. "What about the Dragonwitch?"

"I'll take care of the Dragonwitch," said the scrubber. "Never you fear. Now go!"

Mouse ran. She fled into the Diggings without direction, without a Path, but she held Halisa in both hands, and the darkness kept its distance. Around her she could hear screams. The priestesses and acolytes wandered the Diggings in unprotected fear. Like the Diggers they had sent to perish at the goddess's command, they lost their way. Tears stained Mouse's face. They were her sisters! They were blind, and they were foolish.

They were like her.

She gripped the sword, wondering how she managed to carry it, for it should be far too heavy. But the blade gleamed, lighting a Path at her feet, and she followed without question. "Where is the Chronicler?" she whispered. "Where is the heir?"

"Mouse!"

She turned at the sound of her name, staring into the darkness beyond the sword's light. "Eanrin?" she called, her voice tentative.

"Wait! Wait right there!" called the familiar golden voice.

Mouse planted her feet, and soon two figures appeared in the ring of light around her. "Silent Lady!" Mouse cried, recognizing the woman beside Eanrin. "You're free!"

"Dragon's teeth, girl, don't make such *noise*," Eanrin said, his face ferocious in Halisa's glow. "It's killing my nerves, all this screaming and shouting."

Imraldera gently squeezed Mouse's shoulder. The friendly gesture was enough to make Mouse weep, but she swallowed her tears. "You have Halisa," Imraldera said, gazing in wonder at the weapon that she had never before seen but about which she had written more than a hundred documents.

"How did you get it?" Eanrin demanded.

Scarcely able to draw breath, Mouse explained what had happened, the breaking of the doorway arch, the burying of the high priestess and the eunuch warriors. "They're trapped!" she said. "He gave me the sword, told me to run, then left me, and they're trapped in the dark!"

"That sounds about like Etanun," Eanrin growled.

"Don't, Eanrin," Imraldera said and turned to Mouse. "We'll get them out. Can you lead us to them?"

But even as Mouse nodded, Eanrin scowled. "What are you talking about? We must find the Smallman so he can gather all his impish might and slay our foe, remember?"

"If these people are buried alive, we have to free them," Imraldera said firmly. Eanrin opened his mouth to protest but stopped at the light from the sword glinting in her eyes. "Don't think you can dissuade me."

"Dragon's fire!" he cursed, and Mouse flinched and looked down at her feet. Then he turned to the girl, and his eyes were catlike in the half-light. "Tell me where they are," he said. "I'll dig them out."

"By yourself? It's not safe—" Imraldera began, but he held up a hand.

"I can manage unearthing a dozen crazed warrior eunuchs on my own, old girl. You take Mouse and get to the surface. I know we need to find the Smallman!" he hastened to add before she could interrupt. "But there's no point in any of us wandering around in the half-light. If anyone will find him, it'll be his blood kin, and we'll have to wait to see if that works.

Meanwhile, you two need to get the sword as far away from Hri Sora as you can. Lumé knows what she plans to do with it!"

"What of you, Eanrin?" Imraldera asked.

"I'll follow quick as thought. Find the miners' path and stick to it. Don't listen to ghosts, hear me?"

Imraldera nodded, swallowing hard.

"The cave-in was not far behind me," Mouse said, pointing. Her tear-stained face was hopeful now. "Please," she said, "find the Speaker. She . . . she doesn't know better than she's done."

"There's a new excuse," Eanrin sneered.

Imraldera gave him a look. Without a word, she took Mouse's hand and led her through the half-light, back the way she and Eanrin had come.

Eanrin stood alone. He watched until the light of Halisa was a dim pinprick in the shadows. Then he turned and darted in cat-form down the path, seeking the broken chamber. "Dragons blast that Imraldera," he muttered.

"Dragons blast that cat," Imraldera muttered as she led Mouse back up the path. Mouse, confused and exhausted, blinked in surprise. She would never have expected such language from an ancient prophetess. But then, nothing ever was quite what Mouse had expected.

They entered a cavern. The sword's glow could not reveal the vastness of its proportions. They felt tremendous emptiness surrounding them, an emptiness full of wraiths and woes. Imraldera faltered and Mouse's stomach dropped with terror. Were they lost already? Standing there in silence, with only their own breath in their ears, it was easy to imagine the echoes of lost ones resounding in the depths. Lost miners. Lost slaves. Lost worshippers. Voices echoing . . .

And suddenly Mouse realized that it wasn't the echoes of lost ones she heard. No, this was a present, ever nearer howling.

"The Black Dogs!" Her grip on the sword tightened.

"No," said Imraldera. "Just one Black Dog. It is alone."

"They were sent to find the Smallman," Mouse said. "The Dragonwitch sent them after I freed him."

Imraldera licked her lips and glanced over her shoulder as though even now Eanrin watched her every move. Then she said, "In that case, it must be on his trail. If we find it, we'll find him."

"What? You mean follow the *Black Dogs*?"

"It won't be the first time I've done so," said Imraldera, taking a firm grip on Mouse's upper arm.

"They'll kill us!"

"I doubt it."

"The cat-man told us to go to the surface!"

"Eanrin doesn't always get what he wants, does he?"

Then they were off in a new direction, plunging away from all traces of the Near World Diggings, down and down into the Netherworld. Immediately Mouse became aware of the phantom presences on the fringes of her conscious mind. But fear of Halisa kept them at a curious distance, where they could watch but not interfere.

The baying grew louder until it rattled every sense in Mouse's body. She wondered how she'd make one foot fall ahead of the other.

Suddenly she felt something like a pulse through Fireword's blade, down to the hilt she gripped in both hands. It startled her, and she stopped, yanking back Imraldera, who still held on to her. "What's wrong?" Imraldera demanded, her voice sharp.

"The sword," Mouse said. "It said something."

"Said something?"

"Like . . . a name."

"What name?"

"Asha," Mouse whispered.

The Midnight fell upon them. Like the overwhelming sweep of a tidal wave, it crashed over their heads. The two women drew together, and Mouse lifted the sword, her only defense against oblivion. Yet where the light of Halisa fell, the Midnight tore away, and Imraldera and Mouse stood in a small, untouched haven in the darkness.

But the baying of the monster increased.

There were two eyes. Two red eyes like pulsing suns, and a wide, gaping mouth full of dark teeth and blood. Mouse faced it, pointing the sword like a warrior preparing for a last stand. And she saw something she did not expect.

The Chronicler, the Smallman, running before the pursuing beast with a silver lantern swinging from his hand. And the light of that lantern reached out to the sword like brother calling to brother. Though she heard nothing, Mouse knew that the sword answered and that its answer was joyful.

Halisa.

Asha.

"Chronicler!" Mouse shouted.

He saw them. His face was desperate, and the Black Dog was hot at his heels. But he saw them and ran toward them, his short legs unable to make the strides he needed, at any moment expecting to be overcome, to be devoured, dragged down to the Dark Water and beyond.

Imraldera strode forward to that place between the points of light that were the sword and the lantern. She looked at neither but fixed her gaze upon the torrent of fury that was the Dog. As it approached, its great neck straining, its jaws slavering for the kill, Imraldera raised her arms and spoke in a voice of command.

"Be still!"

The Dog came to a halt.

The Chronicler ran on past Imraldera until he reached the pool of light where Mouse stood. There he stopped, panting, his face full of the expectation of doom, and whirled about to see what Mouse, her eyes round and staring, watched.

Imraldera stepped forward, her black hair glinting red in the light of the Dog's eyes. It was a vast monster, towering over her like a bear. But it whined, a piteous sound in its thick throat.

"Down," said Imraldera.

The Black Dog collapsed to its belly.

The Chronicler and Mouse exchanged glances. For the moment, her betrayal was forgotten by both in their extreme surprise. They looked at each other, then back at the small woman commanding the great dark monster.

"Stay," she said.

The Black Dog growled. But it did not move.

Imraldera hurried back to the waiting pair. "You did not need to run," she said, addressing the Chronicler. "As long as you hold Akilun's lantern, the Black Dogs cannot hurt you. Now tell me, where is the other one?"

"It—I saw it—"

"Where is Alistair?" Mouse demanded, releasing her hold on Halisa with one hand to grab the Chronicler's shoulder. "Where is your cousin?"

He turned to her. Here in the Netherworld he could understand her words once more. More important, he understood their tremulous meaning. He found he had no answer.

"Where is he?" Mouse insisted.

Imraldera looked from one face to the other. Then she stepped between them, separating them. "We have the sword," she said, "and we have the heir. Come, let us find our way to the surface. The Dragonwitch's time is come. Walk before us, Smallman," she said. "We'll follow Asha's lead."

So the Chronicler, every limb atremble, stepped forward, and the three of them walked as the lantern directed. Imraldera cast a last glance back at the cowering Black Dog, and it snarled at her. She turned away again, her heart heavy. For she had known that Dog long ago, and she had offered it love, which it rejected. But even now it would obey her. She knew it would not try to follow them.

Mouse, her stomach roiling, wondered at the Chronicler's silence. Her mind nearly burst with a storm of reasons why Alistair was not there. Good, healthy reasons, none of which involved rending or blood or any of the horrible, nightmarish visions that scratched at the edge of her imagination. No, he was fine. He must be!

And the Chronicler wondered why no one had offered him the sword.

The Flame at Night sat upon the altar of her fire. Smoke drifted from her mouth and nostrils, and heat glowed in her eyes. But she sat in dead embers, her fingers digging into the cold ashes. A weak sun gleamed in the sky above. She could not see its light. Her fire burned her from the inside out, driving away all senses save those of flame, of power. So she sat, seeing nothing but her own pain, seeking nothing but control.

"Greetings, Hri Sora."

The Dragonwitch stood up, scattering ashes in a cloud from the altar top. The ends of her hair momentarily blazed and burned away. She could not see him, but she felt him, every last piece of him.

Etanun walked in several worlds at once.

He walked in the realm of legends, ever a legend himself, more than human and larger than life. In that world, he was beautiful, well muscled from his broad shoulders to his lithe and limber calves. In that world, he was the hero, the dragon slayer, the rescuer and defender of the weak.

In the world of memory, he walked in shame, and darkness hooded his brow. There he was equally strong as his legendary self, but his hands were stained with fresh red blood. And falling like burning oil onto his skin, scalding away those stains, were his own wretched tears.

In the decaying world of mortal dust, he wore the form of a dust-made mortal. Bowed and burdened in this body, he tottered up the long stairs of the Spire, taking each step with gasps and surges of his old, old heart.

Yet in each world equally true and vital, Etanun walked. And the Dragonwitch, standing blind upon her altar, perceived him clearly in her mind through all disguises and assumptions.

Immortal. Faerie. Knight of the Farthest Shore.

"Murderer," she hissed.

Etanun crossed the flat rooftop. She snarled at his approach but did not otherwise move. Her fists clenched so hard that her talon nails drove into the flesh of her palms.

"You have not brought me your sword," she said, spitting sparks between her teeth.

"No," said he. "Did you really think I would?"

She hadn't. But it did not matter.

"I will kill you," she said.

"I know," he replied.

He put his hands on the altar and pulled himself up to sit with his legs dangling over the edge. She joined him. Side by side they sat, like two old friends who had not spoken in years. Neither was willing to break the silence of time, time which they, though immortal, felt stretching between them. But the moment of slaying must come.

At last Etanun said, "Tell me, dear queen, why do you burn?"

She turned to him, and for a breath, the smoldering coals of her eyes dissolved, and the real eyes that had once been, dark and liquid and beautiful, were visible. For a breath, she could see him through a film of tears.

But with the second breath she spoke in a smoldering voice:

"Have you ever watched an immortal die?"

16

You asked me why I burn. Do you recall it now? Do you recall the story of a queen who loved but was not loved in return? Do you recall how you hunted her down, she who had been your friend?

Do you remember the answer to your question?

"Do you?"

The Dragonwitch sat beside the Murderer on the altar, and her body quivered with every stray wind, threatening to break into ashes. Etanun listened silently. Even after she finished her tale, he kept his peace, hearing the rasp of uneasy breath in her lungs, watching her eyes smolder blindly, unable to see even the dark truths she had brought into this mortal realm. The stink of her death was upon her. Yet her body lived on in a death of a life that had driven her to the brink of madness and beyond.

"I am strong," she said, her voice quavering with vulnerability. "I am neither wholly woman nor wholly dragon, but stronger than either. My fire is hotter even than when I destroyed that mortal woman you chose, hotter than when I burned the Houses of Lights and sent the smoke spiraling to the heavens."

Etanun looked upon her and saw everything again as though it were all new. The beautiful, frightened creature who came to him and his brother at the Haven. The pain of rejected love in her eyes that he had ignored, even scorned.

He saw the dead body of Klara, the girl he had loved. The dead body of Akilun.

"I am a goddess," the Dragonwitch said, and her voice was hoarse and shattered. "I am so strong!"

"I am a murderer," Etanun replied. "I am so weak."

"See then how the Spheres have sung the cadence of our lives," said she, and there was cruel laughter in her voice: laughter . . . or tears. "You have paid for your deeds, and I have been rewarded."

"Is this your reward?" asked Etanun. He indicated the desolation surrounding the temple and slowly spreading across the mountain-encircled land. Not even the rivers, powerful guards on the Near World against the forces of Faerie, could hold it back.

"No," the Dragonwitch said. "My reward is you. Your life at last in my hands. For you are weak and I am strong, and I shall kill you now as you have killed me thrice already: first, when you broke my heart; twice more when you plunged that cursed sword through my armor and into the furnace of my breast."

Etanun nodded. "Well," he said, "I expected as much. Being killed by you at the last, that is. It's poetic. The stuff of ballads to come."

"Ballads you will never hear," the Dragonwitch said.

"Thank the Lights Above," he replied. "I've ever been a man of action, not so much for the finer arts. But one thing, Hri Sora, before you kill me. One thing I want you to know."

Her lips twisted back from her teeth. Ash poured like saliva over her chin, ash that glimmered with building heat. "What is it, Etanun?" she asked. "What excuses do you make for yourself?"

"No excuses," he said.

She could not see him. But her ears, sharply attuned to his voice, heard the change in it. The loss of age, the melting away of disguises so long assumed as to have nearly become reality. She heard the voice of the Etanun she had once known. The Etanun she had loved. The Etanun who had killed her.

She trembled at the flood of memories that rose inside, choking her, drowning her. He sat there, a being of immortal power and beauty, his skin bronzed, his eyes like star sapphires, every bone, every muscle exquisitely crafted as by the hand of a master sculptor. She recalled it all, and she felt it now, the overwhelming pain of loving this creature, this hero, this slayer.

"I have no excuses anymore, dear queen," he said. The liquid gold of his voice washed over her, and she shuddered at the dangerous sweetness of it, at the longing it stirred even now in the trembling core of her ashen frame. "Only this." Etanun took her ravaged face between his hands.

"I love you."

A perfect silence hung upon the air.

Then the Dragonwitch exploded in a roar of flame.

The sound of fire filled the world above and echoed down to the world below, where the Chronicler hastened along strange Paths as the lantern light revealed them. His two companions followed, Mouse bearing the sword, which still no one had thought to offer him. When the roar of the Dragonwitch boomed above them, the three crouched in the dark, huddling as near Akilun's lantern as possible. Its light gleamed off Halisa's blade.

The roar of the dragon above was deeper than the Midnight of the Black Dogs. They waited, expecting the sound to pass. But it did not. It went on and on with such destructive insistence, the Chronicler began to wonder if he would ever again find the strength to rise.

Suddenly he felt his hand clasped, and he looked up into Dame Imraldera's drawn face. "Take it!" she said. Her other hand grabbed Mouse's arm and drew her and the sword to the Chronicler. "Take it! You *must* defeat the Dragonwitch! Take it and slay her!"

Mouse and the Chronicler's eyes met. The moment, then, was finally come. The moment of truth or lies; he could not guess which. The moment when he discovered whether or not his life had a purpose. He set Asha down upon the stone floor.

"Take it," Mouse whispered, her voice an echo of Imraldera's. And she pressed Halisa's hilt into the Chronicler's trembling grasp.

The sword fell.

The Chronicler believed his heart had stopped. Even the roar of the Dragonwitch above vanished in the ringing cry of Halisa as it crashed to the stone, too heavy for his arms to lift, too big for his hands to hold.

The two women said nothing. They did not look at him.

"I knew it," the Chronicler whispered. "I knew it all along. I'm not the one. I cannot bear this sword."

Without a word, Imraldera picked up the weapon. It did not shine in her grasp, did not even seem to reflect the light of the lantern anymore. Indeed, it had lost all its silver glow and returned to a form of chipped black stone, a dull, lifeless weapon without power or trace of glory.

"Come," said she. "We'll follow the light."

The Chronicler did not reach for the lantern again, so Mouse took it up and set the pace, and Imraldera fell in step behind her, letting the Chronicler follow last of all. No one spoke. But Asha shone, and they pursued it.

Eanrin found the place where the chamber door had fallen in, recognizing it at once though he had never seen it. Springing to the nearest of the broken stones, he listened, and sure enough, heard the sounds of those within scratching away at the rubble. They were close. It would not be long before several large and angry eunuchs with spears freed themselves, and then what? Eanrin shuddered, but he had promised, so he took his man shape again and began picking up loose stones and tossing them to one side. He called out as he worked: "Fear not, my fine mortal fools! I'll get you out in a trice; then you can have a go at skinning my furry hide."

The work on the other side paused, and Eanrin heard a murmured conference before the prisoners set to work once more. Eanrin grimaced as he labored to free those who would gladly slit his throat. He called to them again, hoping they'd take some comfort in his cheerful voice. "Not long now!" he said. "Soon you'll be able to push your way free."

No answer. He tossed aside the last few stones, rolled one of the greater boulders away. There were pieces of intricate carving and tile broken into bits here, but Eanrin threw them away without a care. Only a thin barrier remained now. If he placed his shoulder so and gave a shove, he would be through. But he hated to risk a tumble into that dark chamber full of armed men.

He stood back, brushing dust from his hands and debris from his fine clothing. "All right!" he called. "It's your turn now. Feel out the weak place and give us a push."

Nothing. Eanrin, rubbing the back of his head, wondered if perhaps he'd lost track of time. It was possible, even probable here in the Netherworld.

"I should go," Eanrin muttered. "I should retrace my steps and find Imraldera and see to it that all is made right—"

He had scarcely spoken when the roar of the Dragonwitch struck his ears. Even down here in the deep place, the sound was as present as a living thing, and Eanrin dropped to his knees, horrified by the pain of it. How that fire must be tearing the poor, sad creature apart!

Then, near at hand, he heard a voice cry, "The Flame!"

It was a woman's voice, full of devotion.

Eanrin grimaced and braced himself. Harshly barked commands rang beyond the broken wall, and finally warriors with lances broke through the remaining rubble and climbed over. Others came behind, and the last of all turned and assisted the high priestess as she climbed up and out of Halisa's chamber.

They stared at one another in the half-light of the Netherworld. Now that their torches were gone, they were surprised at how improved was their ability to see. The voice of the Dragonwitch continued to echo down through the thickness of dirt and stone above, from Near to Netherworld, and the mortals cringed away from it.

But the high priestess said again, "The Flame! We must go to the goddess!"

She started climbing down the rubble pile, nearly falling in her hurry.

Her slaves reached out to help, but she refused their offered hands. She stumbled and landed on her knees.

When she rose, she was eye to eye with Eanrin.

She dove at his face with a scream, her fingers tearing for his eyes, and he leapt back, grabbing her wrists. "Calm yourself, woman!" he bellowed. "I dug you out. Can you show a little courtesy?"

The eunuchs rushed upon him, lances at the ready, long knives drawn. He twisted the Speaker's arms so that she lost her balance and fell again, liberating him to loosen his own knife from its sheath and face the oncoming mortals. He saw death in their eyes, but he hated to hurt them. They were so utterly lost.

"See, now," he said, "I'll lead you to the surface. You can't find it yourselves. Let me help you."

They set upon him, bearing down like wolves upon prey. But their weapons found nothing but empty air. Eanrin, in cat form, darted between their legs, made for the high priestess, and took man shape when he stood before her once again.

He saw, even in that half-light, how like Mouse she was. And consequently, how like Imraldera.

"Please," he said, "let me help you."

"Kill him," she said. And her slaves closed in.

"Fool!" Eanrin again ducked into his animal form and eluded the lance blades. One, quicker than the others, caught a tuft from his tail. Then he darted into the shadows behind the rubble, and as they scrabbled over to pursue, he slipped around behind them to watch as they allowed themselves to separate from one another. One by one, they were swallowed by the beckoning Netherworld.

He turned to the high priestess, who stood watching as well, unaware of his near presence, aware only of her lost slaves. He saw her lips move in what might have been a prayer. He felt no qualm about interrupting.

"I can't save them," he said, and she startled and turned to him, her eyes wide and black. "Thanks to you, they've gone beyond my help. But I can still guide you to the surface if you'll accept my aid."

"Devil in the dark!" she snarled. "Shape-changer! *Amarok!*"

Then she whirled and darted away, possibly believing that she pursued the upward path, possibly not caring even if she did not. Eanrin hastened after her, shouting, "I am not Amarok! Not all Faerie folk are your tormentors! Come back!"

She ran faster, her bare feet slapping on the stone. So Eanrin gave chase and paused only once to consider that he was racing headlong into the Netherworld. By then it was far too late.

The Chronicler felt his mind being slowly swallowed up by the roar of fire above and by the clamor of self-loathing within. Why had he hoped it would ever be otherwise? He'd vowed never to live on dreams. He would not cherish hope of ever being more than the disappointing son, the unnoticed lover, the disregarded and despised. He would spurn legends and prophecies and the idiocy of the chosen one trope. Such things weren't for the likes of him. One such as Alistair should have fulfilled that role!

But Alistair lay mauled at the bottom of the pit.

"I think I recognize this place." Mouse's voice, no more than a whisper, should have been drowned out by the ongoing clamor above this world. But the Chronicler heard her clearly.

"I do too," said Imraldera. "In fact, I think . . ."

She turned suddenly where Asha indicated, the blade of Halisa pointed before her. Mouse followed, still bearing the lantern. In their wake came the Chronicler, so heavyhearted he could scarcely drive himself another step. The darkness closed in, becoming a rough-cut tunnel through real, solid stone. Imraldera and Mouse began to run, and the Chronicler might have been left in the dark if the light of Asha had not been too strong for him to lose. So he caught up with them at a place where the tunnel broke into two parts. He saw a pile of rubble. Beyond it, he saw a broken doorway.

Beyond that, he saw a large black stone.

"This is the chamber," said Mouse, "where the Speaker was buried. The cat-man must have got them out!"

"But where's Eanrin?" Imraldera said, Fireword held high in her grasp. "Where are the others?"

"Where's the Speaker?" said Mouse.

The Chronicler passed between them. Unsteady on his hands and feet, he climbed through the rubble and looked into the chamber. And he heard the roar. Not the roar of the Dragonwitch, which was the voice of fire. No, this was a deeper, darker, stronger sound.

Not fire but water.

"Call up the rivers, Smallman King."

Stronger than death is life. Stronger than hate is love.

Stronger than fire is water.

"Give me the sword, Dame Imraldera," the Chronicler said, suddenly turning.

The lady knight started, opened her mouth, then closed it again at the sight of his face illuminated by Asha. Without a word, she placed Halisa in his hands. It tilted. He staggered, adjusting his grip. It was still too heavy, and the blade fell with a clashing ring to the stones.

But the Chronicler held on to the hilt, his face set, his jaw clenched.

The black stone flaked away, revealing the silver beneath. Halisa began once more, gently, to glow. A light that reflected Asha's own, a light that it drew down into its heart, like blood racing through veins.

"Go," said the Chronicler, staring at the blade. "Get out of here. Get to the surface."

"What about you?" said Mouse.

"Run," the Chronicler said, still without looking up from the blade. He took a step toward the doorway, dragging the heavy sword across the rubble. "Now."

Imraldera grabbed Mouse's hand. "Wait!" Mouse cried. "He cannot do it alone! He cannot lift the sword!"

"That's not for us to say," said Imraldera as she dragged Mouse and the lantern away from the door, leaving the Chronicler behind.

The roar of Hri Sora was dreadful in their ears.

17

A STAR'S VOICE COULD NOT BE IGNORED. It was far too many voices rolled into one being, and it was full of song.

Leta lay on the cold library floor on a pile of scattered parchments and an ink stain like red blood, staring up at the window through which the blue star gleamed. The air about her face billowed with the whiteness of her quick breaths.

How may I serve you? said the star once more, and this time it drew near to her window.

She did not scream. She had enough presence of mind to recall her goblin guards without, and she did not wish to bring them running. So she clasped her throat with both hands as though to somehow catch her voice there as she watched the approach of the star.

In blinding whiteness, it moved from beyond the world Leta had always known, from a place where stars may have voices to be heard by all with willing ears. It was too huge for comprehension, yet it passed through the narrow window opening and stood before Leta. The walls of the library seemed to fall away, for nothing so transient could contain the radiance of a star.

It has been far too long since I was able to stand in the Near World, it said, its shining head turning this way and that, curious. *The goblin has made this slice of the mortal realm a piece of his own nation now, and for a space at least, I may manifest here.*

"Please!" Leta gasped. "Please, don't talk! You'll kill me!"

Oh yes, it said, and if a star may be embarrassed, this one was abashed. *I almost forgot.*

The next moment, a unicorn took the place of the shining being, and it was so luminous and so fair in the world of broken mortality that Leta still found it difficult to look upon. But it was solid, and it stood upon the stone floor and cast a shadow. "There," it said. "Is this better?"

Its voice was now like music Leta could understand, like the sweet strains of a flute at midsummer, full of lightness and warmth. Though her eyes were dazzled, she found the ability to stand. The coldness of the chamber melted away in the unicorn's presence. Even in her ragged gown, Leta felt warm. Furthermore, though she wore rags and her hair hung in straggling limpness across her face, she had never felt more beautiful than when standing before a creature far more beautiful still.

Its eyes, like the depths of an ocean in which stars have melted, fixed on her with all sweetness. "Tell me, fair maid, how I may serve you?"

She put out a hand. Without asking, she knew somehow that it was right for her to touch this pure being, to run her hands through the glossy strands of its mane, even to touch the coiled horn, though it turned away before she might prick her finger.

"Ceaneus," she said, using the North Country name for the star, "I am imprisoned by the goblins."

"So I saw from above. And so I sang with my brethren," said the unicorn.

"I know where the House of Lights hides," she said. "I saw by your light. Corgar will wrest the secret from me if I do not escape. I know he will."

"It is not for Corgar to open the House of Lights," said the unicorn. "That is for the Smallman King."

"But he's not here." Leta took hold of the unicorn's mane like a child clinging to its mother's hand. "He's not here, and I am the one who holds the secret. I must protect this knowledge! I must escape Gaheris."

"The door is not locked," said the unicorn, delicate lashes sweeping as it blinked, momentarily hiding those luminous eyes.

"It is guarded," Leta said.

"Ah." The unicorn tossed its horn, and the movement itself was like song. "Very well. I will sing them to sleep, and then you must follow my light. I will show you a way from the castle and take you to the Haven of my Lord."

Leta nodded. Anything the unicorn said seemed right. While moments before she had desperately considered death her final option, she saw now the possibility of life, of escape, and even—though this was a more desperate hope—of Gaheris's rescue.

"Lead me, Ceaneus," she said. The unicorn, its soft oval ears cupped forward, stepped around her, cloven hooves gently tapping on the floor, and moved to the door. It passed through as though the heavy wood were mist, and Leta felt bereft without its light.

She hastened to put her ear to the door. She heard nothing. Without the unicorn directly before her eyes, it was difficult to believe what she had seen. But she closed her eyes, drew a long breath. Then she took hold of the latch and pulled.

The goblins sat one on either side of the door. Their heads were down, their jaws slack, and one snored as it slept.

Feeling as though she passed the very guards of hell, Leta stepped between them and stood free of the library in the cold corridor. Even in the dark, she could see how the goblins had scored its walls and destroyed all furnishings and tapestries.

A breath of wind touched her face. Ahead, up the passage, she saw a light like a white candle hovering in the darkness.

"Ceaneus," she whispered.

Though her knees were weak as violet stems, Leta hastened after the light, pursuing it down the passage, down the stairs, and down another passage. Everywhere, she smelled the stench of goblins and felt the weight of her enslaved mortal kindred as though she herself wore their chains. But she followed the light as fast as she could. Down another stairway, her feet making no sound on the stones. She saw no one either mortal or immortal, though sometimes she heard the heavy sounds of goblins.

Suddenly the light turned a corner. Pursuing, Leta rounded the bend in time to see a little gleam on a certain small door. Then, just as the unicorn had slipped through the library door, the light melted into the wood-and-iron fastenings of this one.

Leta put her hands to this latch and found it also unlocked. She pulled, and the hinges screamed in the cold, a sound like razors to her ears. She looked over her shoulder, expecting goblins to come running at any moment. She ducked inside and hadn't the courage to shut the door for fear of what noise it might make.

She stood in the damp chamber of the castle well.

"The most prized possession of all within Gaheris," Alistair had boasted to her that day long ago.

Leta looked at it now. It was like a mouth in the darkness, a mouth from which shone a light that illuminated that dank chamber with a ghostly glow. She stepped up to the opening and looked down and down.

Deep within, she saw the flicker of the star.

She'd come too far to second-guess her decision. Taking her courage in both hands, she found the bucket. It was big enough and strong enough to hold her, she thought, and the pulley was rigged in such a way that she might have the strength to lower herself into that black mouth.

"Lights Above!" she whispered. Then she sat on the lip of the well, her feet in the bucket, her hands on the chains, which bit into the flesh of her palms. Her fingers were so cold, she doubted she'd be able to hold on. But she swung out anyway, feeling the drop beneath her, the emptiness waiting to swallow her up.

The chains and her grip on them held.

Whispering prayers, she began to lower herself slowly, hand under hand. The metal bit into her shivering flesh. She dared not look for comfort down to where the star gleamed. She squeezed her eyes shut and focused on her work, and though the sides of the well were frozen with ice, her forehead dripped sweat.

Don't worry, practical Leta said. *If you fall, you'll drown, and Corgar will never get the secret from you.*

"Shut up and concentrate!" she growled aloud. And down she went, deeper and deeper.

Strangely enough, the farther she went, the less afraid she felt. Perhaps because she knew that the drop, however great, was no longer as great as it was when she'd started. Perhaps because the increasing brilliance of the starlight warmed her and melted the ice on the sides of the well so that it dripped with light *plink, plink*s to water below.

The bucket turned. The chain creaked. And Leta's eyes flew wide.

She had come level with a hole in the side of the well. A hole large enough for her to climb through. Furthermore, the starlight now shone from within.

Swinging her weight, Leta shifted the bucket enough to allow her to get a purchase on the hole and, after a thrilling moment when she thought she would lose her balance entirely, managed to pull herself inside. Here she discovered a tunnel just big enough to crawl through. The stone was sharp. If she'd thought she was dreaming until then, the pain of those biting stones would have convinced her otherwise. But the star winked on ahead, and she crawled after it, ignoring how numb her ears, nose, and toes were, or the dreadful crick developing in her neck and shoulders. She crawled until the tunnel opened up and she was at last able to stand.

Here she found a dark staircase carved of rock. The secret passage of Gaheris Castle, winding down to the river.

The starlight vanished. With it went all the warmth and comfort that had been holding Leta's fears at bay. She fell against the wall, feeling a wellspring of panic and despair swelling in her bosom, ready to explode.

"Don't be a fool, Leta," she growled as she made her feet take the next few paces in the dark, feeling for the edge of the steps.

But two steps down, the stairway vanished. As did the cold and the dankness of heavy stone surrounding her. Leta stumbled and nearly fell as her third footfall landed on crackling twigs, leaves, and undergrowth.

Another step, and she stood in an old forest.

It was warm. It was full of shadows. It was still.

Leta stared about, her eyes disbelieving, fingers and feet aching as her blood warmed and began to rush through her body. "Ceaneus!" she called, but somehow she knew the star was no longer near. It had served its purpose and guided her from Gaheris. But guided her where?

"Ceaneus!" she called again, without hope. Her voice was strangely small, as though the great trees around her and the heavy moss beneath her feet caught it up and swallowed it. She staggered forward, her head spinning with colors and smells and a quiet filled with the whispers of the trees.

Two steps more, and she stood at the doors of the Haven.

18

EANRIN FELT THE SURROUNDING PRESENCE of the Netherworld's phantoms. He heard their voices faintly crying; though they sounded miles distant, they may have been near enough to touch. He tried to ignore them, straining his ears after the footsteps of the high priestess ahead of him.

"Fool, fool, fool!" he muttered. "Slow down now. You'll not catch her, and you're lost enough as it is. Slow down and find your footing."

It was then he saw a light ahead, a light he recognized.

"Asha!" he gasped and ran for it, seeking the brilliance of white hope that might yet be found in the deep places. He could not help the phantoms nor even the priestess, so long as they fled from him.

But he could help bring about the end of the Dragonwitch's reign! He could serve the Smallman King.

The light was drawing closer. Was it Alistair, he wondered, searching in the darkness for his kinsman? Had he found the grave of Akilun and taken the lantern to guide his way?

But soon Eanrin recognized a face and form highlighted in Asha's brilliance. "Imraldera!" he cried, his voice angry. "Dragons blast your mortal stupidity!"

"Eanrin!" The lady knight and Mouse stopped and waited for the catman to catch up. The white glow of Asha revealed his pale face smeared with dirt and with the darker stains of Netherworld shadows and fears. His eyes were bright and flashing, however, and they saw that he was whole.

For an instant, Imraldera's face openly displayed all her relief and worry rolled into one. "I thought . . . when I saw the chamber open and you nowhere near, I feared . . ." Then she shook her head and hid behind a frown. "What are you doing here?"

"I could ask the same of you!" Eanrin replied, glaring furiously from her to Mouse and back again. "Did I not tell you to take Halisa to the surface? Where is the sword? Where is the dragon-eaten Smallman? Why can't you *ever* listen to an order?"

"You're not my superior," Imraldera growled, but she put out a hand and touched his arm, glad to feel him solid and warm in this world of cold wraiths. Then she and Mouse explained, stumbling over their words.

"The Chronicler told us to run," Mouse said, her voice shaking.

"Why?"

"I don't know. I don't know what he intends. But he seemed to know. And he has Fireword."

Eanrin rubbed his face with both hands, suddenly as tired as a mortal at dusk. Imraldera squeezed his arm again. "He is the Smallman," she said, "chosen by our Master for this purpose. We should trust him."

"Trust him and what?"

"Trust him and do as he says." Her grip tightened on his sleeve. "Run."

Asha illuminated a Path, and they followed it, uncertain where it would lead. The roar of the Dragonwitch above pursued them like the Black Dogs themselves, but the phantoms made no effort to impede their progress. And then the Path led uphill and became difficult. Eanrin took Mouse's hand to help her, and Imraldera struggled behind. But the light shone steadily even as the lantern swung wildly in Mouse's grasp.

Then they saw another light ahead of them: the light of day. They made for it, their strength renewed, and the Dragonwitch's bellows faded behind them into nothing.

Eanrin felt blinded as he fell through the opening of the cave mouth, landing on his knees upon hard rock, high on a mountain face where the wind blew sharply. Mouse emerged behind him, realizing then that she no longer held Asha, though she had no memory of setting it down. She caught her balance and looked around, recognizing the scene to which they had come. There was the trail leading down to a weather-beaten hut. There were the goats straggling about with little interest in anyone or anything but themselves.

There was Granna, standing with her arms wrapped about her middle, her cloudy eyes suddenly bright. "Granna?" Mouse called, but the old woman did not turn to her.

Imraldera stepped from the darkness. She stood, blinking and blind like the others, her hands shading her eyes. Granna stepped forward slowly, every limb protesting as though the exhaustion of her age had caught up with her. Her voice crackled as she spoke.

"Starflower. You've come home at last."

Imraldera's hands dropped away from her face, and her mouth and eyes opened wide.

"Fairbird!"

The next moment, the two of them were in each other's arms. Eanrin turned his face away, unable to watch for fear of the tears that threatened. But Mouse stood and stared and could not believe her ears when she heard Dame Imraldera saying:

"Darling! Little sister!"

The problem with dreams come true is the question they leave behind. What next?

Alistair sat in the darkness and frowned. His dream had only ever brought him up to the point of death, that moment of unbearable pain. Nothing beyond.

He lifted his hands and tried to feel his face. But he was no longer certain he had hands, much less a face. If he recalled correctly—and this was questionable, considering—he was fairly certain the Black Dog had torn it off.

"Well," he said, relieved to find that he still had a voice, "this is a bit unpleasant."

Something moved in the darkness. Alistair hadn't the wherewithal to be frightened anymore. Now that his dream had come true, he doubted he would ever be frightened again. Or happy. Or sad or hungry or anything. So he sat quite still, and someone else sat down next to him. They remained like so for what felt a long time.

Then Alistair said, "Hullo?"

"Hullo" came the response.

It was a friendly voice. Encouraged, Alistair said, "I'm Alistair Calix-son. Former heir to Gaheris."

"I am the Lumil Eliasul, Prince of the Farthest Shore."

If he had a throat, Alistair was fairly sure it was too dry for swallowing. Sitting there, he considered many things. Then he said, "So you're real too, eh?"

"Very real. Yes."

Once more Alistair considered. Then he snorted. "Funny how a fellow has to die before he starts to understand what's important."

"You're not dead."

"It's awfully dark. I figured I must be."

"You're in the Netherworld. It's always dark here for those without a light. But you're not dead."

This was a heartening thought. One that definitely bore mulling over.

"I wish I had a light," Alistair said at length.

"You'd have to open your eyes," said the Prince of the Farthest Shore.

19

THE DRAGONWITCH FLAMED LIKE THE END OF THE WORLD.
In days of old this fire would have torn apart her woman's body, revealing the powerful dragon beneath. But now, her dragon form stripped away, she stood in the frail, wingless body into which she was bound, and the fire was too much for her. It destroyed her from the inside out, and yet she could not die. Her hair fell away in tongues of flame, and her fingers were torches, her eyes blazing coals.

She set the temple ablaze. Her tongue spilled forth lava, which engulfed the Spire, scorching it into a vast torch visible throughout the Land, even to the mountains, where two knights and their mortal companions watched with horror. Fire fell like rain upon the temple city, rooftops caught and blazed, and the air filled with black smoke. Slaves and priestesses alike fled the destruction. The time of the goddess's final wrath was upon them. It was flee or perish.

On the altar, untouched by the inferno, stood Etanun, immortal Faerie, in his true form.

"Hri Sora!" he cried.

But she stood with her back to him, her torched arms upraised and blackened, her mouth open as she let the furnace inside her billow out. She could not hear him; her agony was far too great. She gave herself over to it and to the desolation of this world she had created.

Fire fell even to the deep places, illuminating the blackness of the Diggings. Stone melted and roiled bloodred, then flowed like rivers of fire into all the crevices of the Netherworld. The phantom ghosts fled screaming, the shadows chased from hiding by flames.

The Chronicler stood in the broken chamber of Halisa, the sword in his hands. The subterranean air heated until his skin felt as though it melted with sweat, and his palms were so slippery he feared he would drop the sword. But he struggled to the center of the chamber where the black stone stood, and even above the cacophony of the Dragonwitch's suffering, he heard the roar of water below.

Clutching the sword in both hands, he placed his shoulder against the rock and pushed. It was like trying to move the world. He was too small! He was too weak!

He ground his teeth. "No man," he growled, "no matter his size, could move this stone."

In that moment of extreme humiliation, this thought encouraged him. His stunted growth and graceless limbs did not matter, not now. Not even the greatest hero could accomplish this impossible task in his own strength. No muscle or might would move this rock.

"Let me be weak, then," the Chronicler whispered, resting against the stone. The ceiling above him boiled with heat, but he did not look. "Let me be weak so that you may be strong."

Even as the screams of the Dragonwitch shattered his eardrums, the Chronicler braced himself and pushed again, crying out as he did so: *"Lumil Eliasul!"*

A voice he knew responded:

"I am the one who chose you."

The Chronicler, his forehead pressed against the stone, one hand clutching the heavy sword, the other a fist resting beside his head, closed his eyes as the words washed over him.

Then he opened his eyes and uncurled his clenched fingers. He saw still lying in his palm the little pool of water, unspilled, unevaporated. For an instant, it flashed through his mind that he held whole rivers.

He lifted his hand to his mouth and drank the water down.

He felt it rushing through him: the power of rivers, the power of eternities and the great, pounding Songs of the Spheres. It was enough to bring him to his knees. And yet, as it swelled in his breast, pouring tumultuously into every vein, he felt the rising strength of living water.

"I am the one who chose you."

This time, when he put his shoulder to the stone and pushed, it gave. First the shift, then the crack of rock on rock. Groaning with the effort, the Chronicler pushed again, the mighty rush of torrents pounding his temples. The stone shifted, unbalanced, and then rolled. The Chronicler staggered and would have fallen had not his grip on the heavy sword held him anchored. Well for him that it did, for as the stone crashed away and broke into pieces, it revealed a hole in the floor.

Flowing below was the black current of many joined rivers.

The Final Water.

The Chronicler stared, and he felt the heat of Halisa, different from the heat of the reddening stones around him or the heat of the Dragonwitch's shrieks above. The sword pulsed with might, with the truth of purpose, and the Chronicler felt that pulse flow up his arm and into his spirit.

"Call up the rivers, Smallman King!"

The Chronicler heaved the sword, and suddenly he was able to lift it, to stand with the blade upraised before the churning rivers below.

"Wait!"

The Chronicler braced himself and looked around. Someone stood in the chamber doorway. "Wait," she said and stumbled in, fell to her knees, rose, and fell again. She raised her hands in desperate supplication. Burns covered her bald scalp, extending down her neck and arms, showing between the shredded remnants of her once-fine robes.

The Chronicler recognized her. "High priestess," he said.

"Please," said she, crawling across the chamber. Her eyes were wide with the shattering terror of her deity's tortured voice. Her blistered, raw skin looked red in the light of the heated stones. "Please, don't do this thing. Don't kill my goddess."

The Chronicler swallowed. Sweat poured down his face into his eyes, and he blinked it away as best he could. The weight of Halisa was tremendous in his small hands. "I must," he said.

"Please," said the Speaker, no longer the powerful figure she had been, drawing her feet back from the deformed prisoner cast at her feet. She was a picture of self mutilation, of womanhood denied, of humanity broken. "Everything I've worked for all my life. You would bring it to an end?"

"Everything about you is a lie," the Chronicler said.

Her eyes swam with tears. "But the lie is all I have," said she.

The Chronicler saw then the final depths to which this creature had fallen. And his heart broke as he gazed upon her.

"I am sorry for you," he said.

Then he turned to the Final Water and plunged in Halisa, up to the hilt.

The rivers ran.

From the mountains above the lowlands, Eanrin, Imraldera, Mouse, and her grandmother saw the rivers of the gorges surge away. From the Near World they coursed down to the Netherworld, pouring into the source of all rivers. Water, pure and powerful, filled the caverns, flooding the Diggings, where mortals had dared root their way into Death's own realm. And the rocks, heated almost to the melting point by the Dragonwitch's flame, hissed with the sudden cleansing coolness.

The power of rushing, surging water tore into the stone, accomplishing the erosion of centuries in mere moments. The temple's foundations cracked, and buildings began to fall as the earth opened up beneath them. The Spire wavered in the wind.

Caught off balance, the Dragonwitch staggered and fell to her knees. Her flaming stopped as she felt the sway of her world giving way. She looked over the roof's edge and saw her temple falling, saw the rise of water, a relentless, churning white foam that drowned her flames.

"Ytotia."

At the sound of that name—that name that had once belonged to a lovely Faerie queen—the Dragonwitch turned stricken eyes and saw Etanun approaching. Even as the Spire swayed and stones fell from its walls, he crossed the rooftop to her side. He reached down and took her under the arms, lifting her to her feet.

She was small again, like the delicate creature she had been long ago, watching the life of her father, her mother, her brother drain away before her eyes. Only now she was without her wings, and the immortal glow of Faerie was long gone from her face.

Yet Etanun looked down at her and saw what he had seen when first he met her.

"Ytotia," he whispered, "in my anger I slew you twice. I saw you only as the dragon, and I forgot what you were meant to be. Can you forgive me?"

Her face, burned and scarred by Death, upturned to his.

Then she snarled, and there was a dragon in her eyes.

The foundations shattered. The Spire fell, crumbling as it collapsed into the Final Water. The rivers fountained to the heavens, a white curtain of foam between the mortal realm and the Netherworld shimmering in the sunlight. A million crystal droplets glimmered in Lumé's light.

There was a rush, a final roar.

And the Dragonwitch, held in the arms of her foe, died with him her third, her final death.

My true name has been forgotten, the name given me by Citlalu and Mahuizoa. It is lost in the fires of Hri Sora. I am the Flame at Night! You could not love me, Etanun. Neither could you kill me. But I did love you and I will kill you.

And if I must perish in my own flame, so be it.

20

"THEY'LL BE UNPROTECTED NOW," SAID EANRIN.

He stood beside Imraldera, looking down from the mountain to the expanse of lowlands below. They and the two mortal women standing nearby could see the steam of the Dragonwitch's doused fire even from that distance. A great cloud of ash and smoke hung over all, darkening that part of the world. They guessed at the destruction of the Citadel and the final death of Hri Sora.

The two knights, their eyes more farseeing than those of their mortal companions, could discern how the rivers, which had cut across the landscape of this realm in deep gorges, were gone. The gorges themselves were dry and deep.

"The Wood will grow up," said Eanrin. "Without the protection of the rivers, more Faerie beasts will penetrate this realm."

"My people have dealt with Faerie beasts before now," said Imraldera, though her voice shook.

"With the Wolf Lord, yes," Eanrin agreed. "But he could not cross the borders of the Near World on his own. He had to be invited."

"And Hri Sora."

"She was different," the cat-man said, and his face was, for once, somber. "The Dragon's firstborn could burst through even the river gates. But now, with the rivers gone, this country will be far more vulnerable to Faerie. If the Wood grows up, how many beasts will notice and see it as easy prey?"

"Our Lord will not leave them unguarded," said Imraldera, her voice confident. "If he allowed the removal of the river gates, he will put other protections in their place. You will see."

Eanrin turned to Imraldera with a smile. She stood there before the bigness of the worlds, her body frail from imprisonment, her hair hanging in long snarls. In that moment she looked like the weak mortal girl he had, once upon a time, found lost in the Wood Between. Yet she was different too. There was a greatness in her earnest gaze, the greatness of purpose that made her strong indeed.

He wanted to reach out and take her hand. His fingers even made the first twitch. But she turned to Granna and Mouse, and the opportunity was gone.

"Fairbird," Imraldera said to the old woman, "I must go again."

"I know, sister," said Granna. "I know you must. But you did come to me once more as you promised. I knew you would."

"What happened to you?" Imraldera asked. "Since the death of the Wolf Lord and the liberation of our women. What happened to you during all that . . . time?"

"I did as you said," Granna replied. "I journeyed across the Land, proclaiming our liberation, teaching the women to speak. But there was war. War and bloodshed. Many preferred the slavery of the wolf to the freedom of which I spoke."

"Oh, Fairbird—"

"Don't be sad, sister!" Granna insisted with a faded smile that could look back on times past and see the fair amid the foul. "I found a good man, and I had good children, grandchildren, great-grandchildren. We fled to the mountains when the Flame came. We watched the wars give way under her rule, and we saw a power more deadly than the Wolf Lord's take hold of the Land. I heard the lies she spoke of you, but I never believed them.

And up here in the high country the smoke clears, and I could wait for your promised return."

Tears welled in Imraldera's eyes, and she looked far younger than she had a moment before. "I did not realize how time was passing," she said. "I did not feel it in the Between. I never expected to return and find you so . . . so . . ."

"Decrepit?" Granna suggested with a wry grin. "Well, age does have a way of creeping up on us mortals."

"But not on me," said Imraldera, bowing her head.

"Who says you're mortal now?"

Granna took the lady knight in her arms, and they stood holding each other. Mouse, standing near, saw then how alike they were. It was difficult to discern through the extreme age of the one and the agelessness of the other. But as she watched them, Mouse thought she glimpsed the sisters that they were, the one brave and protective, the other trusting and loyal.

"*Your hair is like hers,*" Granna had told Mouse more than once.

Like Starflower's. Like her great-great-aunt's.

It was too much. Mouse turned away and gazed back across the distance, where the Citadel lay in ruins beyond her range of vision. A column of smoke rose as a memorial. The Dragonwitch must be dead. And many more besides. The Speaker, the priestesses, the slaves. Even the Chronicler.

"And Alistair," she whispered. "Alistair is dead."

For the moment she could not cry. She merely watched the smoke churning in the sky until she felt Eanrin's hand upon her shoulder.

"It's time," he said. "We must journey back and see what we may find."

It was difficult to believe there had ever been anything more than this deep, deep blackness on the far side of dreams.

Alistair sat, his mind spinning with too many thoughts. He wasn't certain he possessed a body, wasn't certain he even wanted one. After all, the last he'd known, his body was being torn apart. Hardly a thing worth having anymore.

"I wonder," he said after a long silence, "what will happen if I open my eyes?"

The Prince of the Farthest Shore, sitting beside him, answered, "You'll see things as they are."

Alistair shuddered. Since that moment of red mouth and black teeth and pain like ripping fire, he wasn't convinced he wanted to see things as they were. "Maybe," he said, "I'd rather sit here in the dark."

"No, you wouldn't," said the Prince, and there was a smile in his voice.

"You're right," sighed Alistair. "I wouldn't. I would like to know. But I'm scared of what I'll see."

"If you open your eyes, Alistair Calix-son, you will see me."

So Alistair turned to that voice. After a struggle, he discovered his own face, felt his own eyelids pressing down, shielding his vision. That moment took more courage than any other in his life so far, more than the climb into goblin-infested Gaheris, more than stepping into the Netherworld, more even than throwing himself at the slavering Black Dog. For once the deed was done, he knew there could be no going back.

But then, really, when all was lost, what had he to fear?

Alistair opened his eyes. And he saw the Lumil Eliasul.

21

THE CHRONICLER SAT ATOP A PILE OF RED STONES, and he could see nothing. The smoke was so thick around him, he thought he probably should have asphyxiated in it long ago. But somehow, though it engulfed him, it seemed to be part of some other world and could not affect him.

So he sat atop the rubble, the sword in his lap, and wondered where he was. When he closed his eyes, he saw in his memory the waters rising through the chamber floor, flooding the room, catching him by the legs. He saw the high priestess, her face filled with hatred and pain, dragged away in the same current.

But he'd kept his grip on Halisa.

And now here he was. He recalled nothing after the rivers closed over his head. Was the Dragonwitch dead? Somehow he believed she must be, and the smoke around him was the last of her final destructive act. The stone on which he sat was the red of the Citadel Spire. It all must have collapsed, fallen into the Netherworld.

Where that left him was anyone's guess.

The Lumil Eliasul stood before him.

The Chronicler nearly fell over backward. But the next moment he was on his feet. "My Lord!" he cried. Then his tongue failed him.

What could he say? How could he apologize for his doubt when all his life his doubt had been as much a part of him as his own heart? Until the Lumil Eliasul moved in his spirit, the Chronicler had been incapable of believing what, to his mortal mind, was impossible. He was as helpless to save his people as he was to save himself.

And yet here he stood, the despised dwarf armed with the sword of legends, hero and dragon slayer, fool and doubter. Every contradiction of his existence weighed upon his shoulders so that he could scarcely stand.

But the Lumil Eliasul looked at him and smiled. "Will you be king now, Smallman?"

"If you ask it of me."

"Then go. Return to the home of your fathers and set your people free."

Like a gusting breath, the wind picked up and blew the smoke away. The Lumil Eliasul vanished, and the light of the sun shone down fully upon the destruction of the sunken Citadel, gleaming brilliantly on the red stone and the brilliant silver-white of Halisa.

The Chronicler looked around and saw the wide, desolate plain, so dry with the Dragonwitch's spoiling work. He saw the mountains in the distance and thought this country might one day be green and growing again. But he would not see it. He must hasten home. Home to Gaheris.

He began to climb down from the rubble, his head dizzy, and found that the sword was no longer so heavy as it had once been. In fact, though it was still the broadsword of a hero, it was simultaneously the right weight and balance for his small frame. Limitations such as size could never hold it captive. As the Chronicler began to understand this, he bore the sword as well as Etanun ever had.

While descending from the ruins, he wondered how to begin this journey. Where Eanrin, Mouse, and Dame Imraldera might be he could not guess. He knew only that his road would lead north, so north he would march.

A stone shifted beneath his feet. The Chronicler unbalanced and was obliged to leap to keep from falling headlong. His foot came down hard on something soft, and someone yelled: "Ow! Have a care!"

The Chronicler's eyes widened. Then he was down on his knees, digging through pebbles and dirt and debris. He heard more grunts and growls, which served only to make him work faster. "Is that you?" he cried. "Is that really you?"

Up from the rubble, covered head to toe in red dust, came a long and leggy figure that was almost familiar.

Almost. But not quite.

The Chronicler sat back and stared.

"Well, Lights Above us burning!" cried Alistair, rubbing dust from his face and coughing violently. "I thought I'd had it there. I really did! Unless, of course, you're dead too and we ended up in the same place?"

He turned to the Chronicler, and the lower half of his face twitched into a smile. But what the Chronicler saw was not the familiar grin. Alistair seemed to feel the difference too. His brow fell, and he lifted both hands to feel his face. He drew a sharp breath at what his fingers told him. The next moment he sat down hard on a stone.

"Is it as bad as it feels?" he asked.

The Chronicler could not find words. He shook his head, licked his lips, and looked away. Then he said, "You searched for me. In the dark. You came after me."

Alistair, his skin gone a sick shade of green, squeezed his eyes shut. "Did you kill the dragon?" he asked faintly.

"I don't know," the Chronicler said. "I think so."

"Good. That is good."

"You went over the edge. I saw you pull the Black Dog over the edge."

Alistair nodded.

"But you didn't die."

"No." Alistair let his hands fall away from his face and once more attempted a smile. "I didn't die."

Despair threatened to overwhelm him, and he hung his head. But then he felt something he had not noticed before. With tentative fingers he felt for the puckered scar on his shoulder where the goblin dagger had bitten deep. But it was gone. Tucking his chin to better see, Alistair looked but could find no signs of that poison.

He breathed a sigh and felt the despair flowing from his body. His old self was dead and gone. And yet, he was renewed as well.

The sun was dipping behind the western mountains before the Chronicler and his cousin climbed from the last of the rubble. They had met no one else, and both wondered how many had fled the destruction of their life and faith, and how many had been buried along with their goddess.

At last they stood upon the dry plain, the ruins behind them. Their faces set to the north, they started the long trek, neither trying to think too far ahead, neither ready to consider what they would do when they reached the gorge.

"Oi! Mortals!"

Both started and turned. They saw a familiar figure, small and fluffy, step into view seemingly out of nothing. The cat streaked toward them, tail upright and eyes wide as saucers. "You're alive!" he cried, taking man form as he reached them, his arms outspread. "You're both of you alive!"

Then he saw Alistair and stopped, and the smile fell from his face.

"Is the dragon dead?" the Chronicler asked.

"She is," said Eanrin. "We saw the smoke of her final passing even from the mountains. The others are near." He waved a hand vaguely behind just as Dame Imraldera and Mouse stepped off the Faerie Path, becoming visible in the Near World even as they took stock of their surroundings.

Mouse's gaze fixed on Alistair.

The next moment she was running. She did not care how little it befit her dignity. After all, she'd gone in unsuccessful disguise as a slave boy for months, and it hadn't killed her! So she ran, ignoring the gazes of Eanrin or Imraldera or even the Chronicler. She could not slow herself at the last, and nearly toppled Alistair as she fell into him.

"Steady, Mouse!" he cried. His voice was not as cheerful as she had always known it, but that didn't matter. She reached up, caught him by the ears, and pulled his face down.

She paused when she saw it. She hadn't, after all, expected those changes scored across his features where the Black Dog's ravaging jaws had torn his skin, riddling it with scars puckered in ugly lines over his cheeks, down his jaw, swelling one eye so that it nearly disappeared. She hesitated; his brow constricted, and she felt him try to pull away.

But her hold on his ears was strong, and she gave him a kiss that was no less passionate for its lack of experience. When she let him go, Alistair gulped back a laugh, and his scarred face flushed crimson.

"What was that?" he cried.

"Please, mortal," said Eanrin, crossing his arms, "do you really need me to translate this time?"

They walked to the gorge together, the two knights, the two North Country men, and Mouse. The Chronicler saw how Mouse and Alistair stayed near each other, and this eased his stride even when his spirit champed to hasten.

But when they stood at the edge of the gorge and looked down on the empty riverbed, Eanrin said, "All right, the time has come. We must enter the Between and hasten on. Gaheris won't rescue itself, and the prophecy is only partially complete. So, if you can pry that girl's fingers from your arm, young master Alistair, we should be on our way."

Imraldera frowned at him. Then she turned to Alistair and to Mouse standing close beside him, her eyes downcast. Imraldera spoke in her gentle voice. "You don't have to go, Alistair. You can stay here if you wish."

Alistair shook his head. His ruined face was difficult to read, but Imraldera saw the firmness of resolution set there. He took Mouse by the shoulders and tried to make her look up at him.

"Well, Mouse," he said, "the time has come when friends must part."

She didn't know what he said. But she heard the tone. She knew he would go.

"I may not be part of this prophecy fulfillment," he said, "but Gaheris is my home." The death that had passed over him in the Netherworld weighted his voice . . . the death and the glimpse of life. "I will never be what I thought," he continued. "I will never be earl or king. But I am a North Country man, and I must see the North Country freed. Maybe one day . . ." Here his voice faltered, for he wasn't certain he dared continue.

Mouse licked her lips, feeling the weight of words she did not under-stand. Then suddenly she looked up. Her eyes glistened with tears, but they were not weak tears, not anymore. The lie that her life had been was gone, and though she was feeble in the truth, at least truth was firm ground on which she might stand.

She took hold of Alistair by the back of his neck and, standing on tip-toe, put her mouth to his ear. "Sight-of-Day," she whispered. "My name is Sight-of-Day."

Alistair looked down and saw many things in her face. He repeated the name as he had repeated the name of the star when they stood on the walls of Gaheris. It was strange in his mouth, but she smiled through her tears and let him go. Her shoulders were back now, her head high. Even so, she was grateful when Imraldera stepped to her side and placed a hand on her shoulder.

"I will stay here for now," the lady knight said. "I will see Mouse safe, and I will spread the word of the Dragonwitch's death to the tribes of my people."

Eanrin nodded, though his heart was heavy. But he put on a bright smile. "You enjoy that," he said and slapped Alistair on the shoulder. "Ready, lad?"

They began climbing down the narrow gorge path, the cat-man first, the Chronicler after, bearing Halisa. Alistair went last of all. He allowed himself a final look and wave, and called out loudly, "Farewell, Sight-of-Day."

Then he was gone. The red shock of hair vanished like the setting sun.

Mouse turned to Imraldera. Her eyes were tearful, but she managed to smile and realized it was sincere.

"You were right, Silent Lady," she said. "My name is big and full of hope."

Imraldera smiled. "And I am not silent," she said.

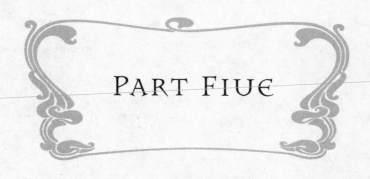

PART FIVE

KING

1

EVERYTHING SHE HAD BEEN TOLD as a child was true, though the tellers themselves had long since ceased to believe.

Leta pushed through the door of hanging greenery and branches and stepped into a hall that was both a corridor of tall trees and a solid structure of wood and stone. She saw windows that were leaf-draped boughs; she saw carpet that was moss and ferns. And it was all true. She knew it with more certainty than she had known anything before now. It was more real than her life at Aiven, even than her life at Gaheris. It was full and rich, and every sensation in her body experienced that fullness and richness to a degree she had never thought possible.

Leta had now spoken to a star. She had stood up to goblins and passed from the Near World into the Between. Now she could almost see the Brothers Ashiun as they labored to build this Haven in the dangerous Wood, could almost hear the lingering whispers of their voices. In this place, past and present were not so greatly divided, for Time was not master here. She felt herself caught up in the greatness of a story far too big for her mortal understanding, caught up and carried in a rolling current. But she was unafraid. For the first time, she believed she was truly alive.

She recognized Dame Imraldera's library from nursery tales. And she found the poem on the good dame's desk and read for the first time the strange Faerie letters.

> *Fling wide the doors of light, Smallman,*
> *Though furied falls the Flame at Night.*

"Come home," she whispered as the words took shape in her mind. "Come home and accomplish your purpose, Smallman."

At first there was no answer but the golden stillness of the great library. She breathed in that stillness and felt it, warm and calming in her heart.

Then she heard a voice she did not know speaking from the hall beyond: "There's someone here, I tell you, and we're not going back to your world until I know who it is."

"Very well, Eanrin. But I wish you would hurry."

Leta whirled about. That second voice she knew well indeed.

The next moment she flew from the library, calling, "Chronicler!"

"M'lady?"

They met in the passage, between two rows of towering pines, and light fell through the needles and cast them both into green shadows. And they stared at each other as though they were strangers. For Leta saw the Chronicler standing with a sword in hand that should have been too large for him, but which he wielded now with unnatural grace. All traces of his protective silence had fallen, and for the first time, she thought she looked on the man he was born to be.

And the Chronicler saw Leta, tattered and worn, exhausted and yet . . . strong. He saw a woman not a girl. A woman who had faced monsters and not crumbled. A woman who would never again be told what she ought to be.

They stood across from each other, and pine shadows fell between them. "I thought you were dead," Leta said.

"So I thought you," he replied.

Alistair and Eanrin looked on from the end of the hall. Eanrin folded his arms and rolled his eyes ceilingward. "Of course. Prophetic destinies can't be played out without the proper sense of poetry. Even the girl must be here at the end! Though, Lights Above, I don't know how she managed it. I don't think I could have fixed it that way even in verse!"

Alistair made no reply. He hung back, hiding his face, and watched yet another vestige of his intended life disintegrate before his eyes. His dream had indeed come true, he thought, and one hand touched the ravages marking his face. And yet somehow, he wasn't as sorry as he supposed he should be. After all, he had never thought that destiny was meant for him.

"Your mother knew," said Leta to the Chronicler. "I found her letters to you. I read them."

The Chronicler nodded, and though he flushed, he did not look away.

"You saw what she wrote," Leta persisted. "Why did you not believe?"

"I was afraid," he said.

"But not anymore?"

"No. Not anymore."

"And you will be king?"

"I will drive out the goblin."

"And you will open the House of Lights," Leta said, and her eyes shone bright as stars. "I found it, Chronicler. I know where the last House stands. Shall I tell you?"

"Please," he said.

So she whispered the secret in his ear, and though Alistair and Eanrin strained to hear what she said, even the cat-man's sharp ears could not quite make it out. But the Chronicler's eyes widened, and he stepped back, surprised but undoubting. "Lumé's crown!" he exclaimed.

Leta laughed. "It was there in front of us all along."

The two goblin guards snapped to attention outside the library door when they heard their master's footsteps. They exchanged glances as they did so. This was the day, they thought. This was the day when, finally,

Corgar did away with the mortal inside. They'd heard his threats and they'd heard her responses. No goblin would stand for such disrespect from a human! Today, then, must be the day when he broke her scrawny neck.

They stood with weapons upraised when Corgar approached, his head down like a hunting animal's, his eyes fixed on the door. It was as well for them that they backed away, for he would have barreled through them unseeing, so intent was his stride. He flung open the library door, ducked, and entered.

Instantly, he felt the emptiness. But he did not believe it at first.

"Where are you?" he growled. The floor stones shook beneath his heavy footfall as he crossed the room. With a heave, he tossed over the big table, scattering books and pages without a care. Then he turned to the desk, and his claws tore into its surface, digging trenches. "Where are you?"

The tapestry covering the secret door was next, lying in shreds within moments of Corgar's touching it. But the door beyond was shut, its lock secure. She could not have escaped this way.

The stairway to the loft was too frail to hold his bulk, and it broke before he had taken three steps. But he could see that she was not there. And even had he not seen it, he could smell it, he could taste it, he could sense it with all his being. The girl was lost to him.

He stood in the center of the library, his chest heaving, his wild eyes staring at nothing, and no thoughts could fit in the tumult of his brain. The guards looked inside, saw what was happening.

Then they turned and ran for their lives.

One was slower than the other, and Corgar caught the luckless lagger by the back of the neck, flinging him to the ground. "You let her go!" he growled, drawing a stone knife as he towered above the screaming guard. "You let her escape!"

"No, captain, I swear!" the goblin cried, and these would have been his last words had not Corgar's attention been caught by a shout going up outside in the courtyard.

"It's him! It's him! The mortal king!"

Corgar gnashed his teeth, and his aim with the dagger went wide, cutting the guard across the face rather than plunging into his heart. With a roar, the goblin captain left his wounded prey lying on the stones and hastened down the stairs and out to the courtyard. Human slaves shrank back with the clank of many stone chains at his passing; it was not they who had set up the cry but their goblin drivers.

The walls of the inner yard were almost completely demolished, but the outer wall was still high and strong. Corgar climbed to the battlements of the outer gates, demanding, "What is this noise I hear? What is this rabble saying?"

No one dared answer him, so he tossed aside any goblins in his way and looked for himself to the winterbound land beyond Gaheris's walls.

Four figures stood on the road below. One was a redheaded youth with a shattered face, another a golden immortal clad in a cat's body. Eanrin of Rudiobus, curse him and all his kind! One Corgar recognized with a lurch in his gut as Leta, standing with a borrowed red cloak about her shoulders, shivering but defiant even at that distance.

And stepping from among the other three was the half-sized mortal who was their king.

"Corgar of Arpiar!" the Chronicler cried. His voice was bold but small in the coldness of hastening morning. Nevertheless, he took the forefront position and stood with his shoulders back. "The time of your tyranny is ended. You will leave Gaheris, you and all your goblin kin."

Corgar drew a hissing breath. "I will send my warriors out to slaughter you!" he called, then hated himself, for his voice was that not of a captain but of a petulant child. "They'll stick your heads on their lances!"

Alistair and Eanrin exchanged glances, and the cat's ears went back. But Leta did not shift her gaze from Corgar's face above. And the Chronicler, calm as a cloudless sky, replied, "Send them out, then. Send them out if you are afraid to face me yourself."

"Me? Afraid?" The stone of the battlements crumbled to powder beneath Corgar's tightening fingers. "These braggart insults become you little, mortal. Especially when you are incapable of backing them with your own strength. Do you intend to pit me against your Rudioban comrade? Did you bring an immortal to do your work for you?"

The small man shook his head and took a step forward. Corgar drew back like a threatened dog, crouching a little behind the ramparts. He snarled at this, aware of the gazes of the other goblins upon him, and drew himself to his full height again. He wanted to hurl broken stones at the head of that mortal but dared not forget himself so blindly.

"I need no friends to do the work that has been purposed for me," said the Chronicler, and his voice was clear and deep. "Step down from those high walls, Corgar, and face me. Fight me in single combat, and he who carries the day will be Master of Gaheris."

He should laugh. Corgar, feeling his servants watching him, knew he should laugh in the face of such a foolish proposition. He should laugh and accept the challenge, then pound this mortal nothing into dust. He should break him and enchain him as he had done with all the powerful warriors of Gaheris, and when the little man's shame was absolute, he should tear off his head.

They were waiting. All his warriors who looked to him as they might look to their king. They waited for that mocking laugh they knew must come.

Somehow Corgar could not find the breath for it. Instead, he growled, "So be it, mortal. If you are so eager to venture into Death's realm."

"Oh no," said the Chronicler softly so that the goblin could not hear. "I've seen Death's realm, and I have no intention of returning."

Corgar disappeared from the wall above. In the moments before the gate opened, Leta moved forward and placed a hand on the Chronicler's shoulder. He felt it there but did not turn to her. His face set into such lines that anyone who looked upon him would have seen the lineage of earls from which he was sprung—earls and fighting men and masters of great lands. Yet his body was still that of a dwarf, and he looked no more than a child when he stepped toward the gates to meet the monster emerging from within. Corgar's hand could have crushed his whole head without apparent strain.

Yet it was the goblin who trembled as he took the field beyond Gaheris's walls. In one hand he bore his knife, still stained with the blood of the goblin guard he'd slashed. In his other, he carried a club fixed with spikes after the fashion of goblin-kind. He wore no armor, for what was the need? His hide could break the blade of any mortal weapon set against him. Indeed, most immortal weapons as well.

"All right, small man," he snarled as he approached. His gaze flickered momentarily to Leta standing beyond, but he did not allow it to linger there. Time enough for such dealings when the pest was duly squashed. "I hereby lay claim to the mastery of this land once and for all."

The Chronicler drew his sword.

Corgar saw it and knew it, and he breathed out a curse. "Halisa!"

2

It was the sword of prophecy and of power. It was the sword that slew dragons and drove darkness before it like dawn chasing the night. It was far too big a weapon for the Smallman's hands, yet he grasped it and held it high and was made stronger for bearing it.

"Fight me, Corgar!" he cried and approached the goblin with the assured pace of a lion. He was not the rejected son he had always been; he was the Netherworld walker, liberator of nations, final death of the Flame at Night.

He was weaker than any man in Gaheris. Yet, bearing Halisa, he was mightier by far.

Corgar roared and charged, his club upraised, his knife swinging like the lash of a whip. Just as the mortal weapons had broken against his skin, now his goblin weapons shattered as they connected with the bright blade of Etanun's gift. Stone shards strewed the ground around the Smallman's feet, and Corgar stood weaponless before him.

His future flashed before his eyes. He saw his queen upon her ugly throne, saw her face as he told her of his failure. He saw the darkness of underground caverns, where goblin eyes might be shielded from the sun, where beauty was a lost dream.

His awful eyes lifted beyond the sword and the Smallman to the girl, the girl he had intended to kill if necessary, standing with stern face, her shoulders back. And she met his gaze and did not flinch, for she was no longer afraid of him.

He heard himself asking her, *"Was I meant to be more?"*

With a howl that would rattle stones from mountains, he hurled himself at the Smallman. He felt the sword bite into his left arm, but his right shot out and grabbed the mortal by the shoulder and lifted him from his feet. Still there was no terror in that frail, dust-bound face, only ferocity and faith rolled into one. Halisa swung and Corgar screamed as it sliced through his right arm, through bone and all, freeing the Smallman from his grip.

The severed hand broke into bits of stone upon the ground.

Red filled Corgar's vision. The red of pain, of rage more dreadful than pain. He fell away from his opponent, clutching his mutilated arm, unwilling to believe what had happened though his whole body cried out with the agony of it. He felt the eyes of his goblin warriors watching from above. Even at this distance he felt the terror of defeat sweep through their ranks. They would never hold Gaheris now.

"You've lost, Corgar," the Smallman said, and even as his body quaked, he raised his arms and pointed the blade at the goblin's heaving chest. "You've lost. Will you die now?"

Although the shame of defeat was as keen as the pulse of pain rushing through his broken limb, Corgar was not yet ready to face the Final Water.

With a scream high and dreadful in his throat, he turned and ran for the gates, barking orders to his goblins. And they, too frightened at the sight of Halisa to spare a thought for the certain wrath of their queen, flooded down from the ramparts, poured out of the castle, climbed over the ruins they had instigated. The mortal slaves shouted insults and wept with the hope of liberation, with fear of false hope. They saw Corgar and his maimed arm pass through the gate; they saw his mouth open in an animal scream. And the next moment they saw the Smallman, the dwarf, the despised one, pursuing their foe with sword upraised. The great goblin fled from him to the shattered remains of the mausoleum.

The goblins dragged back the ruins of the door, opening the black mouth of the descending stairway. And they flooded back through even as the Smallman set upon them with the sword; and though some few turned to fight, those who did never saw the Wood Between or their homeland again. Corgar himself plunged first into the darkness and, for the time, his shame was lost in pain and wrath and vows of unreal vengeance.

In his hatred, he lost all memory of what beauty might have been.

Alistair and Leta approached the remains of the outer gate, and Alistair swore violently when he looked in and saw for the first time the destruction the goblins had wreaked upon his home. Leta saw only the Chronicler, strong in the midst of mighty terrors.

She whispered: *"Not in vain the hope once borne."*

The goblins were still screaming, still running, when the Chronicler turned to the chained mortals and cut through the stone links, freeing them. Men and women both shouted and grasped what weapons they could, and though these were useless on goblin hides, they chased their enslavers and beat their backs and shoulders, however ineffectually, as they ran. Then mothers turned to find their children, men to find their wives. Friend sought out friend, and by the time the last of the goblins had fled into the dark, Gaheris, which had been silent, save for the noise of whips and ringing rock, was filled with the sound of tears and laughter and hundreds of upraised voices.

The Chronicler was lost to Leta's vision. Alistair took her arm and plunged with her into the throng. They tripped on piles of rubble and broken chains, pressing their way through the haggard, laughing crowd. Alistair ran into a woman, and when she turned, he found himself face-to-face with Mintha.

"Mother!" he cried, letting go of Leta, who pressed on into the crowd. "Mother, you're safe!" Alistair reached out to take her in his arms as he might comfort a child.

But Mintha's gaze flickered across his features, and her eyes were glassy, as though she did not quite see what was right before her. She shook her head and ducked away, and soon she too was lost in the press. Alistair cried out and tried to follow her. His large frame could barely find a path through the crush of bodies. Suddenly he was quite alone in the crowd.

Leta, however, made her way quickly. She knew where she wished to go, and no one tried to stop her. At last she reached a clear place in the crowd where the gates of the inner courtyard had once stood. Ahead she saw the Chronicler.

He approached the dilapidated shack, the scrubber's shed, unthought of, unseen, unworthy. The Chronicler stood at its door, which hung loosely upon ill-made hinges.

"Fling wide the doors of light, Smallman!" Leta cried.

The Chronicler, the sword of Etanun still high in his grasp, reached out and opened the door.

The mountains trembled.

The river churning below the stone roared. Its voice was the voice of all the rivers, of the Final Water, rushing across the worlds, across the arch of the heavens. The people of Gaheris turned as one and saw the House of Lights standing where it had always stood, though they had never before seen it. It towered above them, above the greatest heights that remained of the castle, and its doors, east and west, were wide open. Within shone a lantern suspended from massive red beams.

The sun broke through the clouds. The moon turned her gaze from night and looked upon the mortal realm. And they, the monarchs of the sky, shone their lights from east and west, joining within that mighty House.

Once more the Songs of the Spheres were heard in that realm. Lumé and Hymlumé sang, and the voices of the stars above rained down upon mortal ears. It was a bigger sound than the whole of that world, and the people fell to their knees.

"Do you hear?" cried the Smallman. He stood upon the doorstep of that mighty House, small and weak, and the power of the weapon he bore was all the greater for his weakness. "Do you hear, my people? Do you hear the Songs of the Song Giver?"

The people fell upon their faces and then rose up again, for the Songs of the Spheres filled them with a greatness. They saw the heavens opened.

They looked up and saw worlds beyond their world, life beyond their lives, and they wept with joy.

For the first time in centuries of mortal years, men, women, children, young and old, opened their mouths and joined their voices with those of the sun and the moon. Songs poured from their throats, from their hearts, from their upraised hands. Songs of hope, songs of joy, songs of truth victorious. And the Smallman stood in that doorway and looked out upon the ragged throng. He saw that as they sang, they were clothed in riches far beyond the rags of their slavery.

His eyes filled with tears and his heart broke with love.

"Do you hear?" he whispered, and though none near could discern his words in the thunder of the swelling music, the one to whom he spoke did. "My people know the Songs once more. They see the rivers roaring; they hear the anthem of the skies. They hear the stars, and they proclaim with them the glory of the One Who Names Them."

The people declared before the worlds: "We are frail; we are dust; we are bound in dirt. But we hear the Sphere Songs rising!"

The goblins, fleeing through the darkness below, stopped up their ears and screamed, falling over each other to escape that for which they had vainly sought.

3

THERE WAS NO CROWN, for the North Country had never before had a king.

But they took the seat of Earl Ferox and placed it at the eastern door of the House of Lights. Upon it they set the Smallman and placed the shield of Gaheris in his hand. One by one, the gathered earls—as broken as slaves, though their liberated spirits shone anew behind their eyes—took up their own shields and placed them at the feet of the man who was now their sovereign. And they swore oaths of allegiance, pledging their swords in service and protection; their new king, in turn, pledged his life for theirs.

Before the hugeness of that ancient House, the dwarf son of Ferox looked smaller still. Yet, Alistair thought, it was his weakness that brought the earls to their knees before him. They knew that he was king not by right of might nor even by their will. He was established by a Power far greater, a Power they must now acknowledge as the Songs of the Spheres still echoed in their hearts and the remnant light of Asha glowed from the lantern high in the rafters of the House.

The Smallman sat with Halisa across his knees and Ferox's shield leaning against him. It was Earl Aiven who stood before those gathered and, holding out his arms, declared for all to hear: "Long live Florien Ferox-son, King of the North Country!"

"Long live King Florien!" the people cried, and the earls raised what weapons they had recovered from the goblins, and the women, servant and lady alike, waved rags like banners.

Alistair bore no weapon. He stood at the back of the throng near the ruinous outer walls of Gaheris. The House of Lights, its disguise dropped away, rose in majestic glory above the river, and Alistair wondered why he had been unable to see it before.

"You'd have to open your eyes," he whispered with a wry smile.

He saw all now with a clarity beyond understanding. He saw the whispered councils of the earls at last brought to light, united in a kingdom none had ever fully expected. And under such a king!

"You have a look about you," said Eanrin, appearing suddenly at Alistair's elbow, "like you're trying to think. A strained, exhausted sort of look. After such an effort, I do hope you intend to share."

Alistair grinned at the cat-man, feeling the strangeness of his scarred face as muscles with which he was no longer familiar moved. "I was thinking," he said, "how unreal this is. How like the Faerie tales the Chronicler—that is, King Florien—once made me read."

"Unreal, you say? Well . . ." Eanrin shrugged, his cloaked shoulders rising beneath his ears. "There's no excuse for you now, my boy. You've heard the Sphere Songs. You know that Faerie tales are far more real than the reality to which you once clung with such vigor."

At this, Alistair nodded. Then the smile fell from his face, replaced by a pensive expression. He saw Lady Mintha standing not far off. Like him, she remained separate from the gathering. She had somehow, between the moment her chains fell away and now, found some of her old finery and bedecked herself in brocade and veils. But, even after only seven days of slavery, there was something altogether broken about her. Something that said she would never be the lady she had once been. She stared up at the House of Lights, but it wasn't the House she saw. Instead, her gaze filled with the sight of the king upon the makeshift throne.

Leaving Eanrin where he stood, Alistair made his way to her side. He was obliged to touch her elbow to make her aware of his presence, and even then she refused to turn to him. "Mother," he said and saw a spasm cross her face.

"Do you see that?" she said, her voice trembling. "That king over there?"

"Mother, please, look at me."

"That was supposed to be my son. I had planned it. I had seen it all."

"Sometimes dreams must die so we can live," Alistair said, feeling again the deadly dream that had torn apart his face. "You must let it go, Mother. Let it go so that we can find our place in this new world."

He grasped her shoulders, turning her to him. She fixed her eyes upon the ground, and he flushed with frustration. "I know," he said, "I have not become what you always hoped. But I have become what I am supposed to be, which is better. I have a purpose of my own to discover, and it's not *his* purpose." He tossed his head to indicate the Smallman on the throne. "He must live this life and rule Gaheris and all the North Country. I must move on."

Still she would not look up. He felt her quivering in his hands and realized how frail she had become since Ferox's funeral. It seemed much longer ago now. From her expression, it might have been twenty years. "Mother, look at me. Accept who I am. And let me accept you."

For an instant her gaze moved to his face, perhaps for too brief a span even to see the changes wrought there. Alistair glimpsed the Sphere Songs in the depths of her gaze and knew that she had heard them. Then her eyes rolled in her head, looking again up to the throne and the House. She had heard the Sphere Songs, yet already she had forgotten. Fixed as she was upon that one dream of her heart, she could not let it go, not even for something far grander.

"Why do you call me *mother*?" she asked, and her voice was that of an old woman. "I'm no one's mother."

"You're my mother," said Alistair.

"I had a son once," she said. "The goblins killed him. He would have been king, but the goblins killed him, so they made the dwarf king instead. Isn't that sad?"

Tears clogged Alistair's throat. Mintha stepped back, and he let her go, his hands falling to his sides. He watched her vaguely wander away, her eyes fixed upon the throne. She passed like a lost soul into the throng, and people parted ways for the grandly clad Lady Mintha, the king's aunt. Soon Alistair could see her no more.

Eanrin's hand fell upon his shoulder, and Alistair was surprised to find it comforting. "It is the hardest thing in the world to let go of a dead dream," Eanrin said, his voice more serious than Alistair had ever before heard it. "Many people cling to their dreams and watch them die again and again rather than release them entirely. Don't think too harshly of your mother after you've gone."

"Gone?" Alistair gave the cat a quizzical glance. "What do you mean?"

"What do you mean, what do I mean?" the cat-man replied, some of the natural sarcasm returning. "Don't tell me you intend to sit around here watching another man live the life that was to be yours? That would equal any nightmare your mother makes for herself."

"The king might need me," Alistair said.

"The king will get on well enough. I'll be keeping an eye on him, making sure those goblins don't return. Though I doubt any man of Arpiar will have a taste for the mortal world for many generations to come, not after seeing Halisa borne in a mortal's hands. Ha!" The cat-man laughed and shook his head, but his eyes were wide and wondering. "It's not a sight I'll soon forget myself! The will of my Lord is strange indeed, and he does seem to place high value on your lot."

He shrugged again and passed a hand over his face as though suddenly tired. "It's strange," he said, "but I think I'm beginning to . . . I don't know. Understand a little, perhaps. I never much cared for mortals, what with all your living and dying and so forth. But you have pluck, don't you? Not a Faerie alive would've marched into the Netherworld more boldly!"

Alistair sighed. "Not a Faerie alive is so foolish."

"That I'll grant you." Eanrin clapped the lad's shoulder again. His eyes looked to the House of Lights, and his ears filled with the Sphere Songs. The mortals gathered had already grown accustomed to the sound, and some, like Lady Mintha, began to forget. But Eanrin heard them as though with new ears, and they filled his soul with an inspiration not unlike when he had first knelt before the Lumil Eliasul and taken up knighthood.

And he could see, even from that distance, that the Smallman King heard them as well. "He won't soon forget," Eanrin muttered.

"What was that?" asked Alistair.

"Nothing. Well, my friend, I must off!" Eanrin fixed a final smile on Alistair. "I can't say it's all been grand, but I can say that I'm glad I stopped the goblin poison from killing you and . . . yes, on the whole, I'm pleased we've met. We might meet again. I'm finding myself far more interested in mortal affairs than I once was. Maybe I'll keep track of your flow of Time and have a look in on you now and then. Remember what I said: Get your feet moving and find out what you were meant for. Cheery-bye!"

With that he became a cat once more, and before Alistair could say a word, he had slipped away, vanishing between skirts and boots across the ruined courtyard of Gaheris.

If he was going to take the Faerie cat's advice, he needed to do so at once before he talked himself out of it. So the following day Alistair made his way to Gaheris library, where the king had holed himself away for some privacy. Men stood guard and earls and retainers lined the halls, for much needed doing in this land that was now a kingdom. But, respecting their sovereign's need for some quiet, they stood patiently without, waiting for him to emerge.

Alistair did not wait. Though the guards protested and refused to let him knock, he called out in a loud voice that carried through the heavy door, "Your Majesty! Will you see me?"

The door opened. The king looked out and said, "Let him in . . . please." Though his voice already bore a tone of command, years of deference had ingrained certain habits. He winced at his own "please," but the guards obeyed and Alistair stepped into the quiet of the library.

It was strange to see it in such a state of destruction, tables overturned, papers strewn, book covers torn into shreds of leather. The king looked far more the chronicler as he moved about the chamber, gathering pieces of his and his predecessor's work, sighing over them as over friends now dead. But he paused to ask, "What may I do for you, my lord?"

Alistair shook his head. "I'm not your lord," he said. "Remember, you are king now."

"Yes." The king frowned and took a seat on his stool, his short legs dangling. "It is difficult to grasp. They don't talk about after the crowning in Faerie tales, do they?"

"Not that I recall," Alistair said. "You might write it down yourself. For future chosen ones and prophetic kings to reference one day, eh? They would appreciate it."

"I might just do that," said the king, his voice serious. He looked again about the room at all the work to be done. Work that he himself would not have opportunity to perform. His heart was heavy at the sight. After all, he'd never asked to be king. Sighing, he turned to Alistair once more. "What may I do for you, cousin?"

This was perhaps strangest of all, this familiarity, this kindred they now shared, linked less by blood than by experience. For the one had died that the other might sacrifice his life to the needs of a kingdom. They were cousins indeed, Alistair realized. They were brothers.

Even amid this realization, his resolve was firm.

"I have come to take my leave," he said.

The king nodded as though he had expected this. "You'll return to the South Land, then? Behind the mountains?"

"I'll try," Alistair said. "It's a much longer journey overland than through the Between, but . . . well, I don't feel quite up to Faerie forests just now! I think a long trek might do me good."

"A long trek?" The king frowned. "Long indeed. You may never reach your destination. And from what I know, there is no path to the South Land through those mountains."

"I shall have to see when I get there," Alistair said.

"You are determined?"

"Quite."

"Will you take horses? Men? Provisions?"

"I'll take a sack on my back and a stout pair of boots. And I'll follow the blue star. That seemed to work well enough for Mouse. It'll suit me fine."

The king looked at him a long moment, unspeaking. His eyes said things he dared not speak aloud: *You should be in my place. You should be king.*

But Alistair, his scarred face beginning to relearn what it had once known, smiled. "Long life to you, King Florien," he said. "May you rule with mercy and justice, and your heirs after you."

The king opened his mouth to speak, but nothing that seemed right to him would come. So instead, he said only, "Farewell, cousin."

The library was quiet in the wake of Alistair's departure. The chronicler who was king sat awhile upon his high stool, staring around at the stone walls, trying not to think, for any thought might be too overwhelming.

"I am weak," he whispered. "Too weak for this."

And in you, my might will be made visible to all people.

"Give me the strength, then," said the Smallman. "Give me the strength and the wisdom I need."

A knock at the door. Sighing, the Chronicler slid off the stool and opened it. One of his guards stood there. Beyond him stood Leta.

"Your Majesty, this young woman insists you would wish to see her," said the guard tentatively, for he was uncertain of required protocol when it came to kings. "She says you need her to put the library back together," he added, glancing back at her.

"Oh. Yes," the Chronicler said, opening the door a little wider. "You did well. Let her pass."

Relieved, the guard stepped back. Leta entered the library, proceeding to her usual place under the window, though the table had been overturned and broken and all the inkpots scattered. The Chronicler shut the door.

"I can't imagine how terrible this looks to you," said Leta, gazing around the chamber. She met the Chronicler's eyes, and he saw sorrow equal to his own. "All your work."

"I shall have to transcribe it again. If there's time," he said. Then he shrugged ruefully. "Or hire my own chronicler."

"I thought about that," said Leta. "I thought maybe . . ." She hesitated, then hurried on. "I thought maybe you'd consider me for the position. I know I'm not very skilled," she persisted, seeing him open his mouth and, in that moment, not caring that she'd just interrupted a king. "I know I still have much to learn. But I am *quite* familiar with this library now, and I should like to be part of its restoration. Even if you can't commission me as official chronicler, I hope you will allow me to help. . . ."

Her voice trailed off, and he thought perhaps there were tears in her eyes, for she no longer was willing to meet his gaze. He sighed and bent to pick up several loose sheets lying at his feet. They were torn as though by great claws. He pretended to read them but for some reason couldn't discern the words.

"I think," he said, "it might be best if you returned to Aiven. To the home of your father."

"You'd send me away?" Her voice was sharp.

He bowed his head and shuffled the papers. "There's no place at Gaheris now for an unwed maiden."

He felt the power of her stare full upon him, and he dared not meet it.

"What did you say to me?" Leta asked.

His throat was too dry to swallow. "I simply don't think it would be wise, my lady."

She did not speak for a long moment. She felt rebellious Leta rising in full force and fury, ready, after all the dreadfulness of the last week, to explode.

But practical Leta reminded her, *Do be reasonable. A little reason never hurt anything.*

"Very well, Your Majesty," Leta said, her voice as prim as any lady of the court's. "As concerns my return to Aiven, there is a legal question I should bring to your attention."

"A legal question?"

"Indeed. As you may recall, I am contracted, by the will of Earl Aiven and your late father, to marry the heir to Gaheris." She waited but could not discern from the side of his face presented to her whether or not he understood. So she added, "Which is you."

He turned away and marched across the room, pausing to pick up a torn volume and tracing the damage with his finger. "Never fear, my lady," he said. "I have no intention of holding you to such a contract."

"What do you mean?"

"I am not unreasonable." His back was still to her, though his head was up and his shoulders straight. "I would not expect any maiden to hold herself to a legal arrangement intended for another."

Leta's eyes narrowed. "Do me the courtesy of plain speaking, Your Majesty."

He sighed and half turned to her. "I wouldn't ask you to marry a dwarf."

Leta couldn't breathe. Her rebellious side took up all the breath remaining to her, shouting: *Tell him! Tell him what you think! Tell him now!*

She waited. Practical Leta, after all, should have a chance to whisper reason into the tumult of her mind.

But practical Leta said only: *Do it.*

"Chronicler . . . Your Majesty . . ." She ground her teeth, eyes squeezed shut. "Florien, do you love me?"

The hot rush of blood flooding her face was almost too much. She felt him turning, looking her way, but she couldn't quite raise her gaze to meet his. She rushed on before she could collapse with embarrassment but found that her courage rose and the words came more easily. Soon they spilled out quite beyond her control.

"Because I love you. I love you very dearly and have for . . . I don't even know how long! Since you taught me that silly alphabet. Since you looked at me and saw more than a bargaining chip, more than an instrument for your use. Since you saw me for who I *am*, the rebellious, the practical, everything. I love you for seeing me, and I believe you love me too. You'll tell me, of course, that what I believe has no bearing whatsoever on the truth, and I'm ready to hear it. Still, you needed to know. Before you break your contract with my father, you needed to know."

The king stared at her. He saw so many things as she stood there before him, things he could not quite understand. He saw that she was strong though vulnerable, courageous in her fear. Every contradiction filled her face, and all he saw was true and real.

"M'lady," he said, finding his voice at last. "M'lady, I love you."

Her smile was quick and brilliant as sunlight, filling his whole world.

"In that case," she said, "if you don't want me for chronicler, what do you think of queen?"

EPILOGUE

LET ME TELL YOU A STORY.

Ever flowed the Final Water, through the high lands of the moon's own garden, along the warm vistas of the sun's great realm. Into the Boundless it swept, reaching at last to the very banks of the Farthest Shore.

Before the water stood a man, and he watched intently, his eyes shining bright. None could guess how long he had remained in this attitude. A thousand years, a handful of moments—it did not matter. Here he would stand until he found what he sought.

The Final Water swelled with many burdens and sorrows, washing them far and away.

Suddenly the man gave a glad shout and stepped out into the shallows, wading deeper and deeper. The rushing torrents, though mighty beyond all mortal comprehension, could not sweep him away. He put out his hands and caught up something from the water, a figure dressed in rags.

"Etanun!" the man cried. "Etanun, you've come at last!"

The ragged figure coughed up water from his lungs and, with the aid of his companion, stood on trembling feet. His face was scarred with terrible burns, and he dared not raise it but whispered with his head bowed:

"Akilun."

Whole worlds lived and died in his voice. For a moment, he stood in the haggard shreds of his disguise, the scars of death marring every feature, and he could say nothing more.

But Akilun caught him up and held him close. There, with the Final Water flowing about their knees, the two reunited were made whole as they once were. Beneath the watching gazes of Lumé and Hymlumé, they embraced. As they stood thus, Etanun's frailty melted away, and he was transformed, stronger, more beautiful, more complete than he had ever been.

"Welcome home, my brother," Akilun said and took Etanun around the shoulders.

Together, without another word spoken between, they waded to the shore. They put their backs to the Final Water and ran together up the green and golden slopes, vanishing into the lights of the sun and the moon and the greater, ringing light of the Song ever singing.

And nevermore were the Brothers Ashiun seen by mortal eyes.

Ever flowed the Final Water, bearing with it all burdens, all sorrows. It poured down into the deepest reaches, cascading into the depths of the Netherworld. At last it came to the Dark Water. There it cast a carcass up upon the shore and left it, sodden and unmoving.

The Black Dogs stood over the body of their mother. First one, then the other nudged and pawed at her still form. She was broken. She was burned. She was drowned.

As though one animal, her children threw back their heads and howled. It was a sound unlike the baying of the hunt: a sound of mourning, of loss, of devastation. These monsters with their gaping jaws and red eyes howled the cry of the forsaken and rejected, and they could know no comfort.

The Dragon found them thus. He gazed at the broken form of his firstborn, lying wet upon the stones of the Netherworld. Her flame had been more brilliant than tongue could tell. Even at her final death, the

Dragon had wondered if her fire would be enough to burn away the waters rushing in.

But no. She was finally dead. As they all must die.

"Enough," the Dragon snarled, turning to the Black Dogs and cuffing them both with his clawed hand. "Enough of this weeping. She never loved you anyway. Come. I have need of you."

ACKNOWLEDGMENTS

With special thanks to my David Rohan, who not only designed Gaheris Castle and the surrounding countryside so I could have a clear mental picture, but also wrote both versions of the Smallman nursery rhyme.

ABOUT THE AUTHOR

Anne Elisabeth Stengl makes her home in Raleigh, North Carolina, where she lives with her husband, Rohan, a passel of cats, and one long-suffering dog. When she's not writing, she enjoys Shakespeare, opera, and tea, and studies piano, painting, and pastry baking. She studied illustration at Grace College and English literature at Campbell University. She is the author of *Heartless, Veiled Rose, Moonblood, Starflower*, and *Dragonwitch*. *Heartless* and *Veiled Rose* have each been honored with a Christy Award.

If you enjoyed *Dragonwitch*, you may also like...